Every Hidden Secret

Reese McPherson

Published by Reese McPherson, 2024.

EVERY HIDDEN SECRET

First edition. October 4, 2024.

ISBN: 979-8223210467

Written by Reese McPherson.

Table of Contents

For someone very special who has stood by me in every
aspect of my life. Stay humble and kind...

Chapter One

September 13, 2023~5:54 AM

I refuse to get up. This living situation won't work for much longer, but quite frankly, I have no other options.

I reached over to the flimsy rose-colored cart by my bedside and felt around in the dark for what felt like forever, finally grabbing my phone off the charger. Its bright screen was just enough to signal a slight daze of the eyes, worsening an already forceful morning wake-up. Once my eyes finally adjusted to the blinding light, a text from Kelly caught my eye, something I must've missed before I went to sleep.

Meet you at six fifteen?

I replied quickly, hoping she sees it when she wakes up. Well, that is if she actually wakes up on time; it's always fifty-fifty with her.

Yeah, meet you at the corner:)

I sat up just enough to see the numbers displayed on a black and white clock across the room, my back aching immensely from the surprisingly uncomfortable mattress padding. It still sits on the filthy ground just as it has for weeks, because my stepfather, David, hasn't made the time to come upstairs and hang it for me. Unfortunately, that's no big surprise, he never makes time for anything that doesn't come with a "Drink Responsibly" label attached.

5:54 AM, twenty-one minutes before I need to meet Kelly for our run.

Kelly Gibson lives down the street from my mother's house, a mere five miles from David's new place. Without fail, we go for a run every Wednesday and Friday before school like clockwork, been doin' it for the past three years. We met summer following eighth grade after a gruesome scooter wreck her little brother, Dean, had just outside my house. We both ran out to help him and became instant friends. Rarely do I ever click with people that quickly now, but a lot of things have changed since then.

I finally worked up the energy to get out from underneath my warm cream-colored sheets and put on a pair of green shorts sprawled across the static-filled floor. Size small, stretch waistband, just like every pair of hand-me-downs I own from Kelly's older sister, Amber. Kelly's much too luxuriant to wear old clothing, but I can't complain. It saves me from having to go out and buy new clothes.

I grabbed a tank top from underneath my bed and put on the same pink Brooks I've been running in ever since this started. The left sole has begun to wear down and the logo is completely rubbed off the right, but they do their job. I'm not jealous of the new shoes Kelly got last month, nor was I surprised when she pulled out new headphones to match. She comes from old money. The Gibson family used to own over half of Stonson, the town where we live. Her grandfather, Jay Burgess, was the mayor for over thirty years, retiring only last month. Her mother is a high-profile car saleswoman over in Raleigh, but she stays in Stonson with her family most days. Kelly lives a very spoiled life, but in her mind, so do I. She has no idea what goes on behind the scenes in the Cassidy household, and I want to keep it that way.

I walked downstairs to grab some water and get my bike, careful not to creak the noisy floorboards beneath my feet. Fake hardwoods, I assume, as they lack the shiny top coat one would expect to see on authentic ones. This weekend I'm staying at David's new place on Walker street, two miles from the neighborhood where Mom and

Kelly live. This means many things have, and will, change, but only one thing really threw me for a loop—I have to ride my bike to meet Kelly, since my car was "collateral damage" in Mom's most recent divorce. David bought it for me last year, a real piece of junk that barely got down the road, but at least it was a car. When the bank took everything in the divorce, the car had to go too. He's been too busy wasting his rarely found income on shots at the bar to save up for a new one. I hope that's where he is right now, at the bar. He never came home last night, and I see no new woman's car parked out by the road.

David always tells the women he brings home to park underneath the old willow tree at the end of our street so that I can't see them come or go. But I know the things he does when I'm away, and so does the rest of the town. If only he could see how much his actions affect the people he claims to love.

Ignoring the smell of cigar smoke coming from the porch next door, I hopped on my faded blue bicycle and began the short ride over to Kelly's house. When I get there I'll have to stash it in the bushes behind Mrs. Boulware's backyard so Kelly doesn't see that I didn't walk to the corner.

No fiber of my being wants to explain to her anything about the divorce.

The Gibson children go to Southpoint, a private school about thirty minutes north of Stonson. Because of this, Kelly doesn't know about my parents' divorce, nor that I'm being split between both houses. I want to keep it this way; she's one of the few people who hasn't heard yet and doesn't judge me every second I'm in her sight. I don't have to listen to all the whispers no one thinks I hear, I don't have to answer all the nonsense questions people ask, and I certainly don't have to hear any new rumors. She's never in contact with kids from my school, profoundly despises social media, and rarely is she home at all for that matter—she likes to spend the night away a lot.

I guess it's just a teenage thing, tryin' to be rebellious and all. I never really went through that stereotypical teenage phase; I never had the chance to. Anyhow, the chances of her finding out about the behind the scene decisions of my distorted mother are very low, and I like those odds.

Over halfway to Kelly's street I saw the Hampton's back porch light flicker on, at first quite bright, but slowly dimming as the morning's still dark sky seemed to absorb the blinding hue. I stopped pedaling immediately, an odd feeling overcoming me as I walked my bike over to their white fence to get a closer look. I get a feeling every time I think about that house—about all the memories I made in it, all the laughs its walls retained during my childhood, and most importantly, all the regrets its residents have caused me to have—it's puzzling. This will probably backfire, but I can't help myself. Something about the Hampton family just doesn't sit well with me, but somehow I've yet to turn away a chance to see them. Well, more like stalking them. Each morning that I pass their house, it has a total of three cars in the driveway, two on the concrete and one pulled only partially inside the small garage. However, only one of them actually piques my interest; a navy-blue Jeep Cherokee. I always make it a point in my head to notice the Cherokee in all its greatness.

It's Cade's car.

Cade Hampton and I have known each other since we were infants. Our mothers became friends during a town hall meeting to save the trees. Odd, I know. We think it was the pregnancies that made them crave environmental awareness action, a form of unusual cravings of some sort. We also share a birthday, born just four hours and thirty-eight minutes apart, so we became close friends during all the shared parties we were forced to have at preschool.

I've always felt like we're supposed to be in each other's lives. How else could you explain such a coincidence? Then again, I don't really believe in coincidences.

I know, of course, that it's a work of God, but God never does anything without a reason.

Cade and I used to make so many memories together, I wouldn't trade them for the world. Him, on the other hand, he'd throw our memories out a third-story window if he could. The minute we hit middle school, everything changed. Our mothers had a falling out over some property they invested in together. The survey came back with results confirming that the land was covered in toxic metals, meaning they couldn't build anything on it, much less resell it to an industrial company. It was a waste of money for them both, though it's not like they didn't have plenty to spare. Cade and I were never allowed to hang out after that, but even if we had been, it wouldn't have mattered much. He was the only boy in our grade to make the baseball team, sky-rocketing his popularity in an instant. Of course I was popular too, but the town was smaller back then. Once the Rivian plant came in and more families relocated here, he had much prettier girls to choose from.

I had a few offers from young boys to "date", although they weren't really relationships considering we were twelve. But once everything happened with my dad, nothing was ever the same. I stopped talking to Cade even more than I already had, along with the boys who took a liking to me.

In fact, I stopped talking to much of anyone.

I always figured that Cade would make the effort to come find me in the hallway, or maybe one day we would talk if he saw me in town, but he never did. We continued living our lives as if nothing ever happened, as if we were complete strangers, and as if his parents weren't accused of murdering my father.

Of course, they were eventually cleared of any involvement with his disappearance and murder. Turns out it's hard for authorities to convict when no one can figure out who did it.

Suddenly, the Hampton's back door swung open, and out walked a large man, one leg slightly dragging behind the other. A pretty broad guy, I'd say, not fat, but stalky, wearing a white button-up shirt and blue tie.

Carl Hampton, Cade's dad.

He set down a glass of what I believe to be bourbon, though it's an odd hour to have a drink. In his left pocket seemed to be a phone, that of which he quickly pulled out at the sound of a vibration and answered a call. He had to have seen me lurking by their fence, because as soon as he turned towards the road, he hung up.

I grabbed my bike and rode away, but I know his stare could very easily still be fixated on me.

As I rode up the street, I could see Cade's bedroom window open and his lamp on, something which is not unusual. When we were still friends he used to wake up early every morning to read his books, and despite the fact that he acts all tough at school, I know who he is at heart.

Now all I pray is that his father doesn't relay the fact that I was stalking them to Cade. I can only imagine the level of awkwardness I would have on my hands then.

TURNING THE CORNER after passing the Hampton's cookie-cutter house, the Gibson's estate comes into full view, cinematically sitting dimly lit beneath the rising sun. The walnut colored Earlpark welcome sign gleans off the red signal lights stabbed into the ground beside it, a recently instated protocol so that no more drunk drivers casually ram into it like last summer. Kelly waited for me on the corner where we always meet, the starting point of our three-mile loop. Today's run is supposed to be a steady pace since we're both too tired from school starting back to try any harder, although I doubt Jane Fonda here will allow me to follow through on that.

"Well, hello Sunshine! As George Washington Carver once said, 'Nothing is more beautiful than the loveliness of the woods before sunrise.'"

Here we go, Kelly's philosophical mindset leaking into my crappy mood once again. I can't ever just be down in the dumps when I'm with her. She always feels the need to be hyper and happy. Nothing against that, I guess, though sometimes it's too much to handle. Her Carver outburst is a daily occurrence, she announces it every time I walk up still wiping my tired eyes.

After that she didn't say nothin' else, just put on her new headphones and began to move her long, pale legs as fast as they could go underneath the morning mist's coverage. And so we ran in silence, each of us pressing our headphones harder into our ears with every step. *That's My Job* by Conway Twitty echoes through my head, all four minutes and fifty-one seconds of pure joy. All those nights lying in bed as Daddy sat across the room singing it as if it was his own flood my brain, emotions of both joy and sadness coming all at once. It's tiring, trying to focus on both steady breathing and the devastating memories, but I'm used to it by now.

Just about every song before 1990 reminds me of my dad and his corny, yet classic taste. I tried my best to sync every step with a different beat of the tune. Left, right, left, right, left, right...Kelly is already way ahead of me by now, her thick ponytail swaying back and forth effortlessly.

Kelly's life is very different from mine, but at an eagle's eye view, you'd think we're pretty darn similar; wealthy families, fortunate lives, strong friendships. We even excel in the same athletics, cheerleaders since we were kids. The only difference in that is the fact that she goes to a school which actually has an all-girls team. They don't have to deal with guys who don't have a sport for their senior year and try to join just for the roster spot. That's not even to mention how different Kelly and I really are at home. Her life consists of a grand house with a happy family full of loving siblings, parents who genuinely want to watch her compete, and friends that smile when she walks in the room. She never has any trouble managing to find the perfect outfit every day. Her figure is what every girl wants, her skin without a blemish to be found. She's the only person I have ever met without a single acne spot. It's like she came outta nowhere, her complexion and figure much prettier than her sisters and mom.

But we're living two entirely different lives, despite how both she and I may appear on the outside.

Finding a true friend has become an impossible task, as I'm constantly surrounded by people who have an insatiable curiosity about my personal life. My face is chock-full of acne, but I can't use most medications because I'm allergic to benzoyl peroxide. My mom couldn't tell you what grade I'm in, every guy who likes me is a top-tier jerk and jock combo, and my dad is six feet under. What an origin story.

"You comin'?"

Kelly continued running, her body now turned to check on me rather than facing ahead as it should be. I'm fine. Gassed, but fine. But despite my ability to finish the run, it's probably best if I let her go on ahead. It'll give me some more time to think.

"You go on, I'm gonna walk for just a second."

Kelly headed towards me, her feet still shuffling as she got closer. "You sure? I can wait while you catch your breath."

"I'll catch up, I promise."

She shrugged her shoulders and carried on, that silky ponytail still flopping as she bobs her head to the beat of her music. That's another thing that's so different about the two of us; our taste in music. Kelly always listens to pop or country music, which I don't mind. But my version of country is Conway Twitty, Billy Ray, you know, all the oldies. Kelly's version is Taylor Swift attempting to be country. And then there's her pop music, her fallback when she has nothing else to listen to. I always catch her mouthing the lyrics to a new Olivia Rodrigo or Jessie Murph song, never getting them all correct, but still confidently dancing about. She loves to pour her heart out to breakup songs, today especially. I heard *Seeing You With Other Girls* blare through her headphones when we began our run, but I'm sure she's found a better song by now.

Kelly listens to music to find another reality, a much happier one in which she finds joy. Me, on the other hand, I listen to music in order to think. Thinking not so that I can avoid the rest of the world, but so that I can understand it. How am I supposed to leave a good impression on others' lives if I can't even figure out what to say about my own?

You can tell a lot about a person by who and what they listen to. If I ever walked up to someone who was listening to *Angels*, a true classic by Alabama, I would think they were my soulmate. I mean that genuinely, no joke intended. To me, the song represents two things: the innocence that we're blessed with as children, and the purity that is sadly washed away by the sinful world in which we live. The boy in the song—let's call him Lyle—gets lost on his way home late at night. He cries, growing more and more upset as the sky darkens with each hour. Then, doing all that he knew to do, he prayed. He prayed dearly to God that he would make it home safely, that He would take care of him. As he carried on with his hunt for the road home, he met a man, a complete stranger to him before that night.

Let's call the man Mitchell.

Mitchell led the young boy home, leaving him safely in his worried mother's comforting arms. When the boy tried to show his mother the kind man that helped him home, she couldn't see him. That's when young Lyle realized that there are angels among us. They're here to lead us on the right path, to offer words of kindness when we need it the most, and to guide us with the "light of love".

I watched as Kelly continued to run off into the depths of Earlpark, plentiful white and red houses lining her route. I wonder what Kelly thinks about when she wakes up, what her very first thought is. Does she ever think about her special person, if they wake up thinking the same thing as she is? Maybe it's just me, but I've always been fascinated by others and how their minds work.

Their past.

Their present.

Their future.

People say that your true self is determined by what you do when no one else is watching. I agree with that, for the most part, but not entirely. I believe that in addition to what you do in private, we must take into account what you do when you're surrounded by others. Wandering eyes, judging peers, and friends that depend on you. When put to the test, how do you react? What do you do?

That, my friend, is what truly determines who you are. What you do when everyone is watching, and when all eyes are on you.

I deal with this a lot more often than I'd like, with times at which I feel like everyone is looking at me; judging me, judging my past, judging every little detail about my appearance. Kelly loves to ask me why I don't wear a lot of makeup. The simple answer is that I've realized something she has failed to recognize; everyone is going to stare and judge no matter how I look or who I am, so why would I change myself just to try to lower the frequency of that occurrence? She also asks why I don't have an obsessive interest in men as she does. Well, not in those exact words per se, but pretty close.

"I'm sure there's someone at that school who wants to date you," she often says. "Just one date, go on one. What's the worst thing that could happen? You get a free meal?"

I understand where she's coming from, wanting me to be happy and all. But men aren't what make us happy, especially not for me. Every man who has ever been in my life has either been taken away or has screwed me over; Dad was killed, Cade was ripped away, and David is a douchebag. That's enough to keep me away from the male species for quite some time. Kelly will understand my reasoning one day, maybe.

That's another difference between her and I. She cares too much, and I don't care enough. Better put, there's a difference in the things we choose to care about. Kelly and I very clearly choose to put our time in different areas. She chooses left, I choose right. She dates for a month, I dream of dating for a lifetime. We're remarkably different people.

Events change lives. Kelly has loving parents and siblings on whom she can lean in her darkest hour. It makes sense that she hides behind her music, her makeup, her men. It's because she fails to recognize just how blessed she actually is in comparison to those around her.

Blessed, what a beautiful word. A holy combination of letters, with a holy meaning. It's amazing how many meanings such a basic word can have.

I find it extremely interesting to see how few people recognize that. The simple concept of ignorance is a beautiful thing.

"The greatest enemy of knowledge is not ignorance,
it is the illusion of knowledge."
-Martin Luther King Jr.

Chapter Two

September 13, 2023~8:00 AM

Science class with Mr. Daniels. My least favorite subject, and for good reason. The small gum-infested desk in first period will be my residence for two hours as I sit and watch rain trickle down the only window looking outside. Its white plastic rims, covered in pollen from years of allergy seasons, remain untouched by weather, forming a mustard yellow color that seems pleasing to no eye. It hasn't rained in Stonson for weeks, but of course it pours now, on today of all days. Tomorrow night is SHS's homecoming dance, and if it doesn't stop raining soon, the precious night adored by every teenager in the county will be postponed until next week. We just started painting banners for it last night, a task every cheerleader must do before we can participate in the festivities.

There's only one bad thing about being a cheerleader; the leering football players who love to take their pick of preppy girls wearing a royal blue school-issued uniform. My lack of ability to be properly social doesn't mean I'm never hit on, it just means I hate when it happens. They're all jerks. I, however, must admit that I am a bit different from most of the girls on our squad.

I do one thing that no one else does. *I don't flirt back.* I see no point in entertaining someone who I know in the end would dump me at the drop of a hat, though occasionally I find a bit of pleasure in the feat.

Every guy in this school has one thing on his mind, and I refuse to let that be the reason I date someone. And quite frankly, no male here could handle the encounters I have during my short sixteen years. I believe that God will send me the right man when He is ready to, and I will be fascinated by him and who he is as a person and follower. So far, I've never met anyone like that.

Well, there is one person who has fascinated me in such a way, but I have a feeling that relationship could never be.

"Tatum," I heard a deep voice whisper my name from behind, almost startling me. No one has had the nerve to confront me about much of anything ever since news of my mother's divorce got out, unless it was with malicious intentions. It is incredibly embarrassing being the known daughter of the most hated woman in Stonson. No, embarrassing isn't the right word for it. Shameful. Yes, that's what it is, shameful.

When I turned to the left, Beau Citroy's steamy persona came into clear view, leaning himself over his desk in my direction. He's taken the opportunity to press his arms against the gray and blue football hoodie that lies beneath them, as if he wants me to notice it, along with the definition in his biceps. I turned my head a little more until we sat face to face.

Beau has been hitting on me for as long as I can remember. He moved to Stonson when we were in fourth grade, only he was just a short white kid with shaggy black hair back then. Now he's seventeen, he's lost all his baby fat, and it's obvious that he spends more time in the gym than he does studying.

"Yes, Beau?" I always talk to him in an annoyed manner, just for fun, though I'm never truly bothered by his player demeanor. Just a little agitated.

"Did you think about my offer any harder?"

Weeks earlier Beau came up to me in the hallway by my locker and proposed a question; be his date to the homecoming dance, an "honored" position in the eyes of every female enrolled here. So, of course, I gave him a flirty look to turn down the intriguing offer and walked away. Absolutely no amount of money could get me to go anywhere with him. All he'd do is make fun of me for the divorce and ask about my dad. I can see it now, envision it with me...So, Tatum, how did he die? Why don't you wear makeup? Ever thought about going blonde? What number husband is this for your mom, third, fourth?

Honestly, I think he was shocked when I said no. No girl in their right mind would ever turn him down.

Guess I'm not in my right mind.

"You know my answer, Beau. I don't go out with guys like you."

He turned his head to the side, his pearly white smile shining as he casually sat back.

"And what kind of guy might that be?"

"Let's take a look at your last five girlfriends, shall we? Blonde, tall, all cheerleaders. You clearly have a type. Oh, and that's not even mentioning how long you dated them for. Who was the longest, Callie? What was that, a month?"

He bit his lip, thinking through his response before answering. "Now that was uncalled for," he said, laughing. "How can you say that when you're not blonde?"

He's right, my wavy dark brown hair remains damp from the shower I took after my run with Kelly, my yellow and blue cheer bow slicking it back to stay in place. I hate wearing it to school wet. It steadily remains curly until lunchtime, but by then it's too frizzy to bring back to life.

I've thought about my bike ride encounter with Mr. Hampton a lot today. I apologized to Kelly for lagging behind in our run, but she didn't mind. We were both exhausted, and she could probably use some alone time of her own after her recent breakup with Eddie, her boyfriend of over a year.

"You know what I mean," I finally replied. He smirked at me, flipping back his curly black hair so that the scar on his left cheekbone could easily be seen. I remember when he got that scar. Well, when he supposedly got it. Beau was a bit of a train wreck a few years back, fighting all the time and skipping school regularly. His side of the story was that he got into it with Stanley, a foreign exchange student. Every girl was fascinated with Stanley and the mysterious Australian lure he brought along with him. I never cared for him much, but then again, I tend to not take comfort in the arms of men who spend every waking moment displaying themselves.

One day after school, a Thursday I think it was, Beau and Stanley had an argument about Shannon, a girl in our grade they both wanted dibs on. I can't blame them; she was new at the time, the first redhead to catch anyone's eyes. Her skin was perfectly clear, although she complained about her non-existent acne all the time. At five-foot eleven inches, her long legs made even her child-like figure appear stunning. I won't lie, I was momentarily jealous of her style. She always wore the coolest shoes, high-top sneakers that no one else had or could fathom to afford. She even owned this one pair she called the "Christmas Edition", green and red Nike sneakers with white fluff surrounding the heels.

The next Friday Beau came to school with bruised fists and a black eye. His face was extremely swollen, beyond badly beaten, and a large cut encompassed most of his cheekbone. I remember it well. I was in the nurse's office getting my inhaler when his teacher sent him in to be re-bandaged. He told everyone about his fight with Stanley, and that his victory was great. Of course everyone believed him, and he proudly let them feast their eyes on his "battle scars". And it stayed that way, because Stanley never came back to school. I never really bought the story; Stanley was a much bigger guy than Beau, and his heroic version of what happened just didn't line up.

We all heard that Stanley went back home to Australia because of a family emergency, but I've always suspected that something else might've spooked him off.

"C'mon, Tatum. It's just a dance, and I haven't asked but one girl. You." Even though he's right, it's odd that I wasn't his second choice, or that he doesn't have a backup option at the very least. He must have someone to fall back on; Beau Citroy would never allow himself to be seen at a public event without a girl on his arm.

"Why do you want to take me so badly? There are plenty of other girls who'd go with you in a heartbeat." He smirked, my slip-up seemingly amusing. "Don't take that as a compliment."

He still sat back smiling, his legs spread so he appears tough in front of the eavesdropping friends I've so kindly pretended not to see.

Then, just as he began to open his mouth to respond, someone chimed in from the front of the classroom.

"It's because you're the first to say no."

That's all that was said. The person in front said just eight little words. Then it hit me. Surely it isn't. It can't be. He wouldn't choose for this to be the first time he talks to me in almost four years.

Would he?

Sure enough, as I turned to see who had spoken, there sat Cade, positioned sideways in his seat, letterman jacket hanging loosely off the shoulder of his gray t-shirt.

Now that's a jacket I'm willing to notice.

A face chock full with concern and agitation covered his usually perky profile; he didn't like what he'd overheard in our conversation. It took me a minute to gather my thoughts, all the things I hoped I would one day get to say to him bouncing off the walls in my brain like tennis balls at Wimbledon. But before I could say anything, Beau chimed in.

"Hampton, don't be upset just because you lost your chance with her."

I saw something change in Cade's beautiful blue eyes as he moved his glare from me to Beau. When he was looking at me, his eyes begged in desperation for a response, yet they were almost shocked at what had just done. Now, he's just pissed.

"That's not true, and you know it."

"Oh really? Then how come you're interjecting?"

Interjecting. Wow, that's a big word for Beau.

"Because you clearly don't know how to take a hint."

I can hear the subtle voices whispering from the back of the room as Cade defends himself. He continued, "Tatum is the first girl to see right through your little act. That's why you keep hounding her to go out with you. C'mon man, grow up already." Cade spoke the entire rant very sternly, like a real man would as he stands up for someone he once cared for.

Once; what a strong word. I *once* loved to go to school, I *once* had people that cared for me, I *once* had a loving father. *Once upon a time,* my life wasn't so unbelievably screwed up.

He turned back to me, glancing up and down slowly as if to solidify what he'd just said to reality. I can feel myself turning a bright shade of red as I look up at Beau now hovering above me. Maybe he's protecting me in his own odd manner, but there's no need for that, especially not from Cade. He would never physically hurt me, at least not on purpose anyhow.

Before I could blink both boys were standing within a foot of the other and deep in argument. Cade hasn't spoken to me in years, and yet he seems ready to fight over a guy who is nothing more than a minor issue. It certainly doesn't help that Beau loves to fight, especially if it means getting the girl.

Now fixated on Cade, I moved my bookbag from its place on the floor over to the top of my desk, simultaneously noticing his dark blonde hair tousled from all the excitement. His jawline remains defined as he yells at Beau. I don't need to look at his eyes again to feel the anger in them.

Then it hit me; this feeling is *attraction*.

But to Cade of all people, it can't be true. It must be something else, another feeling I've uncovered in this mess of high school.

I have a lot less of those things—*feelings*—because regular girls haven't been through what I've been through. They haven't seen the things I've seen or heard the things I've heard. Their parents bought them toys and taught them that cuss words are wrong and that you make friends by showing kindness to others. My parents—well, my mother—taught me that friends never last, introduced me to corruption at much too young of an age, and is the reason that I know the world is not as forgiving as it's made to seem. God is the only one who truly always forgives. I had to learn that one on my own.

As I looked up one last time I saw Cade aggressively take off the royal blue letterman jacket he once wore so proudly. He rolled it up for just a moment before throwing it in my lap. I held on tightly to the patch on its sleeve reading *2021 State Champs*, then one line down, Star Linebacker. I stared at it in awe, careful as I ran my fingers against its pure white stitching. I was there when he made the tackle that helped win that game. Minutes before he'd been throwing water bottles, helmets, gloves—basically anything that was portable and could fit in his hands. It was the first time I caught a glimpse of what I couldn't have known was a childhood full of bottled-up anger and eagerness to understand what happened on that cold winter night.

I gather a lot about people from the little things they do.

The evening my father disappeared was the same one that the cops showed up at Cade's front door instead of just mine. It was the night he began to recognize the existence of the same sixth sense I was blessed with then too. The sense that something wasn't being told to us, that the story wasn't complete. We were sheltered from the truth because of our age, but little did those protecting us know that we would only grow more mature and unwilling to trust than we ever would've otherwise. And we both know it.

Then, just as I turned once more to look at the man whom I used to call my best friend, it all started.

The first punch was thrown.

*"What a lovely surprise to finally discover
how unlonely being alone can be."
-Ellen Burstyn*

Chapter Three

December 8, 2019~9:57 PM

Isat there, beyond quiet, on the bed I've peacefully slept in so many nights before. The copycat treasure chest from my favorite pirate cartoon, 'Jake and the Neverland Pirates', sits in the corner in front of me, untouched ever since I hid shards of glass from my mother's broken vase inside. Everything in my room is the same as it's always been, perfectly positioned and clean, just as our housekeeper Meredith left it earlier in the day. Except now, blue and red flashing lights decorate its crisp brick walls, and sirens ring out as far as I can hear. Even several streets over, the once quiet neighborhood of Earlpark is swarming with incoming police cars and panicked neighbors.

Stonson is a small town, even I know that—surely everyone wants to know why the Cassidy residence has the entire police force outside our garage.

I can see my mother outside talking with Mr. Davidson, our police chief, but her expression is not at all one of joy.

Mr. Davidson's daughter, Jenny, is in my class at school, a very beautiful girl. Her long blonde hair is always in perfect pigtails or a cute French braid, never without matching bows. Her mom, Mrs. Brooke, dresses her up in ruffled pants and hemmed skirts, never an outfit worn more than once or twice. How I wish that my mother would do the same for me rather than pay someone to buy my clothes so she doesn't have to.

Though I doubt she could pull herself away from arguing with Daddy long enough to notice this desire of mine.

Mr. Davidson walked back to his car and later returned to take my mother to the station, his ludicrous brown cowboy boots covered in what I hope is mud. I turned to my bedroom door as it slowly opened and in walked a social services worker who introduced herself as Catiey Hathaway. Catiey was very sweet, even bought me a hot chocolate to sip on while we talked about my dad. She says he's just out right now, but I know better than that.

They can't find Daddy. No one can.

Maybe they thought he told Mama where he was going. If they think she knows where he is, they're terribly wrong. She doesn't know where he's at, and I know when she's lying, trust me.

She lies a lot, to a lot of important people—me, my dad, people she works with—in fact, she does it so much that I swear she must be immune to caring what other people think of her. When she lies, she tries to cover it up, making more stories to cover her first. But Mama walked outside to the cops with a straight face. No tears, no retaliation, just a blank slate. She doesn't care what happened to Daddy, and she doesn't care what might happen to me. She isn't trying to lie about it or cover anything up. She genuinely doesn't know where he is.

And she won't lose a minute of sleep over it.

Catiey doesn't have to shelter me just because I'm a kid. I'm not clueless like the rest of the girls on my street. The Cassidys may look to everyone else like a normal family, one who is wealthier than most and lives an almost Hollywood lifestyle. Big backyard, perfect landscaping, successful jobs. But to those inside it, it's nothing more than a screwed up, distorted version of what used to be a happily married couple.

My mom, Jessica, met my dad, Michael, during an intense game of dodgeball in their high school gym. He was new to town, and she wanted to be the first to go out with him, since everyone found him rather attractive. She always planned to break up after prom, but she fell in love. They used to tell me this story all the time; at the dinner table, on picnics, even on my birthday. Daddy loved to say that if it wasn't for his dodgeball skills, I wouldn't be here. I would laugh and he'd join me, Mama worrying that he'd scarred me for life.

Everything changed when my Papa passed away. Some kind of cancer in his liver, I believe. I was four, so I don't remember much from the time, but what I do know is that his death altered the course of my life forever. I don't know how people really get cancer, I just know that you lose lots of hair and feel really sick. We weren't very close to my mom's side of the family when Papa died; she always said that I didn't need to be spoiled by their money like she was. However, despite the few years of silence between them, Papa left my mom the family business. A realty company, Shargold Homes; Shargold was her maiden name. Getting ownership of Shargold meant that she got millions, money that changed both her and our family forever. She became corrupt, obsessed with her work and a need for success in the business. She cheated on my dad a lot—still does—I always hear them arguing through the thin wall between my bedroom and theirs. But my daddy, he's a kind soul. He always forgives her, and even though she was never again the same woman he met in that sweaty gym, he stayed for me.

He's never missed a play, a talent show, or even a ballet concert. He makes sure I'm in the front row at church every Sunday, even quizzes me about the sermon after to make sure that I was listening well.

He keeps me innocent, as much as he can.

But I hear every argument, every time Mama screws over someone at work and makes another enemy, every time she puts herself over Daddy and I. I know that everything will change if he doesn't come back. No more nights filled with ice cream and giggles as we watch a movie, no more ballet recitals, and no parent left willing to give me the love and attention I look forward to.

Catiey can tell me that it's all goin' to be fine a hundred more times if it makes her feel better, but that isn't going to change the fact that I know my life may never be the same again.

That's when another cop walked in. I don't recognize him, but he sure seems to know Catiey. He walked over and placed his hand on her shoulder in an almost flirtatious manner, nodding for her to follow him over to the other side of the room. They exchanged a few mumbled words, those of which I could barely hear. But what I could make out was about Cade's parents. I know I'm not allowed to hang out with Cade anymore. His mother and mine had a fight about something and they talk no more. My dad said that Mama and Mrs. Lanie, Cade's mom, couldn't agree on what to do with land they bought together; the old property out by Hirsten Court. Daddy has taken me only once before because of the purple flowers growing on a hill there.

Purple is my favorite color, he knows that. I had never seen flowers quite like these in my life. They amazed me more and more with every step I took into the slightly itchy field full of them. Each pink stem was no more than knee-high, a beautiful array of small purple ovals blooming at the top. When looking out across the field violet buds encompassed my view for as far as the land seemed to stretch, green grass only showing itself after descending back down the hill.

I can still see the picture Daddy took of me laying in them framed on the kitchen counter a few yards away. He loves that photo, even says that I look like Mama when she was my age in it, maybe a bit younger. Last time Cade came over he said he liked it too; I showed it off like a prized trophy.

Now the new cop says they're going to Cade's house in order to talk to his parents, but I don't know why. Wait, I like that name.

"New Cop", that's what I'll call him.

But nevermind that, why does New Cop need to go to Cade's house? The Hamptons can't possibly have anything to do with my daddy leaving. They give me apple juice and crackers every time I visit their house—it's a snack we all enjoy.

Catiey gracefully made her way back over to me, her gold hoop earrings moving with the motion of her body as the blue and red lights outside reflect off of them.

"You up for a ride?" she asked.

"To Cade's house?"

She smirked, slightly tilting her head to the right as if to signify a combination of annoyance and pride towards me. "Ahh, so you've been eavesdropping."

I smiled, twirling my hair a bit.

"I just need you to look at some people and tell me what you know about them."

"I guess that's alright."

So we rode in her car all the way to Cade's house—a real nice gray car with a little green tree hanging on the mirror up front—radio turned down low. Daddy has a tree just like it in his truck. On long car rides I like to watch as it swings from side to side, the thin thread of cream-colored yarn moving with the wind. It's always there, rain or shine. The little tree isn't like people, it can't just up and leave if it doesn't want to stay. Maybe that's why I like it so much. I can depend on it being where it's supposed to be.

But more importantly, I envy it, because the tree doesn't have to worry about sudden change.

Before I knew it we were pulling into Cade's driveway, only a few minutes away from mine. I could even ride my bike here if I wanted to, but Daddy says I can't do that by myself until I'm older, high school maybe. I bet high school is fun. All the big kids get to go places by themselves, or to football games with friends, no barreling parents crowded around them. I can't wait until I grow up. Life will be easier then; it's gotta be.

After all, it can't be much harder than this.

New Cop had just walked up to Cade's front door when we parked in the pebbled driveway, knocking by the time I got out of the car. Mrs. Lanie opened the door, Cade sitting in his pajamas at the dining room table behind her. He smiled so big when he saw me, even left his bowl of late-night cereal to run over, but was abruptly stopped by his concerned mother's arm as he tried to run out to me, her lime-colored nails inches from his blonde hair. She turned to him and said something I couldn't quite hear, and then he left, cereal and all.

New Cop continued talkin' to her, but she seems upset about whatever he's saying.

I hope he isn't being mean. I'm sure she didn't do nothin' wrong.

Soon, Mr. Carl came upstairs, probably just leaving his office in their basement, and joined Cade's mama with New Cop. Suddenly Mr. Carl had a real mean look on his face, the same look he made when Cade and I dug holes in their backyard to look for "buried treasures". We were in trouble for weeks after that, but the gold rock I found made everything completely worth it.

New Cop walked inside for a few minutes, soon walking back out with Mr. Carl and Mrs. Lanie by his side. He took them in his police car, forcefully, probably to go see Mama.

Catiey told me that she has to go inside and talk to Cade for a little while, so I went with another man who took me to the station. This officer was very grumpy, didn't give me hot chocolate or nothin'. He wouldn't tell me anything about my daddy either, or about Cade, or about anyone else, just kept suggesting I take a nap or somethin'. I guess he figures that's what kids do all the time, obviously a sign that he doesn't have any kids of his own. Or maybe he does, and he's just like my mama, meaning that he enjoys his job more than seeing their ballet recitals or going to church with them every Sunday.

I don't care much for people like this cop, nor like my mama. They remind me of sad hearts, and hearts are always supposed to be happy.

Our heart is what lets us care for people, it's what lets us love. But if our heart is filled to the brink with sadness and deceit, it cannot love others as God made it to. And if there's anything that this world needs more of, it's love.

"In a world full of fear, be courageous.
In a world full of lies, be honest.
In a world where few care, be compassionate.
In a world full of phonies, be yourself.
Because the world sees you. The world hopes for you.
The world is inspired by you.
The world can be better because of you."
-Doe Zantamata

Chapter Four

September 13, 2023~2:19 PM

To my own surprise, I woke up in a musty hospital bed, no larger than a few inches over my full height. I've only been in the hospital once before, when I broke my nose back in third grade.

I had been running on the playground, the old elementary school one with brown mulch sprawled out across the entire slide. My teacher, Mrs. Cape, had just yelled for my class to come back inside from our recess break. So, as any eight-year-old would, I decided that Cade and I should race back to the classroom. We took our starting positions along the fence as Andrew, one of our closest friends, counted down from three. We started to run back together, giggling and snorting the whole time, knowing good and well our teacher would not find it amusing.

Suddenly, I tripped over an old root sticking out from underneath the raggedy picnic tables lined up by the school's red brick wall. When I got up, Cade began to holler and cry, Mrs. Cape quickly running over to discover my face dripping thick, red blood. I didn't know at the time what was broken or from where I was bleeding. All I remember after that is my dad meeting Mrs. Cape and I at the hospital to talk with the nice doctor who fixed me up. I was so scared that I would get in trouble for not listening to the playground rules, but Daddy didn't do nothin' but come over and give me a big hug.

"Did you at least beat him?" he asked, referring to the traumatic race.

I giggled, telling him that we didn't get to finish, but that I would if we got the chance later on. All he cared about was my safety. The hospital bill wasn't even a thought in his mind.

I can see the same look Daddy had back then now prominently apparent in Cade's eyes as I awake, but this time, he's the one with a banged-up face and bruised nose.

He'd been perched in a faded green chair across the room, something you would expect to find at an estate sale or landfill. He jumped up from the old chair once he realized I was awake, and within seconds our bodies were inches apart. It almost startled me that his hand was touching mine, but then I noticed the IV in my arm, and suddenly Cade's presence wasn't exactly my first priority.

I looked around to see who else might be in the room, but it's just Cade and I. It hasn't been just the two of us since we were twelve, and a flood of memories quickly began to fill my throbbing head as I reminisced those joyful times.

I turned to Cade, finding yet another cut on his neck that I hadn't noticed before. He can tell that I'm worried about him, but I'm more concerned with what happened than I am with his minor cuts.

"I'm so sorry, Tatum, this is all my fault. Beau and I got way out of hand. I should have never gotten involved."

I guess he's referring to the argument he and Beau had today during first period, over exactly what, I'm not even sure. But no matter what got into him, it still doesn't explain why I'm the one lying in a hospital bed.

Suddenly, I felt a sharp pain below my bra line. I reached over to grab my ribs, removing my hand from its spot next to Cade's. I can feel bloody bandages seeping through the thin blue and white dotted hospital gown I now wear.

"That's courtesy of Beau and I," said Cade, moving his gaze away from my face and to where my hand now lays. "When we were fighting he pushed back against the desk behind yours, then the leg snapped. Long story short, the desk fell on your foot, and you were trying to move it when he stumbled back and fell. I swung at him, but I had no idea you were pinned behind him. That cut is from my class ring, quite the piece of machinery."

Trying his best to make a joke of the situation, he slightly smiles, but I can tell deep down that he knows he messed up. I looked at his other hand, and sure enough there lie a silver class ring, surrounded by bruised knuckles and a torn fingernail.

"When you fell, your head hit the desk, and you wouldn't say anything to me. Beau reached over to check on you, but you were out." He stood silently for a moment, refusing to make eye contact with me, but also appearing uncomfortable looking away. His eyes did all they could to find a spot to land, but they never did, and so with one last blink, he closed them and tilted his head down in regret. "I'm so sorry."

I'm not sure why I didn't react at first to what Cade told me. Probably because I'm stuck in an unfamiliar place the day before my junior year homecoming dance, and I'll surely miss tonight's game. Neither Mom nor David has the decency to show up, and I'm sure they were called by the school. Although, in all honesty, that might be a good thing. If my stepdad, David, had shown up, the nurses might've called DFCS because he clearly isn't suited to care for a sixteen-year-old right now—or any kid, for that matter. He would reek from the bourbon stains on his flannel that he hasn't washed since the divorce, and if my mom showed it would be with some filthy rich lawyer friend of hers because she can't handle anything by herself. She'd probably want to sue Cade's family, especially since she still holds a grudge against his parents. To be honest, I'm not quite sure that she doesn't still blame them for what happened to my dad. But she might be right to blame them. It's the one thing we agree on.

"Where's Beau?"

I said it before I could even think through everything swirling in my chaotic mind. He opened his turquoise rimmed eyes and looked down at the ground, pulling his hand away from the bed. It was a stupid thing to say. He has been so kind to stick beside me, and I know he doesn't have to. I probably offended him by asking such a careless question. Why do I even care where Beau is anyhow? Cade is the one showing remorse. He's the one who made sure I was alright.

Maybe I'm just not used to having someone like that around, a guy there for me for a reason other than the outfit I'm wearing or the fact that I'm still single.

I desperately wanted to apologize and tell him that, but it was too late. His expression had already changed as he told me that Beau went home after the fight.

"He felt bad, Tatum, I'm sure of it. He just isn't guilty for the same reasons I am. It's not his fault that I couldn't control what I said, couldn't stick with the fact that it wasn't my conversation to begin with." He said this as he grabbed the mustard yellow bookbag he's had since fifth grade off the green chair. I can still see the fading frog sticker on the front pocket we got at his favorite restaurant, Leaper's Cove, down in Charleston.

I was just about to ask him why he got so upset about Beau not being able to take no for an answer, when suddenly he stopped at the foot of my bed and tilted his chin up from its saddened position looking at the cold hospital tiles. It's like he read my mind, like we were kids again and still in the habit of finishing each other's sentences.

"I don't know why I did it, Tatum. I just don't like seeing guys keep going when you're obviously not interested. I see it all the time in the hallway, in class, at lunch. You don't like it, I can tell. I've just never had the nerve to say anything before now."

Say something, Tatum. Say something. Say anything.

He continued, "But to be honest, I'm glad I did, and I don't regret tellin' him off. I just wish it didn't have to end with me not having you in my life again."

And then he left, taking his bookbag and half-full gallon of water with him. Every football player is told to hydrate by their paranoid coaches, but Cade always takes everything to the extreme. He looks stupid carrying the gallon around every day, but I don't think he minds the embarrassment. "Embarrassment is fake," he used to say. "Things are only awkward if we make them awkward." He always did find the good in things, he thinks so differently from everyone else. I do have to give him a little credit for how I turned out. After all, he was basically my brother for twelve years.

Why does he think we have to keep living life ignoring each other? He's the one who hasn't talked to me since that night out at the police station.

But before I could ask, he was gone, already a mile down the hall by the time I comprehended his leaving.

And so here I sit, left in a room at night once again, someone else in charge of what happens to me next. God is always in charge, of course, and I'm grateful for that. But what I don't love is the feeling of a sickly germ-infested building being where I lay to rest all by myself, the occasional nurse coming in to inject me with God knows what. The feeling is oddly like what I remember feeling that night, when I knew that my dad was never coming home again. I felt it in my gut, even when Mr. Davidson and the other officers wouldn't tell me anything. And my gut was right. It has been ever since. What I didn't know was how much his disappearance would alter the course of what could have been a pretty solid childhood.

That tan little girl who sat criss-cross applesauce on her polka dot bed sheets as she watched her mama leave and never come back the same; she had no idea how to handle anything, no helpful tips from her parents or even from Google. But now I do, yet even older, I still don't always know what moves to make.

Alone and silent, sitting in a hospital bed, legs crossed like I used to do as a child. Maybe I am a child, and everyone else has simply aged while I've stayed in the same state I was in that night. Maybe this is all a dream and tonight I'll go home to the gold-framed photo of me in violet flowers on Mama's marble kitchen counter. Maybe it will no longer remind me of what I've *lost*. Daddy will be sitting on the floor by our fireplace waiting for me to join him for movie night.

But I know this is still the same tragic reality I have dealt with for four years, and if I'm being honest, reality sucks.

"Sometimes you look like a human scribble.
Like a two year old has colored you in.
Like you've got too many feelings to fit inside the lines of your own skin.
But that, my friend, is the masterpiece."
-"What Love Is" by Andrea Gibson

Chapter Five

December 8th, 2019~10:41 PM

My eyes remain fixated on the black-plated vending machine standing against the wall in the station's lobby, my arms fully covered in chill bumps from the fan rapidly rotating above. The rude cop, whose name I later found out was Mr. Jackson, gave me a bottle of water from his office. He said I should be very responsible with it. It's the only one I'll get. But I didn't listen to him and got a few more dollars from a gracious lady for a snack to accompany my drink. I'm set on a small bag of Fritos on the third rack. Mama never lets me have them. She says they'll make my breath stink, but personally I think that's what mints are for. And right now, Mama is with Mr. Davidson, not me. Plus, I don't think she's goin' to be done anytime soon.

I watched the chip bag drop and went back to my seat, precious snack in hand. The chair Mr. Jackson left me in has a large tear towards the back, but I don't mind. He put it right next to a real nice old lady, who even gave me a cherry red cough drop to suck on while I sat. She smells like the preacher's wife, Mrs. Kathy, from church. Burnt coffee and Cheerios, I think. She told me her name is Carla and that she's waiting for her grandson to get off his shift. I don't know who her grandson is, but I gladly listened to all the stories she told about him. By the fourth story, it felt like I'd known him for years.

Daddy always says to be humble and kind, so I just sat there and smiled while she carried on with her plots. Soon enough, New Cop came strolling out of the gray doors that lead down the hallway where they took Cade's parents, water of his own in hand. Those doors scare me. I don't care for them much at all.

"David!" Carla exclaimed as she grabbed her purse and got up to greet him.

He hugged her and motioned towards the door, blowing right past both me and my Fritos. But Carla, being the sweet woman she is, stopped him and introduced us to each other. Little does she know that I've already met New Cop.

"Nice to meet you Tatum, I'm sorry I didn't ask your name earlier." He shook my hand, wiping off Frito dust after he was done. As I pulled my hand away, I noticed the purple nail polish on my right hand chipping, but I was planning to take the paint off soon anyhow.

"It's okay, you were busy." I said, trying to be polite. "I like your name. I know a guy who works with my mama named David, but he's always coming over and bringing her bottles that Daddy says I can't know about until I'm twenty-one."

Officer David laughed, saying he bet he'd like my daddy.

"Maybe one day you can come over and meet him!" I exclaimed, excited at the thought of making a new friend. When he heard me, his eyes grew saddened as he looked at Carla compassionately.

He smiled, the bags underneath his eyes darkened from a long shift. "I hope I get to do that for you, sweetie. You have a good night now." And then he left, Carla on his side, her leather magenta purse swinging from her frail arm covered with dark, circular moles.

I felt all sad inside when they left. I liked talking to them, plus, I'm out of chips. I don't like this feeling of loneliness. I never get it when Daddy is around. But this time he isn't around to talk about my day or make sure I'm not hungry from a long day at school. In fact, he's nowhere to be found; not in the lobby, not at Mama's office, and not at our house.

But the one person who I can see is Mrs. Lanie, sitting in a room right past the gray doors New Cop came out of. She's crying, but I'm not sure why. To be honest, I don't even know why she is here at all. All I know is that the police officers who came to my house can't find Daddy, but what they do have are his dog tags found at the Winn-Dixie in town.

You can learn a lot by eavesdropping in on adult conversations.

Daddy used to be a marine, says he still is at heart. He always wore his dog tags, told me that if he ever lost them, it would be like a part of him was missing. I always felt that was a very dramatic thing to say, but now I get it. I feel like a part of me is missing knowing that he might be hurting somewhere without them.

I guess he told Mr. Davidson about how important his dog tags are to him as well. So when Mama called to say that Daddy never made it home from work and he discovered the unclaimed dog tags sitting in his evidence room, he put two and two together.

I was eating spaghetti I had heated up from last night's dinner when he knocked on our front door. Mama walked outside with him and told me to go shower, get ready for bed. When I got out of the shower, I grabbed my pink koala bear towel and walked across the hall to my small bedroom.

I used to have a much bigger room upstairs, but Mama said she needs that room for her office now. I don't mind though. Daddy painted it for me and made it all pretty and nice.

I opened the door to my room and put on my pajamas, unfolding the creased bed sheets and fluffing my pillow as I finished. When I opened the curtains, the same thing that Daddy does for me every night, I saw a mob of cop cars in the driveway. A few officers talked to neighbors while others talked to my mama. I stood watching for a while, hoping that she would eventually come back inside and tell me everything would be alright.

But she never did. She just stayed outside, whether a cop was talking to her or not. It's like she wanted to do anything and everything except come in and comfort me, like she didn't want to tell me what they said to her.

The same thing is happening now, except this time my place of comfort is a musty torn chair, as I wait for anyone to come and get me. It doesn't even have to be Mama, I just need someone.

Then, just as I was close to losing hope, Cade and Catiey walked in from a small blue door directly in front of me. The door reminds me of a sunflower, light in color, yet seeping with beautiful mystery. I can tell that Cade has been crying, not hysterically, but still enough to leave tear stains on his pajama top. He doesn't seem too happy to be stuck here either.

Join the club.

Catiey motioned for him to sit with me while she talked to some lady behind a glass counter in the middle of the room. The woman's name tag read JADE, and below, FRONT DESK. I like that name. It reminds me of a necklace my Gigi once got me when we visited her in Montana. I used to wear it all the time until one day Cade and I decided to bury a time capsule in the woods behind his house. We both had to put something special in it, so I put in my necklace and he put in his blue Power Ranger figurine. I knew it was his favorite toy, but he was so excited to put it in the little pink chest I had bedazzled for us the night before, so I didn't object.

Cade sat in the chair that Carla occupied only minutes ago, wiping his tears with a tissue pulled from the box on the round table between us. In his hands is a small white bear, a NETS basketball logo sewn onto its paw.

"My dad got it for me when he went to Brooklyn last week on a business trip," he said, still sniffling. "I named him Tres, because he's my third favorite bear. Wanna hold him?"

He reached out his left hand, still holding the bear, and offered it to me. I grabbed Tres and gave him a great big hug. He laughed, but I can tell he's still upset. Before I could ask what was so upsetting, Catiey walked over and reached for my hand.

"Ready to go?" she asked, smiling.

"Go where?" I replied. I hope she doesn't make me leave Cade. I never get to see him anymore. I just want to make sure he's okay.

"We're going to have a talk with some of my officer friends. Is that okay?"

Against my wishes, I nodded and walked with her through the big gray doors, sadly waving goodbye to Cade. I still have his bear tightly gripped in my shaky hands. I hope he doesn't mind me borrowing Tres for a while. I have a feeling I might need a friend.

Once we walked through the doors and past the room where Mrs. Lanie sits, I saw a large glass door swung open on my left, Mr. Davidson sitting at a wooden desk inside. He looked very serious when he waved Catiey and I in, almost scary. Mama calmly sits across from him in a chair just like the torn one in the lobby, only this one is much bigger, and a matching one sits beside it. I sat in that other chair once I saw that Catiey had left, careful to shut the door behind her. When I turned back to Mr. Davidson's desk, I noticed a tan colored file sitting in front of him, but the room still stood silent. It stayed that way for a few more seconds, he and Mama exchanging glances back and forth, occasionally looking at me.

Eventually Mama said that she had to use the restroom and left me all alone with Mr. Davidson. This isn't an unusual occurrence, her not being here when I need her the most. This is usually the part where Daddy comes in and talks to me, or compassionately dries my tears. But he isn't here this time. I don't really know where he is.

Finally, Mr. Davidson spoke up, saying, "Tatum, do you believe in God?"

It was an extremely random question, but I answered rather quickly, nonetheless. "Yes sir. My daddy takes me to church every Sunday. We go to the one off Derek Drive."

He nodded. "So then you know about Heaven?"

I laughed at his silly question. "Of course I know about Heaven! That's where my Papa is. Daddy says he's probably up there right now fishin' away. He used to build houses, you know, probably even built himself a big ole' mansion up there!" He smiled for only a second before his face saddened, just as Cade's had.

"Your Papa was a good man. He used to help teach my Sunday school class every week when I was about your age. I have no doubt that God let him in those golden gates, but Tatum..." he stopped.

This is the first time I've ever seen a grown man shed a tear. He looked back at me after taking a sip of water from his bottle and frowned.

"He got a new buddy up there tonight." I'm very confused by what he means. Of course my Papa has friends up there, but I don't know how Mr. Davidson knows if he made a new one or not.

After a few seconds, I think he realized that I don't quite understand what he's getting at. "Sweetie, your daddy got to meet up with him tonight." He stopped once more, taking a deep breath before continuing. "He must've missed their fishing trips too much."

He tried to make a joke out of what he said, lighten the mood a bit, but I still don't understand. Why is Daddy with Papa? He was supposed to come home early tonight and finish a movie with me. He knew that.

"Why is he in Heaven? I thought you only get to go there once you die."

Then it hit me. Even a scared little girl can figure out the last piece to a puzzle.

A deadly puzzle.

I looked up, my eyes filling with tears, and saw that Mr. Davidson's were doing the same.

"I'm so sorry, Tatum, but he's in a better place now. God will keep him safe and make sure he can watch over you every day. If you ever need anything, Jenny and I would be happy to—"

The sweet conversation he kept attempting to have with me was now being abruptly interrupted by the glass door violently swung open on my right. It's my mother, no tears in her eyes, makeup just as it was before she left the house. Her face remained stiff as a board, only forgotten memories and severe oppression seen on it. She moved her perfectly straightened hair behind one ear, allowing her gold hoop earrings to be proudly showcased.

I remember when she bought them for a New Year's party, telling me that the ones Daddy and I got her for Christmas weren't going to work with the outfit she planned to wear. She wanted a new pair, more expensive ones. She's always wanting more; more money, more clothes, more out of Dad and I.

But at this moment, she seems to want nothing more than to snatch away the small sliver of innocence I still possess.

"He's dead."

Two words I never want to hear again, words out of a bad dream. No, not a bad dream, a nightmare.

"Jessica," began Mr. Davidson. He looked just as shocked as I was to hear that she would so abruptly say such a thing.

"What? She needs to be introduced to the real world, John. Life's hard, it's not always fair." She turned her gaze to me, a stern expression on her face. "Tell her how they found him." She was clearly directing her speech towards Mr. Davidson, though her eyes remain fixated on me. He hesitated before eventually speaking up.

"Your dad was hunting in the woods just before he passed away. We found him barely outside of town, near the barn on the old hunting grounds."

The old hunting grounds? Cade and I used to play in a treehouse out there all the time as kids; his dad owns the land. Everyone in town knows you must alert Mr. Carl if you want to go out there and hunt.

Maybe that's why Mr. Carl and Mrs. Lanie are here. Maybe Daddy talked to them about visiting the land. But I doubt it, especially with how rude Mama has been to them recently.

There's something I need to tell Mr. Davidson, but before I knew it he and Mama were arguing back and forth about what I should and shouldn't be told. I kept trying to butt in, but Mama would just shush me and put her hand up to stop my interruptions. Finally, Mr. Davidson noticed my need to speak and addressed it.

"Tatum, I know you must have a lot of questions and probably want to ask me all of them, but right now..."

My turn to interrupt.

"No sir, no questions." Of course I'm lying, I have so many questions. How did he die? Did it hurt? When will I get to go to Heaven too and see him and Papa? But for right now, I only need to let him know one thing. "I just thought I'd let you know something."

He smiled, my lack of questions clearly bringing him relief.

"What is it, sweetie?" It's becoming obvious he feels remorse for snapping at me moments ago. I sat up a little straighter and held onto Tres tighter, then I said it.

"My daddy doesn't hunt."

Chapter Six

September 14, 2023~1:03 PM

They released me from the hospital at one in the afternoon, the bright sun painfully shining through my patient's room window. I didn't sleep all night, I couldn't. I found that it's hard to lie down comfortably when you have a bruised rib on one side and a gash the size of a quarter above it.

My phone sits still beside me, brightness on high, messages app open to Cade's contact. Eight hours of sitting in silence, the occasional visit from a nurse or doctor, and I still can't decide whether I should text him.

I still had his name pulled up when I walked outside to the hospital's entrance, simultaneously running into quite the character; a woman in a cheetah-print jacket and black heels, cigarette in hand. She looks like Kim Novak in Bell, Book, and Candle, only a little more drunk.

"Are you Tatum?" she said, smacking a single piece of gum just a little too violently.

How can she possibly smoke and chew gum at the same time?

I almost want to laugh at how much my new acquaintance reminds me of the washed-up stepmom in every teen drama movie ever, but I held it in.

"Who's asking?"

"Name's Bailey, I'm a friend of your dad. He sent me to pick you up. Guess he couldn't make it." What that really means is that she's one of my dad's many girlfriends and he's passed out drunk somewhere. I hate when people refer to David as my "dad". To me, he is nothing more than some name on the same custody paper as mine.

"No thanks, I can find a ride home."

I never accept the rides David finds me, and it probably wouldn't end well if I did. Bailey didn't seem to care much about my decision, leaving without a second thought. She peeled off in an older black Camry, a long white scratch down the driver's side door, a detail that oddly caught my attention.

I hitched a ride on the city bus, which was fine. My step-dad's house is only six or seven miles from the hospital. Another perk of living in a small town; you're never more than twenty minutes away from anything. When I got there, David was sitting on the bed of his truck wearing the same flannel he's always in, beer in one hand and phone in the other.

Mom married him a few years back after Dad died. She met David through work, he was the youngest worker she'd ever employed. But I'm sure they were "involved" long before he was hired, and long before my dad passed. This isn't news to me, but David doesn't know that.

He officially adopted me last year, against my wishes. I have better judgment than to put any part of my life in the hands of a man like David. But it was what Mama wanted, so I complied. That's the last time I listen to a woman who can't get her own life in control, much less someone else's. When they filed for divorce, he got partial custody since I'm technically his daughter by legal requirements.

That's what happens when the only judge in town happens to be married to his divorce lawyer. But I'm only his kid legally, not biologically. I would be ashamed if he was truly part of my bloodline.

"Where ya been?" he said, slurring almost every word.

"You know where I've been. You sent a drunk to pick me up, did you not?" I regretted saying it the minute I finished, but at the same time, it felt so good to get out some of the anger I've been bottling up.

"I sent Bailey over an hour ago. The hospital is ten minutes from here."

I told him about my taking the bus, even though it meant having to lie and say that Bailey's car got towed while she was inside getting me. And somehow it worked, so he carried on with his beer without a care in the world. He never really cares what I do unless it impacts his life.

Trust me, I do anything and everything I can to avoid crossing paths with him.

I walked inside and headed straight to my bedroom. Well, I call it my room, but it's really just an old laundry in which I set up a twin-sized bed frame and mattress. The frame only cost me thirty bucks from a yard sale, but that shows in the rust lining its black rod headboard.

Hung up on an old coat rack I found in the garage is my hot pink dress, cinched at the waist. I've waited weeks to put it on, along with the matching silver heels that sit below its fragile fabric lining. Kelly and I bought it when we went shopping at the outlets for homecoming dresses, it was the only one that fit my oversized hips. Kelly's school is having their homecoming dance tonight too, except she chose a baby blue long-sleeve dress hitting right below her upper thighs rather than one similar to mine. My dress, on the other hand, came off the clearance rack in the back of our Macy's outlet store, something I can afford. Everyone thinks that since my mom is loaded, I must be loaded too, but she never cared about my needs when Dad was here, and she certainly doesn't now. She says the money would spoil me, make me a brat.

Money does change people, but I'm not the one she needs to worry about it changing.

She usually leaves me twenty bucks on the counter whenever it's my turn at her house, for dinner food, since she's never home to cook. Most nights I just pocket it and eat an extra yogurt in the morning to fill my appetite. Believe it or not, it's hard to find time for a job when you have practice all week and no car to get you there.

I bought the dress with what I saved from a weekend at mom's, three nights getting me sixty bucks. Tonight I have to be at the school by seven o'clock. That gives me over six hours to find something to do with myself.

I threw the dress and shoes in a plastic bag I found balled up in the corner, along with some makeup and a curling wand.

When I walked back outside, David was pulling out of the driveway, probably going to do some freelance work by the mills like he has every Saturday since Mom fired him from the company. That means I'm left with no ride and an empty house all to myself. Not that I would've asked David for a ride anyhow, but it's always nice to have the option.

I can't possibly ride my bike to the school and carry all this nonsense; my brush, dress, and plastic bag all at once. I look over to the end of the driveway, two mailboxes positioned beside each other. 151 and 153, David's house and the Whitlock's house. Dixie Whitlock and I are friends. She's honestly one of the most genuine people I've ever met. Her family's farm is by far the prettiest in Stonson, not too many acres to handle, but just enough, each plot thick with cows and horses alike. Every animal they own is bred to the finest standard possible, fed and housed with care by Dixie and her eleven siblings. If I get blessed with children of my own, I'd want a family like the Whitlock's have, charming and genuine, but still goofy when needed.

I can see Dixie and her perfect matte black hair from here, gracefully playing with some massive four-legged thing in the field beyond our driveway. She looked over, effervescently waving her dirt-covered hands from side to side until I finally waved back. I would ask her for a ride, or maybe even her older brother Madden, but I don't want to be a bother. I know they've heard about the divorce by now, and I know that my mother wasn't exactly the kindest person when selling them their property a few years back, but they don't know what's really going on. I doubt they see David's raggedy old pickup pulling out the driveway at three in the morning going Lord knows where, his bright headlights blinding me through the windows. I doubt they can see my plastered and broken face from this distance, hopping on my makeshift bike way too early just so that no one sees me on the road.

Dixie has always been there for me when I ask for help, but I've asked too much recently. She can't do anything about my situation now, none of my friends can.

So I pray. It's all I can do, and it's all I know how to.

I pulled out my phone and texted some girls on the cheer team. They should still be at the school painting more Homecoming banners. I figure I'll walk over there since I can't possibly ride my bike and carry this crap. The school isn't that far from here, but that doesn't help the fact that it's eighty degrees outside and not exactly walking weather.

So I started on the walk, sweat dripping through my already pierced pores and into the seams of my shirt. My bandages will have to be reapplied after this, but unless I can get a minute away from everyone, I won't do it. If they see me hurting, then I could lose everything I've worked for, everything towards maintaining this tough exterior. Nothing phases Tatum Cassidy, right?

On my left is nothing more than cotton fields as far as the eye can see, little white particles effortlessly flying through the humid summer air. On my right, acres of land filled with verdant plants and resplendent flowers blooming ever so crisply underneath the radiant sun. The birds chirping above force me to look up towards their euphonious chimes, distracting me completely from the heavy bag in my perspiring hands. Their evocative steady tone reminds me of days in the park with Dad, those halcyon days of my past more bittersweet than ever before.

I hate being left alone to do everything by myself, but at times like this, it doesn't seem so bad. Quiet, isolated, stunning beauty surrounding me. I've done nothing to deserve such moments as this one, silence filling the space between me and the trees with such ease.

Despite my continuous efforts to stay in this moment and enjoy the sublime natural beauty of Stonson's vacant back roads, the never ending vibration in my back pocket eventually won the battle, snatching my attention disgracefully. An unnecessary text from Riley, my favorite cheerleader. She's also our only senior on the team, but I've known her since we were little.

COME IN THRU BACK DOOR, FRONT ENTRANCE BLOCKED OFF.

The front entrance to SHS is probably blocked off in preparation for the dance, our student council's way of getting a head start on decorating.

When I got to the school, I saw Kate Hatfield's red Toyota 4Runner parked out front, her monogrammed initials placed swiftly across the back windshield in a glitter cursive font. Kate and I haven't spoken since her ex-boyfriend Mack asked me out last September. If I remember correctly, the thought of him moving on so quickly after their breakup pissed her off. So she blamed me instead of her "perfect dream guy", who in her eyes could do no wrong. Kate is also the head of our student council, a classic mean girl. You always think the movies dramatize those characters. Surely girls would never act so petty in real life, but this one does.

I walked past her car and headed towards the back of the gym so Riley could let me in. I'm sure everyone knows about the fight by now. I'd be surprised if there aren't even a few videos, different angles and all. If there's one thing you can count on high schoolers to do, it's video fights. We may not pass our classes or stop bullying from happening, but trust me, we're professionals with a camera.

"Tatum! Where ya' been?"

When I looked up the door had already been swung wide open, Riley's strawberry blonde hair blowing behind it. That's when I realized that she definitely hasn't heard about my lovely little trip to the emergency room. Apparently, neither had half the team, because when I walked in, not a single soul asked if I was okay or what happened. Actually, only one girl ended up asking, a freshman whom I recognize as one of our flyers. We've never really talked before, maybe once when I borrowed a hair tie or something.

"How's your side?" she whispered to me, as if she didn't want anyone else to hear. I leaned down, figuring I'd whisper too, just to join in the fun.

"It's fine, just a little scratch. No biggie." I said this knowing good and well it was a lie. I took three or four ibuprofen before leaving the house, not to mention all the medicine I got at the hospital. The girl, who I now know goes by Lauren, explained why no one else knows about my little incident. When the fight broke out, the rest of the school was in the gym for our pep rally. I guess Mr. Daniels didn't get that memo. I totally forgot to meet the team during that class, but no one called or texted to remind me.

Goes to prove how little I mean to this team.

Quietly giggling she continued, "All we heard was that Beau got in another fight, but this time he didn't win so big. No one knew about you getting hurt. Cade told me that your class was asked not to spread the word.

I find it hard to believe that word wouldn't spread quickly in a public high school, especially when the word is that a cheerleader got knocked out by two guys double her size, but I played along. "So, why did Cade tell you?" I didn't mean to come off as rude, but in all honesty, I've never seen Cade talk to Lauren in his life.

"I bumped into him on his way out of the principal's office yesterday afternoon, said he was headed to meet you at the hospital. Looked like he was in a hurry too, dropped this when he ran out."

She dug around in her green Lululemon backpack and pulled a blue and yellow bow out, eagerly showing it to me. That's when I realized that my hair isn't pulled back anymore, no bow keeping my thick ponytail in place. It must've fallen out during the fight, assuming Cade picked it up for me.

I grabbed it from her pale hand, thanking her as I walked over to help Riley with the banners.

Why isn't Cade here? Most of the football team is helping us finish up banners, even Beau. Given he hasn't looked up from his paint bucket one time since I walked in, but at least he's present. Although he is on crutches, so it doesn't look like he would've made much of a dance partner tonight anyhow. Lauren said that Cade and Beau were suspended, but they managed to talk our principal, Mr. Roberts, into letting them come to the dance tonight.

I'll never understand how some kids can sweet-talk adults like that. I can't even convince myself to be more open-minded most of the time.

After hours of painting, everyone eventually started to pack up and head home to get ready for the dance. I told Riley that my ride was on its way, but in reality, my plan is to use one of the school restrooms as my personal dressing room. It's too hot to walk back to the house, and Mom would never stop her busy work schedule just to come pick me up. I could ask Riley for a ride, but then I would have to explain why David's drunk self can't come get me, in addition to why I don't have a car of my own.

So I watched passively as everyone left the gym in a chattering mob, no one glancing back to see if I was following. The boisterous football players squeaked their overpriced shoes across the freshly waxed floors as they filed through the gym's large double doors, each step deafening for every female in the room. Soon enough it was just me sitting on the gym floor with my bags, battered cheer bow still grasped tightly in hand. Here I am, left to sit in silence with my thoughts once again. This seems to be a much too frequent occurrence nowadays, but quite frankly, that's never really changed.

I've never been a major priority to anyone in this school. Well, anyone except for Cade, but I guess that doesn't matter now.

Not much matters now.

*"Beginning today, treat everyone you meet as if they
were going to be dead by midnight.
Extend to them all the care, kindness, and understanding
you can muster, and do it with no thought of any reward.
Your life will never be the same again."*
-Og Mandino

Chapter Seven

December 8th, 2019~11:01 PM

The observation I told Mr. Davidson about Daddy's lack of interest in hunting sent what felt like a sudden shock wave through the entire Stonson police department. His eyes immediately grew big, and he ran out of the room, almost knocking over Mama on his way out. The passionate shove forced her to turn back at me after watching him run down the hallway, offering nothing more than a nasty look. It wasn't exactly a look of anger, nor was it one of disapproval.

It was a look of pure rage.

Her expression is the common result of a cluster of events happening much too fast for one woman to handle. She began to scream, pointing her finger as if I'm the one in the wrong, but I'm used to it by now. She went on and on about how I'm just a child, how I don't know nothin' compared to her. Apparently, I should have just kept my mouth shut and held onto the stupid bear I'd acquired. She reached down and snatched that pretty white bear from my grip, holding it up as if it was a trophy she'd won.

"Where did you even get this piece of junk?!" she yelled, inching closer and closer to my face with every word.

I don't know why, but I didn't answer Mama's question. I always try my best to listen and do what she and Daddy tell me to, but I don't think she's right this time. She stared at me for a second before following up with, "Are you gonna answer me or not?"

But I still didn't.

Daddy says that violence will get me nowhere, but he also told me to always talk through an argument civilly in an effort to resolve it. Sorry Daddy, I don't think that's gonna work this time.

I stood up from my chair, no longer having anything to hold on to but the sorrow in my heart. By now Mama had put Tres down by her side, still leisurely waiting for my response. I don't ever want to do anything like it again, but in that moment, I reached over and snatched Cade's bear from her hand. She wasn't holding onto it very tight; her focus now on me rather than the bear.

"You know what, Mama? I bet you're glad he's dead, one less person to tell you when you're wrong."

And that was the last thing I said to my mama all night. I walked out through the open glass door and followed Mr. Davidson down the hall, shaking from the fear that she might come after me. But when I turned back, my headstrong but terrified self shaking as I held Tres, Mama still stood in the doorway of his office, probably shocked by what I said.

I'm sorry, Mama, but you aren't right this time.

I turned forward and watched as Mr. Davidson entered the room where I had seen Mrs. Lanie crying before. I'm not quite tall enough now to see through the glass as I had been in the lobby, but tippy toes are a pretty magical thing.

Mrs. Lanie sits at the grayish metallic table towards the center of the room, Mr. Davidson and one more officer across from her. The room looks very much like the one in a show Daddy used to watch all the time. It even has cops in it, just like now.

Whenever I'd walk into the bedroom to visit him, he would turn it off and say I'm too young to watch. I hate when people tell me I can't do something because of my age. I see people all the time a lot older than me doing much dumber things. Age doesn't matter a whole lot, in my opinion. What really matters is how you carry yourself. My teacher says that some kids aren't as fortunate as I am, that's why they act out or say rude things.

But I don't think that money has anything to do with it, at least not when it comes to someone's character. It's the problems that God gives you to figure out that make a person who they are.

Do you get all sad and say that the task is too hard to do? Do you lash out, or do you stand up for what is right? I don't know yet which of those is the best thing to do, but I'm not sure any of us can answer that question with total certainty. Maybe the right answer is something in between; the best of both worlds. Maybe God wants us to handle the problems He throws at us in our own way, with a lot of prayer and a bit of patience.

That's something it looks like Mr. Davidson needs to work on. His patience, I mean. He asked Mrs. Lanie, Cade's mom, a question, but all she did was cry. Over and over, more tears than I have ever seen one person emit in a single sitting. Then he began to scream at her, a little louder each time.

To my surprise, within a minute, Mrs. Lanie just stopped crying. It looked almost as if he had broken her, yet her eyes didn't look too broken. They just look dark, as if she's too tired to know what to say. But I guess I was wrong, because she sure did answer Mr. Davidson's question, and with a kick of enthusiasm, too. Although he clearly doesn't approve of her answer. I'm not very good at reading lips, but I know she's asking about Mr. Carl, Cade's dad. I haven't seen him here at the station yet. Maybe he's just in another room with a different scary table. I hope he isn't gonna get screamed at like Mrs. Lanie did. He doesn't deserve that.

"They must thunk she killed em."

The words came unexpectedly from a slurring voice behind me, the grammar terribly incorrect. A woman's voice, very southern and very drunk. When I turned around, I saw a police officer holding the woman in handcuffs, her long black hair falling over the left side of her face.

She looks a lot like my aunt, except this woman is much taller, and my auntie is a Mormon, so she says she can't drink.

Auntie lies a lot.

"That's enough," said the officer holding her, quickly apologizing for the inappropriate outburst. "She isn't thinkin' straight." I smiled, saying it was fine. I watched intently as they left through those same gray doors I came in through, the woman practically dragging her feet across the floor as they walked.

Surely she was wrong; Mr. Davidson and the other cop couldn't possibly think that Cade's mama hurt my daddy. Daddy was hunting when he died, or at least that's what they all think. But I know that must be a lie, because Daddy always said that killing animals for fun is a bad thing to do. The only thing he liked was fishing, but he always released them back into the water once he caught em'.

At first, I thought Mama and Mr. Davidson had just made that up so they would have a story to tell me about what happened to him, but maybe I was wrong. When I explained that Daddy doesn't hunt, it looked like a surprise to them both. Maybe Mama doesn't know about Daddy's rules against hunting, which actually makes sense. She isn't home enough to hear him tell me things like that. Actually, she isn't home to hear him tell me much of anything. Maybe that's why she got so mad—he didn't want to hear any news she didn't like.

If that's the case, someone else is bound to get yelled at eventually, because Mama also hates Cade's parents with a passion. They in the same building will not end well. It's been that way ever since the land on Hirsten Court couldn't be resold. If they had something to do with Daddy going missing, she'll have their throats. Well, that's what you would think, them being married for over twenty years and all.

But when Mama finally left Mr. Davidson's office, she kept on walking right past both me and the scary room where Mrs. Lanie sits. In fact, she kept going until she was no longer in the police department at all.

This moment is one that I know that I will remember forever. I can tell even standing here now.

This is the first time I can remember my mom crying over anyone other than herself. She cried all the way out to the Uber she'd called and left me standing all alone in that quiet hallway. Alone with a stuffed bear and crying, right behind those big gray doors.

"If I showed you my teardrops,
Would you collect them like rain,
Store them in jars,
That are labeled with 'Pain',
Would you follow their tracks,
From my eyes down my cheeks,
As they write all the stories,
I'm too scared to speak,
Would you stop them with kisses,
Bring their flow to a halt,
As you teach me that pain,
Isn't always my fault,
Would you hold my face gently,
As you dry both my eyes,
And whisper the words,
'You're too precious to cry',
If I showed you my teardrops,
Would you show me your own,
And learn though we're lonely,
We're never alone."
-"If I showed you my teardrops", by Erin Hansen

Chapter Eight

September 14th, 2023~7:41 PM

It took me an hour to figure out how to do my hair the way I saw on a Pinterest video. The girl who posted the tutorial called it a "waffle cone", but mine looks more like a messy braid plopped aggressively atop my head. It's the only hairstyle I could find that I knew would show the blonde highlights underneath my hair, something very few people know about. Besides not complimenting the bronze-colored eyeshadow I found at the general store for two bucks, all-in-all I'm proud of how I manage to clean up.

When I left the women's restroom on the second floor, I could already hear music coming from downstairs. The clock above the east wing staircase flashed seven forty-one with a slight red hue, the dance has been going on for almost thirty minutes now.

I turned the corner to go downstairs, careful not to slip on the freshly mopped tile, when into my eyeline came an uncontrollable line of people, guys and girls alike. Their suits and dresses vary in color from charcoal black to chartreuse yellow to boysenberry purple, everyone waiting to show their tickets at the table up front. I headed to take a spot in line with Riley and some others, all sharing a bittersweet moment over the fact that it's her last homecoming night.

Just as I approached the group in the middle of a photo with Teresa's new digital camera, she announced, "Four years and I still never get tired of these dances."

Riley's personality is somewhere in between a heavenly angel and an overwhelmingly dramatic diva. Some days she offers the most engaging and intellectual advice, while others she rolls into school looking everyone who passes her up and down with a stern glare as if she's just threatened to put them on a red list. But I can't say much. I'd pay a killing to have a body like hers. Thin waist, toned legs, and hair unlike anyone else at this redneck school.

When we got up to the front of the line, Kate Hatfield and her younger brother, Jonathan, were running the booth. She wasn't too happy to see me, but I'd already prepared myself for this before I walked into the vicinity.

Quickly pulling up the QR code ticket on my phone, I showed it to her, still keeping a good few feet in between us to be safe. She scrunched up her nose as if it was a disgusting sight—or maybe she thought I was the disgusting sight—but let me in anyway, only after mumbling under her breath to both me and Riley.

"Hit on anyone else's boyfriend recently?"

I don't want to engage with her already inflated ego more than I have to, but Teresa, on the other hand, would have a field day with this if we let her. She whipped around, carelessly smacking me in the face with her hair, and scowled, "If she has, at least we know it couldn't be yours. He's been on a leash for the last two years."

Astonished, Kate stood up and slapped the plastic card table with great force, getting ready to say something in response, but Teresa shoved us all into the gym, giggling before it went any further.

The once brown and yellow gym walls are now decorated intricately with neon colored streamers and banners, a wobbly green DJ table at the center of it all. As we enter, Cruel Summer plays obnoxiously over the loudspeakers to match the theme for this year's dance, 80's Retro. The apparent clicks reside in each corner of the gym, the kids who do sports and those in academic clubs on opposite ends.

I swear, high school is starting to feel more and more like a hidden camera reality series by the day.

I followed Riley over to where most of the seniors sit casually talking, by the stage on the far end of the gym. I'm not a senior just yet, but most everyone who I've befriended over the past three years is, so it's no problem that I join them.

I went to take my seat on the stage steps, a deep voice exclaiming, "Tater Tot!" from a few feet away. Devon, our starting quarterback, who also happens to be the son of my mom's secretary, Martha. Martha and Devon moved here from the West coast two summers ago, both still talk with a classic surfer accent, except Devon looks the part too.

"Who knew you'd have the guts to show your face here after last week's beat down?" I said this referring to our gym class last Tuesday when we played flag football. All it took was one precise yank at his belt and he was out like a light. If you ask me, he was too busy flirting with the new student teacher to play much of anything.

"You just got lucky, my friend," he said, attempting to bring me in for a hug. I don't care much for physical touch, so I transitioned to a pat on the back instead, but he didn't seem to mind. We sat and caught up on life for almost an hour, leaving only once to get pink lemonade from the back table by the restrooms. I was just about to fill him in on the fight yesterday when I noticed something bulky walking in our direction from the corner of my eye—a tall, dirty blonde, his blue eyes practically gleaming off the ceiling's spotlights. No doubt it's Cade, a small plate in hand, holding up a single chocolate cupcake. His face still appears scraped up, but how can anyone possibly focus on that when he's wearing such a slick black and white tux? Thin layers around his ankles, a neutral-colored belt with a gold clip; I'll admit, I'm impressed. His mom likely had tailored it for him—after all, she always has him dressed for the part—no matter who paid for it, Cade's owning it.

He walked over to some boys sitting behind Devon, a few of whom I recognize from this afternoon's banner decorating. After greeting everyone kindly, per usual, he quickly burst out in laughter over something his friend, Andrew, said, a row of perfectly straight teeth coming into full view. I had only a few seconds to admire them before he closed his mouth and continued socializing.

I wonder what all those lips have said in the years I've missed. I remember the long conversations he and I used to have, every syllable and vowel exchanged from my mouth to his, now long forgotten. Does he miss our friendship like I do? Or is it something else entirely? Is he grateful he cut me out when he did?

This is also the moment when I realized his beautiful blue eyes looking directly at me, an awkward situation for us both. Cade changed his demeanor quickly at the sight of my glare, now much more upset than before. In this moment, my brain could only think of one thing to do.

Run.

"I'm so sorry, Devon. I have to go. I'll tell you all about it later, okay?" I excused myself from the conversation and headed straight for the doors, Devon shrugging my sudden outburst off and moving onto the next group of girls.

No matter how much I hate the thought of passing Kate's table again, I hate the thought of confronting Cade even more.

Knowing Cade, he would've tried to come over and talk to me earlier, probably apologize for running out of my hospital room so rudely, but when I turned back to see his sunken face once more, he wasn't moving. He still stands where I left him, watching as I trot out. I usually have no problem confronting people, the world needs more face-to-face conversations. If people would just learn to sit and talk with friends from time to time, rather than texting, we would all know so much more about the people we surround ourselves with.

But maybe this time I've overestimated Cade's concern with making amends.

I grabbed the door handle leading out of the gym and walked outside, hands profusely sweating as I hurry away. 9:13 PM, officially dark outside, only a few people leaving the dance early like me. I can hear and smell others tailgating towards the back of the parking lot, drinking what I know isn't the pink lemonade from inside. I walked through the doorway and into the sultry summer air, easily finding a spot to sit while I gather my thoughts—the old bench outside, completely covered in leaves and bird droppings. It's usually where I tend to be pulled to. Places that are lonely or run-down, abandoned by those who once cherished its presence. Kind of like me.

As I sat contemplating, I saw a few more girls come out from the dance together, giggling and taking selfies as they walked. One girl flaunted a mint green dress, two spaghetti straps loosely holding it up, her butt dramatically poked out. The other two girls wear blue dresses, one with a pure white cardigan covering her frail arms and the other without a coat at all. The girl with the cardigan split off from the others and watched as her friends headed for the parking lot, phone and purse covering a small waist.

I recognize the girl; Brynlee, I think. Her mom is Stonson's only dentist, a real young Indian woman who moved to the States around the time my parents got married. If I remember right, she started dating Mr. Berkley around the time Cade and I were born. He works at the bank in town, a very successful man to this day.

I've seen Brynlee around school a few times, maybe once or twice at her mom's office, when I went to get my teeth cleaned. She's a sophomore, very wholesome to the naked eye, only two piercings in each ear and not a mole to be found anywhere on her skin. Her complexion is dark, but clear, the same hazel eyes as her mother's only adding to her natural beauty. They look similar in that way, but also in the manner that they both have such petite figures.

Brynlee definitely recognizes me, but I guess it isn't too hard to notice a random chick staring at you from afar. She came and sat beside me, sighing as she plopped herself down forcefully.

She smiled, "Rough night?"

At first I was confused as to why she would think that, but when I looked down, I realized what she meant; a huge stain on my dress from where I must have spilled my drink on the way out.

"You know, you'd think pink lemonade wouldn't leave a stain like that on a pink dress." I laughed, Brynlee joining in as if we've been friends for the longest time.

"We all have those nights every once in a while. Some more often than others," she said, wiping a tear from her face. It was almost too direct of a statement for me to comprehend, but I asked what was wrong, nonetheless. She reached over to her right shoulder, removing a part of the cardigan that once sat there in its place. She revealed a bruise on her upper arm, still light in color, not yet healing by the looks of it.

"What happened?"

While I am intrigued by the bruise, I already know the answer to my question. Someone would've had to grab her arm and hold it real tight in order to make a mark like that.

"He didn't mean to," she said, almost whimpering too low for me to fully hear.

"Who did?"

I've only ever seen Brynlee with one guy before, but he's still dating Hannah Damon from West Cove High in the next town over. If she does have a boyfriend, I don't think anyone else is aware of it.

"His name is TJ, he's a junior. I met him last year at a soccer game we both went to see over in Richmond. We've been dating ever since."

"TJ Barrett?"

"Yeah, you might know him. But last week we had a fight, and I ended up breaking it off. It was over something stupid, but he always made even the slightest disagreements a big deal. I thought it would be fine when I noticed he showed up tonight wanting to talk, but..."

She stopped for a minute, looking down at the ground, her eyes dropping a tear or two every few seconds. "He just couldn't accept the fact that I didn't want to talk. He grabbed me as I walked away, but he didn't mean to grip me so hard. At least, I don't think he did. That's why I was walking with those girls, just so I would have an excuse to leave." She inched a little closer to my seat, still wiping tears from her face, then whispered in my ear as if to make sure no one else could hear. "I don't even know them."

I know TJ from biology last year, a real introvert. I always thought his look was—how do I put this—unique, to say the least. Brown curly hair, tall, slender, the same black leather jacket draped across his narrow shoulders every other day. I'll never forget the rattle that echoed through our small lab room every time he walked in wearing silver dog collared boots. He's very hairy, almost to a point that it seems unnatural, but he kept to himself for the most part. I never pinned him to be aggressive with women, just figured he could use some manners.

Brynlee now leans into my shoulder, still crying, but more on the side of uncontrolled sniffles rather than sobs. Looking up, she introduced herself, realizing I'm clearly not as familiar with her as she was with me.

"I'm Bryn. I've seen you in my mom's chair a few times. Always thought you had real pretty hair. I would kill to have highlights like yours." I'm shocked she noticed them. No one ever has before.

"Tatum," I said back to her, although I'm pretty confident she already knows my name.

I was just about to compliment her dress when the doors a few feet behind us abruptly swung open, and out walked a large group of guys, each with a date on their arm. Towards the end of the group stood Cade, no girl attached to his hip like that of his friends. He looked out into the parking lot as if to look for someone, but his eyes immediately stopped wandering once they met mine. Brynlee noticed my stare, turning around to look at Cade as well. She softly smiled and stood up, glancing back and forth between Cade and I.

She understands.

"I'll see you around Tatum." Almost smirking, she turned to the doors and looked at Cade once more. "Hampton, nice seein' you." Cade laughed and waved her goodbye, leaving just the two of us to be alone.

She headed into the parking lot, the cardigan now hanging off her arm a bit, threatening to hit the ground unless she pulls it up quickly. Cade awkwardly took his seat on the now silent bench, both of us waiting for each other to start the conversation.

"I guess I should apologize." He looked at me and shrugged. "For earlier."

I want nothing more than to tell him how his leaving really made me feel, to tell him everything I've ever thought about saying to him over the past four years. All the nights I spent in tears, knowing none of my friends cared enough to notice my pain, knowing he was perfectly fine without me. Every time I passed his house and relished in remembrance of our memories, every time my heart broke a little more because he walked by without so much as a glance in my direction. But I didn't. I took the coward's way out and told him it was fine.

No harm, no foul.

"No, it's not fine. Even though I didn't mean to hit you, it doesn't make what I did okay." He began fidgeting with a rubber ball in his left hand, a makeshift stress releaser. It looks much like the ones

Bryn's mom has in her office, styrofoam balls she sold to raise money for the volleyball team last year. Now the leftover ones just sit in a bowl on the front desk for advertisement.

He must've seen me looking at the ball and noticed my confusion, because of course he felt the need to address it.

"My dad left it on the counter the other night. I think he had an appointment with Dr. Berkley. Probably grabbed it then." He threw it up in the air to catch again, a little higher with each toss.

This is stupid, making small talk when we both know what really needs to be said.

"Cade, stop." I said it before I could register the words in my head, but one of us needed to. He glanced away from the ball and directly at me, his new toy rapidly dropping to the concrete. "Let's just get the elephant out of the room. We both changed that night. It's not your fault we grew apart."

I think I sounded convincing enough, but I know deep down that it is his fault, and he knows it, too. He's had every chance to speak to me, every chance to say sorry for ending our friendship and acting embarrassed, whether his parents are actually guilty or not. But he never did. He simply put on a straight face every time I walked by, or turned the other way if our eyes "unfortunately" met. To everyone else, he may look like a jock whose biggest priority in life is football, but to me, he's still the twelve-year-old boy who sat by my side crying in the police department lobby. The same vulnerable kid who fell off his bicycle countless times, who never learned to swim, and whose biggest fear is wasps. The boy who gave me his chocolate candies when he brought them for himself, the one who pushed away others at the risk of his own status if I didn't care for them.

Not every "tough guy" is as tough as he may seem.

"I just never knew what to say to you, Tatum. How do I even begin to apologize for not being there? When I saw that you were hurting and had no one there to help, all I did was watch." He wouldn't look at me as he said this, and yet somehow, I still understand his fear. Sometimes it's the people you admire from a distance that you care about the most.

"Can I ask you a question?"

He smiled, "Sure."

"What do you think happened that night?"

He seemed taken aback by the question, but he had to know it was coming sooner or later.

I'll always have my opinion of the stories that were told, every rumor and cruel myth people fabricated about my dad's murder. What the town believed happened versus what the facts actually proved. People said it was a hunting accident, or that maybe his car broke down and he was mugged, but for that to make sense, the police would've found his car near his body. But they didn't. It was most certainly something *more* than simply being in the wrong place at the wrong time. People don't just die on the side of the road with no one else in sight, much less without a car of their own nearby. Especially not in Stonson, of all places.

It took me a few years to understand the technical parts of the investigation, the evidence, and official terms. From what I remember reading, Stonson's medical examiner at the time, Dr. Ainslie, found blunt force trauma injuries to Dad's skull. Those don't just show up out of nowhere.

Someone put them there, someone hurt my dad that night.

But Cade doesn't know that. No one does. Only the police, me, my mom, and Dr. Ainslie. Mom said she didn't want the information released because it'd be terrible publicity if her investors knew that someone might be attacking her family. She always makes everything about herself. Even his death was an opportunity for advertising.

"You want the truth?"

I nodded.

He slightly pinched up the corner of his lip, then continued, "Looking back on everything we know now—all the questions they asked my parents—it wasn't an accident." He paused. "But you already knew that, didn't you?"

I looked back up from the puddle I'd been staring at and turned to face him. "Why would you think that?"

Squinting his eyes and sticking out his lip, he sarcastically observed, "If you thought even for a second that he really died in a hunting accident, you wouldn't have asked me that question in the first place."

He's right, if I knew what really went down that night, I would possess enough closure to leave it be. But I don't have enough closure. In fact, I don't have any at all.

"Do you ever wonder?"

"About what?"

"About what happened on the land. How he felt, what he saw, if he knew that he was about to die?" I directed the questions toward Cade, but they were more for me than anyone else. I'm not looking for reassurance in his answer. I just want to get it out in the open.

"Not the last one, but the other two, of course. I always find myself wondering how he died, who killed him." He stopped, then shakily continued. "Wondering if it was my parents."

We looked at each other wearily, realizing it's the first question we can agree neither of us have an answer to.

"The important thing is not to stop questioning.
Curiosity has its own reason for existing."
-Albert Einstein

Chapter Nine

December 8th, 2019~ 12:53 AM

Mama never came back to the police department. The rich lady who lives across the street from us, Mrs. Gibson, came to get me from Catiey. I've only met her once, but I always see kids running around in her front yard, and in all honesty, I'm a little jealous. One girl looks about my age. It seems she's the head of the roost when her siblings are around. Although, I'm not allowed to talk to strangers alone, so Daddy said he would walk me over there one day to meet her. Guess that isn't going to happen now.

"Are you hungry?"

"No ma'am."

"You sure? I don't mind grabbing somethin.'"

"No, it's okay. Daddy says it isn't smart to eat after nine. The food sits in your belly all night."

"Sweetie, eat if you're hungry. I promise your dad would be okay with it just this once."

Hesitantly, I gave in. "I guess that's fine. But just this once."

Mrs. Gibson drives a real nice black Range Rover, even has four cup holders instead of two. Not sure why I notice things like that, I've just always been this way.

I don't want to seem needy, but I'm actually starving. I never got to finish my spaghetti at home, and one bag of Fritos won't hold over any kid for long. Soon enough, she had pulled into the first McDonalds on our route home.

"Here's twenty bucks. If you wouldn't mind getting me a Diet Coke, I'd appreciate it dear." She reached over and carefully placed a crisp twenty-dollar bill in my hand, softly smiling as we made eye contact. It felt like when you have something on your face but no one wants to tell you, so they just stare and smile instead.

Daddy never lets me go inside restaurants alone, but I guess Mrs. Gibson isn't aware of that rule.

The man at the cash register had a crazy beard, kind of like Santa Claus, but without all the gray coloring. The name tag on his shirt read CHRIS, but he doesn't really look like a Chris to me. He's more of a Bill. Yeah, that's it, Bill.

"What can I get you, ma'am?" I've never been called ma'am before.

"Can I have nuggets and fries, please? Oh, and a Diet Coke." He looked at me as if I'd said something wrong.

"What meal?"

I guess he wants me to be more specific, but I don't know what to say. Daddy always orders for me, even makes sure I get a girl toy and not some transformer or dinosaur.

"The one with six nuggets." I handed him my cash, and he gave me a number for my order. Number 113, I like that.

My favorite number is three because of God being the Father, the Son, and the Holy Spirit. My Sunday school teacher calls that the Trinity, our church, is even named after the Trinity. Although I like the number one as well, it seems like God would pick that as His favorite number. The beginning of an infinity of possibilities, just like God. He's the reason we're all here and an infinity of different people who have been blessed with unique lives exist. I hope Chris' dad taught him about Jesus like mine did.

I waited a few minutes before he called my number and handed over my meal, along with Mrs. Gibson's diet Coke. When I got back to the car, I could see that she was on the phone with someone, but not sure who. Once I opened the car door, she told them goodbye and hung up. Great, one more person hiding something from me.

"You got my change?"

I don't think she meant to sound rude on purpose. I gave her the nine dollars and fifty-six cents I had left over, and she dropped it in one of the platinum cup holders. We sat without speaking for the rest of the ride home, the only sound bouncing around being a Kenny Chesney song playing low from the stereos beneath my feet. When we got to Earlpark, our neighborhood, she hesitantly pulled upwards into the sloped hill that is my driveway. I see the light in our kitchen still on from when we left, but no other cars outside. Mama clearly isn't home, probably went out again after the Uber dropped her off.

"Are you gonna be okay here by yourself?" It was very thoughtful of Mrs. Gibson to be concerned, but I don't think she would've done anything if I had said no. So I told her I'd be fine and she reminded me that she's in the phone book if I need anything. I don't know what a phone book is, but I nodded anyway.

The front door was locked when I wiggled the frigid handle, so I went in through the garage. Daddy never told me the passcode to get in that way, but I always watched him put it in. 1191. I pressed the pin numbers, and it slowly opened, louder than I remember. It's the date my parents met, November 1991. When I found out that was also their senior year, I told Daddy that they're much too old to be my parents. He thought it was the funniest thing for a child to say, considering they're a fairly young couple compared to most of my friends' parents, who already have four kids and a corgi by now.

When I walked into the house, I turned off the kitchen light and went straight to my room. I introduced Tres to my other stuffed animals, Courtney and Linda, as my favorites. My Pawpaw gave them to me, my dad's daddy. Before he died, he won em' for me at a carnival up in the mountains. We went to visit during fall break. It was a blast riding the Ferris wheel over and over again. It reminded me of my color wheel from art class, a beautiful array of vibrant shades pounding at the walls of my brain, each one a little more vivacious than the last. When we finished, he and I walked over to a water balloon game, three shots for five bucks. I let Pawpaw shoot since he was older—much older—and told him that I wanted nothing more than the pair of unicorns hanging on the prize wall. Of course, he hit the target with ease, the winning alarm suddenly blaring for everyone to hear. He gracefully picked me up and gave me a big ole' kiss. The game attendant handed me a pink unicorn attached by a single white string to an identical purple one, both only about the size of my fist. I named them Courtney and Linda after the characters on my favorite show, 'How to Build a Friend'. I started watching it when it first came out three years ago, mesmerized by what Daddy called the "plot". Cade and I discovered it one afternoon while eating Goldfish crackers on my couch. He said it was too girly for him, but watched it anyway because I enjoyed the childish drama in every episode.

I wish Cade was here right now. I could give him Tres back and make sure he's okay. He always makes sure that I'm okay when I get upset, so I hope he doesn't think I'm being a bad friend by keeping my distance. After all, it isn't my choice to stay away.

I wonder if he knows about my daddy going to Heaven. Maybe that's why he was crying at the station. But why didn't he tell me? I would've told him if his daddy went to Heaven, his mama too. But thankfully I won't ever have to, because it isn't his daddy who died, it's mine, and I don't know what to think about that just yet.

This isn't something they teach you at school. In fact, I don't think anyone prepares for something like this to happen. I certainly haven't been prepared. Turns out the prince doesn't always win, and the princess isn't always rescued.

All I knew to do was cry.

So that's what I did. I cried all night until I fell asleep. Maybe I'll cry some more tomorrow. I know that Daddy wouldn't want me to be sad, but I'm not sad. I'm just lonely. Lonely without him here, lonely as I lay in my room in silence, lonely without Cade. Unfortunately, I have a feeling that I might be lonely a little more often than I'd like.

But I'm learning now that some steps need to be taken alone. And that, as hard as it may be, is something I must accept.

"There's a reason we feel lonely even though we're not alone;
It's because loneliness is not about how many friends we have
or how many people there are in the room with us...
It's a disconnection from other human beings.
Being social doesn't cure loneliness;
Many people socialize when they don't really feel like it
just to keep up appearances.
We all have layers and we all pretend we're okay when we're not,
but loneliness comes when there is not a single person
close enough to see past those illusions to who we really are
and what we're really feeling inside."
-Ranata Suzuki

Chapter Ten

September 15, 2023~10:31 AM

I went home that night with more stress than I'd felt before I went to school. Cade and I haven't spoken in years, yet we carried on a full conversation as if nothing ever happened.

I've never felt as connected with another human being as I do with him.

I spent the entire remainder of my weekend thinking about it, even at church. Mrs. Kathy sang beautifully alongside her husband preceding the sermon, but even those notes of harmony couldn't distract me from the intrusive thoughts flooding my brain. His face, his voice, his persona; everything about this man intrigues me. It's weird, I've never felt this like before, not even when we were kids. Cade has always just been my best friend; nothing less and nothing more. Of course, that was before the murder tore us apart. I know everything there is to know about this boy, and yet here I am longing to learn more.

I tried my best to listen to the sermon and block out these thoughts, but halfway through, Mom called, needing me to run her lunch by the office. Every day I am more and more tempted to tell her how I feel, that she has officially ruined my life once again with this divorce, and that she'll have to fix it all herself. But once again I withheld my thoughts, then rode my bike all the way to the farmer's market a few miles away and grabbed a turkey and cheese sandwich from inside. Cost me eleven bucks that I know I'll never get back, but that's reality. No matter how rich my mother is, she never reimburses me for anything.

I hopped back on my bike, careful not to drag the flowy dress I wore to church across the hot pavement. It's my favorite; violet in color, cinched at the waist, and slightly puffy at the sleeves. The Shargold office is only about three miles from the market, but it took me all of an hour to get there with traffic. Small town with no bike lanes, hungry church-goers, and no one willing to give a ride to the talk of the town's school-girl daughter. The peach colored front doors leading into the office are being repainted on account of the crusted eggs splattered across them one night last week. Mom seemed shocked that kids would have the nerve to egg her "place of work", as she called it, but I'm not in the slightest. Someone was bound to pull something like that sooner or later, considering the manner in which she handles her business affairs. The painters had to stop and let me inside, something I'm sure has been a frequent occurrence all day.

When you enter Mom's building, all that most people see is a long hallway lined with glass office doors and a grand staircase to the right. Each step is lined discreetly with blue and white custom tiles no more than a finger long each, a sizable gold chandelier hanging above. They don't see what I see. I see bricks that hold so many stories, so many memories of those who left their words within these walls.

This used to be the town's only library, somewhere my parents would take me after school to pick out a book for the weekend back when our family was still whole. When Mom inherited the business, she picked the first place available for lease, and the one place she knew I loved.

I'm still not sure whether or not that last part is a good thing.

I never quite grasped whether she deliberately meant to take away a place I deeply enjoyed, or if she picked it because of my love for it. I guess I'll never know, just like I'll never know if I would have grown to be an avid reader.

Another opportunity Mom has managed to take away from me.

I took to the staircase and climbed what felt like ten flights, all the way until I got to the fourth and final floor. It's not a dirty yellow like the rest of the building. Instead, it's painted an almost coral pink color. Dad used to say that it made Mom feel happy to have a bit of color around when she's working, but in my opinion, it makes her feel like she has superiority over her colleagues when it's painted that way. As if somehow the vibrant coloring of her work area is better than theirs. Or maybe I'm just overthinking it. Probably the second one.

"Special delivery..." Knocking on the already opened door of her office, I watched as Mom sat typing away on her laptop. What you would expect from a mother who hasn't seen her only child in almost a week is an overdramatic jump from her chair, maybe even a trot over to give me a hug. Instead, she never even looked up, but simply flashed a thumbs up in my direction as if I needed permission to enter her ever so glorious space. At first I didn't come in past what the doorway permitted, but eventually she looked up, shooting me an almost judgmental stare. I swear she can see into my soul when she does that.

"Well, are you gonna come in or not?"

Unless you count her silent, yet rude, gesture, I was never told to come in. I hate when she acts like a teenager, sarcastic answers and stern glares as if she's quietly rating me. It's beyond childish. I walked over to her desk, an old pine one that my dad hired a high school friend to make for her. He wanted to surprise Mom when the office first opened with a fully furnished space, wanted to make it feel more like home. To this day, that desk is the only thing she kept from him. The minute Dad and I left that day, she cleaned out all of our hard work and replaced it with "newer, more modern decor," as she described it.

And yet, she kept the desk. Sometimes it feels as if she held onto it tighter than she did me. I've always wanted to ask her why, but maybe it's better that I don't know.

"Did you get my sandwich?" Practically reaching out already, she pretended like I was to hand it to her on a silver platter.

"Yes, but they were out of the chips you like." That was a straight lie. I never even looked for the brand of chips I know she enjoys. I used to feel bad doing things like that—even the tiniest of wrongs—but not anymore, not when it comes to her. I would say that I learned not to lie from my parents, but in all honesty, my mother's moral compass has been broken for years.

No, not just broken, *shattered.*

She looked up at me again, disappointed in my failure to retrieve her chips. I have little to no issue bringing her lunch. I'd even bring her dinner if she needed it, but most people expect at least a brief conversation in return. I barely even got that, no smile at my presence nor an expression of gratitude for what I brought.

"Did someone give you a ride?" This is the first time she's asked a question implying concern for me. It's almost exciting to hear that she might actually somewhat care about my safety.

"Yeah, Riley dropped me off. I spent the night over at her house last night." Another lie. If my pretentious mother knew that her daughter was riding around on a childhood bicycle for everyone to see, she'd have a fit. She tells me constantly that we have a standard to live up to in this town as the Cassidy family, that she can't have me running around actin' a fool; I wouldn't want to ruin her reputation. And yet she refuses to buy me a car. She assumes that I have enough people to get me where I need to go, but I can barely keep a friend long enough to maintain that, much less get their number. She would also have had my head if she knew I spent the morning at church.

Mom says that God loves us even if we don't go every Sunday. Of course she's right, but I also know how important showing God that I can make time for Him is, even if it's just once or twice a week. She tells me to spend my Sundays doing other things: being more productive, reading, going to the gym. I refuse though, because I know that church is much more important than any worldly thing, no matter what she says.

"Good, you need to pay her back for gas."

And there it is. There's the real reason she asked. I should've known that she didn't really care about my safety, she didn't want to know about my day. All she cares about is that I'm not pissing off any of her rich friends' kids by wasting their gas.

So I left. I dropped the red and white thank you bag along with the sandwich on her desk and I walked out, slamming the glass door behind me just hard enough to emphasize my rage, but not so hard as to damage it. The worst part of all this is that she didn't come after me. No text or call to make sure I'm okay, no holler down the hall to see if she could catch me before I left.

She just stayed in her stupid office like she does every day.

Every time I need her, every time I'm hurting, when I need to ask a question—the moments a mother should see in her daughter's life—there she is in her office.

It's usually parents who are let down by their children, not children let down by their parents. I see kids at school bringing their mom and dad to awards days or to pep rallies just to see them during a favourable moment, parents who work nine-to-five jobs just like the rest of Stonson. But somehow, some way, they find the time to be there for their kids when they need it most. They see the moments in their lives that they'll remember forever; meeting the first boyfriend, driving them to their first day of high school, holding them after the first breakup. I try my best not to complain or hold grudges, but I get none of those privileges. I'm lucky if my mom even asks if I have a boyfriend in the first place, lucky if she calls an Uber to take me to school. Maybe that's why I don't date often. Maybe it's not because I don't want to deal with what this world has to offer when it comes to men, nor because dating means a seemingly unavoidable breakup and extreme heartache.

Maybe it's just that I don't want to have to go through it *alone.*

I would rather avoid relationships all together than have my heart broken any more than it already is. Sometimes, unfortunately, you have to shelter your heart in order to protect it.

My Latin teacher once told my class that as teenagers, our first instinct is to protect ourselves, both socially and physically. "It's how y'all survive," she said, and at first I didn't agree. When could there ever be a time when it's necessary to be selfish, when we're forced to think of ourselves before others? But now I understand. It's not to put ourselves above others or to be egotistical, but to keep us from getting hurt.

She might just be the wisest person at that school.

Avoiding connections is how we protect our heart. More than that, it's how we protect others. Maybe that's the key to life, why Mom feels the need to remain so focused on her work. She simply doesn't want to hurt me any more than she already has, wants to keep her darkened world away from the one she believes I've kept so bright. Only this life she left me to mend is far from bright. I guess I can understand that hypothetical reasoning, so I think that's what I'll stick with. I would rather spend my life thinking she acts the way she does to protect me rather than to harm me.

It's a better explanation than reality.

Sometimes reality isn't all it's talked up to be. *Sometimes* you need to let your mind wander a bit. The difference in that concept versus the world's version is that I can keep the line between the two clear and concise. I won't let it become blurred like it often is by influencers on social media or those with false beliefs. That's the key. Be clear with your thoughts and do not let them become fuzzy or hazed.

I just wish I would've realized that before what happened the next morning. Before I walked into the school building.

Before all chaos broke loose.

"I accept chaos.
I'm not sure whether it accepts me."
-Bob Dylan

Chapter Eleven

December 10th, 2019~9:13 AM

Days. It was days before Mama came home. I laid in bed alone the morning after Daddy died, then did the same all night. I couldn't sleep, but Daddy said I'm not old enough to have a phone, so I couldn't call Mama either. I debated walking over to Mrs. Gibson's house, but she must've been at work, because no one was home the whole day. I had no breakfast when I woke up, no cereal or chocolate chip pancakes like Daddy usually prepared for me.

I guess you really don't understand what you have until you lose it. Or in this case, who you have.

I heated up some soup for lunch and did the same for dinner. I know that there are other neighbors I could ask for a phone, but I don't know many of them well. The only time we went out and talked to our neighbors was when we first moved into Earlpark. The whole family baked oatmeal cookies and walked around, knocking on doors to see if anyone wanted some in exchange for a quick conversation or invitation inside. In return, a few families brought us presents, "housewarming gifts", as they were later labeled. We got one gift card for a restaurant in town, countless kitchen utensils, a few candles, and a beautiful set of monogrammed towels for my parents' bathroom. Those two lavender towels still hang on the metal rods in their bathroom to this day, although they're never actually used. Mama says they're for decoration

78

only, but if that's the case, a lot of things in our house must be for decoration only, because she barely touches any of it.

Now that I think about it, he's never actually home enough to use much of anything; not to cook or clean or play with me, nothin'. Mama hasn't stepped foot inside my bedroom since last Christmas, not even to ask if I needed a snack or water. But that hasn't changed much, I guess. She still isn't home, and no one cares enough to come to check on me.

Until they did.

I heard the garage door open, jumping from bed in hopes that it was Mom. I stood by the kitchen counter fidgeting, anxiously waiting to see my pretty mama walk through that door, but she never did. When the door opened and a woman came walking through, it was not who I'd expected.

Mrs. Lanie stood there, staring, holding a white and red bag by her hip as she chaotically reached to hang her tan parka on our metal coat rack.

With the biggest smile on her face, she asked, "Hungry?"

It's very exciting that someone possesses enough kindness to give up some time for me, but I'm also a little concerned because of what the drunk lady at the station said. Mr. Davidson and his cop friends think that Cade's parents may have killed my daddy, and even though I disagree, the feeling of not knowing leaves my already empty stomach unsettled. But if she's here, I guess that means they cleared her. Hopefully. No matter what the truth is, I still need food.

"Whatcha got?" As Mrs. Lanie walked closer, I could see that the bag in her hand was from Chick-fil-a, my second favorite restaurant. I would tell you what my first is, but I think I'll keep that a secret for now.

"Okay, I've got two orders of hash browns, one biscuit, and a few nuggets." She laid it all out on the counter, separating each item into its own area. I reached over to grab the biscuit, but my hand was suddenly stopped before I could get to it, those unforgettable lime green nails coming into full view once again. Mrs. Lanie tightened her grip, her

teeth grinding as she spoke, "Silly girl, that's mine." Her smile is clearly fake, all but plastered on. Mama always said that she was fake, but now I see it.

Still, I didn't flinch when she grabbed my hand. No one really scares me like that, not since I began to understand that the world is harsh, just like the people in it. In her mind, wrapping her fingers around my wrist shows authority, but not in mine.

No one really has much authority in this world except God. However, lots of people are pretty convinced that they themselves do. Authority is the first lesson I've been taught since Daddy went to Heaven, the A of my new alphabet.

They taught us letters and numbers when I was younger, at school and at home. My teachers always said that I would never make it in life if I couldn't read, if I couldn't write. But I don't think you need to be the smartest person in the room in order to leave the greatest impact. In fact, it's usually who you expect the least; that's the one who creates the biggest waves. Sometimes God allows our lives to be used in ways that help others, and I believe that's what He did for my daddy. His life, and death, they're gonna change my life in so many ways. Whether those ways are good or bad, I can't yet tell. But what I do know is that events help chart the course for the rest of our lives, and I believe that this is one of my core events.

Even in such a small manner, Mrs. Lanie has just shown me her true colors, and I must say, they are not pretty. They aren't pure like Cade's are, nor like I hope mine will be someday. I pray she knows who Jesus is. I hope she's best friends with God, because right now all that she has shown me is the false authority she's convinced herself she's in possession of. She has no authority, not over me at least.

Not over me, nor over my mama, nor over anyone else in this town, so why do I get the feeling that she's given that power before?

Maybe she had authority over my daddy. Maybe she does know what happened to him. But I guess I'll never know, because I didn't ask.

I refuse to entertain adults who act like children, and I am certain Mrs. Lanie is one of them.

"It would be too easy to say that I feel invisible.
Instead, I feel painfully visible,
and entirely ignored."
-David Levithan

Chapter Twelve

September 16th, 2023~7:56 AM

Character says a lot about a person; how someone acts when faced with adversity, how they act after being humiliated in front of those they care about. The length at which one person is willing to go for someone they love can define them in that person's eyes forever.

We see all movies where the couple makes it through together, the ones with perfect circumstances and a happily ever after ending. But life isn't always a Hallmark movie. God doesn't allow us to date every guy we come across until we find the right one. He already has them picked out for us. He knows exactly how we will meet our person and I pray that He has one for me, along with everyone else. But He knows how we can be. It's hard not to become fixated on the couples that seem to have it all; big white house with a matching picket fence, a perfectly bred dog to sit by their side during family photoshoots. We've all seen 'em. I'll even admit I've wondered what it would be like to already have that perfect husband I pray so deeply to be blessed with one day. I imagine he would be tall, handsome, characterized with intense dark hair and tan skin. But I would love him no matter his appearance, and I would do my very best to care for him always. However, there is one trait that I consider a must-have.

Lots of girls say their boyfriend loves God, that he goes to church every Sunday and sits right by his sweet mother in the velvet green chairs or wooden pews. He wears a pristine patterned blue flannel, all cleaned up, even poses appealingly for cute pictures afterwards. They recall the classic "country boy" story every chance they get, telling how they originated to friends and family alike. But, in my opinion, love is very different. It's not just a matter of whether he goes to church, or if he says that he loves God as he should.

The Bible says that a woman's husband, if he is the one God wants her to be with, will be a man of God. There is a distinct difference between being a servant and devout follower of Christ versus just sitting in the front row at church every Sunday. "Head of the household" does not mean ruler, it means leader.

It doesn't imply male *dominance* or *superiority*. No man should ever lord his demands over a woman wanting everything he wishes to immediately come true. God never viewed women as the next step down from men. He made us all equally His children, and we all hold worth beyond what this sinful world can offer us. The husband, as the leader, makes the decisions with his wife concerning what is best for their family. He values her opinions and is willing to compromise, even if it isn't exactly what he originally had in mind. He puts God above his wife and children, giving thanks for them every day. He is not afraid to call out the wrongs of his peers, yet he also accepts when others point out his flaws. And his wife should do the same as she loves him properly.

That is a man of God. He doesn't talk down to others, man or woman.

But Cade would never treat me as an inferior race, and trust me, I know many boys who would. Cade always knows how to make me smile on a bad day. He recognizes my struggles and comforts me, whether he knows exactly what they are or not. And although he comes from a family that has its issues, he's the odd one out.

We all make mistakes, especially myself, but Cade is aware of his few flaws. He doesn't try to hide them behind a screen or pretend to be perfect until no one else is around. He is straight with what he says and there is always truth behind what and who he thinks should have priority over others. Twelve-year-old Tatum would believe that Cade would never ignore her or hurt her by choosing silence over confrontation. Sure, anyone can play nice with others and throw out a few empty compliments to satisfy egos, but having respect for someone takes a deep connection.

I once thought that this boy was honestly and truly one of the few people whom I could respect in such a corrupt world.

Turns out I was wrong.

Who knew that someone you once woke up everyday excited to see would also be the person *forcing* you to lock up your feelings? Not on my watch; not in this world, and not after ignoring me for years. Anyone can blame an unpleasant situation on someone else, blame it on the choices of their parents or friends rather than themselves. And I must agree, sometimes that blame is well overdue. But after a while it becomes easier to take ownership of how you handled the situation, whether it was in a poor or fair manner, because if you truly care for someone, you won't cut them out as if they never existed. You won't make them question whether or not they were right to care for you and make sacrifices in order to do so. But Cade did. He made me question every little thing he ever said to me.

This is what I spent the entire night pondering over, a sad memory rerunning in my head as I slept.

The mind brings crazy things to our attention; some even say that dreams reveal what we truly think of the world. Whether you see the world as a cruel and dark place where evil lingers until it finds the right time to attack, or as a peaceful and charming bubble, your inner thoughts still tell the truth. And God, God shows you as well.

Tonight my mind had quite a few questions like these; a multitude of things to say, but never through words. Only through pictures. Except this wasn't exactly a lucid dream of sorts, more like a cloud of thoughts, flashing images in my mind narrated by the voice in my head, all with one person in common: Cade. For a reason that I've still yet to find, my mind has quite a lot to say about him.

More questions than answers, might I add.

I am not an overwhelmingly philosophical person, but tonight I am, or at least my inner thoughts, decided they would be. These images are what I truly think about Cade. Even after everything that happened regarding the murder, I still believed he cared for me for four years.

Four years I'll never get back.

I guess sometimes your heart needs more time to accept what your mind already knows.

Maybe I was simply led astray by the hope that my best friend had finally come back to me, that he surely wouldn't allow years to go by without speaking to me or even reaching out to see how I felt, not my Cade. Even though we were just kids, he will always be my favorite *platonic* movie.

Maybe platonic is a strong word.

As I walked up to the front of the school, it was déjà vu, more flashes of memories racing through my mind with each step I took. That cold winter night all over again, but swap out the frigid snow and ice chips for jean shorts and a blazing sun. As far to my left and right as the property goes, shine blue and red lights, yellow crime scene tape around over half the parking lot, along with the entire front entrance bollards. A mob of students stand crowded inside the doorway, a few more arriving close behind me. Almost everyone has their phones out, cameras on and recording. What it is they're recording, I can't quite tell.

I continued to stand where I was until I felt a hand, somewhat cold, on my left shoulder. Cade; I know by the distinct class ring now inches from my face.

"It's happening all over again, isn't it?" He hasn't turned to face me yet, but I can hear the extreme distress in his deep voice.

He continued, "Something's happened, I just know it."

He's right, but whatever happened will be just like my dad's murder. The cops will probably spend months searching for the answers we all want, the ones that would finally give a little girl closure about what happened to her daddy so many years ago. But they won't find anything. They'll blame it on a lack of resources or a faulty system that's never going to give them help no matter how hard they try.

As I walked over to the front entrance, I saw the bench we sat on only two nights ago, now engulfed in little yellow and black markers and enclosed by cops and tape galore. My mouth is *heavily* weighed down as it remains wide open, staring at the scene, the disbelief that anything could have possibly happened at a place where I stood not long ago quickly overtaking me. I looked up from my gaze at the bench to see Mr. Davidson walking towards us, Cade having waved him over.

"Kids, you need to go inside. You know you can't be over here." He spoke as if he was directing the words to Cade, yet his eyes remained dead set on me. He's thinking of the same night I am, the same case that changed Stonson forever.

"Sir, what happened?" Cade moved his hand from one shoulder to the other, side-hugging me as if we're married and waiting to hear news about our newly expected child. Mr. Davidson looked around for a few seconds, making sure that no one could hear whatever he's about to say.

"A girl went missin' from here Saturday night."

My heart stopped. Saturday was the night of the dance. The minute I took a second glance at the bench, I knew who he was talking about.

"Who?"

Cade must've known too. I felt him pull me closer into him, both of us tense awaiting Mr. Davidson's answer.

"You know I can't tell you that. You're just gonna have to wait until the media releases it like everyone else. Trust me, I'm not happy about this either."

No way Mr. Davidson turns me down, not after everything we've been through together. I nudged Cade on the shoulder, a hint to watch and learn. I relaxed my posture a bit, rubbing my eyes as I spoke.

"Please. I need to know."

Mr. Davidson closed his mouth, twisting it inwards as one would after eating something sour. That's the same face Jenny used to make when I would try to convince her to race during recess. It means he's thinking, pondering maybe, but I've learned not to make too many assumptions when it comes to the Davidson family.

He sighed, looking to Cade for help, but Cade just stood there, his eyes somehow saying, "you're on your own man." He's probably right. You don't want to mess with me when it comes to my dad.

Dad was the only person who ever really cared.

Taking one last scan around, Mr. Davidson leaned into our huddle a little closer, motioning for us to do the same. "Town dentist's daughter, Brynlee, I believe."

If there was ever a time to burst into tears, this would be it. Cade was right. Here we go again. Someone just got away with another life-changing crime, something you can't simply undo with a little White-Out or water. I guess in hindsight, we all make mistakes that can't be erased. But usually, and thankfully, they don't always end in another family left without its third member.

I don't understand why things like this happen to me, and of course, when my life is finally starting to become normal again. Well, as normal as my normal can be; Cade somewhat acknowledges my existence. I'm having a great junior cheer season, and my grade in science is officially passing. Life is particularly uneventful, yet I could not be more content. And now this horribly unimaginable event is about to disrupt my extremely average lifestyle and shatter whatever broken relationships God has managed to piece themselves back together.

Another story I hope to laugh about one day. Maybe then I can laugh through the pain.

Bottom line, Brynlee is nowhere to be found, and Cade and I were the last people to see her alive.

I took a deep breath in, gathering my composure just enough to walk away from Cade and find some water, then exhaled what might just be the most painful exhale I'll ever experience. *Breathe.*

"I fear that I am losing my mind.
But really, it would not be such a precious thing to lose,
as it only causes me pain."
-L.A. Meyer

Chapter Thirteen

September 17th, 2023~3:17 PM

After it was announced that Brynlee Berkley was missing, the whole town went off the rails. People who grew up in normal households began behaving in ways that would make you question their mental stability.

For a town where most everyone supports their neighbors and friends, there isn't much of any help going around at all.

Parents have been posting inhumane comments online, making assumptions that have probably traumatized Brynlee's parents for life, and keeping their loved ones closer than ever before. Kids sit at home terrified, swearing off all high school dances as if they're acts of the devil.

Those of us who are at school have heard every rumor you could conjure up, crazy stories you'd never believe. But people sure seem to be believin' them, they've put the living fright in even the most mature of children. As I passed the cafeteria before fourth period, I even overheard some kids say that they heard traffickers took Brynlee, another saying she was kidnapped at birth and her proper parents simply took her back. They're all lies, even I know that.

Mr. Davidson said he couldn't release all the details for security reasons, but Cade and I know that the real reason is because they don't have anything to release. They have no clues, no evidence, and certainly no leads on whoever took Brynlee or where they went. Just like my dad's case, no one seems to have seen much of anything the night she up and disappeared.

Stonson's only high school hasn't been renovated since 1967, when it was first built, and the security cameras haven't worked since the circuit shortage back in 2008. But then again, there's never really been a reason to get new ones. Unless you count my mother, rarely does anyone have the nerve to piss off people in this town by doing wrong.

I met Cade by the old storage shed across the street from his house because he wasn't allowed to go to school, just like half the kids in our twenty-mile radius. He might be gettin' older, but he's still a true mama's boy at heart, follows her rules to the letter.

The old shed, once painted a pale blue, is now faded and filled with cobwebs and dust bunnies. The metal door has rusted, but the doorknob somehow looks to be pristine. I can still see the chalk letters Cade and I drew as kids underneath the tin awning that wraps around the small building, untouched by the elements that corroded the rest of the structure. We used to come out here and pretend we were detectives. This was our office. We would knock on neighbors' doors and ask if they had any crimes in need of some solving, always in our matching investigator t-shirts Mrs. Lanie made for us. It was usually the older ladies who found us a problem to help with, whether it was a "lost" shoe or "stolen" garden hose in their backyard.

I remember this one time I was sitting on a little pink beanbag in the corner of our shed, when suddenly Cade busted through the door, a huge smile on his face. He was beaming with joy at what he had found; a thin stack of seven or eight tan office folders.

"We can write down our cases and put the clues in these!"

His voice was still high-pitched on account of those pre-puberty years. I remember thinking how silly he sounded. He handed me a folder and a green sharpie marker to label it with, and I took it, because I always trusted his intuitive ideas. On the front of the file I wrote 'THE MISSING BONE' in big fat letters, practically to the point that it took up the entire cover. At the time we were searching for clues to find a bone, Mrs. Ethel across the street told us her dog, Jacky, had lost. We were happy to help because of how cute Jacky was.

Jacky was a Russell Terrier, as Mrs. Lanie called him, loved to bury things in the yard. We spent so many afternoons looking for that bone, running across Mrs. Ethel's backyard like kids high off processed sugar. "Little maniacs", as she used to call us, always said we were much too hyper and needed to teach her how to have so much energy.

"It's easy," Cade would say. "Just eat lots of chocolate!"

Him saying that made his sweet neighbor laugh so hard, tears profusely running down her face by the time she'd finished.

Cadence Ethel passed away last year at the ripe old age of seventy-six. I wanted to go to her funeral, but I knew that Cade would be there, so I chose to stay home.

Now, staring at that mildewed pink bean bag still slumped in the corner, I deeply regret that decision.

"Lots of good memories in here, huh?" Cade waltzed in behind me, my mind still reminiscing the days of our once wonderful childhood. But we're grown now, life changes, things happen. I know that, I just wish ours would've ended a little differently.

"So what do we do?"

"About what?"

Turning to face him, I said, "About Brynlee. What are we gonna do about Brynlee?" He's sporting the same red Under Armour shirt I've seen him in a million times before, perfect to go with the black forming shoes he wears when lifting. Everyone makes fun of him for wearing them, but I know he'll never throw them out, no matter how many uncalled for comments he receives. He's much too sentimental to do that. A man on the outside, but at heart, he's just a sweet kid waiting for someone to show him the love he sees everyone else getting. He can act tough for as long as he wants, but I see who he really is.

I just wish he knew that. I wish he knew how much I *care*.

"I have no idea," he finally answered. Much help that was. I rolled my eyes at his lack of effort, stepping closer to him as I began to speak.

"I won't let this happen again. No more families need to fall apart before it ends." I can't tell if he's annoyed by what I'm implying or if he's thinking the same thing.

It was silent for a few moments as we exchanged serious glances, then Cade finally spoke up.

"Oh Tatum, please tell me you're not about to say what I think you are." He moved his hand across his mouth as he said it, shifting from one hip to the other.

"Say what?"

"You don't seriously think that, do you? I mean, the chances of that being the case are very slim..." I stopped him mid-sentence.

"Cade, stop. What are you talkin' about?" He gave me a sarcastic look, his lips poked out like a female's would at the sight of an attractive guy. I know exactly what he's thinking, but I want to hear it come from his own mouth. His own devastatingly perfect mouth.

"You think Brynlee's kidnapping and your dad's murder are connected. Well, stop, stop thinking that right now. You're jumpin' to conclusions before we can even..."

"How can you rule it out when we don't know who was responsible for all this the first time around? I mean, my dad's case was never solved," Now he interrupted me, this time as still and stationary as can be.

"It was one of a kind, Tatum. Your dad's case was one of a kind. That's why they never solved it. It's not because someone managed to pull off the perfect crime, and it's not because we have a mass serial killer on the loose. That's pure nonsense. It's Stonson, the biggest scandal since then, was a stolen pack of gum from the Winn-Dixie. It was just a rare and really unfortunate occurrence. This is completely different."

Is it? Is Brynlee's disappearance and my dad's death completely different? Or are the thoughts that have been lingering in the back of my mind since we first found out not so wrong after all?

"Cade, I'm right and you know it."

Maybe if I'm the one being stern with how I speak, it'll jolt a sincere and honest response out of that tough exterior he flaunts so well. He stared at me for a good ten seconds, his pure and defined jawline clenched as he grinds his teeth deep in thought.

"What makes you think they're similar? Because as far as I'm concerned, there's only one thing in common with the two: you."

"Think about it. My dad and Brynlee may not be the same person, but whether you want to accept it or not, what happened to him is no different from what's happening to her. They both were great members of our community, beloved by many people. And then, with the blink of an eye, gone. No apparent reason, no apparent suspect with a grudge against them, and nothing but silence after they went missing. Listen, I know it's a little crazy, but you have to at least consider it." Breath Tatum, breath. "Please Cade, for me."

He slowly swallowed, his neck bulging for only a moment. I can see his desire to ignore what I said, his better half telling him to turn around and run. *Run* from this shed, *run* from me, and *run* from any chance that this might ruin his life all over again.

Realizing that he can't find any reason to disprove my theory, he looked down at me vulnerably.

"You had better hope you're wrong Tatum, because if not," He paused, careful with what he said next. "Then someone just got away with it twice."

So from then on it was decided, we'll think about every detail of what happened the night of the dance, assuming that the cases are alike. Assuming that the same person, or people, who killed my dad also took Bryn.

I feel as though we are heading back to the days as children where we played detectives until odd hours of the night, drinking apple juice and Capri Suns until one of us had to go home. Except now we've grown; more mature, less naive. We know better than to trust the world. We've already learned that it is a terribly cruel and unjust place where all we have is God.

But truthfully, God is all we need.

The secret to life that everyone has been trying to figure out isn't in social media or the internet, it isn't on TikTok or Instagram; it is found in our Creator and King, Jesus Christ.

If only the soul who killed my dad was aware of this truth, maybe then I could sleep at night. Maybe then Cade and I wouldn't spend every waking moment looking over our shoulder, praying and pleading that they don't prey on us next. Never knowing who we can and cannot trust, never being able to decipher truth from the lies. Maybe then the life of a fifteen-year-old girl wouldn't have just been changed forever, and the town's fear wouldn't be finding her cold and isolated somewhere on the side of the road.

"We need to find God,
and He cannot be found in noise and restlessness.
God is the friend of silence.
See how nature– trees, flowers, grass– grows in silence;
see the stars, the moon and the sun, how they move in silence...
We need silence to be able to touch souls."
-Mother Teresa

Chapter Fourteen

December 15, 2019~1:18 PM

That Sunday was Daddy's funeral. Mrs. Gibson drove me to the funeral home, said that Mama would meet us there, but she never did. Her petite figure never walked through the two white French doors leading to the small room where we sat for his service. She never came to my side and comforted me as I cried, nor explained everything the pastor said about Daddy. Every story he reminisced, every accidental grocery store run-in or church softball game he relived, it all made no sense to me.

Mrs. Gibson and I sat in the third pew, only a few others occupying the rows ahead. The first five rows are draped with velvet red covers, "reserved" embroidered with gold stitching across the center of each. The scent in the funeral home is peculiar, not exactly musty, but noticeably aged. Stained glass windows that surround the podium must be the most beautiful things I've seen in a while. Yellow, purple, and gold scenes depict what I believe to be a story—the glass contains two women down on their knees, clearly praying to God. One is shorter, stalkier, a little broader, but still majestically gorgeous. The other woman to her right is lean, taller, her thin legs stretched out across the dirt as she prays. I too do that every night. They must be saying their bedtime prayers. Then, in the center of the two women stands a man, much taller than them both. He is clothed in a long white gown, a blurry halo of sorts above his head. I believe the man to be Jesus, which would make the two women Mary and Martha.

I love the name Mary; if God blesses me with a daughter one day, I want to name her that. Mary Cate, Mary Morgan, maybe something along those lines. It reminds me of Jesus and His eternal pureness, something that I hope He blesses those children of mine with. I will pray for them to have a good and peaceful childhood daily, along with happy memories to look back on when they're older, not sad ones. No sad memories like the ones engraving themselves in my head today, the ones where I have to put Daddy's frail body in the ground. I know this should be a merry time because he's in Heaven with Jesus and God, yet I can't help but cry. Crying is just about all I can think to do. Well, that and pray.

I sat in the wooden pew for over an hour watching photo slideshows of Daddy and listening to old friends tell funny stories about him. One man got up and told my favorite story, one about Daddy in high school. He explained with great detail how one afternoon after practice, he and Daddy went to the locker room to shower off and change before heading home.

"Michael had just told me all about some hot date he had that night. I'd never seen him so excited over somethin' as casual as dinner." He looked out across the room as if to search for someone, probably my mama, but he didn't find her. I saw the man on stage make eye contact with a woman in the back, who then discreetly shook her head. Then he looked at me compassionately, a sad expression painted across his face, but quickly continued on with the story.

I've never seen this man before today.

"I walked to the other side of the locker room to set down my bag, when suddenly I heard a girl scream from the entrance. I ran to see what was happening, and sure enough, there he was, standing on top of the old bench by the lockers. Michael let out the girliest yelp over a single roach beneath him! My sister's scream is more masculine than his!"

The entire room erupted with laughter at the funny tale, the man himself all but peeing his pants. I never knew Daddy to be scared of roaches, but then again, he never leaped at the chance to kill one for me.

After the man left the stage, Pastor Mike got up to speak. He talked all about Daddy's life and about how he was a man of his word.

"Michael Cassidy rarely faltered in his faith, and if he did, an extremely rare occurrence, he always found time to sit and pray about his mistakes."

That's true. Daddy always made time at night to sit down with his Bible and pray; about life, about me, even about Mama. He would tell God about his day and discuss how he could've done better, how he could've touched more hearts with the holy word.

"He always said there weren't enough hours in the day," exclaimed the pastor. "Michael yearned for more time to spend with his daughter, Tatum, and his lovely wife, Jessica."

This is the first time I've ever heard a pastor lie. "Jessica", as he called her, is my mom, but Daddy and her absolutely never spent any extra time together unless they had to. Of course he would try, but it never worked, and how I see it, he eventually just gave up on connecting with Mama any longer.

"This was a man who was not ashamed of his faith; a man of God."

And that was the last thing he said about my daddy. No girl should ever have to bury her father. She should never have to watch in silence as they lowered his casket into the dirt, afraid that if she lets out a tear, it will only bring attention to her. And to help with it all, she should never have to do so alone. I appreciated having Mr. Davidson and Mrs. Gibson accompany me, but was not the same by any means; they are not my flesh and blood. What kind of wife doesn't come to her husband's funeral, let alone leaves her daughter to figure out his death on her own?

Jessica Cassidy does.

Daddy isn't here anymore, but no one can tell me why. Everyone says that God called him home, and I know they're right, but even then, they can't explain how he died, but not for a lack of effort. They've all tried, attempting to offer me comfort by telling stories their own better halves have created to avoid seeing the evil that actually surfaced with his sudden death. Lies are what they are; fibs made up to restore the innocence of a young girl whose innocence will never truly be restored.

Oh, the lies we tell for the sake of those we care about. How they grow.

"Absence is a house so vast that
inside you will pass through its walls
and hang pictures in the air."
-Pablo Neruda

Chapter Fifteen

September 17th, 2023~6:37 PM

"So where did they see her last?" If Kelly asks me the same question one more time as if I haven't already explained the story four times, I'm gonna lose it.

We sit on the couch in my living room, Mom's house, of course, catching up and de-stressing each other. I would never invite Kelly over to David's place; she doesn't even know that I live there half the time. I want it to stay like that too, less drama that way.

"At the school. She was headed into the parking lot." It doesn't get any easier to say the more I explain it. Each sentence hurts more and more, knowing that with every breath I take in the comfort of my home is another second that Brynlee is out there suffering, begging to be brought back to hers.

"She probably just ran off or something. They'll find her."

I shot her a nasty look. She doesn't understand. Kelly hasn't even met Brynlee, and yet she seems to already know her entire life story. She's so sure that Brynlee is just a runaway.

I just know that's not the case.

She cocked her neck in response to my gaze. "What? Kids run away all the time. Plus, you said she just broke it off with her boyfriend. Probably needed some time to think."

I answered harshly, "Kelly. When you're going through a breakup, you cry and egg his house." I paused. "You don't skip town without a trace."

Bryn can't even drive yet. Someone picked her up from that parking lot and took her, that I'm sure of. Who that someone is, though, I have no idea.

"Stop actin' all depressed." Kelly moved from her spot on the couch over to a new seat on the floor. She turned back around towards me and laid her head on the couch by my feet as if she's a simple schoolgirl waiting for a gift from her secret admirer. "She'll turn up, trust me. In the meantime, tell me all about Cade."

There it is, exactly what I've been waiting for all day. She asked in a giggly voice, fingers tingling in the air and everything. I'm not used to being the one asked about boys, much less having something—or someone—to talk about.

Of course, I acted annoyed at her request, but in reality, I can't wait to tell about our interactions.

"He's definitely grown up a lot. I'll give him that."

She winked. "He sure looks like it." I hit her on the shoulder as she fell back, laughing.

It's true, if anything, Cade has most certainly enhanced his appearance since we were twelve. Now, instead of the scrawny pale arms he used to lug around, he proudly flaunts forearms triple the size they should be, complemented by perfectly toned skin.

Kelly drove by the shed near Cade's house earlier to pick me up. Needless to say, they hit it off. Well, that's how she describes it. If I didn't know any better, I might say she's more intrigued by him than I am.

But no, no one is more intrigued by Cade Hampton than me.

"Okay, but in all seriousness. What should I do? I haven't had a relationship with him in years and here he goes fighting someone all because he thought I was uncomfortable."

Cade didn't even have all the details about me and Beau's conversation, and yet he stood up for me when Beau wouldn't take no for an answer. I would say that's just the kind of guy he is, one willing to stand up for others at the risk of himself. But I know better than that. He doesn't act like that with other girls. Maybe I'm just getting ahead of myself. I know he doesn't like me.

"It's like we're learning about each other all over again, but at the same time, there's nothing new to learn."

I don't need Kelly knowing that I might actually be considering thinking of Cade in any way other than with pure hatred. For so long, I've spent nights ranting to her about how awful he is, how all he does is ignore me. I guess people can change after all. Or maybe it's not people that change, but the circumstances those people are in.

"There ain't nothing awkward about the two of you, the way you both act, please. It's obvious you don't hate him anymore."

I don't want to confirm what she said, but I can't quite deny it either. I truly don't know how I feel about Cade randomly deciding to act civil towards me. We're just now getting back to a point where we can talk again. I don't want to screw it up this time. I want to have a connection with him whether or not it's just like when we were younger.

"You've seen us together once. You don't even know how we act around each other." I laughed as she hopped right back up onto the couch next to me.

"Trust me Tatum, I know you. You certainly don't hate him." Before I could combat her incorrect yet somewhat correct remark, a catastrophic thud abruptly interrupted us from the front door.

Someone continued pounding as if their life depended on it, and if I hadn't run to it as fast as I did, they would've broken it down in no time. As I cracked the entrance, I saw my mother's car parked in the driveway, the front bumper falling off from her recent run-in with a deer. Before I knew it, I was being pushed back into the coat rack as she busted through, brown leather briefcase in hand. I saw Kelly stand up out of the corner of my eye, her face pale as a ghost. I guess not everyone is used to seeing my maniac mother as often as me.

"Tatum, I've been standing out there for ten minutes, waiting for someone to let me in. Where were you?" She took her position impatiently beside the kitchen counter, one hand on a barstool, the other on her hip. It's like she's preparing for war.

She most definitely has not been knocking for ten minutes. Kelly and I would've heard her, especially considering how loud she was.

Her short temper calls for a curt response in return, "We didn't hear you, sorry."

I began the short walk back over to our couch so I could finish my conversation with Kelly, when without warning, I tripped over something by my feet.

What could I have left on the floor? I just swept twenty minutes ago.

I slid across the ground, finally hitting my head hard against the small table settled behind the couch. Reaching my hand to rub my head, I felt the warm surface soften as a stream of thick red blood ran down the left side of my face. I turned around to see what I had tripped over, and there stood my mother, black three-inch heels sticking out from where she'd tripped me. That's Jessica Cassidy for ya, doing petty things in order to get her way.

"I was in the middle of speaking to you." She acts as if I'm a servant bowing to her highness. This will happen no longer. I'm tired of the mind games she plays. I originally planned to ignore our minor incident at her office, but now she's gone too far. Every time she pulls some stupid stunt and ticks off a client, I take the heat for it. Everyone she does wrong ends up hating me. They tell their kids and friends to do the same. They say things like I'm a "bad influence", or that I don't come from a pleasant home. Actually, part of that might be true. But nonetheless, I'm done being associated with her selfish efforts. She is nothing more to me than an immature and ignorant woman.

I slapped the ground, then, with every ounce of rage I could muster from my aching body, I got up, now inches from her face. "You know what? That's it."

Kelly frantically stood, beginning to grab her things as she dropped every other item in her possession while scattering toward the front door. As much of a gossiper as she is, it's surprising that she doesn't plan to stay and see this unfold. But I didn't object as I watched her leave, her thin build occasionally turning back to make sure my mother hadn't killed me yet.

"Excuse me?" Mom finally realized what's going on, realized that for once someone has worked up the nerve to call her out.

"I'm sick and tired of you acting like this. You handle everything with the utmost disrespect and have no awareness for anyone you take down with you! Or you know what, maybe you are aware, maybe you know exactly what you're doing and who you're hurting by doing it."

Her face slowly turned red. Probably not the best sign for me.

"I work so hard to provide for you and this fami..." I stopped her. There's no way I'm about to allow her to call this 'bloodline' a family. We haven't been a family since Dad died, and even before then, we weren't much closer.

"What family? Look around Mom, you've lost everyone. Everyone's gone! Anyone you let into our lives ends up hurt so badly that they ditch us, one after another. Don't you ever sit back and wonder what life would be like if you weren't so inconsiderate?"

Even I know better than to pop off that harshly to my mom, no matter how rude she may be. Oh well. We both began screaming, each statement louder than the last.

"Well, maybe if you worked harder to learn about my career, we wouldn't have so many issues!" She said this as if I'm the reason we're falling apart at the seams.

"Maybe if you cared enough about your own daughter to glance in her direction every once in a while, you'd see that she needs you, and that she has for the past sixteen years. Maybe then we wouldn't be like this. Maybe if, if..." I stopped, careful to think about what I plan to say next. "Maybe if you weren't so self-centered, Dad would still be here."

And then there was silence. The kind of silence that eerily digs into the innermost parts of your ears, burying itself in the deepest cavities of your heart.

She stared at me, a furious look on her face and hot blood running through her aging veins. I can practically see the pure anger pumping throughout her body, her pitch black pupils throbbing back and forth, pulsing to a quick beat. Finally, she spoke, surprisingly, in a calm and hushed voice.

"I didn't kill your father, Tatum. I'm not responsible for what happened." I looked at her, her gleaming eyes filled with years of bottled up sorrow and regret. I see now that the anger I once thought had finally surfaced was really just *pain*. Yet still, I can tell that she does not understand how much her decisions have affected me.

"No, but you certainly didn't care enough to help give him justice."

And that was that. She didn't say another word to me. I threw one last demeaning stare her way, no longer than a few seconds, and walked out.

An oddly cold gust of wind blew my tangled hair across the wooden door frame as I left our house. Well, I say "our house", but this is not my home anymore. I don't really have a home at all.

With one forceful pull, I closed the front door and marched down our rocky steps and towards the declined driveway. Once again, Mama didn't yell after me, didn't chase me, didn't even come outside.

It breaks my heart when she doesn't see me, doesn't help me—doesn't love me.

I jogged around the neighborhood for hours thinking about everything that happened, wondering how it's possible for someone to be so blinded by hate that they can't even see what's right in front of them; a hurting young woman, still a child at heart, in need of her mother's comforting arms.

How does she live with herself, walking around everyday knowing that she has no idea what goes on in her own daughter's life? No idea who my friends are, what I like to do, or even where I like to eat. Does she go to sleep at night not knowing or caring what her child's struggles are, what MY struggles are, not having the slightest clue whether I would go to Heaven if I were to die? I would like to think that I would go to Heaven, but only God knows.

I deeply pray, dear God, please help us all make it to Your Kingdom one day.

After a while of sightseeing, kicking myself for not saying more, I called Cade. My bike isn't here and I have nowhere to go, so his ignorant and confusing self might just be my best bet. David headed out of town this morning with one of his "lady friends", instructing me not to bother his house, and there's no way that going back to Mom's will end well, no matter what angle you look at it from.

I'm not sure why I thought of Cade first, but he's the only person that I know will make sure I'm okay.

I trust him. I may not always respect him or agree with his decisions, but I trust him.

"Hello?" He picked up the phone after the third ring, quite a quick answer for someone who is usually too busy to talk.

"Hey." His voice is so alluring. I'm almost infatuated with him, every aspect of him; the dusky voice, carelessly perfect hair, toned physique. Snap out of it, Tatum.

"Listen, I'm at my mom's, but I need a ride. It's a long story. I'll explain when..."

"I'm on my way." He hung up the phone.

If there's even the slightest hint that I need help, he is the kind of person who doesn't ask questions. He never hesitated to respond, nor had a second thought about if he wanted to assist or not. Mom could learn a lot from someone like Cade. No matter who his parents are, they raised him right.

It was dusk when Cade arrived, the daunting sky appearing cerulean blue as it floated softly overhead. We drove around for a long time before speaking. Cade pulled up in his navy blue Jeep Cherokee, but seeing it this time feels so much more surreal than it did watching from a distance. I ride by it every morning, wondering how Cade is doing, wondering whether or not he's okay. It always sits awkwardly parked in their pebbled driveway, usually an athletic hat inside the windshield or some cleats left by the driver's side door. Now, here I am sitting in the passenger seat beside him, internally yearning for him to ask me about my day or talk to me at the very least. The mere sound of his protective voice brings me a smile that lasts for days.

But he didn't. We rode around Stonson in peaceful silence, watching as the sun set behind rows of houses and shops. If the mood was better, it would've been the perfect night, a gorgeous scene and a long drive down summer back roads, but unfortunately my life is not the ending scene in a romantic movie. In fact, it's anything but that.

Finally, I decided it would be best if I was the first to say something. To control the narrative, if you will.

"Thank you."

C'mon now Tatum, that's all you could come up with? Thank you?

He looked away from the road quickly at the sound of my voice. I thought for sure we were bound to crash. But he didn't let that happen as he frantically grabbed the wheel and straightened it back out, all the while looking at me. All those skills he learned at football might've actually done something for the poor boy's once underwhelmingly awful hand-eye coordination.

"Anytime. I'd never leave a friend hangin' like that."

A *friend*?

Deep down I know *that's all* we are. It's all he wants us to be. But I guess that's good news.

So why do I feel so weird around him? Why do I keep getting these odd feelings whenever he's near? I don't know how to explain them. It's as if my ardent outer layer wants so badly to push him away, to project every hateful thought I've ever had about him and his sorry parents out into the surrounding atmosphere. And yet every innermost part of me wants to grab him and never let go, never loosen my grip. It wants to proclaim every detail I notice about him that no one else sees. Every glance away, every missed day of school, every tear I've seen fall discreetly from his glossy blue eyes. Every secret he holds so tightly within, every rambling conversation he desires to have, every idea he hides away, fearful that if he shows his colors he might be shamed. And if that happens, if others see how he truly wants to act, he could easily lose the one thing he values more than anything else in the world: *secrecy*.

Cade Hampton may seem like an open and shut case to anyone else, but to me, his chivalrous persona is clearly nothing more than a way to hide his pain.

The idea of him and I hanging out again, going on dates, having the same conversations we did as kids, it's all too much for me to think about at once.

"I didn't know we were on the same page about that."

He turned back to look at the road as I said it. Maybe I said the wrong thing.

"I'm lost. On the same page about what?"

"You know, about us talkin' and all. I'm just glad you consider us friends again."

He sighed, the most painful and sorrow-filled sigh my ears have ever had the task of hearing.

"Listen, Tatum, I know everything with your dad affected you negatively, and I know how me not being there during it hurt you. I'm sorry for that." He seems sincere about the apology, and for a moment I even thought I saw a shimmer of water in his eyes sparkle as he spoke, but it's probably just a reflection from the streetlights. "But you have to understand, I was a kid too. I didn't think about things like that. Kids should have to worry about what to wear to school or what stuffed animal to buy, not about what happens if their parents are convicted of murder."

I've never thought about it like that.

Even though I was the one who lost a parent that night, Cade lost something too. He lost the innocence that every child should never lose, stripped of the safety I know he once held onto so dearly. Most importantly, he lost trust in the fact that his parents are good people. No matter how many people tell him they're innocent, or how little evidence was found, he'll always have that thought in the back of his mind. The little voice in his head saying, "Well maybe they did do it, maybe they're not the people I think they are," repeating in his brain over and over again until he eventually begins to question whether or not he's actually safe with them at all.

"You're not the only one who had questions that night." We both had unanswered questions, still do, just very different ones, about very different people.

That's when it hit me. "Cade, turn left."

"What?" His voice cracked as he spoke, well, more like yelped, reminding me of when his voice hadn't gone full blown man on me yet.

"Turn now!" He jerked the wheel to the left as fast as he could, all but a few feet from passing the road I need him to turn down. The yellow diamond-shaped caution sign violently fell over as he slammed into it, quickly flying over the car roof as we continued on.

He began to yell, not out of frustration, but out of desperation, and the hope that maybe then I could hear him. "You don't just yell things out like that, you scared me! I could've run us off the road!" The dirt road we turned down is more than quite bumpy, and the noise now being emitted as his wheels roll over it is neither pleasant nor discreet.

"My bad."

"Well clearly. Where are we anyhow?"

"You don't recognize it?"

"No, not really. Should I?"

"I'd hope so."

We drove on the unkept path for a mile or two before I motioned for him to turn right. I'm surprised that he still can't tell where I'm taking him, that he doesn't recognize it. Sure, vines and bushes have grown over the road since four years ago, but it's still a pretty discernible area. "One more turn, go left." After a few minutes more, it became clear in his face that he now recognizes where we are.

He pulled over on the side of the road right before we crossed the old red bridge, our wheels close to tilting into the ditch below.

"Tatum, we shouldn't be here. You know what Mr. Davidson would say if he knew that we were…" I opened the car door and got out.

"Shut up alright, just let me look around for a second." I closed the door and watched as he rolled his eyes dramatically, still choosing to follow me only moments later. I all but gracefully jumped across the drainage ditch below my sopping wet feet, only a foot or so wide, but pretty deep compared to those in town. Cade jumped next, a few feet to my left. I let him catch up as I carried on, keeping my eyes wide open as I cautiously moved deeper into the brush. The treeline starts a hundred or so yards from where we left the car, lined with poison ivy plants and the occasional squirrel or two. Cade ran up from my left, picking me up to lift my legs over the plants. In all honesty, it caught me off guard more than he will ever know. As he went to set me down, his hand got caught in the pocket of my hoodie, an awkward situation for us both.

"Sorry," he said, letting go as quickly as possible, followed by an embarrassed stare at the ground. We all have some unique quirk we portray when we get embarrassed. That's clearly his.

He leaped over the plants himself and we continued on our trek through the overgrown woods that will forever haunt my dreams. People say it's not places you remember when you're grown, but what happened at those places that stick with you. I think they're wrong, because I will never forget this place, and I'm not even completely sure what happened here.

All I know is that one minute my dad was here, alive, and the next he was in Heaven.

"What exactly are we looking for? Anything that used to be here is either gone or covered with weeds." He kicked at a root as we walked, obviously not understanding why I've brought him here.

"Where's the closest road?" I stopped between two large trees and turned back to look at Cade, awaiting an answer.

"C'mon now. We just left the closest road." Sighing, I realize that I need to reword my question.

"I meant, where is the closest access road on the property?" He raised an eye at the question, his thick blonde eyebrows somehow staying perfectly in place.

"How am I supposed to know?"

I walked over to an opening only a few hundred yards ahead of us, waving for him to follow. "Well, it is your parents' land after all."

As we cleared the covering of the trees, I could see an old hunting perch across the way, maybe a mile or so from where we stood. The wooden legs are rotting sideways, practically touching the ground at its base. As I look over to the left, I lay eyes on exactly what I came here for; the old gray barn that sits on the back corner of the Hampton's hunting land, still standing proudly isolated and free.

I need to see what's inside that barn for myself. I want to stand where Mr. Davidson once stood searching for any evidence that my father had more than simply a "hunting accident".

I've seen the barn a million times before, but only in my imagination, with a design and layout my head created all on its own. I know it can't possibly be as dungeon-like as I make it seem, probably no real chains or deadly ropes laying across busted floorboards, but that doesn't make it any less triggering.

I began the run over to the barn, expecting Cade to follow behind just as he did. We hurried through the tall grass, our ankles cut and bit every few steps. I can feel the pollen compiling on the soles of my shoes, adding to the already disgusting collection of flooded marsh packed into their crevasses. The end of summer means that no fragrant violet flowers coat the once luscious hill here, only dying weeds and lemongrass.

But we made it, and with only a little less blood than we had at the start.

I stood at the entrance of the barn and tediously looked upwards. I didn't realize how tall it was from afar. Cade had already opened the door when I caught up to him, him having passed me on the way over. The minute he cracked the grimy white door open, an odor filled the air, punching us like a fist to the face. I have never in my life smelt anything quite like this before, and I never want to again.

"Good Lord Almighty, what is that horrible smell?" Cade pinched his nose and tilted his head upwards, as if that's goin' to do much of anything. I've never seen a grown man be so dramatic over anything quite like Cade.

"It's probably just a dead animal or somethin.'" Walking deeper into the musty barn, I can feel the scent slowly becoming weaker, but Cade still lingers by the entrance, now bending over and gagging at the wretched smell.

"Oh stop it, your room has probably smelt worse than this." I turned around laughing, only to see him looking up at me, his nose and lips turned up at my sarcasm.

Finally, walking over to join me, he asked, "Can you please tell me what we're lookin' for in here?"

"We're not lookin' for anything in particular. I just needed to see this place." In reality, I thought that if the same person who took my dad really had taken Brynlee, maybe they would've brought her here. The cops always thought this was where my dad found shelter after his accident, a sensible assumption if you really believed the hunting accident story.

I never did.

I sent Cade to take a look around one side of the barn while I took the other, hoping something would stand out to us, give us some idea of where Bryn might be, but we found nothing—no fallen hair ties she could've dropped, no empty Coke cans or Mountain Dew bottles. I guess I was wrong. Maybe the barn has nothing to do with Brynlee.

Just as I went to call Cade's name, something purple caught my eye in a corner of the downtrodden stables. I navigated around an old barrel, brown in color, careful not to stir up any more dust than we already had, and laid my eyes on a ghastly object, momentarily refusing to believe what I'm seeing.

No, it can't be. It just can't.

I'm not sure why I began to cry at such an underwhelming discovery, but the waterworks sure started flowing. I can't help but let my emotions get the best of me, and that means a lot coming from my mouth; my true feelings don't like to show themselves to the public eye very often.

Cade ran over at the sound of my tears. "What happened?"

I grabbed his hands to calm me, profusely sweating. I looked at his worrisome expression and pointed over to what I'd found, smiling through the tears. When he saw what I'd discovered, he quickly shared my confusing joy.

Sure enough, there it is, only feet from my own emotionally bruised self, a frozen memory that the barn has somehow kept waiting for me to find; growing through the uneven wooden floors sits a small patch of purple flowers. Two beautifully blooming violet sprouts, just like the ones Daddy and I loved so dearly, side by side and intertwined at the stems. Despite the weather, here they are. The same ones that star in a photo which still sits on our kitchen counter, his favorite photo, mine too.

God gave me a sign today, one that nobody can ever dispute—hope. It may not help us find Brynlee, but it gives me the motivation and willpower to keep pushing forward until we do.

I will find my father's killer, no matter how many hours it takes or how many tears I shed in the process. I am no longer the innocent little girl surrounded by flowers as I was in that picture. I may not be searching for a buried bone in some neighbor's yard, but I'm still on the hunt for answers.

And God just gave me my first sliver of hope.

"Hope is the feeling you have that
the feeling you have isn't permanent."
- Jean Kerr

Chapter Sixteen

December 16th, 2019~2:48 PM

I went back to school the Monday after Daddy's funeral. Mama came home that night acting as if nothing happened, pretending that she hadn't missed the entire funeral. She tried to explain to me that life can't just go on hold for every minor inconvenience, for every unfortunate event, but Daddy's death isn't a small issue. This is a life-altering "inconvenience" that will change the way I live, and think, for the rest of my life. She just doesn't want to recognize that yet.

Mama hides away and cries by herself, never letting anyone see her shed a tear. I feel bad for her, but maybe it would be easier to feel genuine sympathy if we felt it together.

I internally mourned all throughout the day at school, and it certainly didn't help to hear the rumors kids spread. They're probably just things they overheard from their gossiping parents, siblings, neighbors—the list goes on. All my teachers pulled me aside during class to offer their sympathies and remorse, but I'm a big girl—brave, just like Daddy would want me to be. I didn't shed a single tear until I left the school building. For all I know, whoever killed him could be there. Sounds like paranoia to some, but not to me.

Cade wasn't at school today. His mom must've let him stay home. I guess she's nicer to him than she is to other kids, like me, for example. Something's off about her, how she acts around everyone else versus how she acts around Mom and I. Now don't get me wrong, I like her, but *ever since that night at the police station, she's been really weird, almost rude, towards me. She won't let me hang out with Cade anymore, not even at the playground after school.*

I don't get to see him at church. That was my favorite part of the week.

I took the bus home from school, something I only do when both Mama and Daddy have to work. I guess I'll be taking the bus a lot more often now that Daddy won't be here to pick me up.

I hate the bus, and for good reason. Every time I get on, it smells like burnt hair and cheap perfume, courtesy of our driver, Shelly. Plus, the seating situation is wretched; if you pick a seat towards the back you're bound to spend the entire ride nauseous, but if you sit too close to the front, you'll spend it listening to Shelly talk about her date the night before, and they're never PG-13 stories. It's usually a summary of why men are all "pretentious lumberjacks" who do nothing more than insult her ego.

How dare they.

Today, however, Shelly isn't very talkative about her troubles. That's how a lot of people seem to be whenever I walk into the room. The minute I stepped on the bus and began my search for a good seat, she flagged me down and pulled me aside, her old-school fluffy blonde hair bouncing as she hopped out of her seat.

"Tatum, I'm so glad to see you today! I saved you a seat right next to Aidan." She pointed to a perfect seat in the middle row next to an open window. A boy, characterized by freshly cut brown hair styled with gel, sits on one side of the seat smiling. His dimples are overwhelmingly cinematic, perfectly shaping his youthful face. I've only ever seen him when I ride this bus, but he seems sweet enough.

I thanked Shelly for her kind gesture and she softly smiled back, thrusting her seatbelt on quickly. Everyone keeps trying to hide their concern for me, if that's what you wanna call it, but I can tell they're only being nice because of my dad. If only care like this was contagious...

"You can have the window seat if you'd like. I'll move my stuff." Aidan reached over and moved his black bookbag along with a blue pair of gym shoes from where I'm supposed to sit. Clipped on his backpack appears to be a sparkly purple and gold keychain, a panda, I think.

I like pandas, but I've never seen one in person. Mama agreed that I could only go to the zoo if I had perfect grades all year, but Daddy said he'd find a way to get me there whether my grades were perfect or not. But now he isn't here, and the zoo will just have to be another thing I'll never get to see with him. All those memories we could've made, gone in the blink of an eye.

When I looked back up at Aidan's face, I could tell that he noticed me eyeing his panda keychain; it intrigues me.

"My little sister and I got it when we went to Costa Rica over vacation. She has one of her own to match." I'm not sure that Costa Rica has pandas, but I'll roll with it.

"It's real pretty, especially the colors. Hey, it matches your shoes too!"

Aidan's high-top white and purple sneakers with a single gold star on the side, Converse, to be exact, discreetly bob against his legs as I still stand waiting for him to scoot over.

Aidan looked down at his shoes and laughed, "Yeah, I guess they do. I hadn't really noticed." He got up and let me in the seat, careful to make room for all my stuff. It was awkward at first since we've never really talked, but eventually he warmed up to me.

This is exactly how my older cousin Tiffany described what happens when you get into high school. She once told me, "You try to talk to a boy, and he can't even respond like a civilized person." It was Thanksgiving, and we had gone to her house to eat, but we haven't visited since. Tiffany says men have no common sense or general social skills once they pass puberty.

I'm not sure exactly what puberty is, but I don't think the boys in my grade are quite there yet.

She announced it to our whole family, "They just sit and stare until it's awkward for everyone or until you walk away. They're ridiculous creatures, no manners. I mean seriously, who raised these boys?" No one else understood the irony, but it was quite funny for someone who, at the time, was cramming three rolls into her mouth to talk about men without manners.

Tiffany has been dating a guy named Nate for as long as I can remember, although I've only met him once. She came down to celebrate Mom's birthday a few years back, and he tagged along, but they fought the entire time. I don't think that fighting is such a good idea, but my parents do it all the time, so maybe it's just what couples do.

"No man is raised right nowadays. They don't open doors or pay for dinner. They all just walk around flexing their muscles and hikin' up their shorts. Sometimes I really question whether or not that's all they're good for." I laughed when she said that. It was such a silly thing to say. Boys don't wear shorts like ours, they're supposed to wear longer khaki ones or sometimes even pants. She gave me a look and said that her boyfriend hikes his up, then rolled her eyes and walked upstairs. Why she even has a boyfriend if she has this many complaints is bewildering. I haven't talked to Tiffany since. She didn't even come to Daddy's funeral.

Maybe she and Mama are more alike than I thought.

When I get to high school, I'm only going to date boys who are nice. Ones who give me hugs and tell my friends how pretty they look, even if we all really look a little crazy that day. Daddy used to say that no one would ever be good enough to marry me, but then he'd smile and make me giggle, unable to keep a straight face. He would put his hand on the top of my head and tousle my hair, then say, "But if you love him, I guess he'll have to do." Daddy knew that if God wants me to get married, I'll get married, and he loved God with all his heart. I believe he still does up there in Heaven.

"Where you headin'?" I forgot that Aidan sat beside me for a moment. It was just so quiet.

"What do you mean?"

"Like, where do you live?"

"Oh! My house is in Earlpark, right inside town. How bout' you?"

Aidan looked at me and pointed out the window. "This is my stop now, 1732 Dreyor Street." He gathered his things, panda keychain still dangling from his bag now being slung across the bus. He jogged off the bus in a goofy manner, accidentally plunging his adored sneakers into a muddy puddle by his mailbox.

I thought he had already walked inside, when suddenly, I saw him run back to our seats.

"Did you leave something?" I asked, looking around in search of anything he could've dropped.

"Nope, I got everything. I just wanted to tell you something."

"What?" Patiently, I waited as he stood for a moment gazing at me, a soft grin painted across his clean face.

"You look really beautiful today."

I sat there for just a second or two, my eyes dilating and constricting at a rapid rate for no apparent reason. Aidan smiled, those iconic dimples gracefully flashing my face before turning away one last time. I watched in awe as he left, for real this time, walking all the way across the road and into his well-lit house. Well, I call it a house, but with the granite stone walkway and white-washed bricks complementing giant evergreen trees that line the fence, it's more of a palace than a home. His perfectly shaped hair lightly blew in the wind, those memorable shoes bouncing to the beat of his own heart.

Aidan never made it anywhere else after that. Not to school the next day, not to the science fair that morning, and never again to my bus.

That night Aidan Courier got to go to Heaven.

Apparently he passed in his sleep, a painless death, I pray. His little sister, Anna, found him the next morning when she went into his sports-decorated bedroom. Anna is a beautiful young girl, not as put together as her older brother, but six-year-olds are allowed to be like that. Her skin is tan, unlike Aidan's, but they both have the same distinct light eyes, recognizable from a mile away. She carries a bit of an attitude with her, but she's still learning, I'm sure of it. I saw her greet her brother at their doorstep when he left the bus, a large doll gripped in her small hands, their outfits oddly matching just enough to force a double take.

No one knows why Aidan died that particular night. He had been battling leukemia for over thirteen months when he went up to Heaven, something I was unaware of until Shelly told me. I guess you never really know what actually goes on in other people's lives. That beautiful brown hair that I'd thought was so insanely handsome was really a wig. His hair fell out months ago because of radiation. His parents said he'd just gone in for a checkup about a week ago and they got the great news that his cancer was finally gone. He beat it, a long but joyful road to recovery ahead.

The doctors don't know what caused him to pass while he slept, but they say the cancer itself didn't kill him, and I believe them. Their guess is some kind of side effect to the treatment, but even that makes me wonder. I don't think Aidan's disease is what killed him. Maybe he just finally finished the plan God has in place for him. He left this world with a gentle and beautiful soul. I could tell that just from our brief interaction on the bus. His last act of kindness was sharing a few sweet words with a little girl who lost her dad, showing me that there's still good left in this world after all, that God is still here, and that He will absolutely never leave us alone.

And that's all I know about Aidan Courier; he was a kind and genuine soul. Well, that and the fact that his body will never be alone in its grave. His precious baby sister left a gift for him; a small stuffed panda, purple in color, with a gold nose and white paws. It was the gift she'd planned to show Aidan the morning she found him dead. It matches the keychains they bought once on a vacation, the same keychain that I will carry around with me for the rest of my life.

I don't know why I got to keep such a treasure, but I found it in my seat on our bus the next day. I must've been sitting on it or something. I picked up that keychain and clutched it in my hands so tightly, an impression quickly being made on my skin, then I looked up to the sky.

"Thank you, God. Thank you."

That keychain has never left my side since.

"If someone comes into your life and has a positive impact on you,
be thankful that your paths crossed.
And even if they can't stay for some reason,
be thankful that somehow they brought joy into your life,
even if it was just for a short while.
Life is change.
People come and go, some stay, some don't,
and that's okay."
-Unknown

Chapter Seventeen

September 18th, 2023~1:23 AM

Da na, da na. Cade tossed blueberries from his bowl, and one by one, they hit the correal vase's outer rim.

"Would you stop that? You're making a mess."

I used to get like this when we were kids, intolerable when I become frustrated. Now throwing blueberries at me instead of at the vase, Cade is hoping to provoke a laugh out of what he calls my "poor mannered exterior".

Hands flailing and fingers ticking, I yelled, "Cade, will you just stop? How can you possibly be playing a game at a time like this?"

I want so badly to get more upset and say something I'll soon regret, but there's no point. I'm not yelling at him out of anger, I'm yelling because I care.

"Tatum, the police are working overtime to find Brynlee. Relax for a second."

"Yeah, well, they tried their best to find out what happened to my dad too, and look how that turned out." I walked over to his fridge and pulled out a bottle of water, throwing away the lid as I chugged it.

"I'm sorry. I didn't mean it like that." He eagerly followed me into the kitchen, simultaneously annoyed and remorseful.

"How could you say that? You know how much this means to me."

"But why?"

"What do you mean, why?"

"Why do you care so much about Brynlee? I mean, I know it's awful that this has happened and all, but I didn't think you two were that close."

"It's not about how close I am with Brynlee. Cade, none of this is about that."

"Well then, what is it about Tatum?"

"I'm not having this conversation right now."

"No really, what's all of this for if it's not about finding Brynlee or about satisfying your need to fix everything all at once? Because as of now, all you've shown me is that you just don't want to get hurt again."

Given how painfully bliss his words are to me, they still hurt.

I walked closer to his face, tilting my head slightly downwards, so he knows how serious I am. "This is not about keeping me from getting hurt again. This is so that another family doesn't have to go through what mine did; what yours did. Got it?"

He gulped, his Adam's apple momentarily bulging inches from my face. "Got it."

This is the first time I've been back inside Cade's house since everything happened, but not much has changed. A new rug lays across the living room floor and a fresh layer of paint coats the front entryway, but for the most part it's the same house I practically grew up in. If Cade's parents knew I was here, they'd flip out, probably curse my name for another four years. Both Mrs. Lanie and Mr. Carl are still out with the town's search party, looking for any sign of sweet Brynlee. They may not be the kindest people, but they sure are involved in our community. I'll give em' that.

"Tatum, you must remember that we still don't know for certain what happened to your dad. Stop freaking out about it." He's right, the cops could never prove who killed him, nor that the Hamptons had anything to do with it, despite it being on their land. But he didn't find his way into that barn by himself. Someone put him out there. I know it might be foolish of me to really think that my dad's killer and Brynlee's kidnapper are the same person, but it would be blatant negligence to not consider it as a possibility at all. There's just too many similarities about the cases, too many coincidences—I don't believe in coincidences.

"And if I'm right, what do you think is gonna happen to Bryn?"

Just a few days ago, Cade and I finally agreed on who we believe is responsible for Brynlee's disappearance. Now he's letting false logic get in the way of recognizing the truth, so we're back at square one.

"If you're so worried, then why aren't we out there looking for her?" Cade doesn't understand how I think at all. The way my brain works—it processes things differently. It's very peculiar.

"Wandering around town in the middle of the night looking for someone who might not even still be in Stonson is pointless. If she's alive at all, we're not gonna find her in the Winn-Dixie parking lot. She's not just gonna pop up."

Cade leaned his hand on the marble kitchen counter, batting his eyes as if to convince me otherwise. "I know, but it can't hurt."

I feel bad when Cade tries his best to be so sweet and I still have an attitude. Yet everything he's said has found some way to upset me. But honestly, it's hard not to be upset when he keeps asking stupid questions.

He sighed and moved closer to where I stand, his eyelids no longer flickering. Smiling, he leaned in and gave me a hug, something I didn't at all expect. I didn't object, of course. It's actually a relief to stop and breathe for a minute.

I rarely like people touching me, but Cade's touch is different. It's warm, welcoming, and unbelievably wholesome. To me, his arms are the safest place to be.

"So, what do you want us to do?" He pulled away from me, leaning back on the counter again. I want to tell him not to let go, tell him how comfortable he makes me feel—but I don't. I simply let him slip away from my grip once again. It's obvious that he doesn't have the same confusing feelings I once hoped we would share.

"Honestly? I have no idea. All I know is that we can't let history repeat itself."

And that's when we got the call.

Cade's phone began to ring, only four times before he made it into the living room and answered.

I yelled from my secluded spot in the kitchen, "Who is it?"

He hollered back, "My mom!"

I barely heard him respond, only a practically inaudible whisper making its way to my ears. You would think that with the massive size of their house, there'd be at least a small echo, but there was none. For a few more minutes, I heard nothing other than indecipherable speech between Cade and his mom. When he walked back into the kitchen, the phone dangled loosely from his grip, a heartbroken expression on his face.

"Is everything okay?"

He didn't answer at first, continuing to stand by the tan woven barstools and shake his head. "Cade, look at me. What happened?"

He looked up from the ground silently.

"They found a body."

"Stare at the dark too long and you
will eventually see what isn't there."
-Cameron Jace

Chapter Eighteen

September 18th, 2023~2:07 AM

I'll never forget today. Just like the day Dad never came home, it's one that will forever haunt my mind.

We got to the warehouse a little after two in the morning, but certainly weren't the first ones to arrive. Half of Stonson's population gathers in the parking lot off York Avenue, the street where an old abandoned warehouse barely stands, if you can even call it a warehouse at all. It's more of an awry pile of pieced-together bricks covered in vines and insects, slowly crumbling as the days go on. No one has used it for almost twenty years now, quite the literal abandoned building.

Cade got out of the car first, me soon following behind, practically using him as a protection device. I don't know what I thought I needed protecting from, or why I assumed Cade could be that for me, but the whole place just gives me a bad feeling.

"Mom?"

Cade walked us over to a woman in a blue shirt and yellow reflective gear, not much taller than me. As she turned towards Cade's voice, we forcefully made eye contact. Eerie eye contact. After that, she never even greeted her son, who so kindly came to meet her at the news, but headed straight for me like a lion hunting its prey.

"Cade, what are you doing with this poor excuse for a..."

Thank God for Mr. Davidson and his nosy instincts.

"No need for that, Mrs. Hampton. We are all here for the same reason. Let's stick together, not slash each other's throats." He looked at her once more and then turned his attention to me. "We've lost too much already."

He then showed Cade and I over to an old rock walkway leading towards the warehouse entrance. People in white and blue uniforms swarm all around us, a medical examiner van arriving next, tires popping from the partial gravel drive. Mr. Davidson is trying his best to prepare us for whatever we're about to see, ending every line with the same two sentences: "I've never seen anything like it. Don't look too long" The silence after that was crippling, time somehow stopping all over again. Just like it did four years ago.

I'm not quite sure why he's allowing Cade and I this close to the crime scene. It surely can't be legal for us to be here. Maybe it's out of sympathy, or some kind of obligation he feels to include me, but I believe he's doing it out of regret for not saving my person; my dad. Curious spectators stand around the yellow crime scene tape, a few trying to wave over stagnant officers and ask questions, while others simply stare in awe and horror. As I scanned the crowd, one couple in particular caught my eye. They've been standing in the same spot since we arrived, only shifting a little with the flow of the surrounding group. The woman appears of darker skin, a green trench coat draped over her compact figure, white rain boots to match. I can't see her face very well, but it's the man who intrigues me more. He continues to cry hysterically, as he has for ten minutes now, yet no one around is offering him any comfort. Everyone in his vicinity acts as if he's diseased, making sure to stay meters away from both him and the woman at his side. I would say he's very attractive for his age, a proportionately muscular build accompanied by a head full of dark, luscious hair. They both appear fit, the woman with a shadow of what I assume is long hair, or possibly a turban, and her partner is no less than six feet tall.

The man continued on with his breakdown, only drawing more attention to himself as it went on. Finally, I worked up the nerve to ask Mr. Davidson who they were, but he did nothing more than look their way and sigh.

"You don't recognize them? I figured you both would've met Brynlee's parents by now, considering how invested y'all seems to be."

Mrs. Berkley—Brynlee's mother—although for someone who has just been faced with the news that her daughter might be dead, she doesn't seem too fazed. I should've known who she was, her being my dentist and all, but the shadow of tonight's dark sky threw me off.

"It's shock. She's in disbelief." He's right, shock can do wonders to a person's emotional state.

I once read about a man who was in a severe car accident, even lost his hand in the wreckage. He wandered off from the crash site before help could arrive and somehow managed to walk all the way to his house over six miles away. He didn't realize the severity of his injury until the next morning when he arrived at work, missing a limb. The man's body had gone into such severe shock that he'd somehow tuned out the pain and aggravation his body was enduring. Maybe that's what's goin' on in Mrs. Berkley's mind; on the outside, she's a full spirited woman with a gorgeous complexion and an enormous amount of energy, but on the inside, her heart is mourning and she doesn't even know it.

Mr. Davidson motioned for an officer to let them past the tape to join us, crying puddle of a man and all. They walked over to us, arm in arm, one bawling his eyes out and the other expressionless. He introduced us to them, although I've already met Mrs. Berkley at her dentistry office. Mr. Berkley slightly smiled after the introduction, his tears halting for only a few seconds before resuming. Brynlee's mom, however, did not seem as pleased to see us, particularly Cade.

"Is this the one who let my daughter walk into that parking lot alone?" She spoke so sternly, so full of anger, even the escorting officer was taken aback. Cade doesn't seem to know how she knows that or why she's making it seem like Bryn's leaving is his fault. I'm not sure what Mr. Davidson has told her about who Brynlee was with when she disappeared, but whatever it was, she must've gotten the wrong idea.

"I think you may be confused–"

"Don't tell me what I may or may not be. You don't get a say in this!"

"Yes ma'am, I understand that, but what you're not understanding is that—"

Bam!

I won't tell you what I thought as Mrs. Berkley walked up to Cade, I don't think I could describe it justly. She did something that I have never seen a grown woman do, and certainly not one of Mrs. Berkley's petite nature. She looked Cade in the eyes and paused only for a moment before slapping him across the face, a harsh red handprint left compressed into his face for all to see, even at this dark hour. I expected for something more to happen after that, expected for Cade to say something sarcastic in response or for an officer to intervene. But no one did much of anything. In fact, everyone simply gasped and stood where they were, exchanging glances and whispers with those around. After a while, too long for no one to say anything, Mr. Davidson finally made the hard decision to continue on with what he actually invited the Berkleys over to do, addressing the couple on a first name basis.

"Tim, Anika, if you're ready now?"

With no words spoken, Mrs. Berkley silently nodded, her husband still tearing up as he gripped his wife's arm tighter.

He opened the door to the warehouse, an odor much like the one from the barn emerging ferociously. The officers inside have decorated themselves with white hazard masks around their nose and mouth, but now I understand why.

The entire inside of the warehouse is burnt to a crisp, only a small part of the roof left uncharred. Mrs. Berkley fell to her knees at the horrid sight, crying now more hysterically than her husband. I've never seen anything so gory in my life. This is certainly nothing any movie scene or documentary could've prepared me for. "Gunk", as Cade calls it, covers every inch of the gray and black walls. I don't think either of us immediately realized that it's human flesh, much less that it came from a girl we sat with only nights ago. Mr. Berkley somehow managed to gather himself enough to walk deeper into the burnt building, leaving his wife kneeling on the ground behind. She began to recite prayers in another language, each one louder than the last. I know the scene is a lot to take in, but no one else around is reacting in such an obscene manner as the Berkleys.

And that's when I saw why; in the corner of the small building lie a thin shadow on the ground, only able to be seen by the sliver of moonlight leaking in from an intact window above.

"Tim, can you identify the body as your daughter?" Brynlee's dad inched closer to the figure, wincing with every new part of her he discovered burnt to the bone. He began to cry again, not uncontrollably this time, but still discreetly into his hands and the sleeves of his shirt.

"Brynlee, you mean. Her name is Brynlee Ray."

The thought of his daughter no longer being alive must be harder for him to comprehend than Mr. Davidson will ever understand.

"It's hard to tell with so much of her, you know, missing." He looked back at the door, his wife still on the floor while Cade and I hover over her, secretly trying to peek inside. I feel sympathetic towards him, of course, but he doesn't seem entirely sure whether it's Brynlee lying below. If it was me, I might not be so sure either—the condition she's in is practically unrecognizable.

As I lean further into the room, I can see that the shadow I first noticed is only partially intact, one side almost fully burnt and the other covered in ash and charred flesh.

Mr. Davidson can clearly tell that it isn't a good idea for Mr. Berkley to look at Brynlee's body any longer. The corpse of his precious child is a sight that will already traumatize him forever. There's no need for him to stare at it any more than what's necessary. He escorted him out past us, helping Mrs. Berkley up as they left. He held his wife as she cried.

Once the building momentarily cleared out of all officers and mourning parents, I looked around to make sure no one was watching before slipping inside.

"Tatum, what are you doing? Get out of there!" Cade exclaimed as softly as he could without coming inside, commands that I will not be listening to. Eventually he followed me in just as I knew he would, still holding his cheek and stretching his sore jaw.

I walked over to the corner where my friend lay, her body torn apart and burnt like nothing I'd seen before, nor want to see again.

I hurled myself over, holding my stomach and burping as I tried not to regurgitate my dinner all over the crime scene.

"I think I'm gonna puke."

"Holy..." Cade's eyes grew to the size of a small melon, his face turning so white it scared me. He remained standing, staring at Brynlee as if she were a prized jewel on display. A very burnt and scattered prized jewel.

I got up very slowly and joined him over her dismantled body.

"We couldn't save her." I feel more frustrated now than sickened, agitated that someone got away with taking yet another life.

"Tatum." As I looked up, Cade's face was no longer an expression of disgust, but one more of utter shock. He turned to face me, now inches from where I weakly stand. I can smell his inordinate cologne coming up from his chest, his breath now hitting my forehead. He may not be paying much attention to how close we're standing, but I sure am.

"It's not her."

He grabbed my shoulders and smiled big, his perfectly whitened teeth blinding my eyes for just a moment before retreating.

"What?"

He began to run out, screaming as he left. "It's not her!"

Cade returned seconds later, practically dragging Mr. Davidson back inside. He's not too happy that we've entered the warehouse, but he seems more interested in what Cade has to say than in punishing us.

"Sir, it's not her. This is not Brynlee." He sighed and looked at Cade like a hurt puppy just begging to be acknowledged.

"Son, I know this is hard to comprehend all at once, but you can't just waltz out there with her parents around and get their hopes up that it's not their little girl lyin' here."

Cade ran around me and stopped on the opposite side of Brynlee's remains, squatting down to get closer.

"No, look."

He pointed at the only arm that's somewhat intact, smiling as if he had made a grand discovery.

"Cade, I don't see anything there." Mr. Davidson leaned in a little closer and squinted, his aging eyes trying their best to examine it accurately.

"Exactly." Both Mr. Davidson and I are officially lost. Cade made no more sense as he kept talking. We need to go home and get him some rest so that he's not paranoid like this in the morning. "Sir, Brynlee fell during field day one year in middle school. I was there, I remember it." He looked at me for support, but I still don't follow. Frustrated, he continued. "She had a steel rod put in her arm."

There's no steel rod. No remnants of rust or charred metal either, just the blackened bone and flesh that we can assume would be there, nonetheless. Cade's right. The body before us has clearly never had surgery for a steel implant.

Whoever this is, it is not Brynlee Berkley, and someone has just tried to make everyone believe that she's dead.

"A woman is always a mystery:
One must not be fooled by her face
and her heart's inspiration."
-Edmondo de Amicis

Chapter Nineteen

December 17th, 2019~12:17 PM

"There simply isn't enough information to work with. I'm sorry, Mrs. Cassidy."

It was a little after lunch when Mama picked me up from school. My name came over the intercom for check-out, something that rarely happens anymore. When I walked up to the front desk near the back of the school, closest to the parking lot, I saw a woman in a red body length fur coat waiting for me. My mother. All she needs now is a facelift and a Brazilian wax and she'll basically be a Kardashian.

Does she not realize how embarrassing it is for your mom to act half her age?

"Hurry up. We're going to the station to talk with Mr. Davidson."

"Why do I have to come?" I was actually enjoying my day at school before she checked me out, and that's hard for me to manage. Today is one of the few days that kids haven't found a new joke to make about my dad or about what happened to him.

"You need to be brought back to the real world, Tatum. It's not all sunshine and rainbows like your father made it seem."

There's so many things wrong with that sentence. Of course, there are bad things in this world, I know that, but she's wrong to blame Daddy for hiding them from me. The world isn't a perfect place anymore. It hasn't been since Adam and Eve. Evil does lurk here, and it shows itself in everyone's lives, but you can still be sheltered from the things that your parents deal with, sheltered from what snatches away our innocence at far too young of an age. And that's what my dad did. He didn't put a blindfold over my eyes to keep me from knowing that the world is full of sin. He simply chose to protect me from it as much as he could.

There's a difference.

We got to the station after about a ten-minute drive, the small parking lot empty except for county issued police vehicles. We walked inside and checked in at the front desk, a different lady sitting behind it now. This woman's name tag read BRYCE, but she looks very similar to the girl working the night Daddy died. Bryce was very kind, very beautiful, too. She told us to go ahead through the doors towards Mr. Davidson's office. As we continued on, I could see the room where Mrs. Lanie had once sat crying, as well as another woman now sitting in her place. I don't recognize this woman, but she definitely looks much older than Mrs. Lanie. Her bleach blonde hair is pulled back in a slick ponytail, lightly colored highlights showcasing thick eyebrows, her emerald green eyes cold as can be. She isn't at all crying as Cade's mama was. In fact, she stares emotionlessly at the wall in front of her. No officers are asking her questions, nor is there anyone else in the room, for that matter.

She just stares, no tears or nothin', not even a minuscule drop of salty liquid falling down her cheek. No expression at all actually, just a blank gaze. Then she looked at me, slowly, but the momentary glance was still enough to send chills down my spine. I jumped backwards, running into Mama.

"Watch where you're going."

She continued walking, dragging me by the hand as she went. That lady in the room seems very similar to my mama; cold, angry, expressionless most of the time. She hasn't always been like this; she used to be such a cheerful person, joyful and peppy and all-around great.

I had no idea how soon I would miss those days.

"*Thank you so much for seeing us today, John.*" *Mama took a seat in Mr. Davidson's office, the same spot where she sat not too long ago. It's surprising that she spoke so kindly when addressing him. I expected a rant about his station's lack of effort, or at the very least a string of unnecessary comments.*

"*Of course, Jessica, anything for the Cassidy women. Especially considering the circumstances.*" *He's referring to the unfortunate fact that it's been over a week since they found my dad dead and no one is being called in about it. No suspects, no evidence, and no idea what really happened. I don't think I'm supposed to know any of this, but word travels fast in Stonson.*

We all settled in, Mama already sitting, and began to talk. First, they discussed the course of action being taken by the department, then what they've found recently, which isn't much. But of course she still requested that he be thorough. Well, more like demanded that he be thorough. Then they got to the part I've been dreading, all the details and information about the murder, violently thrown out for my unwilling ears to hear. Details that no family member, much less a child, should ever have to hear. Mr. Davidson looked at my mom, then at me. We've all done this same charade before.

"*Anything you share with me can be shared with her too.*"

"*Are you sure, Jessica? It's a lot for her to comprehend.*"

"*Tatum can hear it.*"

Sighing, he continued, "Quite frankly, we don't have a lot yet. We know that your husband didn't drive his car after disappearing, we've recovered that. You can retrieve it when we contact you, shouldn't be more than a week or two. We've also confirmed the cause of death: blunt force trauma to the parietal lobe. Massive tissue scarring and internal bleeding were the ultimate heart stoppers." He weakly grinned, clearly sympathetic. "It was quick."

Maybe he thinks that if I know that his death wasn't painful, it'll make me feel better. But it doesn't; it only makes me more upset knowing that he died without putting up much of a fight. Maybe he couldn't fight back, maybe something kept him from opposing. I know Daddy would never just let someone take him away like that, not when it meant leaving me; only if he wasn't given the chance to defend himself would that be the case.

He wouldn't leave me alone with Mama.

"So you're telling me that you can't find any evidence of anyone else at the crime scene, but you know someone killed him? You're saying you've ruled out a hunting accident, but haven't come up with any new possibilities except murder? Please explain that, because right now it sounds like a load of—" Oh, there it is.

Mr. Davidson keeps trying to explain the lack of physical evidence where they found Daddy's body, that he and his team are doing their best to bring him justice.

"I have a question." My lowly sweet voice seemed to shock Mr. Davidson, but he gladly allowed it.

"Yes, Tatum?"

"Were there animals in the barn?"

"No sweetie, no animals. It does have some stables, but horses haven't been kept there for a long time."

Everything they're saying about the barn makes me feel even worse for my dad. When I go to Heaven, if God so blesses me, I pray He doesn't let me die like that, in a scary place with no friends or even animals. I would wanna die in a cool way, like from a shark attack or as a princess while my prince fights to save me.

Mama and Mr. Davidson continued on with their conversation. It was almost dark outside by the time we left. I feel bad for Mr. Davidson. He's trying his best to get answers for Mama and I.

As we left, she kept blurting out very bad words, everyone staring as she continued on. She's practically dragging me out, so I don't have much of a say in the matter. I can't tell if she's mad that they don't know much about Daddy, or if it's just the fact that no one is giving her the attention she so deeply believes she deserves. Of course, as the mourning widow, you'd think she would get at least a little sympathy, but no one gives her a second glance. No one treats her any differently, nor offers leniency considering the circumstances.

Maybe Mama is a bit more misunderstood than I thought. Maybe that's the reason she acts the way she does, because she feels the need to overdo everything—overcompensate, if you will.

Yet somehow, it doesn't appear as if she's mourning, but rather having regrets about how she spent the little time she had left with Daddy. I think she's actually beginning to let the sadness seep in. Even so, not many tears have emerged from her tired eyes over the past few days. I've always thought that if someone feels sad they will automatically cry, it's just what we're supposed to do as humans.

Maybe I was wrong.

Everyone acts as if me crying is the equivalent of a contagious disease, like they'll catch whatever "sickness" I have if they try to help. This is just like how no one paid much attention to Aidan. Maybe the world doesn't want to see all the good people it's losing. Or maybe it just doesn't want to accept how much hurt is being carried within its walls.

Either way, I see them.

I see the people that no one else does. I see how different they are, Aidan and Daddy alike. They differed from your average person. They were unique; two kind souls that I will forever hold in my heart.

Daddy, if you're listening, please take care of Aidan for me. He's one of the few people who showed me kindness when he didn't have to. I don't see acts of kindness much nowadays.

"If we are asking for the world to be kind,
we must first ask what are we doing to add more kindness to the world.
If we are asking for the world to be more loving,
we must first ask what are we doing to add more love to the world.

We are the vessels for the things we seek."
-Joel Leon

Chapter Twenty

September 21, 2023~5:38 PM

I can feel the rain sogging in my boots as I walk to the flagpole outside the high school. The wind continuously blows our royal blue flag in every direction possible, but I don't think anyone is paying much attention to an uncontrollable flag, considering everything else they're thinking about.

I opened the door and entered a room full of disheartened people, all folding up their umbrellas as their squeaky shoes slap the gym floor. Heads hung low, everyone painted a smile as they approach the large group. I took off my raincoat and hung it by the stage, along with others who were doing the same. I noticed Cade waiting for me on one side of the group, now gathered around something in the center of the gym.

There, sitting on the freshly waxed floor, sits two white crosses leaning up against small buckets, each only about as tall as my torso. In front of one cross lay a few bouquets of flowers and a smaller single bouquet, fuschia in color. In front of the other cross is a photo: a beautiful young girl dressed in a flowy yellow sundress, white-washed brick wall behind her.

Brynlee, and the most stunning photo I've seen of her yet.

In a small woven basket beside the cross sits more photos; ones of her and friends, her and family, her at games. Everyone drops in one or two they printed out as they walk by, their kids in photos with Bryn or her teachers putting in something she drew as a child. One girl was particularly memorable, dropping in a small teal book with a bow painted on top as she approached the cross designated for Brynlee.

"This is the memory book Bryn and I made freshman year. She thought that if we put all of our old memories together, then we wouldn't forget them when we made new ones." She paused, carefully placing her hand over her mouth. Tears began to flow from her glossy blue eyes, dark curly ringlets of hair falling in front of her face. "I just wish she knew that I would never forget our memories, no matter how many more I make." She continued crying, backing up into the group now forming around her, all offering compassionate arms as a source of comfort.

I recognize the girl, McKenna; I believe. I've seen her in the hallway with Brynlee a few times. I never really pay much attention to McKenna or Brynlee, lower classmen aren't usually on my radar; I don't mean that to sound rude, but they just haven't matured quite yet.

Then again, not many people had to mature at the rapid pace I did.

We all lit candles and prayed, a pastor from the Methodist church leading. The school committee organized this ceremony in honor of both Brynlee and the woman who was killed in the fire, although we don't know who she is for sure. No one has tried to claim her body, and there wasn't enough tissue for DNA identification. Rumors are it's Isabella Carter, a young girl who went missing a few years back over in Raleigh. Little do they know that Isabella passed away last year, I found the article in an online California newspaper back in January—drug overdose. That's why her family has kept it a secret for so long.

Usually they only hold mourning events like this for those who have passed away, but half the town believes that Brynlee is already dead. It would make sense for me to believe that too, especially with how long she's been gone; no ransom requests, no phone calls home, no trace of her anywhere.

But I can't. I just can't accept that.

I'm not sure if I don't want to believe she's gone, or if I really do feel that deep down, she's still with us. For some odd reason, I just know.

The clock on the wall reads 7:46. We've been at the school for almost an hour now. I don't mind, it's just a sad way to spend an hour of my life.

Everyone gathered is either crying or holding a friend, with the exception of a few people towards the back rudely on their phones. I keep getting notifications from Instagram—people posting photos from the ceremony, photos of the crosses and of kids dropping memories in the basket. What I can't tell is if they're doing it out of respect, or just for the likes. It's so sad how fake this world is now.

But no matter how teachers and students make it appear to their followers, this situation is anything but fake. Nothing about a young girl, still just a child, having her life abruptly altered with no choice, is fake. She didn't get the chance to decide who she went with or where she was going. She didn't get the chance to fight. Cruel people tried to decide Brynlee's fate for her. They still are. Of course, the only one who truly has Bryn in His arms is God.

It's the sad reality of it all, but sometimes, God uses other people's lives as a channel to help those around them. That's the bright side.

It could be someone they know or even a peer they've never met. Either way they affect that person's life in the most genuine of ways, hopefully for the better. That must be what's happening now. Brynlee's life is being used to change the lives of others. Not just the kids posting her story on social media, and not just her teachers, but mine.

Whether she knows it or not, Brynlee Berkley has changed how I view the world drastically. Her story is still changing my life right now. She may appear to be a pretty normal girl, nothing too special about her, but she is no longer just that to me. What she must be experiencing is something I could never handle. She's much braver than I will ever be.

Brynlee may not have aged much in the short time since she's been gone, but she is definitely maturing as it drags on, learning and growing through the trauma.

If only the trauma didn't entail pain.

God, tonight I pray for Brynlee, for any pain that she may be in and any uncertainty she is facing. Please help her through the hard times, the sad times, and the times when she's scared out of her mind. And while I pray that one day she gets to go to Heaven with you, please allow us to keep her for a little longer. I have a feeling she isn't quite done leaving her mark on this town. Not yet.

"I thought about how there are two types of secrets:
the kind you want to keep in,
and the kind you don't dare to let out."
-Ally Carter

The California Women's Rehabilitation Institute of L.A is sad to announce the passing of

Isabella Kennedy Carter

on Thursday, 13th January 2022

A combined service will be held at Whispering Oaks Chapel on Tuesday, 1st February 2022 for Isabella and two of her fellow recoveries, Addison Buice and Sophia Duren.
28347 Balkins Drive Agoura Hills, CA

Chapter Twenty-One

September 21, 2023~8:58 PM

I glanced over at Cade cautiously, and saw that we share the same expression. The cops aren't wrong, there isn't much to go on. There's no security footage from the high school, no tire tracks, and certainly no signal from Brynlee's phone since the night of the dance. Maybe they aren't blowing off her case like they did my dad's. Maybe they really can't find anything to go on.

"It's here. We're just missing it. I know we are."

Cade slammed his hand on the wooden table we set up in the basement, crumbled papers and little blue sticky notes flying chaotically into the air. We're still running on no sleep, and I'll admit, it's hard to think clearly.

The basement of my mom's house looks like an episode from True Crime, a mess of astray notes and information about Brynlee's disappearance flung across almost every square inch. We've only been getting everything together for a few hours, but it looks as if we've been living in this dump for months. When my parents bought the house, the basement was unfinished. We started the renovations four or five years ago to get it done. Mom planned to use the space as remote offices for Shargold Realty, but Dad wanted to build me my own space: a new bedroom and playroom, maybe even a window seat, if he could find the right design.

Once he died, none of that happened. Mom never finished the renovations, and I never got my "special space".

So now we're using the only table as a base of operations for our hunt. It's still coated in sawdust, now matted on permanently. We've managed to get just about every piece of information we could find on both Brynlee's disappearance and my dad's murder, everything from the night he died to the Homecoming dance. Every phone call recorded by the tip line, every accessible photo, and everything the cops already know—or so we hope.

Jenny Davidson has been crushing on Cade ever since he helped her stand up in gym class after a volleyball to the head. Everyone in our grade is very aware of Jenny's crush, even Cade himself. The phone call between the two was comical, her giggling at every word uttered from his mouth and him rolling his eyes on the other end.

"Sooo, could you get them for me?"

She giggled once more, then replied, "Yeah, I can get the files from my dad. But it's gonna cost you."

So now Cade has a lunch date set for next Thursday, one that both he and I are dreading. I don't know why Jenny asking Cade out bothers me so much. It just does.

But we got the files. Everything the police know, and everything they don't. No wonder Brynlee's case is getting nowhere. It's because they have nothing, just like we thought. They have a lot more information on my dad's case, believe it or not, but I guess it still wasn't enough to solve it. The suspects on record are endless. I swear they must've looked at every single person living in Stonson at the time of the murder. However, there are a few that stand out to me, especially one man in particular: Carl Hampton, thirty-nine years old at the time, father to Cade Hampton and dedicated husband to Lanie. Of course, both Cade and I already know about most everything that's in her file.

Cade's parents were automatically put under the microscope because Dad's body was found on property they own, but they never found anything that didn't line up in Lanie Hampton's story. Her alibi was as solid as they come. She was at work all evening, something she has to do often. But in Mr. Carl's file there are a lot more discrepancies and much less order to the madness.

In his first interview, he told police that he had been with Cade at soccer practice all evening. It's not exactly a rock solid alibi, considering they found my dad way after Cade's practice was said to have ended, but apparently, it was good enough for the cops who questioned him. Or maybe it was just his cinematic looks that got him through the questioning.

Then, just as they began to look deeper into his story, they realized that it didn't quite line up. A teacher from the middle school told police that she gave Cade a ride home that night, her son Thomas was on the same soccer team.

So where did Carl Hampton go after he dropped Cade off at six?

That's what the note in the file asked, written in big bold letters by Mr. Davidson. I assume that no one ever found the answer to that question, because that's all that is written. It's the very last note in the file. So where did he go that night, and why did no one ever follow-up on his story after they realized it didn't check out?

These are the things I'm talkin' about when I say that crime is different in a small town. People have connections with uppers in society that no one else even knows about, ties that we still may never be aware of. The Hamptons have lived in Stonson for decades now. There's no telling how many friends they've made. Enemies too.

"What'd you find?" Cade has been searching through other files and notes, but I haven't told him what I found on his dad.

"Not much of anything, you?" I closed the file quickly, shoving it underneath another stack sitting beside me. There's no need for him to know what the police think about his father's involvement, not yet at least. He won't know anything about it anyway. He was just a kid like me when it happened, clueless about the world and incapable of keeping its secrets. And even if he does know something, he clearly isn't aware of it.

"Same here. There's even less on Brynlee than there is on your dad. I get that they've only had a few days to process everything, but it's the only major crime for seventy miles. It's not like they're busy or somethin.'"

If we keep talking about this case, he's definitely gonna want to see the file on his dad. I need to distract him. Time for a change of topic.

"So, who are you planning to ask to Royal Beat this year?"

Of course that's what I immediately thought of.

Royal Beat is a competition held every year at Stonson Town Hall for rich kids interested in competing against other rich kids to be crowned Mr. and Ms. Royal Beat. If you're crowned you're automatically placed on the SHS prom court, instantly gaining your popularity on the rough streets of high school. Almost everyone competes in it, but it's usually just for fun rather than the real competitive spirit. I've never done it, but I know that Cade has. He even won freshman year with Mallory Jones as his date.

If you choose to be a couple with someone, you're basically stuck with them for the entire two-month competition, so you'd better like em', or at least not hate em'.

Mallory and I are good friends now. She's the only person I know whose abs are practically unreal. Ripped, that's what I would describe her as. And yet she's also the kindest person you'll ever meet, a true heart of gold. I understand why Cade picked her.

Sure, Mallory is a natural athlete, and she has the most beautifully full head of brown hair I've ever seen, but I've never been as jealous of her as I am right now.

Cade looked up from the files, leaning his arm on the table to take a break. He seemed to think about my question a lot more thoroughly than I'd expected, taking time to think his answer through well.

"That's a random question." He laughed, his flawless hair softly swaying. Quick Tatum, explain yourself. Think.

"Just tryin' to get our brains off the case for a minute."

Somehow buying it, he continued on. "You know, I'm not really sure. It's way too complicated to find a date nowadays; they either think you must like them or else you wouldn't have asked, or they diss you behind your back. I just want to go with someone I already know. I don't want to be stressed."

I guess I've never really thought about it that way. I get it being stressful for girls; we never know how the guy will react to us, making it known that we want to be their date. But I guess having to ask the girl is a lot to handle too, wondering if we'll say yes or no. Although, I think men stress themselves out a lot more than they actually need to; if they would just casually ask us, they'd be surprised at how quickly we say yes. Our only request is that we have fun with someone we can trust, whether it's as a date or just as friends. We don't need a fancy ask or nothin', no extravagant posters or signs required. Just a simple wave in the hallway, maybe a text to get to know us a bit better. Things like that go a long way with most girls; I know they would with me.

"I get that. There's no need to go with someone just to have a date. Gotta make sure you'll have fun, make memories. God will give you the right person if it's in His plan. No sense in trying to rush it just because of a redneck competition." Cade smiled, looking at me like a child does a sweet treat.

"What?"

He smirked some more. "Wanna make a deal?"

This could either go very well or very badly. Guess I'll just have to see. I nodded, shifting to the center of the table directly across from him.

"If neither of us has a date for Royal Beat by the time March rolls around, let's go together." I'm not sure if I should take this as a good thing, considering how clear he just made it that he wants to go with a friend rather than a love interest. But any chance to hang out with Cade is one I'm willing to take, so I agreed.

"Alright. That sounds reasonable." If only he knew how many beats my heart just skipped. I continued, "Now don't go ditchin' me when Jenny calls you up and needs a date."

He flashed a look of disapproval at my comment, not pleased with it at all, but still ended up laughing, shaking my hand as he finished.

"Deal."

I wonder what our lives will be like when Royal Beat rolls around. Will we have found Brynlee by then, assuming we do at all? Will Stonson be the same quaint town? Will Cade and I even be friends?

If Mrs. Lanie knew that Cade was with me right now, she would have his neck. There's no way she let him take me to Royal Beat. But quite frankly, an enraged mother is the least of my worries. There isn't time to worry about paranoid parents when we have a killer and kidnapper on the loose. As long as the two aren't one and the same, I'll be alright, I just wish there was a way to tell the difference.

But that's something we all wish was true, assurance about who we can and cannot trust. I only know of two people I can trust right now. God first, then Cade.

No matter who his parents are, Cade is still my best friend, has been since I met him. Even through the silent treatment, even through his rude and uncalled for stretches of ignorance, God has been telling me that he's meant to be in my life. It's gonna take a lot more than four years and one fallout to change that.

I just pray we never have to face that possibility.

"Love is a mystery.
We embrace it where we can.
Mostly we do not choose whom we love.
It just happens.
A voice speaks to us, in ways the ears cannot hear.
We recognize a beauty the eye does not see.
We experience a change in our hearts that no voice can describe."
-David Gemmell

Chapter Twenty-Two

September 23, 2023~12:01 PM

School resumed as usual, kids shuffling through the halls complaining about their hair or their boyfriend, tired from an early rise. The cold checkered floors that line the junior hallway seem rather dirty today, trash bags along both walls. Pop-tart wrappers, protein bars, energy drinks, and even a used hairbrush overflow from the uncleanly white bags.

Why haven't the janitors changed out the bags, or swept at the very least?

It's like the whole town slowed down the minute Brynlee disappeared—businesses no longer answering their phones, our school not keeping itself at the usual standard.

I don't think Brynlee's leaving specifically started the downfall. It's just the fact that a child went missing in our little town that has put everyone on edge. How would you feel if you thought your child was safe at their school—small population, minimal chance of any trouble—then the one night you let them go out on their own, a high school dance, they vanished? No idea if you'll ever see them again, ever hear their calming voice, ever get to tell them all the things you regret not saying sooner. Never given the chance to see them get married, or even graduate, for that matter. And it's not that you didn't want to, or that God didn't have plans for them in other areas of life, it's because God called them home. It sounds fine when you put it that way, but to Brynlee's parents, I'm sure they believe their daughter was taken from this world in a sinful and heartless manner. And with no other children to care for, Brynlee is all they have. Facing the harsh possibility of never seeing her again must be crippling.

But I know she isn't gone, not yet. When they told me that my daddy died, I was upset, of course, but I believed them. I could feel it in my heart that something was wrong. I knew he wouldn't be coming home. But if someone told me right now that Bryn was dead, I wouldn't believe it. It just doesn't feel right. Blame it on my age if you want, but even children develop a gut feeling, and right now mine is pretty strong, about more than just one thing.

I headed to the gym once the last bell rang, swerving in and out of mobs in the hallway to avoid getting hit or bumped into. Everyone is just trying to get to their cars or to their bus. No one wants to be at this school any longer than they have to. I don't blame them. Half the kids here have never been outside of Stonson, much less in any real danger. The biggest threat they've encountered is probably a few strange stares in the Winn-Dixie or a crazed deer on the road.

Sheltered, that's what I would call them.

I was the first girl to arrive at the cheer locker room, Teresa and Chloe soon after. Every time I come in here, I imagine my dad standing on the bench, scared of a bug the size of his toe. A man who went to school with Dad told me all about it at his funeral. I don't remember much of what anyone else said.

But I remember that.

"Five bucks says Hadleigh doesn't get here until four." Teresa Bartlett always says what she thinks. She's been like that since we were kids. Her dad owns the farmer's market a few miles from my mom's office, one of the kindest men you'll ever meet. He'd never hurt a fly, never say a mean word, he just nods and smiles as you speak with him. Her mom, on the other hand, Good Lord. Tracy is quite the talker, loves to know everything about everyone. I've never seen a couple as opposite as the two of them, but somehow they match so well. True love for sure. Teresa takes after her mom in many ways; how she acts, how she talks, even how she looks. They have the prettiest dark, curly hair and hazel eyes, both taller than most women, but somehow manage to pull it off with ease.

"Oh, you're goin' easy on her, I'd say four-thirty at least." Chloe Parker is the same way, a busy talker, and quite the loudmouth. She means well, it's just a little too much for me to handle more often than not. The two of them have been close friends for as long as I can remember, since the day Chloe moved to Stonson from her home state of Minnesota. Deep down, I know that Chloe only cheers to be with Teresa, but she'll never admit it.

We start off practice with the basic stretching and warmups, a few less laps around the gym than usual. It's been a draining week for all of us, in case you can't tell.

"Alright ladies, bring it on in." Coach Mandy called us into a huddle as loud as she could, her sweet southern accent bouncing smoothly off the gym walls. Mandy has been coaching us for three years now. I've grown to like her. She's changed a lot about the Stonson cheer program compared to what it used to be, which was practically a circus, but I guess that's for the better. Mandy is always very peppy, hyper more often than not.

She sighed, "Girls, as I'm sure you've heard by now, we've lost one of our own. Our sweet Brynlee has been taken from us much too soon, but we must keep our heads up. The town is handling it the best it can. It just needs a hype cheer team to get it through, and that's what we've got to be! So stay positive, smile, and keep your eyes open. You never know what God might show you."

She said all the right words, even the slang ones, but it's the way she said them that has me worried.

Brynlee isn't actually a part of the cheer team, but she is Mandy's favorite student. I knew that I recognized her from somewhere other than just the dentistry office. Now I realize it was from Coach Mandy's classroom photo collage.

We went over the routine we just learned last month, adjusting a few girls' positioning here and there. We're all just going through the motions, no facials or pep from even the best of us. Our eyes are tired from the recent onset of sleepless nights, wondering if someone is out to get us the way they got Brynlee.

"Alright, time to stunt." Coach separated us out into new stunt groups since we're missing a few of our regular bases. I got Riley, Kelsi, and Jenna, all very capable cheerleaders. I love Riley and Jenna. I've known them forever, it's just Kelsi who I don't know all that well. She moved here last year, joined the squad as a late tryout. We rarely allow newcomers so late in the season, but Coach Mandy made an exception for her. I'm not sure why. She seems normal enough, but no one knows anything about her. She's turned down every lunch invite, party, or trip we've invited her to.

That's what worries me. Kelsi is one of those people who only does what she has to in order to get by. The bare minimum, and that doesn't bode well with me. Doing the bare minimum never gets you far in life. I learned that the hard way.

"What are the counts?"

See, she doesn't even know the counts to go up on. Another red flag. We spent an entire day running over them two weeks ago. No way she doesn't remember them, especially as a flyer. I looked at Riley, exchanging an annoyed glance, then finally turned to answer the ridiculous question.

"Step in on three, dip five, up on seven." She flashed a thumbs up as if to say "got it". I can't tell if she's being genuine or sarcastic; she's got an elite poker face, I'll give her that.

It took us twice as long as the other groups, but we finally got up, an extension to a cradle. After several more successful attempts, the clock finally read 5:15. Time to go home, if you could even call the sloppy stack of bricks under which my head rests a home.

David's house is somehow dirtier than it was when I left it days ago. He only just got back from his trip last night, yet he's managed to trash it twice over. My "room" is the only place still as I left it, an alarm clock on the floor and a light pink toothbrush by the sink. David wouldn't dare come up here. Why would he make the effort to bond with his daughter more than he has to? That would be too much stress in his life right now, with all the work I'm sure he has to do.

He's an underachiever, was even when Mom married him. I don't know why she thought David would be a good match for her. Any stranger could've seen the fault in that assumption from day one.

To this day, I swear I even saw the reverend marrying them sigh as he performed the ceremony.

"Why are you back so late?" David stood at the bottom of my staircase as I came down, waiting for me like his prey, weak and fragile.

"Practice was til' five-fifteen. We just finished." I began to walk into the kitchen for a glass of water, but apparently he wasn't done talking yet.

"When did I say you could go to practice?"

He stopped me in my tracks by saying something like that, acting like he's ever actually parented me prior to now.

"I've always had practice after school. Why would this time be any different?" As I turned back around to face him, the scent hit me like a freight train, and I quickly realized why we're having this conversation.

He's drunk. No, not just drunk, he's *wasted.*

He always feels a little more confident with some alcohol in his system, but that's usually the case these days. David would never initiate a confrontation unless he wasn't thinking clearly.

He walked closer to me, close enough that I can smell his breath even stronger now. Yep, he reeks of booze.

"Because I said so." He put his finger by my face as if to assert control of the situation. But if you were to look at this situation as an outsider, you'd see that David has never once been in control, and he certainly isn't now. He isn't in control of his drinking problem, his job security, or his love life.

I headed for the door behind him, ready to leave the house altogether, but was painfully stopped by an arm to the waist. Where have I seen this before?

"Where do you think you're goin'?"

I continue to push away before the situation gets worse. I refuse to engage with him while he's drunk.

"I'm leaving. You aren't thinking clearly right now."

I looked up at the bulky man hovering over me, his overgrown beard now closer than before. And that was that, the end of any chance he ever had to earn my respect.

I've been hit before, but never like this. His fist came at me faster than I'd anticipated. No time to dodge it or even fight back. I felt his bony knuckle hit right below my eyeline, the discontinued wedding ring from my mother scraping my brow as it swept past. Out of the corner of my eye, I momentarily saw a small spurt of blood hit the bottom stair to my right.

Is that mine?

The crusted carpet below feels a lot less comforting against my skull than it had underneath my weary feet.

"You don't get to question me like that." He walked away, his muddy boots pounding against the floor now level with my eyes. No remorse whatsoever.

I didn't know what to think of David after that day, just like I didn't know how to hide my freshly bruised eye from Cade or from anyone else. But I know one thing for sure; I will never call him Dad.

That position has already been filled.

Chapter Twenty-Three

September 24, 2023~9:27 AM

Apply evenly across face and pat dry. Avoid contact with eyes and open wounds. Product may contain irritating chemicals or chemical solutions. If irritation occurs, contact your physician before continuing use.

What is the point of makeup? Half of the labels are unnecessary instructions, while the other half is a list of a hundred skin diseases you could get from usage. I understand the inner desire to want to impress others, especially men, or give the impression that you're more mature than you really are, but if a guy thinks that you aren't pretty enough without makeup, you should kick him to the curb anyhow.

So yes, makeup can enhance your external features, but true natural beauty is found within.

But Cade knows that. He likes being my friend because of who I am, not who I try to be. Good thing I'm not putting on makeup for him. I'm only using it out of dire need. Emergency situations call for emergency measures.

Once I finished you could barely see the purple and black bruise around my eye. It now resembles shadows from where I didn't sleep all night. No one will think much of this abnormality, considering half the parents in Stonson look about the same. Community groups still spend their nights searching for any sign of Brynlee. You can still hear sirens passing by houses at all hours. From what I can tell, everyone would love for her to just be hidden in plain sight, somewhere obvious. That would be the easiest way out of this. But if they haven't found her by now, that hope is likely pointless.

We can cross off any old buildings in town, dirt roads, and hopefully most of the wooded areas, those have already been searched. The only other places to check would be homes, but no one would be stupid enough to take her to their house.

Would they?

Still pondering this, I got to second period only three minutes before class started, so technically, I wasn't late. All the blinds had been closed, and the classroom was quiet, only a few students chattering towards the back. My seat is closer to the front, a single whiteboard and one other desk to the right, a wall to the left. When I got to my isolated seat, I noticed something lying in my chair; an envelope with a large brown splotch in the top left corner. Coffee, I think, or perhaps lipstick. I moved it to my tabletop and sat in its place. As I examined the envelope, I saw the familiar chicken scratch on its seal, Cade's child-like writing that I've critiqued so many times before. The letter inside was short, getting to the point rather quickly.

Got something I need you to see.
Meet at my car after school. Bring your phone.
Make sure no one follows.

Why he couldn't just text me that, I'll never know. The art of mystery is an illusion within itself. Typical Cade.

So I met him there in his car only after seven hours of painful class time. The school day may feel pointless, but at least I had this to look forward to.

You know, seeing Cade didn't always give me butterflies like this. It used to make me angry.

When I got to the small space where Cade chose to park, I saw him sitting in the front seat, arm resting on the worn black console and an empty water bottle sitting in the first cup holder. But rather than waiting on his phone or doing homework, his wrist flicks against the leather, almost antsy.

"You good?" I opened the car door, swinging both myself and my bookbag into the passenger seat. Cade sighed for what must be the eighteenth time this week, each one making him seem a little more vulnerable than the last.

"I'll let you answer that after I show you."

"Show me what?"

He put the car in drive and started out of the parking lot rather fast. "What I found."

Pressing on the brakes at a stoplight by the school entrance, he turned to face me.

"Whoaaa, wait, Tatum, what is that on your face? Are you wearing...makeup?" Of course he noticed the makeup but not the giant fist sized bruise it so efficiently covers up.

"Yeah, I'm tryin' something new." I was about to try to explain further, a lie I've been manufacturing ever since first period, but I never got the chance to before Cade reached over, lightly rubbing my eye with his finger. I would otherwise take this as a sign of affection if I didn't know what he was actually doing.

"Tatum." He rubbed off more makeup around my eye until I couldn't help but wince at his touch. I don't like physical touch anyhow, but this is different.

"Did someone hit you?" The light ahead has already been green for a while now, the line of cars behind us blowing their horns louder by the second, but Cade doesn't care. He's so focused on me that I'm not even sure he notices the noise.

At least someone notices.

"Cade, the light." He broke his stare and stepped on the gas, all horns finally coming to a halt.

"Tatum, who hit you?"

"No one hit me. I just fell."

"Please."

Our drive down Crawley Street was a hard one, me refusing to tell and him refusing to give up.

"Cade, I told you, no one hit me. You need to calm down."

He raised his voice at me, almost frustrated that I won't tell him my business. "That's bullcrap. No fall would leave you with a bruise like that. Why won't you just tell me?"

I've had people yell at me before, probably more than most, but I don't care for it much when it's coming from Cade. He's never gotten this upset with me before, and I don't like it.

"Cade, it's not a big deal alright. Just let it go, please."

He began to driveway too fast, his mind focused on me rather than on paying attention to the road ahead of us. "Slow down. You're driving like a maniac!" He stepped on the gas more, as if to scare me into telling him. I know that he isn't intentionally trying to arouse my fear, but it sure feels like it.

"Tatum, I'm not going to 'calm down' knowing good and well someone hurt you. You don't understand. I can't just let that go. I care about you. A lot." I waited until the car finally slowed and he took control of the wheel before answering.

"Now, how am I supposed to believe that?" I shouldn't say this, don't say it.

I'm gonna say it.

"You've never cared before."

Cade's sun-kissed face looked at me so intently, his eyes filled with both sorrow and hurt. He pulled over into a littered cul-de-sac and parked the car so he could truly focus. My response probably wasn't the best thing to say.

He locked in his stare on me, turning his body to face my seat. He took a deep breath in, let it out, and then began the conversation that will forever remain one of my favorites.

"Tatum, I've cared for you since the day we met. I didn't become friends with you because I *had* to. I became friends with you because I *wanted* to. You were—you are—beautiful, both inside and out. You don't look like any of the other girls I know, and you certainly don't act like them. You're perfect just the way you are. Perfect for me." He paused. "Not that I was looking for 'the one' in kindergarten or anything, but I always noticed you, even then. I remember every birthday party we shared, every trip to the playground. Trust me, you don't forget the memories you make with your favorite person."

I sat there for a moment, taking in everything Cade said, his rant telling me so much more about him than I was ever aware lied beneath his rock-solid exterior. Maybe he's due more credit than I've been giving him. Maybe he has paid attention to me the past few years. Every time I thought he was avoiding me, every bad thought my mind conjured up about him, it was all just a misleading game I unknowingly played. I don't think the game is very funny, but maybe that's the point.

Maybe he didn't want me to know that he still cared for me after everything that happened.

I guess that's how men protect their egos by bottling up everything inside until they unintentionally hurt someone they love. In this case, Cade hurt the one girl who actually cared about him, and I think he's beginning to regret that now.

If only he knew how I feel inside. Like an umbrella after the rain is over, I somehow become a burden to everyone.

He still sits in his seat patiently awaiting my answer, but I don't plan to respond any time soon. I know it seems rude, but how am I supposed to answer adequately? I've been waiting for him to tell me that he still cares for years, to tell me that I did actually mean something to him at one point. And now that the moment is finally here, I've frozen, because no matter what I say, it won't be the right thing.

And then he did something that will change our entire relationship forever. Not too drastically, but enough that it's obvious we'll be different now.

He leaned over and touched my face, as he had earlier, but his hands feel much softer now, much more delicate. He examined my eye closer, as if to note my damages like one would a wrecked car. Then, with no warning at all, he stopped looking at my wounds and finally began to look at me, smiling. The me that has experienced more pain than he could ever imagine, the me who has spent countless nights on her knees begging for God to forgive her. I feel *calm* as he looks at me, as if for once I have nothing to worry about.

And then it happened. He leaned in and kissed me. I think this is his way of letting me know that he really did think about me all those years. Maybe the confusing feelings that I've been having for Cade weren't very far off from those he felt as well.

I turned to face forward and stared out the front window, unsure of how to feel or what to do next. My eyes refused to look at him, so tears of confusion quickly came to blur my vision. He doesn't understand what he's just done; as much as I have waited years for this to happen, it comes with a lot more than he is ready to commit to. I think I love him. *Truly.* I would write a billion pages about him just to get the words out, then burn them so that the wind around can feel the smell of love too. But loving him is like trying to love something as delicate as the sun; I know that I could get destroyed, but my heart fails to understand.

He looked at me and laughed, leaving me confused about what could be funny.

"What?"

He smiled, then answered. "Guess I just sealed my date for Royal Beat."

"Love is patient, love is kind.
It does not envy, it does not boast, it is not proud.
It does not dishonor others, it is not self-seeking, it is not easily
angered, it keeps no record of wrongs."
1 Corinthians 13:4-5

Chapter Twenty-Four

September 24, 2023~3:51 PM

Cade's house was only a few minutes from the school, but somehow the ride there felt much longer. Maybe it was because of the kiss, or maybe it's just because he found something I haven't seen yet. The radio plays softly, but I don't recognize the song; an older record by a woman who sounds very southern, a feel-good vibe. Her accent is almost a tangy southern, not similar to my accent, nor that of anyone I know from North Carolina.

When we pulled into his driveway, I saw a car in the garage, a white Toyota Corolla that I know belongs to Mrs. Lanie. Cade must've seen it too. He quickly grabbed my hand and motioned for me to duck down below the windshield's covering.

We took his car down an unkept path behind his house, for why I can't yet tell. I haven't been in these woods for years, but they look practically the same. The last time I remember bein' out here was when Cade and I played "Survivor" in order to hide from his parents at dinner time. We made some good memories in these woods, but Cade doesn't seem to remember them as well as I do. He's clearly more upset about where we're headed than he is about where we've been. I can tell by how tense he's driving. His arms practically locked themselves out two minutes ago.

"You can sit up now. We're here."

He pulled over by a fallen tree, far enough from his house for us to avoid being seen, but close enough that I can still see the humble bench on their back porch swinging aimlessly with the wind. I got out and followed where he led. No apparent spot of interest in sight. Suddenly, he stopped about ten yards from where we left the car. I joined him, but saw nothing.

"What exactly am I supposed to be looking for?"

He bent down and picked up something from behind a tree, covered in leaves and dirt. I almost didn't recognize the familiar white woven fabric with all that muck on it, but then it hit me. I know exactly what Cade has found, and I know who it belongs to; and that means that somethin' bad has happened. Somethin' very bad.

"Brynlee's cardigan."

"When did you find this?" I snatched the cardigan from his trembling grip while he explained everything, all the way from the beginning to now. I ran my finger along its seam lines, every stitch a little different from its predecessor. Knit under, then over. Under, over, under, over, until a beautiful pattern of imperfectly perfect lines created the pure portrait I so anxiously hold.

"It was along the treeline by my house, but I moved it back here once I realized what it was. You know, to make sure no one would mess with it." He could've just put it in his car, but I guess throwing it in the woods works, too.

"Why would it be at your house?"

"That's what I'm tryin' to tell you. I don't know."

His face tells me that he knows more than he's letting on. "What is it?"

"What is what?"

"What aren't you telling me?"

"It's not that I won't tell you. I just don't wanna be the one to say it."

"I'll find out anyhow Cade, just tell me what you're thinkin.'"

He sighed, "I don't know for sure why it was by my house, but there's really only two reasons I can think of."

I looked up at him and reluctantly asked the question that we both know needs to be brought about, "Which are?"

He stopped and frowned, grabbing onto the cardigan as I am.

Weakly, he answered. "Well, either she took an awfully odd shortcut home, or..."

We have to accept what we both knew was bound to happen eventually. So, in an attempt to spare him some emotional attachment, I finished the sentence for him.

"Or someone brought her here. But who?"

We made eye contact, more intensely now than ever before, neither of us wanting to say what we're both thinking. He turned back to look at the house, now vacant from all Corolla drivers, and closed his eyes.

"Two people come to mind."

"Sometimes you think you know someone,
but maybe it's impossible to really know everything about a person,
even someone you love.
Maybe good people – the very best people – are
just better at keeping secrets."
-Julianne MacLean

Chapter Twenty-Five

September 24, 2023~5:56 PM

The concept of uncertainty is a complex thing.

We deal with uncertainty every day; when we wake up, when we go to sleep, even when we go out with someone new for the first time. None of us know what will happen for sure, other than of course God. We have to maintain a strong faith, trust that the unknown is the best thing for us, that's what everyone keeps telling me. And I know they're right, in fact, I've never known anything to be so true. It's just a heck of a lot to comprehend all at once.

No one ever talks about the struggles they face when they're left alone, they only discuss their successes. Ever heard an author complain about how they once struggled to pronounce the word "presumptuous", ever heard a fighter proudly proclaim the lowest point in their career? Rarely, because as humans our first instinct is never to announce our failures or struggles, it's exclaiming our successes and capabilities. We're sinners, but God forgives.

Hebrews 11:1 says, "Now faith is the assurance of things hoped for, the conviction of things not seen." God does what is best for us in all aspects of our lives, whether it's what we planned or not. I keep trying to understand that.

They say that you get wiser with age, but I don't think that's entirely true. How I see it, it's not solely a contemplation of years that helps you accumulate wisdom, it's also the overlooked concept of simply figuring out what you're supposed to be doing. You learn to avoid doing stupid things a lot more often than you used to.

Would you consider trying to find answers to an entire community's question of distress as a half-developed teenager stupid? If so, nice to meet you. I'm stupid.

"You have to ask them Cade. It's the only way to find out anything more than what we already know."

We now stand in Cade's father's office, a place that was forbidden as a child. As he scrambles through drawers and frantically runs his eyes over messy folders, I can see how upset he's becoming. Any kid would naturally refuse to believe their parents might be involved in something as serious as kidnapping, he has a right to be frustrated, but he doesn't exactly seem frustrated by it all, he's just irritated that he has finally met a problem he genuinely can't find the answer to.

If there's anything the two of us share, it's our dislike for not knowing. Not knowing what happened to my dad, not knowing who we can and cannot trust, and now, not knowing what happened to Brynlee.

"No, that'll only make things worse. If we want any chance of finding out why Brynlee's cardigan was here, we need to find out on our own. Got it?"

Fine, if that's how he's gonna act.

"What exactly are you looking for? If they had anything to do with it, I'm pretty sure there won't be a record of it or nothin.'"

"Well, there's no such thing as the perfect crime. They messed up somewhere, I just know it."

That's true, no matter how intelligent the Hampton family may be, they didn't just go out for a drive and decide to kidnap someone. Something like that takes planning, motive, reasoning. How could Cade not have known anything about it? Is it even possible to live under the same roof with such cruel people and not know it?

However, deep down, I know that Cade has been waiting for something like this to happen for a long time. He never really trusted his parents again after my dad died. I guess I wouldn't either, and in a way, I don't. I knew that my mom didn't kill Dad or anything like that, but she sure didn't jump at the chance to catch whoever did. In fact, I can only remember one time she actually involved herself with the investigation. But to not know if your mom took a human being away from her whole world, robbed her of her right to freedom, that must be a much heavier burden.

There's no way Cade doesn't have my dad in the back of his mind as he struggles to find proof, especially since we just concluded that Bryn's kidnapper is probably also his killer. That means his parents could be involved in both a kidnapping and a murder, and that's something I get chills simply thinking about.

"Okay, let's start at the beginning. Where were your parents the night of the dance?" He walked past me and headed straight for the door. I followed like a stray puppy until we finally got to the front entrance of his home.

"I haven't the slightest clue. They rarely share their date night plans with me."

"So they were out on a date?"

"Yeah, I think."

"Kind of odd to plan a date on the one night every restaurant in town would be packed with high school kids. Any idea where they went?"

"Nope. Like I said, they didn't tell me much about it."

"What about that place they used to go to down by the square, the Italian place? Could they have gone there?"

Cade opened the door and walked outside, not even holding it for me; that's how lost in thought he's been lately.

"Yeah, let's try there first."

"What do you mean 'try there'?"

He turned around to look at me, almost offended that I'm confused by his remark. "Well, we have to find out where they were, so we're gonna go ask around. If we start now, we should be able to hit all the restaurants by nine."

I think he might be going crazy. I know that Stonson isn't a huge town, but it would take more than just one night to visit every restaurant. Plus, how is anyone going to remember seeing one couple on a night during which they probably seated hundreds?

"Cade, this doesn't make sense. I think you should just get some rest tonight and we can go in the morning." He's clearly mad, maybe at me, but I doubt it. It feels more like he's upset with the world.

"Would you be saying that if the situation was reversed? If there was a chance that your parents knew where Brynlee was? Don't worry, I can answer that, you wouldn't. You would be throwin' just as big of a tantrum as I am, and you know it."

Should that offend me?

After a second of silence, both of us contemplating the words we'd exchanged, I gave in. "Fine, but I'm driving."

I expected him to object to my demand, but he didn't. He swiftly threw his Oregon State lanyard and black keys over to me. Cade is in no position to be driving right now. He can't even focus enough to finish a mature conversation without having to stop and calm himself.

I drove to the Italian restaurant first, but of course there was no parking; maybe Bryn's disappearance hasn't scared everyone inside as much as we thought. I let Cade out while I drove around to the parking deck, a decision that I know I'll regret later. There's no telling what he might say when left unsupervised.

As I pulled into the grimy sienna brown deck, I stopped at the white rustic booth in order to explain my situation to the attendant. I don't want to pay for the whole night if I'll only be parked for a bit.

Plus, I'm beyond broke.

As I got closer, I saw Graham working the booth, smiling as always. Graham Waltson was in all of my classes last year. We got pretty close for a while. His dirty blonde unkept hair slightly covers his light eyes, but it doesn't seem to bother him much. He always has a smile on his face, never a dull moment when Graham is around.

"Well if it isn't the infamous Tatum Cassidy, how's life been treatin' ya?" I closed my eyes and smiled; it's so nice to hear a familiar voice—a very, very southern familiar voice.

"It's been better, how bout' you?"

He grinned and laughed. "Pretty good so far. Need a parking pass?"

I tried to explain everything, about dropping off Cade and driving to the deck, but he wouldn't even let me finish before stopping the conversation. "No need to pay. I got you covered."

"You're the best."

"I know it. Hey, did you finally get a new car?" I wondered how long it would take for someone to ask me that.

"No, this is actually Cade's car." Sharing that will definitely backfire sooner or later. He smirked and winked at me, something I couldn't help but laugh at.

"Hampton? As in the Hampton you hate?"

"Hate is a strong word."

"Yeah, but it's an accurate one. The way you used to rant about him, I thought you two would never figure things out."

"Honestly, so did I. Guess God had other plans."

"Amen. Are y'all a thing now or somethin'?" I haven't really thought about that yet. I guess that's just another thing I'll have to figure out.

Add it to the list.

"I'll get back to you on that." He laughed, leisurely handing me a yellow parking pass for the top deck. I found a spot by the stairwell and headed back down, eager to meet Graham once more on my way out. I didn't get too far before I heard my name back towards the car; Cade, loudly panting from the lengthy run he must've completed to get here.

"I was just comin' to find you. Why are you in such a hurry?"

He took a deep breath and answered, "I know where they were. Well, sort of." I hopped in the car, as he told me to, and backed out as fast as I could. We saw Graham again as we left, him dramatically holding up a hand-heart as we passed. Why can't more guys be like him? Funny, but kind? That's a rare combination these days.

"Turn left. Head towards the hardware store." I looked over at him, confused once again.

"Why?" He seems annoyed at my question, but I don't care. I want to know why we're heading to the hardware store of all places.

"A woman working at the boutique across the street said my mom came in asking for help with her car. She sent out a coworker who had to give both my parents a ride home because the car needed to be towed."

That doesn't help much. "That still doesn't explain the hardware store." Cade slowly clenched his fist, getting more and more aggravated with my questioning.

"The guy from the boutique said he had to stop at the hardware store, per request of my dad. You'll never guess what he saw him come back with." I'm not sure that I really want to know what he came back with. All this uncertainty is starting to stress me out. I paused before answering, but Cade jumped back into the conversation before I got the chance to.

"A flashlight and duct tape."

I still don't follow. "So what? That's pretty basic stuff to get at a hardware store."

"You don't find it weird that he'd buy that at ten o'clock at night? Plus, have you ever seen my dad step foot in a hardware store, even once, in all the years you've known him?"

He's right, Carl Hampton isn't exactly someone you find in the shop with a hammer and some tools.

When we walked into the hardware store, Willie's Hardware to be exact, I noticed Mr. Scoggins working the register. Bart Scoggins has been working at Willie's ever since it opened. I swear he must be almost eighty years old by now.

"Well, if it isn't my favorite cheerleader! What are you doin' here?" I gave him a hug and introduced him to Cade.

"Ooh, the mysterious Mr. Hampton! Did you two finally settle the little dispute Tatum told me about?" I guess I might've mentioned him a few times before. Cade laughed and answered for me, shaking his hand as he did so.

"Working on it, Sir."

"Good. Now, can I help y'all find anything? We've got a great deal on shovels right now." He laughed, but with what we're about to explain to him, his laughter won't last much longer.

"Saturday night, did you see this couple here?" Cade showed Mr. Scoggins a family photo of him and his parents, zooming in closer on his dad. It's a great photo of him, but rarely do you find one where he doesn't look stunning.

"Never seen his lady friend, but yeah, the guy was in here. I checked him out at my register. Great haircut, I'll give him that."

"Did he happen to say what he needed his items for?"

Mr Scoggins leaned against the metal counter, raising an eyebrow at the question. "Son, I have dozens of people come through here every shift. I couldn't tell you half the conversations I have with them. I only remember that guy because of his hair."

I saw a little more of Cade's heart break as Mr. Scoggins spoke, his hopeful spirit slowly dimming. I thanked him for his time and waved goodbye, promising to come visit more often.

"Well, that was a letdown." Cade seems even more upset now, moping around like his dog just died. I need to cheer him up, although it'll be a hard task to complete.

They don't exactly teach you how to comfort a friend at a time like this in school. I'm sure they teach a class on handling grief, yes, but certainly not for this case. No textbook could possibly relay the reality of what this is, no homework could simulate its depth.

"At least we know where they went and what time they came in. It would've been hard for them to make it to the school in the ten minutes from when they left here to when we last saw Brynlee. Especially if they didn't have their own car." My discovery doesn't seem to make him feel much better, considering how wearily he dropped his head and closed his eyes.

"Hard, but not impossible."

The fact that Cade's parents didn't have a car most of that night makes it harder to confirm if they could've taken Brynlee or not. We don't know where the employee from the boutique dropped them off once the free ride came to an end, leaving the question of their final destination still up in the air.

"They were home not much after I got there, maybe eleven forty-five or so. I didn't hear their car pull up, which makes sense now. I just saw them at the kitchen counter when I walked downstairs after showering. Now that I think about it, Mom was arguing with Dad, but that's not terribly unusual."

This is all beginning to feel too real, like we're starring in the sequel to a horror movie gone wrong. An awful movie where they don't find any clues for years, and only after an innocent girl becomes potential collateral damage do they find even a sliver of hope. This one doesn't star Tom Hanks or Mark Harmon, just two scared kids trying to make sense of an ugly and sinful place.

The world hasn't always been like this. God created it as a pure and wonderful place for everyone to thrive in. I know that God always wins, and I know He knew that it would one day be like this. He always defeats evil. This is just a heck of a whirlwind.

But maybe the whirlwind is necessary in order to find balance. Maybe if you look hard enough, you'll see that the whirlwind is what allows for sunshine later down the road.

Just maybe.

"Life isn't about waiting for the storm to pass,
it's about learning to dance in the rain."
-Vivian Greene

Chapter Twenty-Six

January 3, 2020~8:29 PM

It's been twenty-six days since I last saw my daddy. I want to say he's just been on vacation, that he's somewhere relaxing on a beach, but I can't. I know he isn't coming back. I will never again get to watch him walk through the front door, or run to give him a warm hug and see his big ole' smile as he embraces me, too. Now, instead of telling him all about my day over ice cream sundaes, I tell him about it when I go to sleep. I rest my knees beside my bed every night and pray to God, but last night, I prayed something special.

"Dear God,

Can you send a message to my daddy for me?

Thank you.

Daddy, if you can hear this, just know that I love you.

I love you even though you had to leave me, and I know you would've stayed if you could.

How's Heaven?

Did you get to walk through those pearly gates you once told me about?

I bet it's everything we ever imagined it would be, and more.

Have you met Aidan?

He was really nice to me, so make sure you're nice too.

You're always nice, but I know how you feel about boys likin' me.

Although I'm not so sure that Aidan liked me, he was just different.

He was kind for no reason other than that

he saw my need for a helping hand.
Please be safe up in Heaven, I hope I get to go up there one day too.
Thank you God,
Amen."

The headstone for Daddy's grave still hasn't been placed, something about shipping costs being sky high. I didn't know there were so many options to put on people's gravesites. A cross, a bench, a marker; and then there's the shape and material choices.

Mama and I went to go pick it out about two weeks ago, but it turned into more of a one-man effort the further we got into discussion. Of course she had to take a phone call in the middle of the meeting, work related, I'm sure. So I was left to design it all by myself with a random sales lady named Emma, not sure if that's even legal, but I did.

Every one of my friends are busy designing dresses for their dolls and playing little league softball, which is what I should be doing too. Instead, I'm planning out my father's headstone. What a blast. Personally, I don't think any kid should have to see their dad be buried, much less create his memorial. But this is my life now, and I need to accept it, just like everyone keeps telling me to.

I rarely like to agree with the majority of people, because I know that the world is wrong more often than not. A lot of people don't like me because of that, but it doesn't bother me. I guess this time will be different, though. I have to listen. I can't do everything on my own.

I saw Cade the other day, but he didn't talk to me or nothin'. Mrs.Lanie was holding him so close that it looked as if he could barely breathe. Mama said she's what you would call a "helicopter parent".

I'm not quite sure what that means, but she sounded pretty confident.

Cade looks sad all the time now, his eyes are always red, like after you stay outside for too long and the pollen gets to ya'. But there aren't many allergy triggers right now, no flowers in bloom or nothin', just the cold; the unforgiving cold that leaves every morning covered in frost and *ice. No warmth radiates from the trees as I walk to school, no drops of sweat roll down my forehead as I play at recess. Just chills; man do I hate winter. But not as much as I hate people. Not always, and not everyone, just some people.*

Daddy raised me to be very aware of the world, but he also taught me that its inhabitants are generally good people. He was usually right, but maybe not this time. Maybe just this once Daddy was fooled by outside smiles and laughs that others put on for show.

I may only be twelve, but I think I'm starting to learn some things about life, things most adults don't even know yet. Well, I guess they do know, but they clearly choose to ignore them.

For example, the fact that what you see on the outside is rarely a reflection of someone's true inner self. More often than not, what we see when we look at someone is simply a show. I know that kids in theater usually get a bad reputation, peers saying they're nerds. They're too analytical, but maybe they've just embraced what they're drawn to. Honestly, we should all start to do that, whether it's what the world considers "normal" or not.

In all sincerity, being normal is overrated.

What would you do if you were drawn to acting differently than the average person? If you felt the need to act differently because of your past, or your future, and maybe you would be right to do so. But what I feel right now might be bad. Any psychiatrist would likely agree.

What I feel like doing is closing my eyes as I go through life, never again opening them. I don't want to see any more bad things. I don't want to deal with any more relentless evil. I know that it's still there, but maybe if I just close my eyes. Maybe then it'll seem a little less real. Maybe then everyone won't look at me like I'm a broken toy, like I'm scarred for life, so they shouldn't even try to show that they care. There would be no point.

Maybe they really don't care; another way people love to be fake.

I don't understand why people are fake, especially girls in high school. Kaitlyn says that girls in her classes are fake, that they act all mature and perfect until the boys leave. She thinks most boys are nothing but trouble. Her exact words were, "Stop texting first, and you'll realize just how many dead plants you've been watering." I would never tell her this, but I know that she probably acts fake too. I'm not immune to her true colors just because she's family.

But that's okay, because I know that deep down she's a good person. She's not like the people in Stonson, she's not mean.

I've never met such heartless people as I have here. They truly don't care about a little girl who just lost her dad. They don't care that I basically have no mom either, and they certainly haven't noticed that I need a helping hand. No one wants to spare even a second of their day to show me just a glimpse of kindness.

Trust me, it would go a long way right about now.

However, God calls us to forgive. Colossians 3:13, "Forgive as the Lord forgave you." So that's what I'm going to do, I'll forgive each and every one of them until they can no longer hate me, no longer glare at me with disapproval, no longer expel hateful thoughts and words out into the universe, no longer despise me.

There's no sense in constantly trying to change someone, but there's even less sense in never trying.

"Intelligence, hearts, grass,
and nails.
I am the fill-in when the
real thing fails.
What am I?"

Chapter Twenty-Seven

September 25, 2023~4:45 PM

"It's not here. None of it is here." Ten minutes into a phone call with Cade and he's still frantically scrambling through his dad's garage workbench. If the new flashlight or what might be left of the duct tape is there, he'll find it.

Trust me, with the way he's searching right now, he could find a single speck of dust underneath a tire if it was necessary.

I'm not really sure exactly what he thinks locating his dad's hardware store items will do for us, but at this point, anything helps. Of course, we're trying to find peace of mind through all that has happened, but both of us genuinely want to find Brynlee.

Deep down, I still hope to get closure about my dad out of this—a selfish but complex desire. But the odds of me getting that closure are even worse than the odds of me getting a car.

I know this seems like no time for jokes, but there's always time for laughter, in my opinion. At least that's what it says in the self motivation book I'm trying to read as Cade screams through the phone.

Victor Borge once said, "Laughter is the shortest distance between two people." I think he might be onto something there, although he never specified if the connection being made was with good intentions in mind.

My turn to step in and stop this uncontrollable rampage, "Check his car." I heard Cade stop and open the garage door, probably headed back inside.

"I can't. He has his keys on him at all times. He would know I'm looking for something." Cade always makes everything more complicated than it needs to be. If I could just come over and take a look for myself, everything would be going much better.

"So just say you left a hat in there, or your bookbag. He'll let you look."

"Tatum, I haven't ridden with my dad since I was fourteen. He knows nothing of mine is in his car."

Cade and his dad have a weird relationship. They always have. Mr. Carl is in his life—he exists—but he's not really what I would consider a "present father". He always stands by Mrs. Lanie's side, hanging on to her every word as if they're pure drugs. They fight a lot, as far as I know, but I think that's just part of their unlikely marriage. Their personalities don't really match, and their interests couldn't be more polar opposite, but they make it work. Most times, it seems like Mr. Carl is only there for Mrs. Lanie, never for his actual kid. If she leaves town, so does he. If she goes out to eat, he comes along.

If she committed murder, he would help her cover it up.

"Cade, calm down. It's okay if you don't find them." I can hear his size twelve feet stomping hard as they walk, probably upstairs to his bedroom.

"No, Tatum, it's not. In fact, nothing is okay, and if we don't figure this out soon, it won't be for a long time."

He hasn't relaxed since yesterday in the woods, and I know he's been downing energy drinks by the liter all day long. I don't blame him, if the situation was reversed, I would be running all around town looking for anything to prove reality wrong. But we aren't investigators, and we certainly aren't detectives. We have no training to figure out cases like this. We're just trying our best to stop change from happening.

No one really likes change, especially if it's bad. Cade and I are a prime example of that, but at the same time, we're the only ones willing to make an effort to find Brynlee in a way other than just through search parties. We're also the only two people who know about Cade's parents, about the cardigan, and about my dad; a deadly trio.

Who better to ask about a murder than the victim's daughter? I'm the one who experienced it all first-hand, the one who had to deal with the grief, and the one who has finally come closest to solving it.

I hung up with Cade after sharing a few words of encouragement, those of which he scoffed at. It's as if my opinion means nothing to him. Hopefully he's just having a bad day. I'm still getting reacquainted to his unforeseeable mood swings.

I lie in my bed in a quiet house, David still unaware that I'm home. I don't want him to know I'm here, but not because I'm scared. I just truly don't have the energy to deal with him right now.

There's something I've been meaning to do anyhow, which in my opinion takes precedence over drunk adult men with a bone to pick. It's something that has sat in the back of my mind ever since Brynlee was taken.

What better time than the present?

So I took my bike and left, garage door still wide open only so that David didn't hear me leaving. It's usually humid outside, but today is different. With the streets now empty, it's like the heat radiating off the cement is the only way for the ground to feel free.

By the time I got to the cemetery it was almost six o'clock, but that's alright, there's no time limit on grief. I walked down the old stone path towards the back of the property, gripping the bouquet I bought at the general store. A neatly wrapped array of beautiful red flowers, although they don't smell nearly as delightful as they look. The small cluster is all Mr.Johanson could offer me at my mere budget of ten dollars, but I don't think Daddy would mind much.

I strolled over to the back corner where a rounded headstone lay fallen over above an overgrown patch of brown grass. The last flowers I set there are now wrinkled and shriveling up, no longer the pure white color they once were. I bent down to stand the headstone upright again, just as it was the first time I ever placed it here four years ago.

"Hey Dad."

The words sound so surreal coming out of my hushed mouth. It's as if he's right in front of me and I'm simply talking to him like it's a normal day. "I'm sorry it's been so long since my last visit. Just been real busy with a few things."

I wonder if he knows about Brynlee, about what all has happened. Can he see me from up there in Heaven?

"I got some new flowers, but they still didn't have the purple ones we love. You know, from Hirsten Court." Considering the significance that horrid place now holds, maybe I should refrain from mentioning it. If circumstances were any different, I wouldn't mind, but they aren't, and they probably never will be.

"Dad, can I ask you something?"

I don't know why I waited for a moment before continuing. It's not like there's anyone alive here to answer.

"Why won't you show me who hurt you, or tell me in some way? I pray to God about it every night, and I know He's always going to do what's best for us. I just really wish you'd let me know. Everything that's happening right now is so complicated, I could use a little extra help. Actually, I could use any help."

I sat by his grave and placed the flowers down against the weathered headstone. It looks much nicer now than it did with the old bouquet, but it's still just a piece of rock. The algae and grass growing around its base take away more than just a few notches of its beauty.

Just as I went to stand up, I felt my phone vibrate in the back pocket of my jean shorts, probably Cade calling with an update. I answered, holding the phone up to my ear in order to hear him properly.

"Cade?" The call was muffled at first, but once I finally heard his voice, it was nothing more than a faint whisper.

"You gotta get over here right now. Something's happening." With every word his voice shook a little more, trembling by the end.

"What do you mean?"

I began to run back to my bike through the stone path I'd admired only moments earlier, hopping on the worn seat as fast as I could. Cade's house is a good distance from the cemetery, but if I start now it should only take me twenty minutes to get there.

"My mom just got home and headed for the woods." I pedaled faster, but I'm still not sure why I need to hurry.

"Why is that such a big deal? It is her property, Cade. She's allowed to take a walk."

He sighed, then moved from a whisper back to his normal, aggressive tone. "Tatum, my mother has never in her life gone out to enjoy nature, and she hasn't just 'taken a walk' since, well, ever. Something's up. *I need you* here."

Well that's new, Cade being so direct about needing my help. "I need you here." He's never said anything so vulnerable in his life, at least not to me. Maybe he doesn't need to have all the answers after all. Maybe he just needs a friend.

"Okay, I'll be there as soon as I can."

I managed to cut my ride down from twenty minutes to ten, upsetting quite a few drivers along the way. I guess it's true what they say about everything mattering more when it's for someone you love, whether that is a friend or a boyfriend.

I'm not really sure about titles right now.

I left my bike by the old shed and ran across the deserted street to Cade's back door, letting myself in quietly. His mother's car sits in the driveway, but she's nowhere to be seen. Cade was staring out the back porch windows when I walked in, still wearing the same hoodie and shorts I've seen him in so many times before.

"Isn't it a little hot to be wearing that?" That's when I realized what I just walked into; a freezing cold house with the temperature set at fifty-eight degrees.

"Sorry, Mom turned the air way down last night. I can't change it, she'll know." Cade seems almost scared of Mrs. Lanie when it comes to how she likes her house. I can't imagine what he would act like if she found out what we're up to.

"Where is she?"

He took a step away from the windows, keeping his eyes towards the woods, although there ain't nothin' to see. "Mom is still out there, but I can't see her no more. She came home and parked her car, then headed for the woods. But it's been almost fifteen minutes now." It's odd that Mrs. Lanie came home separately from Mr. Carl. They're always together, and her office wouldn't be open this late anyhow.

"She was still in her business skirt and blazer from a meeting this morning. Those high heels can't be too great for hiking through the woods."

When Cade and I found Brynlee's cardigan yesterday, we made the executive decision to leave it be. Well, Cade made the executive decision. I voted for us to move it, or at least show it to Mr. Davidson. That seemed like the safest bet, but Cade made a good point. He argued that if we left it where we found it, then we could use it to our advantage. You see, once whoever has Brynlee realizes that they left the cardigan behind, they're gonna have to come back for it. If we watch carefully, we'll be able to see who takes it.

It's not a brilliant plan. Actually, it's pretty foolish, but it's worth the risk. And honestly, it's our best option right now.

He walked back to the windows and opened one, motioning for me to take a look—and that's when we heard it; a terrifying scream coming from the woods, entirely covered in vines and pine straw from years of minimal maintenance. It was clearly a woman's voice, could be Mrs. Lanie, but somewhere in the back of my mind I doubt that. Or maybe I don't doubt it, maybe I just hope it's Brynlee, because I know that if it isn't, we're in real deep trouble.

Before I could even look at Cade, he had blown past me and out the patio doors. For a guy wearing Crocs, he sure can run fast. I followed after him, those early morning runs finally being put to good use. I tried my best to catch up, but he managed to stay a good ten feet ahead of me the entire way. Once we passed the threshold between a friendly backyard and an uncertain forest, I could finally see who the scream came from. Well, sort of.

Laying on the ground about fifty yards ahead is Mrs. Lanie, her gray blazer covered in dirt and pebbles and ripped on one shoulder. Instead of going to help her up, Cade just stood there, shocked at what's happening.

I ran over to her side, and although she's usually prickly when it comes to my presence, I don't think she minded my help just this once.

"What happened?" I grabbed her arm and helped her to her feet, Cade still walking over in no hurry. She blatantly ignored my question and went directly over to her son, brushing off her clothes as she walked.

"Cade, sweetheart. What are you doin' out here?" She's saying all the right things, and yet somehow her tone expresses an annoyance. She reached out to hug him, but he spun away.

"No. Don't act like nothing is happening, like everything is fine. Because absolutely nothing is fine and we both know it." Cade keeps trying to keep a straight face, keep on being the man he knows to be—strong, emotionless, brave.

But even Goliath couldn't stand tall forever.

Mrs. Lanie acted confused, unaware of what he could be referring to, but the charade didn't go on for long before she realized that Cade wasn't dumb. He's no longer a twelve-year-old kid, no longer a victim of the bubble she so intricately raised him under. He knows all about Brynlee, and he knows that if his father really did kidnap her, she's the one person who can confirm it.

"Alright, fine. Listen, I didn't know if your dad was involved for sure, that's why I didn't tell you, but I suspected something was up when I caught him making late-night phone calls to numbers I didn't know. I just didn't think he could hurt anyone, especially not a child, but it all makes sense now. I just found this." She pointed to an object lying a few feet behind me, Brynlee's white cardigan now in plain sight.

Crap.

I told Cade not to leave it out here, but of course, he insisted we leave it to see if his parents would come back for it. I guess he was right, because one of them did.

Just not the *right* one.

I'm usually very good at knowing when someone is lying. Their eyes always flinch a little towards the upper right corner. But for some reason Mrs. Lanie's eyes aren't showing much of anything, nor moving at all. They're cold, still, frozen.

I have never seen but one person's eyes look like this before, and I'll never forget that moment.

She can keep explaining all she wants, but neither of us are the ones she'll have to convince of her honesty.

"Mom, how could you not tell me? If you really thought something was up, you should've mentioned it. Maybe we could've stopped this whole thing from happening."

Cade's deep blue eyes became glossy as he tried to keep the tears from flowing. Mrs. Lanie kept making up excuses, saying anything and everything she could to prove her innocence. But Cade isn't stupid. He's not oblivious to the evil lurking in his own home. We may just be kids, but we definitely aren't idiots. Maturity is an asset in today's society, something that most teenagers haven't yet realized.

Wait.

"What about my father?" My interruption made both Cade and his mother come to a halt, almost like they had forgotten that I'm here.

"What?" Mrs. Lanie's once slicked back ponytail now slowly fell to the side as she turned to face me.

"What about my father? Did he do that too? Did he kill him?" She's acting as if she doesn't know who I am, like she has no clue who my dad was nor what happened to him. But she knows, I know she does, and she quickly changed her expression once everything clicked.

I don't know for sure that she knows anything about my dad's murder, but if she caught onto her husband's part in the kidnapping, there's a good chance she knows about this too.

"Listen here, I ain't got no clue what happened to your sore excuse for a father, so don't accuse me of nothin'. It's not my fault he's dead."

Her manner was beyond hostile, angered that I encouraged her son to stop playing dumb when it comes to her actions. Her deep southern accent makes it hard to understand everything she's saying, but I'm used to it by now. Some people even say my voice is similar to hers.

I hope they're exaggerating.

For the sake of believing that the world is good, maybe she isn't lying. Maybe she really doesn't know anything about that night, the one when a father never came home to his little girl, and his body was found breathless in a ditch. But I'm not naive enough to believe that I've seen far too much proving the contrary. She knows more about my dad than she's letting on. I just know it. She may not be involved this time, but she has to know something.

But for now, just confronting her will have to do. We still need to find Brynlee, and time is running out.

Cade pulled out his phone and called the station, now sobbing, and reported what had happened. He knows that it's the right thing to do, no matter how hard it may be. His mother pleaded for him not to call, but Mr. Davidson was already on the line.

"Hello? Yes Sir, this is Cade Hampton. I need you to come to my address. I've got someone here you might wanna talk to."

I couldn't quite make out what was said after that, but whatever it was, it wasn't much. The conversation didn't last very long after he announced himself. All Cade had to do was mention Brynlee's name, and the whole police force volunteered to be here within minutes. Everyone is still desperate to find her, even if their only chance is the word of a sixteen-year-old kid and his oblivious mother.

Mrs. Lanie seems pissed at what her son just did, not crying, but very aware that she's under suspicion. It just doesn't make sense. Why would Brynlee's cardigan be here if she or her husband didn't have something to do with the kidnapping? They must. It's the only logical explanation.

Then again, I've found that logic doesn't have much weight in the real world.

When the cops arrived, they took her into custody for questioning, talking to Cade and I for over an hour to follow. But the longer we stay chatting, the lower our chances of finding Brynlee become. So we handled things with the department and went our separate ways, me heading to Cade's car, and the officers heading back towards the station. Mr. Davidson agreed to fill us in if Mrs. Lanie shares any further details. Off the record, of course. No one in town will care that confidential information be shared with us. They know we're capable people.

Well, either that or they've just finally come to realize that we might be their only chance of finding Brynlee.

The only thing to worry about is if the case is ever tried in a court outside of Stonson, us knowing about what happened could compromise its integrity, but Mr. Davidson doesn't have the resources to solve it alone, and he knows that, so it's a risk he is more than willing to take.

As we drove down the long stretch of humid road, it started to pour down heavy rain, Cade's window wipers not even capable of moving as fast as we need them to. I don't know how Cade seems so comfortable driving in conditions like these. I would be scared out of my mind.

We got our license around the same time, considering our identical birthday, but he has a lot more driving experience than I do. That tends to happen with people who actually have a car, along with parents willing to take them for a ride or two.

"Do you see them?"

I was given the task of lookout, on the watch for any sign of Mr. Carl's car or of Brynlee herself, but I can barely see the road in front of us, much less another vehicle.

"Nope, nothing yet. Any idea where they could've gone?"

Cade sighed, becoming more tense as he gripped the steering wheel, a bolt of lightning flashing above us.

"Not really. We know all the places anyone else would. The town is only so big." He stopped, paused for a quick thought, and then continued. "I'll be honest. I don't really know where to go from here."

I've been waiting for everything that just happened to really hit him, and the time to comfort him is finally here. Thank God.

"Seriously, how do I handle this? Mom is in custody—she might be in on it—meanwhile Dad is on the run from any and all law enforcement. And to add to it all, he might have another person's life in his hands. A person who I know, a normal girl who never asked for any of this." His eyes teared up just as they had in the woods, but he ain't done talkin' yet. "Everyone should be able to go to a high school dance and not have to worry about if they'll make it home or not. All the time I see how cruel people can be, how messed up we all are, but here I am, allowing an injustice to happen right beneath my nose. I know they say that love can be blinding. I just never thought it would blind me from something as serious as this."

Your parents, unless you had mine growing up, should teach you how to handle a vulnerable friend in their time of need. What to do when someone is crying, how to calm them down in moments of anger? What they don't teach you is what to say when your friend has psychotic parents and is likely about to be an orphan. A dark reality, I know, but it's the hard truth.

"Maybe she's wrong. Your dad might not have anything to do with the kidnapping after all. Just because the cardigan was near your house doesn't mean he knew anything about it."

It's a pathetic explanation, but it's all I've got.

"Please, I think we both know that he's been the one to blame from the start. It just took us a while to accept it."

By "us", he actually means himself.

As humans, our natural response to something shocking is to become emotional and often upset. For seven seconds, our body unwillingly reacts to that emotion before it begins to control it. But when you find out that your parents are criminals, would you experience more shock or denial? What is it they say about heartbreak, that there are five stages?

Denial, anger, bargaining, depression, and acceptance.

However, I don't think Cade is in any of those stages. He's still just trying to figure out how he feels in general.

As a teenage girl who has gone through heartbreak before, not exactly at the hand of a boy, but because of many other things, I would like to make a few slight changes to those five stages.

"We postpone the finality of heartbreak by clinging to hope.
Though this might be acceptable during early or transitional stages
of grief, ultimately it is no way to live.
We need both hands free to embrace life and accept love,
and that's impossible if one has a death grip on the past."
-Kristin Armstrong

Chapter Twenty-Eight

September 25, 2023~7:15 PM

The five stages of heartbreak...

The first stage is pain. I'll label it as that, but just one lousy word can't really define it. This is the part when you're still in shock, losing sleep as you try to make sense of everything. Eventually you comprehend whatever happened, understand who it is that you've lost, and try to come up with a thousand ways to fix it. But none of them are plausible, because if God wants the situation to remain the same, then that's how it's going to be. There's no sense in worrying about trying to change it, but anyone in this stage hasn't realized that yet.

If it's a boyfriend that you've lost, or in my case, a best friend, you'll often find yourself trying to figure out what was wrong with you, why they didn't want to be a part of your life anymore. I could say all of this about my father, but he's not the one who broke my heart by ignoring me. Cade is.

So when did it change for him? Why didn't he like me anymore? Did I do something wrong? Am I annoying? Does he like someone else? Why wouldn't he talk to me all those years?

I still wanted to be friends...

It hurts my heart that Cade ignored me all those dreadful days at school. It hurts to know that at one point we woke up everyday excited to see each other, and the next we looked the other way without a speck of remorse. It killed me to see him flirting with other girls; them telling him about their day instead of me. All my friends say I'm better off without him, but why can't I shake the feeling that Cade and I still have unfinished business? He used to know everything about me. I'd even send a text just to tell him what I ate for breakfast, and he would do the same. I miss the days when I knew what he was going through, and I knew how to help.

But maybe I was never actually helping, maybe I was simply an annoyance for the entirety of our friendship.

Is that why we weren't friends for so long? Because I'm not good enough for him? I know that we're opposites, but don't opposites attract?

His friends used to say that he talked about me often, but then they began to avoid me too. How can you say that you care for someone one minute, and then act like complete strangers the next? How did he move on with his life so quickly after kicking me out of it? Did he ever really care about me? Did our friendship mean nothing to him?

Because it sure meant a lot to me.

I'm sure that when Cade realized all the pain he caused me, he laughed about it with his friends and called me petty, maybe even naive. But when he went home at night and sat all alone, just him and God, I know he realized just how much he screwed up. He probably felt bad about how he handled things, especially about blaming our fallout on others.

Don't blame others for your feelings. Be a man and take ownership of them.

By the end of this stage, if you're like me, you've realized that it wasn't entirely your fault, hence the rant. So what comes next?

That would be rage.

The second stage is a level above anger. It's no longer just being pissed about how everything went down. In this stage you accept your inner adolescent and rage.

You start off with the basics; working out, trashing anything that might trigger déjà vu, blaring music in your car. If you're mad enough you may even take a baseball bat to the punching bag in your backyard. This is when you tell everyone at school your side of the story rather than listening to him talk about his. You stand your ground, lay down the law for how it's gonna work with whoever hurt you. When you get home from school, you'll put together a killer playlist and rock-out upstairs in your bedroom. You delete all the pictures that you have with them, but not all the way out of the recently deleted album—you're not quite ready for that yet.

You take a joyride with your friends and dump all his stuff on the road while it's pouring down rain. Maybe you even egg his house if his parents are chill enough. While this all might sound like fun, it also happens to be the shortest of the five stages. I'd give it a week before you make it to stage three; sadness.

This is a pretty basic stage, but it lasts for quite a long time. By now, you've gotten out all your anger, yet you're still left with so many unanswered questions. What made him decide to dislike me? Is there something wrong with me?

"There ain't nothin' wrong with you. Any guy would be lucky to have you!" That's what everyone told me, but I never believed them.

You simply learn to move past it, put him or whoever hurt you behind. In my case, that meant forgetting about Cade, even if it hurt more than mere words could describe.

But I never really stopped thinking about him.

The worst part, in my honest opinion, is that I wasn't really sad about the cease of our friendship. It was more the fact that Cade was no longer a part of my life that broke my heart. No matter how much of a jerk he might be, I still loved him, even if it was just as a "sister".

As Thomas Day once said, "You don't stop loving someone just cause it's over."

I also had occasional dreams featuring Cade, weird ones that I can't explain. One about his family, one about him dying, one about him owning a pet iguana.

At this point, you shouldn't be surprised if you have a dream about your "guy" being a celebrity and you a washed-up mobster.

During this stage, you'll get the privilege of having those heartbreaking moments when you see them at school. I know how hard it can be when you lose a friend, seeing them happy without you. Whether it was Cade talking to other girls or him simply looking at his phone, it still pained me to see him without me by his side. I could no longer just walk up to him all giggly and smiling, ready to talk about my day. All I could do was walk by silently, maybe offer the occasional smile that was never given in return. I listened to every conversation about our fallout that no one realized I overheard, and I took any glancing eyes from his buddies like a bullet to the chest.

Overall, you're just going to be sad at your person's *absence*. Then you hit the next stages.

The fourth and fifth stages are somewhat intertwined, so let's call them "double jeopardy". In double jeopardy, I finally began to find myself again. I came back to my strong faith in God, something of much greater value than any man's love, and I learned to never stray from it again; that's one of the best life lessons anyone can ever teach you.

God was waiting for me to realize that Cade wasn't the one. He wasn't the best friend I thought he was. God saw things that I never saw, He heard conversations that I never heard, and He knows things that I will never know. So, since you understand that, you can become much more aware of whom you talk to and how you present yourself to them.

As you go through double jeopardy, you also get into what they call the "self-care" stage. Personally, I must admit that this is my favorite stage. You feel like you're on cloud nine. You begin not to care what your lost person thinks of you, and you're no longer dressing to impress them. You wear what you want because it expresses who you are on the inside, not because someone else likes how it looks on the outside.

Anyone who likes you now will like the real you, not the version that was shown in theaters for an audience of one. God made you who you are because He knew that was His plan, and no matter the struggles you may face, you must trust that He's got you. And yes, I know that is easier said than done, but have faith. God will give you, along with everyone else, the right man if that is in His plan. That man will love you just the way you are, no changes necessary.

Be *different*. I promise that life will be more fun that way. There's a reason that God made us all one of a kind, so acknowledge it.

Imagine a scenario with me: instead of making it awkward between you and whoever it is that you've lost, you act how you really feel. You don't want them back in your life. They've already lost all your respect. The friendship would never be the same anyhow, so you might as well just own it. If it's a boyfriend that you've lost, let his mouth drop when he sees you. Walk yourself around the halls as if you own them. Ditching you was his loss, and you need to allow him to see that. Curl your hair an extra day, take a risk with what you wear, because he is never going to realize the girl he left if you don't up your game. I'm not saying you need to become more popular or anything, and you certainly don't need to be prettier. You are perfect just the way God made you, but you do need to be the bigger person, handle everything with peace and maturity. Flip your hair as he walks by, and don't be afraid to smile and wave as if nothing ever happened. He's going to sit down at night and think about how nice you're being, how well you're managing to handle it all. And once he realizes what he's thrown away, he'll regret it, but by then it's too late. You'll be over him and there's no looking back.

Just be your true self and love God. You'll be so much better off that way. There is no man who walks around acting like a movie star that is worth your time, anyway. Let another girl have him. God will give you the right one, and that's what you begin to realize at the end of these stages.

So that's my piece of advice as someone who has experienced heartbreak, not from a boyfriend, but from a best friend. A best friend who I'm finally beginning to let back into my life. I trust Cade, I really do, but everything he's done over the past four years still lingers in the back of my mind. Or rather a lack thereof. He ignored me; he forgot me, he blatantly acted like a stranger towards me. I forgive him, but I can't bring myself to forget.

I know these aren't exactly the heartbreak stages that Cade is going through, but they need to be addressed. Welcome to high school ladies and gentleman, heartbreak can apply to just about anything.

"That's all that you can do in this world,
no matter how strong the current beats against you,
or how heavy your burden,
or how tragic your love story.
You keep going."
-Robyn Schneider

Chapter Twenty-Nine

September 25, 2023~8:17 PM

We drove around looking for any sign of Brynlee until nighttime, the dark sky continuously pouring down rain overhead. I keep getting déjà vu from all the other times we've found ourselves driving around aimlessly, except now Cade isn't being quiet as I am. He's actually rambling on about anything he can think of.

I can't tell if he's nervous, excited, or just plain anxious.

I got to hear about his seventh-grade math class, his first kiss, even about the time he went out to eat with a girl he met online.

He says he's very picky about who he dates, but it's beginning to sound like that must be a more recent habit he's taken up. I've seen him with about eight-hundred different females over the past three years, but in his defense, they usually seemed much more interested in him than he was in them.

As the night went on, we began to hear more and more sirens, police cars circling around the same back roads over and over again. No one has been able to find anything yet, according to Jenny Davidson.

Oh, excuse me, Jenny Marie Davidson, as she sarcastically informed me is her full name.

She's been doing her best to keep us updated, although I think we would know if the police found anything. In the sixty-mile radius

Stonson has to offer, we've passed the same officers for easily the ninth time at this point.

Where could Brynlee be?

I thought back to an episode I watched on this crime show, one where the investigators tried to put themselves in the criminal's shoes in order to get in the right mindset. "If you want to catch a killer, you have to think like one." That's what the lead officer said, his thick Jersey accent bouncing off the television speakers, but I think I'd have to disagree. If you want to catch a killer, you need to think like his victim. Well, in this case, victims. Every time a murder is committed, it happens for a reason, a motive, if you will. The motive usually has something to do with the victim, who their relatives are, or what they have done. Killers, however extreme their crimes may be, tend to grow habits within their kills. I read all about it in an article, they don't like to change their routines unless absolutely necessary.

If something works once, why change it? Stick to what you know, that's how most of America live their lives anyhow. It's the same with psychopaths. Well, a little different.

So, who are these victims?

If I was an outsider reading this case file, I would state that our killer has victimized one older male and one young female. Yes, they are very different people, but they share more characteristics than you might realize at first glance. Out of the two victims that we've identified by name, not counting the warehouse fire victim, both come from relatively wealthy families and the same town. The difference between the two, however, is that one victim had people who cared when she went missing. The other victim, my dad, had only one.

Me.

Of course the police "cared", but only because it was their job to do so. Not even my mother gave two craps that he was gone. She never thought twice about his leaving. But I did. In fact, I think about Dad every night. Every time I sit in church, every time I watch a movie in the living room, every time I see a purple flower.

Wait. That's it, *purple flowers.*

"Cade, I know where we need to go!" The look I gave him told him exactly what he needed to know, we've been through this same scenario once before. He whipped the car around so that we'd be headin' back out of Stonson, specifically toward a little dirt road that I can only describe as anything but silent.

The barn. That has to be where Brynlee is. Police have closed off every road out of Stonson. She has to be within city limits. The barn is the only place that hasn't been recently searched. If not, then this entire search group is out of options and ideas, and Brynlee might be dead soon.

I've never been in a car going as fast as Cade's is right now, and that's taking into account when my stepfather drives like exactly what he often is: a stubborn drunk. Cade's freckle-decorated cheeks quickly turned red, his face clearly flushed from the sudden U-turn. The internet is much too spotty for any decent service out here. I can't get Jenny on the phone.

That's a problem.

If I can't get Jenny on the phone, then we're essentially driving on the outskirts of town in the middle of nowhere, and no one knows where we are. And just to add to the fun, we're likely headin' into battle with a serial killer on the other side.

Wonderful.

We finally got closer to the bridge on Hirsten Court, red rust practically flying off as we inched towards it. I kept my eyes facing forward, trying not to look at Cade's stressed face unless absolutely necessary. But for some reason he chose to stomp on the brakes almost forty yards away from where we parked days ago—an illegal parking spot, might I add.

"What are you doing? Brynlee could really be at the barn. No one has checked there since we first went. We need to get there now!"

I know that my tone probably sounded a bit harsh, but neither of us has ever been in a situation like this, and we don't have an instruction manual. There are no protocols for us to follow, and no one to count on for backup. Of course we have God, but in all honesty, I don't know if He is telling us to keep going or to get out of here as fast as we can. Maybe I'm not listening hard enough.

It's not always the coward's way out if you run. In fact, sometimes it's the smartest option.

As a professor who spoke at one of our school assemblies once said, "Don't do stupid things, and people won't treat you like a fool. Do stupid things, and you gain everything in the world except respect. Ladies and gentlemen, respect can often be the difference between drowning and survival."

I have never known how right he was until now.

But unfortunately, I think I'll have to ignore my better half for the time being, because I'm about to do something "stupid", as he described it. However, I don't think he had quite this situation in mind when he advised us not to be fools.

"Do you trust me?" Cade's eyes locked on me as he spoke, his body only inches away from where I sit in the passenger seat. Of course I trust him. I just don't always trust his faulty game plans.

"Yes, with my life."

Maybe I should've left that "with my life" part out, because my life might really be in danger this time. This poor boy still has voice cracks now and then, and yet here I am letting him dictate how we proceed in a situation that very likely will be the most dangerous thing we ever take part in.

I must admit, this may not be the wisest decision.

Before I could take back my premature answer, Cade had already put the car in drive and pressed full speed ahead. I grabbed the handle above my seatbelt and held on for dear life, or what's left of dear life. He jerked the wheel as far to the right as it would go, running straight through the brush that we once struggled to jump over, and completely clearing the ditch below. I could hear, and see, dozens of branches hitting the outside of his car as he pressed on.

"Slow down! You're driving like a..." the sheer sight of what lay ahead stopped me mid-sentence. I saw her before Cade did, reaching my arm over the wheel in order to avoid hitting the poor soul.

"What?" Cade's breath was heavy, the result of a clear adrenaline rush from the lack of caution he displayed only moments earlier. He stopped the car right before we hit a massive tree head-on, me frantically running out and Cade following soon after.

The rain drops from above hit my forehead like small rock pellets, each one stinging a little more than the last. The once solid pine straw and mud that covers the surface of the forest's floor is now nothing more than a mush of flowy brown water seeping into the soles of my worn shoes. I can hear Cade wiping the splashes of mud from his calves close behind me. My legs are covered with slop and fallen leaves all the way up to my knees, but I don't care. Nothing is going to stop me from getting to what I spotted from Cade's blurry car windshield. Well, who I spotted.

In the middle of the woods, between two large oak trees that hang powerfully above our heads, lies a girl. Her back faced us as she failed to move at the sound of our distressed voices calling out. Her beaten torso is covered by a cropped white t-shirt, now poorly decorated with yellow stains and dirt marks. What's left of the material from her shorts can only be described as a pure blue, somehow appearing untouched compared to the rest of her pitiful clothing. A cluster of leaves and branches covers the small parameter under which she lays above, allowing her body to remain somewhat dry for the most part.

I recognize the shorts logo on her right thigh even from a distance, it's from a boutique in town, Angels Cove; a boutique at which I know Brynlee works.

I continued to run over to the practically lifeless girl, stopping only a few feet before I approached her now stationary body. Cade did the same, reaching for my hand as he got closer. I almost don't want to look, but I know that it has to be done. I would rather it be us than a random officer paid to handle the scene, because quite frankly, this is not just a "crime scene".

This is likely the last place that this child will *ever* see while on earth.

We inched close enough to see her face, a beautiful young girl with dark skin lying beside our feet. Her lashes are considerably long to be so light, scratches on almost every inch of her gorgeously smooth face. Her cheeks have bug bites as well, crawling with ants of endless descent. Her left ear is lined with gold earrings, at least four or five different piercings, although one hole in particular appears to be surrounded by dried blood. Her chest rose and fell to the beat of raindrops hitting trees all around us, but only barely. I don't think she'll last long if we can't get help soon.

I frantically yelled at Cade, although he's only centimeters away from me, "Call Jenny!"

He whipped out his phone to dial her number, but the service is still here and there. I know it isn't his fault, but he better find a way to get someone on the phone before I strangle him myself.

"She isn't going to answer, Tatum, she didn't when you called five minutes ago and she won't now. Plus, I don't think I can call anyone out here, whether I want to or not."

"I don't care who you call or how you do it, just call someone!"

As he walked off to the side to call the station once again, I pivoted around to see the front of the girl I'll soon kneel beside. Her back is home to a nasty scar the size of my shin, running all the way from her tailbone up to just below her ribcage. There are old burns to match, almost resembling that of a waffle iron. This girl is certainly on the brink of death, but she isn't Brynlee.

The child we've found is another girl, maybe two to three years younger than us. She may not be the friend we've so dearly sought after, but it's clear that she has gone through just as much as we once prayed Bryn never would. Who could've possibly guessed that there was another girl out here the whole time, an entirely different person who has been suffering as we sat safely in our homes worried about Brynlee?

No matter whether it's what we expected or not, we now have a whole other situation on our hands, and that raises two massively problematic questions; how many others are there, and where is Brynlee?

At the end of the day, I must acknowledge the possibility that we've been thinking about this all wrong. Whether it's Cade's dad or not, the kidnapper isn't just after fellow neighbors and acquaintances that they can easily prey on. They've been torturing helpless children, and the worst part is that they could have been doing this for God knows how long.

And none of us had even the slightest clue.

Bottom line, they finally took the wrong girl, and they messed with the wrong kids. Trauma changes a person, and I won't let it ruin another family as it has me and Cade's. I don't care who it is, they're still a cold-blooded killer.

No other girls need to have a childhood as detrimental as mine.

I leaned in closer to the girl's ear, extremely careful not to touch her broken skin. Then I spoke, making a promise that I plan to keep, a collection of words that I will remember for the rest of my life.

"We're going to figure this out, all of it. Every detail, every victim, every second whoever hurt you walked free while you laid out here hurting. I promise."

I've never been one to break a promise, and I refuse to start now. I guess it's true when they say that old habits die hard. "Die", that's such a harsh word. I prefer the term "pass on", but I get no such privilege as to choose the innocent route. Cade and I are in too deep now, and I have a feeling that it ain't over yet.

He turned to me, the phone hanging by only three of his trembling fingers. "They're on the way!"

I stood up from my seat by the girl, running to comfort him as he spoke. Before I could fully gain my balance, he bit his lip, clearly scared to tell me something.

"Tatum?"

I finally managed to brush off my dirt-covered knees and rub my hands together, trying to clean them. "Yes?"

He took a deep breath, bringing his phone down to his waist.

"They've got him." I tilted my head, confused by who "him" is.

"They've got who?" At this point, he could be talking about anyone, and not a single name would surprise me.

"My dad, they've got him. But they don't have Brynlee." He sighed, looking down at the child before us, and then back up at me. "She's still out there, and he probably knew that we were onto him."

I know exactly what that means, but just to be sure, I let him finish. He bit the inside of his cheek, his eyes slightly watering as he spoke.

"If Dad knew that we were onto him, he had no reason to keep her alive."

Chapter Thirty

September 25, 2023~10:57 PM

We all need to learn to start thinking more like princesses. A princess isn't afraid of messin' up, in fact, she fails more often than most. Failure is just another box that she must check off in order to become a queen.

S.C. Lourie once said, "You could have grown cold, but you grew courageous instead. You could have given up, but you kept on going.

You could have seen obstacles, but you called them adventures. You could have called them weeds, but instead you called them wildflowers.

You could have died a caterpillar, but you fought on to be a butterfly. You could have denied yourself goodness, but instead you chose to show yourself some self-love. You could have defined yourself by the dark days, but instead through them you realized your light."

If the world would simply listen to quotes like this rather than something a blonde chick posts on TikTok, we would all have a better chance of finding clarity. The dictionary defines clarity as "the quality of being coherent and intelligible".

So, what quality defines *you*?

If a stranger were to approach you and ask for one thing that defines you, what would you say? Would you say sports, relationships, or maybe your job? Would you describe yourself as a stellar student, or possibly someone who can pull all the ladies? You would probably say something of that sort, an aspect of your life that you encounter in this world, whether it be your sports teams or a new crush or even the shape of your body.

Now, imagine a different scenario: you've made it to Heaven and God just asked for one thing that you believe defines you. God, the creator of the universe, maker of all life and nature, and our Savior, and you've just told him that sports define you. What kind of answer is that?

I define myself as a God-fearing, continually growing girl who constantly finds herself in the wrong, probably more often than most. I'm not perfect by any means, and I've said things that I still regret to this day, but if someone were to come to me right now and ask one thing that defines my life, I would honestly tell them that I can't say just one thing. However, what I can do is tell them about my experiences with God and how He has saved my life, along with how I live it, so many times. He has opened my eyes to things that I never used to see. He has allowed my ears to hear things that everyone else tunes out. I feel when people are hurting, and He has blessed me with the ability to put myself in their shoes as accurately as I can.

In retrospect, I would have to take back my original answer. There is one thing that defines me.

My faith in God, that's what defines me.

> I pray that God blesses me with a strong and firm faith and foundation for the rest of my life and for the rest of eternity with Him. I would love to get to Heaven one day, and I yearn for God to look at me and say, "Welcome, my child. I've been waiting for you. You have done well, good and faithful servant." I want that for everyone else too, and I will strive to live my life in order to do that. Whatever God wishes, let it be done in His name.

These are the things I've thought about as I sit in the hospital lobby awaiting any news. The young girl from the woods, Gabriella Hernandez, as I now know, is stable. But she's still unconscious, and we know nothing more than we did when we found her.

Cade finally got Jenny on the phone, her less than concerned voice giggling upon answering. He yelled, probably momentarily deafening her, demanding to send help. She hung up and quickly dialed her dad who arrived within ten minutes of the call. They took over the scene, sweeping up Gabriella's barely breathing body and shoving her in the back of an ambulance. The ambulance's paint was clearly peeling off of the blue and white sides, so I'm not very confident that she got the best care, but unfortunately I would believe it's the best that Stonson has to offer. Her body was pitiful to look at, painful even. My stomach turned and rolled at the sight of the deep gash I discovered on her thigh after checking for any major injuries, blood still gushing from her pelvic area. Although she isn't dead yet, you could probably convince me she's a goner.

Mr. Davidson left to head for the station maybe fifteen minutes ago, Carl Hampton sitting in an interrogation room waiting for him. He still isn't confessing to much of anything, continually blaming every accusation on his wife.

I guess their love isn't as strong as I once thought it to be.

Jenny said Mr. Carl told her dad all about Gabriella, how he found her a few towns over only three short weeks ago. "She was a runaway", he said. "No one would miss her anyhow," yet I can't help but think back to her shorts. That boutique is in Stonson, and there's no way a runaway could afford a pair like hers. Either he's lying or she got those shorts from another source, likely a young friend of mine who is still nowhere to be found.

He claimed that he was contacted by a burner phone, said he tried to trace it but failed. He did his best to explain why he did it, claiming he was paid eight-thousand in cash to deliver Gabriella to the old barn.

I knew that barn had to be a part of this.

He didn't ask any questions, just said he needed the money. It doesn't make any sense. The Hamptons are beyond loaded, and unless they've suddenly come into some massive debt I don't know about, he has to be lying.

Cade's mother, however, is spilling her guts out. All the officers had to say was that Mr. Carl had turned on her, a clear lie, and suddenly she wouldn't shut up. She admitted to knowing nothing about Brynlee, that what she had told Cade in the woods was true. She suspected her husband of the kidnapping days ago, but she didn't really finish the puzzle until she found the cardigan as we did.

Everyone knows that Mrs. Lanie is the man in their relationship, so they didn't offer her any sympathy when she claimed innocence. However, despite everything that she is or isn't unaware of, she still doesn't know the answer to the question we're actually concerned about answering.

Where is Brynlee?

I left the hospital around one o'clock in the morning after a long few hours without sleep, promising the nurses I would return tomorrow. Until Gabriella wakes up and I know that she's okay, I plan to continue visiting. I may not have met her before now, but I feel as if I've known her for years.

I got a ride from Mrs. Davis, a woman whom I know from church. She had been working at the hospital and just got off of her shift about thirty minutes before I needed to head out.

"How are the kids doin'?"

Mrs. Davis and her husband just gave birth to their fourth child a few months back. They may be a young couple, but they sure know how to have their babies.

"I find a new gray hair every day because of em.'" She laughed, turning the car into the police station's parking lot. I thanked her for the ride and gathered my stuff to head inside.

Once I walked through the entrance, I felt almost nauseous. The memories I've made in this building are not ones I'm too keen on reminiscing over. They don't leave me feeling anything other than heartbroken. I know that God is with me, but knowing that I sat here almost four years ago in a situation not much different from this hurts like you wouldn't believe.

The woman at the front desk ushered me through the doors that I dread to see. Her name tag read BRYCE. She looks oddly familiar. But instead of asking if we've ever met before, I kept my head down and let her stare at me, a sympathetic look on her face. Everyone has been looking at me as if I'm a lost puppy who made my way into their heart. I hate it.

Once I cleared the threshold that anyone else would simply describe as two plain doors, I found myself in a familiar hallway lined with rooms of all different intentions. One room in particular claimed my attention, except it's less of a room and more of a cubicle. The window within the wall sits only five or so feet off the ground and looks into a smaller space with little to no lighting. It can't be much bigger than my bedroom, just a single table and two chairs inside, and, of course, three people.

I know this room, except now I no longer need to stand on my tippy-toes to see inside.

One man I do not know, an officer in the east corner almost fully covered by shadows where the light does not reach. The other two men I know very well, Mr. Davidson and Cade's father. Mr. Carl sits at one of the two chairs, Mr. Davidson across from him. I don't remember being able to hear inside when I was in this position a few years ago, but then again, my mind wasn't exactly at its peak. Today, I can most certainly hear every word, no matter how horrid and crushing they are. It's becoming clear that this whole thing is much bigger than I could've ever imagined, far above just kidnapping.

They bickered back and forth about what the truth is and who should be blamed. There's still one thing that I'm surprised hasn't been discussed; nothing has been said about my dad, nor about Cade. If there is anything that will get him to open up, it's hitting him closest to home. My dad is where it all started, where he got away with it for the first time. Cade is his only child. He cares about how he views him as a father. Whether they always get along or not, Cade is still his kid.

The two of them are getting nowhere by arguing, and I've been conspicuously observing for over twenty minutes now.

That's it, I'm going in. Maybe an unruly teenager with questions she needs answered will kick it into gear.

I busted through the door, which shockingly wasn't locked, with ease. It's as if Mr. Davidson was expecting me to barge in unannounced. In fact, I think he's kind of grateful that I did. I stormed over to the metal table and harshly laid my hands on it. Well, more like slammed them into it. The table was cold, suitable for such a serious time.

"Do you want to know what I think about people like you, Mr. Hampton? I think you act the way you do because you feel the need to compensate for a part of your life in which you're inadequate. A time where you aren't a big, strong man anymore. You're just a helpless showboat trying to figure things out. So tell me, what is it that makes you feel inadequate?" I tried my best to sound sophisticated, using words like "compensate" and "inadequate", but in reality I'm scared out of my mind.

I now stare into his eyes, his cold, yet worrisome, eyes. They're the same eyes that I once gazed into so lovingly, or rather those that mimic his son's.

It's crazy how two people can resemble each other so strongly, yet be entirely different within.

He looked at me and stared, expressionless, fear no longer in his blue eyes. I wasn't expecting him to be scared of me. I'm just a child to him, I know that. But he won't stay that way for long, and I know just how to get him to wipe that smug look off his face.

I looked over to Mr. Davidson, who had stepped back from where he once sat, his pale hand now motioning for me to take over. A little of trust goes a long way, and from what I've observed, he trusts me more than I trust myself.

"You're a father, right Mr. Hampton?" He looks at me now as if I'm simply stupid, an absolute idiot, and I understand that the question seems unnecessary for the moment. But I know where I'm going with it, trust me.

"Yes, you know that." His voice came out so deep that it almost startled me. I forgot how manly he seemed to me growing up. He's twice the size my dad was. Another thing that used to confuse the living daylights out of me.

"So tell me, what would you do if your son knew what you've done? I'm not just talkin' about the things you already confessed to. I'm talkin' about the things you knew were so wrong that you somehow managed to convince even yourself that they never happened. What would you do if Cade walked in here right now and you had to tell him about all of it? Every detail, every idea, every little thing that made you the man you are today." I paused while he thought, then added one more thing to trigger him a bit further. "That is, if you consider yourself a man at all."

That did not go over well.

He looked over to Mr. Davidson as well as the observing officer in the corner, almost as if to say "You're gonna let her talk to me like that?", but they just stood there, eager to see how a grown man would handle being interrogated by someone who can't even drink yet.

"I am a man. Honey, I could do things to you that would make you regret the day you were ever—"

I saw both Mr. Davidson and the other officer move towards us as he spoke, bucking up. They were likely about to put an end to it all because he threatened me. But I put up my hand as a motion to stop them. I can handle this. I'm about to pull the smart-allec card, and I couldn't care less.

"What are you gonna do? Beat me like you did with Gabriella, like you did with my dad? Is that why you hurt them?"

"I never felt threatened by your redneck dad."

"Oh grow up, it's time to accept that if you were a real man, you would've been able to handle it without violence. But you couldn't. You know why? Because you're weak."

Mr. Carl looks furious now. He's finally beginning to get worked up over the petty comments I continue to throw at him.

"I ain't weak, and I never did anything to your father that wasn't well deserved." I stared at him, waiting for more than just a single sentence in response. He began to raise his voice as he carried on. "What do you want me to say? I'm not talkin' to a child about this."

"Why? You worried you're gonna accidentally spill the truth?"

"Listen here kid, I don't even but barely remember that night, and I left the bar before he was ever gone."

"Gone?"

"Yeah yeah, disappeared or whatever nonsense y'all called it."

The air quotes he put around "disappeared" make me think he knows more about where my dad went than he's letting on, but I've thought that for a while now.

"What bar?"

"Me and him were drinkin' a little before he up and' vanished. What, is that a crime now too?"

I stopped, shocked, because surely that isn't all it takes to break a grown man.

"So you were with my dad the night that he died? You never reported that to the police. Trust me, I checked." Now we're getting somewhere.

"This station can't even find out what twelve-year-old stole a bike from the Winn-Dixie. They were never goin' to solve any real case."

"I know you killed him! Why? What made you feel so insecure that you couldn't handle him standing up to you? You can call yourself a man all you want, but you're nothing more than a…"

He stood up and slammed his hands against the table, now hovering over both me and my chair. His cold eyes twitched as they stared at me, or rather, through me.

"He deserved everything he got! He could never learn how to mind his own business!"

I have been shocked by many things in my lifetime, but never like this.

The whole room stopped. Even the officer in the corner gasped as the words echoed through the small room. Mr. Carl's mouth dropped wide open at the sound of what he had just said, Cade walking through the door just as everything went silent. After all this time and nothing but sheer hope to go on, we know who killed my daddy.

Maybe I'll finally find out what happened to him on that cold winter night that I've replayed in my head so many times before. Imagining what could've happened, what couldn't have happened, and what logically makes sense to have happened. Every time a room was too quiet, or when I cried out to God praying for a miracle, I thought about Daddy. I guess that God heard, no; I know He did. Sometimes things happen that you never believed could, that you never believed would, and you're truly blessed.

A grown man just admitted to murder after a four-minute discussion with *me*. I'd say that's a miracle if I've ever seen one.

And most all that it took to break him was knowing how to prey on the few things that we all regret keeping only after it's too late; our hidden secrets.

"Holding anger is a poison...
It eats you from the inside...
We think that by hating someone we hurt them...
But hatred is a curved blade...
and the harm we do to others...
we also do to ourselves..."
-Mitch Albom

Chapter Thirty-One

January 4, 2020~7:16 AM

I had an odd dream last night. If I tell you this dream, you must swear to keep it to yourself. Promise? Good, let's begin.

It started off in the woods, no sun out, only darkness. Not the darkness that covers the ground when it's nighttime; it was the kind of darkness under which you can't even see your hand in front of your face. I looked all around, up and down, left and right. It felt as if I was experiencing virtual reality; I couldn't touch anything, but I could see myself standing there, no one else around.

Until there was someone, a single man, to be exact.

He was tall and bulky, much larger than any man I've ever seen around town. He wore a hoodie and pants, but for some reason, the weather in this dream felt extremely hot.

Why is he in such an outfit all bundled up?

I could see not much more than the shadow of his outline, a dark beard hanging from inside his lint-filled hood. Suddenly, a light flickered on below us, allowing me to see him more clearly.

I had never seen this man before my dream, but he certainly recognized me. He began to walk in my direction, and rather fast. As he got closer, something about his figure began to change. He was slowly morphing into a much more rectangular shape, similar to a gymnast's body. By the time he got within spitting distance of me, he was no longer a man, but a beautiful woman. This woman did not hide herself as her predecessor had. In fact, she proudly smiled. She gave off a wonderful aroma. I could somehow smell it through my brain's hazy fog, and her skin appeared flawless. She wore a white dress without shoes, something that I know must hurt her feet as they stand firmly upon the rocky ground.

I called out to her as she slowly stepped back into the darkness. "Hello?"

There was no answer, just silence, but the silence was louder than any response I could've coaxed out of her, tearing through me like a freight train. I yelled once again, and this time, she stopped. She stepped back towards me, still remaining mute. I stared at her deep emerald eyes and she stared at mine, yet I know that they cannot possibly be as stunning of a sight as hers.

Saying nothing, she reached behind her back and pulled out a mirror. It was a small mirror, but one nonetheless. It appeared outlined with a white rim lining and gold jewels where her hand firmly gripped it. She tilted the mirror towards me, upward, so that I was looking down at it.

As I glanced into it, I saw a girl. She was youthful, yet grown.

The girl I saw in that mirror was not me, but a more mature version of the woman I imagine I will soon grow to be. She had brown, wavy hair, and a small scar on the left side of her forehead. Her hazel eyes looked all too familiar, and her smile put even the woman standing before me to shame.

This girl isn't me, but she sure does remind me of myself.

She tilted her head and shifted to the right, now so that I can see her full upper half within the reflection. She looked back and laughed, motioning for someone outside of the mirror's frame to join her.

Walking over was a man, much taller than her, but not any older. He wore a red hoodie and shorts, something tightly gripped in his left hand. His hair was long, blonde, a tad bit on the greasy side. His eyes appeared much like the ocean, yet they seemed to hold more stories than a body of water ever could.

No matter how deep the sea may be, I can guarantee his eyes are deeper. Much deeper.

He continued to approach the girl in the mirror, but as he got closer, her smile seemed to fade. I wouldn't say that it was fading because of his presence, but more because of what his presence meant to her, or symbolized.

The boy's expression was as if he had seen a ghost. I practically felt his heart shatter as their eyes met.

Is he her boyfriend? Maybe her brother?

They don't look anything alike, but they sure seem to care for each other as siblings would. The girl looked down at her companion's hands; her face still heavy with despair. He lifted up the object he held as if to show an audience, that would be me, what he had found; a tightly knit white jacket covered in dirt stains, torn up on the sleeves and wrists.

No, not a jacket, more like a cardigan.

The two exchanged no words. They simply gazed back and forth at the cardigan, then at each other. With one last glance, the girl began to cry hysterically, but her tears were clearly not of sadness. They were more affectionate, as if in that moment she knew nothing other than to cry. Maybe she's already been through too much trauma to handle whatever the cardigan symbolizes. She could take it no more.

The boy leaned closer into her defined body, embracing his friend as if she was his own. Maybe they are family after all, but from what I can tell, it's much more than just blood or lineage that holds the two together.

They both knew what the cardigan meant, and they both realized its importance.

For the boy, finding the cardigan seemed to confirm something he already knew, but for the girl, his finding meant much more than a simple confirmation. That cardigan was the key to unlock her emotional floodgates. It's clear to me that she has sheltered herself her entire life, never letting anyone in.

But this boy must be different, it seems that he allows her to open up and express her feelings. She can let herself be true around him, and knows that there will be no judgment. Whoever that man is to her, she trusts him with her life. She loves him, and he loves her. I have never known what love looks like before now, but I know this must be it.

Suddenly, the surrounding sky turned dark as trees and briars from above engulfed them to toe. Being swept away by the world and its problems, they still were not rattled or shaken. The boy continued to hold her, and she continued to let him. Her tears lasted no more, but I can tell that she is no less sad than she was only moments ago.

Before long, vines and leaves had completely covered the young couple, only a small circle left open to reveal a tip of the boy's blonde hair underneath shadows of the surrounding natural canopy.

The woman holding the mirror suddenly yanked it from my intrigued stare, scampering away. Back into the darkness she went, never saying but one word, "Go." She spoke it as she fled, her voice like that of an angel. Majestic, that's how I would describe her if given the chance.

But I will never get that chance, because now I stand alone in uncharted territory once again. What one person calls a dream, another calls a nightmare.

If I die, quote me on that.

I'm not sure if I'll classify this as a nightmare or not. It was more of an experience, a story told through silence.

Yes, that's a good way to describe it, "a story told through silence". Maybe that's what I've been missing. Maybe life is more of a story unfolding in what has not yet been said, rather than a tune of what has already been spoken. Sometimes a whisper packs more of a punch than the loudest of screams, and often it is the ones who sit back and observe that learn the most. They see all that we do, take note of our flaws, and gather all the facts before they choose to speak.

Maybe we should learn from people like that, people like Andrew.

Andrew is a boy in my class. He's friends with Cade. Well, he used to be friends with Cade. I'm not sure how close they are now. I don't really talk to Cade anymore. But I have a feeling that no matter how close Cade and Andrew may or may not be, he will always be loyal to Cade over me, even though we've become friends recently. "Bro code", as they call it, but now that Cade and I don't talk, I wonder if we'll stay friends.

Andrew is much smarter than anyone gives him credit for. He sees all the little things that no one else does. He truly has his life together, well, as much as anyone can at twelve years old. He's the oldest of his siblings, and it shows in every aspect of his life; how he carries himself, his maturity in every conversation. But thankfully he also knows when to let loose and act goofy. It's my favorite quality about him.

I understand why Cade wants to be friends with him. He's different, unique even. I've always found Andrew fascinating, how his lack of words speaks for themselves. He isn't rude or cocky, he just is who he is—kind, considerate, keen, a true friend.

Maybe he can be my new friend now that Cade doesn't talk to me, maybe we will be like the best friends from my dream one day. But probably not. He knows too much about my life to like me in that way. He's seen me cry in the hallway after Cade ignored me. He's seen me walk home from school with my head drooping. He's seen it all. If I'm being honest, I think he likes to analyze me. He tries to understand why I act the way I do, why I care what certain people think, even why my mind compartmentalizes tasks in such an odd manner.

The downside of someone who observes everything is that they also see every negative thing we try so hard to hide. All the things we hate about ourselves he notes, never calling us out, but always remembering.

I hope Andrew remembers me well, whether he knows that I enjoy our friendship or not.

You may not know this, Andrew, but I analyze you too. I see you, and I'm here for you.

"Likewise", as he would say. Just a single word, no more.

Maybe he can explain this dream to me. Or maybe I'm not supposed to make sense of it at all. Maybe it was simply something to fill my racing mind as I slept.

Guess we'll find out, because it's finally seven o'clock Tuesday morning, and here I am waking up to a life that I pray every day is all just one big nightmare. Daddy will be in the kitchen making breakfast, he'll smile and tell me good morning as he always has.

"Has", that word cuts deeper now more than ever before. Who knew that just by changing one word to the past tense, you can completely alter the way a story is perceived? See, one word. That's all you need.

Just one word to change a story.

Chapter Thirty-Two

September 26, 2023~8:17 AM

Have you ever had something happen that simply rocked your world, for better or worse? If so, I hope it was something good, because now that I know how it feels, I definitely recommend.

Carl Hampton was charged with murder and kidnapping, and his wife faces a conspiracy to commit charge regarding my father's murder. I'm sure that more charges will pile up as time goes on, but for now I'll have to take what I can get.

I never got to hear the full story of how it all went down, but I will soon enough. Now, I know you're probably wondering why I'm not more eager to hear everything, considering what I've been through the past four years just waiting for answers, but simply the reassurance that we've caught Dad's killer has changed my mood from depressed to ecstatic in an instant.

But maybe I'm the only one who feels this overwhelming relief beginning to take place.

Cade's slumped body sits on the ground in front of me, his head leaned back against the cold white walls that line the very same hallway where we stood only years ago, painfully bliss memories flooding back as I stare at him. He hasn't spoken but a single word, "Apples", since we settled down.

When we were kids, we made a pact to never cuss, and we've done our best to keep it to this day. So, we decided on a word to say whenever we began to feel mad or upset: apples. Just as a picture holds a thousand words, one word relays a thousand thoughts. That one word in particular tells me all I need to know about how Cade is feeling. It shows me that he's finally begun to realize exactly how screwed he is.

It's bad enough having helicopter parents, but now knowing that at least one of them is a killer too, and not metaphorically, that must be heartbreaking.

Many people think describing something as "heartbreaking" is dramatic, but they just don't understand. These are our lives, our reality. They are not fictional books or dramatic plays. We wake up to these circumstances every day, never knowing whether it's safe to walk around town or into school. We have no idea if the killer is going to resurface or if the kidnapper will take another victim. No one should have to look back constantly as we're now being forced to.

No one.

"Sooo, where do we go from here?" I laughed, finding the tone in which he asked amusing. He spoke in such a sarcastic manner, something rather odd for Cade to do, but he did not find it funny as I did. In fact, he was quite upset about my laughter. "I'm serious Tatum, how do they expect me to handle this? It was my dad all along. The man we were both terrified of, the reason we weren't friends anymore; it was him."

These are the first full sentences Cade has said for an hour, maybe more. Of course he would be the one to stay worrisome at a time like this. Only Cade, you can always count on him to act a fool.

"I'm sure Mr. Davidson will be done soon. He'll tell us where we need to go from here. Cade, you've gotta trust me on this one. I know this is hard, but it's gonna be okay. I wouldn't lie to you."

He looked up at me and raised a single eyebrow. The one he can lift much higher than its bushy neighbor—it's a little quirk he's done ever since we were little.

Confused, I asked, "What? I ain't never lied to you."

Cade's face became more serious now, not sad, but serious. He wouldn't say anything back to my question, so now I most definitely need to know what he meant. "Cade, I've always told you the truth."

He turned up his lip and watched as I took a seat on the grimy floor next to him. The tiles are coated in dust, and look as if they haven't been mopped since 1986, but no matter. He looked at me and sighed, his eyes somehow appearing deeper than the ocean.

"Once. Just once that I can remember."

"Once what?"

"That's how many times you've lied to me—once."

Unless he's talking about when I pretended not to be hurt by all those years he ignored me, I genuinely have no idea when I've lied to him.

He softly smiled, clearly hurt by whatever he's about to say. "You said that you loved me. When we were kids. That was a lie, was it not?"

Apples.

How do I respond to an accusation like that? He gave me practically no time to prepare an answer or think through any explanation I could've possibly managed to come up with. I know he's only joking, maybe, trying to hide that he actually cares about it.

Before I knew it my lips were moving ahead of my brain and I was throwing out my best attempt at a valid explanation of such a straight-forward statement. "That wasn't a lie, Cade. If I said that, then I meant it."

Was it a lie? Do I actually love Cade, or was my answer solely the result of a default setting my brain resorted to? A setting that protects both him and me from getting hurt. I had never really thought of Cade in any way other than like a brother until we reconnected, and I hate to be the one to say it, but maybe things were better that way.

And yet I can't help but wonder what might come to be if we were ever more than just friends. Those feelings I've been having are definitely not that of a sister's love. They're much different. I've never felt this way before, so if I'm being completely honest, I'm not quite sure what to expect.

I see all these couples at school who seem to be the perfect match, they even finish each other's sentences, but I've never found anyone who does that with me; someone who matches my energy in a way no one else can.

Well, no one other than Cade.

I've always assumed that the husband I pray God will one day bless me with is to be found years in the future, but maybe he's never been more than a street away. Maybe instead of trying to ignore every guy that comes my way, I should've been with the one who has always cared for me. We might not have always been on the best of terms, but he still never left. He grew distant, and certainly more shy than when we were children, sure. But he never left me stranded. He always kept one eye out for me, whether I realized it or not.

God and Cade are the only ones who have never left my side, even when everyone else has. They have never chosen drama over me, or called me inadequate compared to other girls, or judged me for my appearance. With Cade, I can wear absolutely zero makeup every day, and I don't think he would mind. In fact, I can almost guarantee that he would compliment me. He'd find a way to make my day.

Cade is different, and I like different.

And that's when I made the decision to no longer ignore what I know I feel deep down. "Cade, I do love you. I always have."

The look on his face after that said it all, a rapid flood of confusion and relief and concern all seeming to come at once. "What?"

"You hurt me, sure, but even then I still paid attention to you. I've always wondered why you ignoring me for so long still bothered me, but now I know that it's because I cared."

I may have simply reworded what he told me so confidently earlier, but to him, it seemed to mean the world. I have never seen Cade smile so big, not even when he won the class spelling bee in third grade, an accomplishment he prepared for weeks in advance.

I hope he keeps that big, beautiful smile for the rest of his life, whether I'm by his side or not, because for a kid who has just received possibly the worst news of his life, he's still somehow managing to find joy through it all. That's the kind of man you want to marry, the one who knows how to find joy even in the darkest times. The one who prays to God without ceasing, and not just about you, but about every aspect of his short life. He would do anything if it meant keeping you happy, yet he's not afraid to tell you the truth when called for.

That's the kind of man I want, and that's the man I've thankfully found.

Well, maybe he found me. Or maybe we found *each other.*

Either way, God gave us this friendship for a reason, and I refuse to let a little snag, also known as a lousy pair of parents, get in the way of the noble life Cade Hampton has ahead of him.

After all, what am I if not first and foremost his friend?

"When we love, we always strive to become better than we are.
When we strive to become better than we are,
everything around us becomes better too."
-Paula Coehlo

Chapter Thirty-Three

September 26, 2023~9:14 AM

"You had no right to allow my child anywhere near him!"

Mr. Davidson lingers only a few inches past his office door, listening to my mother's rage as she airs him out over just about anything she can think of.

How dare he let me do something so dangerous, how dare anyone other than her control what I do, she is my mother, after all. At one point she even managed to bring Cade into it, raging about how I should have never been allowed near such a futile boy. But instead of flinching as she got louder, Mr. Davidson just stood there, arms crossed, and took the harsh feedback calmly.

"What do you have to say for yourself?"

I thought about stepping in, but if I'm bein' honest, I want to see how this ends.

"Ms. Cassidy, any activities that your daughter took part in were of her own free will. If she did anything to put her or Cade in harm's way, I was completely unaware of it." Mr. Davidson looked past my hotheaded mother and laid eyes on me, winking while she was momentarily turned in the other direction. He knows that no progress would have been made without Cade and I here to help, no matter if our participation was moral or not. That's one good thing I must give our small town credit for. There are very few people who actually care when we bend the rules a bit.

Assuming you take my crazed mother out of the equation.

"That's bull. You knew that what they were doing could put them in danger, and you let them do it anyhow. This is absolutely unacceptable. I will no longer stand for it!" She reached over to the chair where I sit patiently and carelessly snatched up her purse, violently grabbing me by the arm on her way out. I pulled away quickly, as if I'm going to let her touch me. She may be acting like she gives a crap about me now, but I've raised myself for four years without her.

I didn't get her help then, and I certainly don't need it now.

She gasped, putting her hand on her heart, insinuating that she's offended by my attempt to separate us.

"Tatum, what on earth has gotten into you? First you run off with this redneck boyfriend of yours, and now you're actin' as if I'm in the wrong? I am your mother. I'll make your life a living..."

"No."

Apples. All I've wanted to do for years is stand up to her, but I haven't had the nerve to say everything I've wanted to, everything I've needed to. Sure, I've stood my ground before, like back at the house, but not like this.

Never like this.

I continued, "You don't get to boss me around anymore. You have done nothing but avoid your responsibilities as a mother for far too long. What makes you think that'll change now? Just because you finally realized that I can handle myself without you and your mind games doesn't mean you get to step in as mother of the year. We may have been a family once, when Dad was here, but we're not one now."

There it is again, that heart wrenching silence ringing through by already throbbing ears. The silence that speaks louder than words, that shakes the room without being addressed.

After standing appalled for a moment, she scrunched up her post-Botox nose and turned to face Mr. Davidson once again. Instead of actually believing that I just stood up to her, I think she's searching for someone else to blame my objection on.

Seems that Mr. Davidson fits the profile.

"See what you taught her?"

He uncrossed his arms and stood a little taller, now hovering over my naive mother, whose tan broad shoulders look petite in comparison.

"Honestly Jessica? I think deep down you know that Tatum is a better person than you will ever be, and that pisses you off. You're finally starting to feel guilty for all the years you left her to figure it out on her own. And, to add to it all, you know that she's finally found exactly what you regret letting slip away; a man who loves her."

He looked backwards at the window where Cade leisurely stands, softly smiling first at him, then at me.

I have never seen a woman so taken back by just one statement as my mother in this moment, but it's about time someone told her the hard truth.

She looked at me infuriated; her face burning with anger and her cheeks turning darker by the second. I would compare her to a tomato, but that would be an injustice to tomatoes everywhere.

"Fine. You think you're so grown-up now, Tatum? Then you go on and do whatever it is you find best. Just don't come runnin' back to me when your life goes up in flames. In fact, don't ever come runnin' back to me. I wouldn't want to inconvenience your new life in any way—not with my help, not with my opinions, and certainly not with my money. I don't want you comin' back home and don't expect me to change my mind."

That "home" that she referred to hasn't been a home since the day Dad died, so her attempt to scare me doesn't hold much weight.

She furiously stomped away, leaving us all in her angered dust, only stopping just before she approached the end of the hallway.

"Oh, and Tatum?"

I leaned out of the office door and turned to face where she stood, now holding the bottom of her stomach. "Yes?"

I can only describe the smirk on her face with one word; malicious. It's as if what she has to say is intended to leave my life in shambles. But quite frankly, there's nothing she can say that will make me change my mind about kicking her out of my life, that I know for sure.

"I expect you to stay away when April rolls around."

April isn't for another seven months. What does that have to do with anything? I quickly gave in, intrigued by what she meant by her indecisive remark.

"What's so important about April?" I'm proud of myself for staying so calm as I spoke. I ought to be lettin' her have it.

I want so badly to tell her every time I cried at night because she wasn't home, every question I needed answered by a loving mother. But I won't. I wonder if she actually feels guilty for all those years, if that's why she's such a cruel person now. Or maybe she really is just a sorry excuse for a mother.

Which is true, I will never know.

"That's when Bryson will be here. I just need to make sure that you're never a part of his life. I wouldn't want to screw-up another child."

"Who's Bryson?"

"Your baby brother."

And then she left. Through those same industrial doors I so deeply dread. I watched her hair sway from side to side as she stormed out of the station, everyone in the lobby staring as she left.

She arrived here after a call from Bryce at the front desk, but only stayed as long as she needed in order to get her brutal, yet effective, point across. That's basically the story of my life, her ditching me immediately after ruining everything. The only difference, however, is that she's never dropped a bomb quite like this before. This has to take first place for biggest surprise.

She's pregnant? How did I miss that? Better yet, who's the father?

Mom and David haven't been divorced for too long, so it could be his baby, but that's unlikely. That would still leave months unaccounted for, months during which I should have noticed. She still has practically no bigger a waist than she did when I was a toddler. There's no way she is more than a few months.

If the dad isn't David, who is it? Why didn't she tell me before now?

I know that we haven't exactly been on the best of terms recently, but I'm still her daughter. Then again, she had no problem kicking me out, so maybe I've been overestimating the depth of a mother's love.

Well, this mother's love, at least.

I felt a hand come over my shoulder, gracefully rubbing against my cotton shirt in a swift back-and-forth motion.

"That took guts, kid. You're not afraid of much, are you?"

Mr. Davidson is just trying to comfort me, I know, but his words only leave me feeling even more empty inside. I should feel better. After all, I don't have to deal with "mother dearest" any longer.

I was just about to thank him for the comforting words when another voice suddenly stepped in on my behalf, one of my favorite voices.

"She never has been. Even when we were kids she was fearless. It's what I admire most about her." Cade walked over to join us, that goofy smile still painted on his face.

Standing here with both men huddled around me, I feel like I have a family. For once in my life, a real family; people who care whether my heart is in pain, notice when I need help, and work their hardest to get me that help. And right now, I need all the help I can get.

Mama will have her new family, and I will have mine.

I may do my best to appear "fearless", as Cade would say, but I am anything but.

Sometimes, instead of confronting our biggest fears, we try to cover them up with every emotion other than fear itself. It's how we're wired. We never want others to see just how deep our struggles go. No matter if our fears are real or irrational, they still matter to us, and if we let others see that, it makes us seem weak.

If there is one thing you can't afford to be in high school, it's weak.

If you can't handle it, you might as well move counties, because you won't want anyone to know who you are once you've been humiliated. Trust me, I know. Except I wasn't given the option to opt out of high school, just like I wasn't given the choice of losing my dad or not. It wasn't some raffle I won, after which I could decline the prize. It's God's plan for me. I have to trust Him, but sometimes that's easier said than done.

It's hard being a Christian in such a satanic world, but I would much rather be a struggling Christian than a thriving atheist. I thought that in order to focus on God, I had to block out everyone else. I put up steel bars and made only one key to open them, then threw that key into the unforgiving darkness.

No one in, no one out.

This way, my heart could never be deceived again, and no one could take away the little bit of hope I clung to so tightly.

But God knows that isn't how life works. Part of following Him and His teachings is learning how to do so while simultaneously navigating this cruel world and defeating the temptations it offers.

We're meant to let people in. It's how we learn from our mistakes and grow in wisdom.

It's time to find that key, and it's time to let the people that God has blessed me with back into my life, minus a few.

Maybe this time it will go a little better, maybe there will be a little less heartbreak than there was before. Not a lot, just a little.

A little is all I need; *pas beaucoup, juste en peu.*

*"The most beautiful people we have known are those
who have known defeat, known suffering, known struggle,
known loss, and have found their way out of the depths.
These persons have an appreciation, a sensitivity, and
an understanding of life that fills them with compassion,
gentleness, and a deep loving concern.
Beautiful people do not just happen."
-Elizabeth Kubler Ross*

BRYSON CAIN CASSIDY

SATURDAY   MARCH **16**   1 - 3 PM

2024

AT OUR HOME, 1671 EARLPARK. STONSON NC

RSVP TO JESSICA CASSIDY BY 19TH JANUARY 2024

AT 678-908-1432

Chapter Thirty-Four

September 26, 2023~10:47 AM

Cade and I took a seat behind the mesh covering that hangs from the rusted ceiling, sound equipment attached to almost every outlet in sight. The flooring in the electronic room is much different from that of the hallway, black and blue thin carpeting rather than tile, ripped in small spots as a result of wear over the years.

Mr. Davidson is allowing us to listen to Mr. Hampton's official confession from another room as it happens live, the real thing. He originally only offered up the manuscript that would be given after he took the confession, but both Cade and I want to listen to his father tell the timeline of that night with his own cold voice—real, unaltered, and true.

I want to hear for myself the man who killed my father admit to it, details and everything, no matter how gory. I know it'll be tremendously hard to do, but it needs to be done. The hardest things to do are often the ones we remember most.

He handed us both a pair of old-school oliver green headphones and carefully plugged them into the metal box that allows for us to listen in.

"You both know this isn't going to be like what you see on television, correct? This is as real as it gets." I nodded and Cade did the same, both of us coming to the same conclusion, just for different reasons.

"We're ready."

Mr. Davidson reached to turn on the live signal, somewhere in the back of his mind a voice simultaneously telling him this is a stupid thing to do. Maybe it'll scar us, maybe it won't, but nothing can scar me more than what happened on that cold night so many years ago. Nothing.

So he did it anyway, he knows that we need this more than he can ever imagine.

Closure is a pretty crazy thing.

Then he left, heading for the entrance to the interrogation room next door to start the connected live recorder that sits in front of Carl Hampton. After a few seconds of silence, it began to play as he turned it on, a little scratchy, but still audible.

Recording begins

Mr. Davidson: "September twenty-sixth, two thousand and twenty-three. This confession is validated by Chief Officer John Davidson, Station thirty-four of North Carolina. Primary offender involved is Carl James Hampton, resident of Stonson, North Carolina. Pending charges are as follows: kidnapping, assault, and murder in the first degree. Mr. Hampton has also admitted to the kidnapping and delivery of one Gabriella Valery Hernandez, which will be transcribed in a separate confession. Ms. Hernandez was age thirteen, ethnicity was of Mexican descent, and was found brutally beaten near Hirsten Court on the evening of September twenty-fifth. Additionally, the suspect is also under suspicion for the kidnapping of a third victim, one Brynlee Ray Berkley. Ms. Berkley is age fifteen, ethnicity is of Indian descent, and was last seen Saturday December fourteenth, but those charges will be discussed in a further confession if proven that Mr. Hampton was in fact involved. Sir, can you please confirm the name that I have recorded as it is written on your birth certificate, your understanding of the charges you are being accused of, and acknowledge that you have been read your rights?"

Carl Hampton: "Name is Carl James Hampton, and yes, I understand the charges against me. I have also chosen to decline my right to representation during this questioning."

Mr. Davidson: "Thank you for that Mr. Hampton, but this is no longer just a questioning. You have already admitted to the murder of one Michael Cassidy, dead as of December two-thousand and nineteen. I just need to confirm the details of that night, for both our records and legal reasons. Alright, let's begin. Can you tell me where you first encountered Mr. Cassidy the night of December eighth?"

Carl Hampton: "I guess. Michael and I first met a few years back when we were introduced by our wives, Lanie and Jessica. At the time, we were expecting our first child, Cade, and the Cassidys were in the same boat. A little girl for them, but who knew the mess she'd turn out to be? Anyhow, yeah, that's how we met. I never really liked the guy though, he seemed a little too...how do I put this? Stuck-up. Yeahhh, that's it. He was a preppy, stuck-up excuse for a man. Tatum's probably better off without him anyhow, not that I care."

Mr. Davidson: "Forgive me, but I don't think that's your decision to make. To continue, can you explain to me why you found it sensible to commit such a violation against Mr. Cassidy's person?"

Carl Hampton: "Because the redneck needed to be taught a lesson, and no one else was gonna do it. It's as simple as that."

Mr. Davidson: "May I ask why he needed to be taught a lesson? Mr. Cassidy was both a law-abiding citizen and an outstanding member of our community. I can proudly say that I know that first-hand. Michael was a friend of mine."

Carl Hampton: "Well then, if you're so sure he was this perfect man, how can you explain him sleeping with my wife? Yeah, I bet that's something you didn't know, ain't it?"

Mr. Davidson: "Can you please elaborate on that accusation, Mr. Hampton?"

Carl Hampton: "Well sure. When my son was eleven years old, we were told that he's missing his front two permanent teeth, a defect called hypodontia. It cost us over ten grand to get implants for Cade, but you can barely tell that he has em' now, so no regrets. The dentist, Dr. Berkley, told us that the genes required to contract hypodontia must be inherited, so either his mother or I had to be a carrier. Well, I got tested, and it came back negative for the strand that caused Cade's case. Long story short, Lanie's test confirmed that she didn't have it either. Do you get where I'm going with this?"

Mr. Davidson: "No, unfortunately I do not follow. Mr. Hampton, these are some very serious accusations you are being asked to defend. This is not the time to reminisce about your troubling times as a father."

Carl Hampton: "No, you're not gettin' it. Neither of us gave Cade the defect, but he had to get it from someone. Wasn't long before I realized there was only one other way that could've happened. I can't be Cade's father. A carrier of the gene must be some redneck lowlife slept with Lanie. She's always denied it, but I know better."

Mr. Davidson: "So what made you think this "redneck lowlife" was Mr. Cassidy?"

Carl Hampton: "Well, he was the only guy I had ever let around my wife. She was always by my side unless she was with Jessica and Michael. And if that doesn't get you to believe me, Dr. Berkley also informed us that we aren't the only ones in Stonson who struggle with this disease. She wanted to give us the names of a few people she treated for it, just in case we needed to ask questions first hand from someone else who lives with it. When I asked for the names, she told me only three people. Lyla Grayson, Harper Bowen, and Michael Cassidy. In case you didn't notice, two of those names are women."

Mr. Davidson: "Did you ever approach Mr. Cassidy about this issue prior to the night of his death?"

Carl Hampton: "Nope, just that night. It was the first time I had seen him since I found out about his little secret. Boy, did that backfire for him."

Mr. Davidson: "No need for smart remarks, Carl. Just get to the point, where did you first confront him?"

Carl Hampton: "At the bar down on Jared Street, not sure exactly what time, but it was dark. Definitely after eight. I texted his wife Jessica asking if she could tell Michael to meet me there for a drink. I didn't have his number—like I said earlier, we weren't that close. But he showed up anyhow, gave me the benefit of the doubt I guess. What a shame that was. I confronted him about the whole situation; about sleeping with my wife, about keeping it from Jessica and I. Only a weak excuse for a man wouldn't have the guts to own up to something like that, and yet, he didn't. He swore up and down that it never happened, that he and Lanie's relationship had never been anything more than purely platonic. But I know a lie when I see one, and he was lying straight through his teeth, even the fake ones."

Mr. Davidson: "Excuse me?"

Carl Hampton: "Take a joke John, lighten up a bit."

Mr. Davidson: "I will not lighten up, and this is not a joke. You are the sorry excuse for a father, not Michael, and killing him makes you no better of a man than he was, no matter what he may or may not have done with your wife. You took a man's life, you took a little girl's father away from her. You are the reason that myself, along with half this town, have lost countless hours of sleep sitting up wondering if there's still someone out there hunting us and our families."

Carl Hampton: "Good. You all deserve a little wrinkle in your perfect fairytale lives, because guess what? I still won, and you couldn't even prove it was me. You think that I don't know why this case bothers you so much? It's not because of that girl out there left without a father, and it's not because what I did was against the law, it's because you weren't smart enough to catch me on your own, and you know it. Heck, you still aren't smart enough. You let two sixteen-year-old kids do it for you. And that bothers you more than you will ever admit. Pathetic."

Mr. Davidson: "I love the effort Mr. Hampton, but you couldn't possibly be more wrong. You are the one who is pathetic, and you were just cornered by that sixteen-year-old girl an hour ago. And not just any girl, Michael's daughter. That, my friend, is karma if I've ever seen it."

Carl Hampton: "No, karma is what he looked like when I was finished with him. You wanna know what happens when you mess with my wife, Officer Davidson? Let me tell you and feel free to share it with the world. I want everyone to know what he had coming. I let him leave the bar alone, or so he thought. I hopped in my car and followed him until he got only a few miles from his neighborhood, Earlpark, I think it was. That's when I waited for there to be no other cars around and rammed into the back of his truck. He tried to get out and run, but the threat of a gun proves a lot more effective than you'd think. I pointed it and yelled for him to get in the trunk of my car, which he easily fit inside. Poor guy really needed to hit the gym. Anyhow, I drove him out to some land that Lanie and I own over on Hirsten Court. We've got a barn up there that I knew no one would be at. I threw him out into the snow in front of it. He tried to fight back. He really did, but it didn't last long. I almost felt sorry for the guy, but it brought me joy to see him pay for what he did. I dragged him into the barn and laid him on the floor in one of the back corners. It was coldest back there, one of the windows had been busted out. Perfect place to let him sit and think about his short life, or what was left of it."

Mr. Davidson: "So what happened after you brought Mr. Cassidy to the barn?"

Carl Hampton: "I drove back to where I left his totaled car and moved it, but I'm sure you know where that was. Then, I went back to the barn with a pipe I bought from Willie's a few weeks before and gave Mr. Cassidy what he was due. And to answer the question that chick asked me earlier, no, I do not beat up on people because I feel threatened. I do it because they usually have it coming."

Mr. Davidson: "Usually?"

Carl Hampton: "Well yeah, I didn't give everyone you accused me of a beating. For example, Berkley's kid, I didn't have nothin' to do with that."

Mr. Davidson: "Oh really, because your wife told us otherwise. We also have a witness placing you at Willie's store the night she was taken buying items of suspicion."

Carl Hampton: "Oh, this is good stuff, please continue. What exactly are you classifying as items of suspicion? A flashlight? Tape? Man, I'm redoing the frame in our garden. That's why I needed the light. Lanie's been nagging me about fixin' it ever since last year. I finally got up the energy to do it. Is that a crime now too?"

Mr. Davidson: "No, but I had to ask. We will come back to Ms. Berkley, but for now, I need you to finish your account of Mr. Cassidy's murder."

Carl Hampton: "Murder, that's such a strong word. I prefer the phrase "doing what needs to be done". I heard that on a show once, figured I'd roll with it."

Mr. Davidson: "This is not funny."

Carl Hampton: "Hey, I banged him up a little, but that's it. I didn't plan to kill him or nothin', but he just couldn't take anymore. He wanted to stay strong for his family, I could tell, but his body wouldn't let him. Like I said, he should've invested in a gym membership or somethin'. All I did was put him by the road so that you wouldn't find him in the barn. I didn't mean to kill him. But I can't say that I fully regret it either."

Mr. Davidson: "You know, for a pretty intelligent guy, you sure are stupid."

Carl Hampton: "Excuse me?"

Mr. Davidson: *"That ditch is still on your property. You really didn't think we'd search the land?"*

Carl Hampton: *"Well you didn't find nothin' useful, now did you? Exactly, not so stupid after all."*

Paper rustles across the table

Carl Hampton: *"What is this?"*

Mr. Davidson: *"This is a copy of the test Dr. Berkley performed on your wife, Lanie, over four years ago. We found it behind a drawer at your residence. It proves Mrs.Hampton does in fact carry the gene that caused Cade's hypodontia. She just never told you because she didn't want to be blamed for your son's defect. Cade is, in fact, your son, Mr. Hampton, Michael was telling the truth when he denied sleeping with your wife. You could have simply had a paternity test done if you feared otherwise."*

Audio silence

Mr. Davidson: *"Sir, do you have anything else you would like to say during this confession? If not, I am going to end the recording, and you will be escorted out of the room."*

Carl Hampton: *"He still deserved everything he got."*

Mr. Davidson: *"Okay, I am going to stop the recording now. Officer Chesley, will you please handle Mr. Hampton?"*

Carl Hampton: *"Alright, wait. Now I admitted to killing Michael, but I swear I didn't kill no girl. And I ain't got nothin' to do with that one you found in the forest either. Well, at least not her death. I just delivered her, so don't be blamin' me for that, too."*

Mr. Davidson: *"Her name is Gabriella, and she flatlined over twenty minutes ago. You've already admitted to her kidnapping, and I have nothing to prove that you did not commit her murder as well, you will be investigated for her death at a later date. This confession is over."*

Carl Hampton: *"Wait, I didn't kill her, I swear. But I can help you find whoever did."*

Mr. Davidson: "I know you were contacted by a burner in reference to Gabriella's kidnapping, but even you said that you failed to trace it. Our department is working on confirming that, but it's lookin' to be a dead end. If you have withheld information from me about this, I will have no problem finding a few more charges to pile on your record. Don't test me, Mr. Hampton."

Carl Hampton: "Would you rather sit here and argue about somethin' else I did wrong, or would you like to hear what I know?"

Mr. Davidson: "Fine. Let's hear it."

Carl Hampton: "Alright, now I don't have a name, just an address. It was originally where I was told to drop off Gabriella, but it changed last minute. Hold up, I wrote it down somewhere."

Static

Carl Hampton: "Here we go, umm, sorry, I don't have my glasses. They really weren't jokin' about that after forty thing, were they? Let's see here, the Old Garrett Inn, room three-sixteen. There, just check it out, and if you don't believe me after that, then we'll talk. But don't charge me for somethin' I didn't do."

Chair screeches across the floor as Mr. Davidson exits

Officer Chesley: "Sir? What do you want me to do with the detainee?"

Mr. Davidson: "Book em.'"

End of recording

Cade and I threw off the headphones we had temporarily pressed into our ears and raced for the metal door already being swung open by Mr. Davidson. Our eyes met, both my mouth and his, wide open. All these surprises compiling inside the file cabinet that is my brain are beginning to overflow, out of both shock and unexplainable joy.

"Well, whatcha waitin' for? We've got a hotel room to check out."

He ran out of the audio room expecting us to follow, heading straight through the lobby and out to his shop. Apparently that's what they call their police vehicles, "shops".

See, you learn something new every day.

The minute all three of us shut the door was the same time every other offi cer on duty came barreling out the station doors, headed for their shops to join us on the trip. Before I knew it, every siren was blaring and every light was flashing up and down Main Street, all headed to the same place; the Old Garrett Inn, a crappy rundown building just inside city limits. I've only seen it once before, on a field trip my class took back in second grade when we visited all the old Stonson monuments. I'm still not quite sure why the inn is considered a monument. At the time it seemed like nothing more than a dying business, but when we arrived there tonight every light was on and the inn was up and running better than ever before. Sure, it may be halfway caved in, but it's doing well enough.

Mr. Davidson parked the car practically on the curb, telling Cade and I to stay put while he coordinated with other officers.

As if we're gonna to do that.

Instead, Cade and I slipped out of the backseat and headed inside, everyone else still in the parking lot gathering their thoughts. The woman at the front desk is nothing like Bryce from the station, appearing as if she's been on drugs for years.

In retrospect, she probably has been, so maybe I shouldn't joke about that.

She pointed us in the direction of room three-sixteen, filing her hot pink nails as she did so.

Cade leaned closer to my ear, whispering, "Charmer."

He still manages to find a way to make me laugh even in the scariest of times, and I think this definitely makes at least the top three. Honestly, the fact that it isn't first on the list says a lot.

When we got to the room, there was nothing out of the ordinary, just a DO NOT DISTURB sign on the handle. The door has been painted a mustard yellow, only a bit better than the brown color that coats the hallway leading up to it. This whole place gives me the creeps, even more so than when I came in elementary school.

Cade scoffed, "If this is a monument, I'd love to see what they consider an eyesore."

"Kids, what did I tell you? I specifically asked you to sit in the car! You have no idea what might be in there."

Mr. Davidson finally caught up to us, and he's not alone. Twelve other officers followed close behind him, each holding a weapon of their own. They wore vests almost like the ones I've seen on television shows, black boots to match. I've never seen the cops from our little town so serious about anything before. They must really think this guy is dangerous. But what are the chances he's actually in there? With our luck, he's probably long gone by now, and my guess is that Brynlee remains with him.

Mr. Davidson and the other officers motioned for us to step back, taking their positions to approach the door.

Bang bang. "Police, open up!"

They knocked once more when there was no answer. Bang bang. "We're comin' in!"

Before I knew it, that mustard colored door had been busted to pieces, proof that it was rotting for years. All thirteen of them filed into the small room, guns drawn and brains on high alert. About thirty seconds went by before we heard someone yell, "Clear!", meaning that it's safe for us to come in.

I walked into the crowded room, Cade following behind me. He stood so close that I could feel his breath against my neck, fast and short. He's scared too, but he has every right to be.

Once we got all the way inside the room, I noticed Mr. Davidson staring at something on the opposite wall from where we stand, others joining him. I finally made it through the crowd and took a spot next to his tall stature, gaining a clear view of what he'd been staring at with such intense concern.

"Holy mother of..."

I won't tell you the words he used next, but let's just say that God would not approve. However, the sight before him definitely warranted an "apples" or two.

There, on the clandestine wall, hangs something out of a horror movie. At first glance, it almost seems like a joke, appearing much too cookie-cutter to be real.

In front of us is a collection of photos, every three or so separated into their own area on the wall. Every cluster is of a different girl, four clusters total. I don't recognize two of the girls, but I sure know the others. One photo in the highest cluster is of Gabriella holding up a drawing she must've made in school. Another is her yearbook photo, a gorgeous picture considering the poor quality school photographers come in nowadays. But sadly, the last photo is the most heartbreaking. The image depicts Gabriella balled up in the corner of a dark room, tears in her eyes and dirt on her face.

To the left of Gabriella's cluster hangs three more photos. This time they're of a slightly older girl, Brynlee. One photo is her winning a math competition at school, another her yearbook photo. The last photo is almost identical to the one of Gabriella, but this time it's Brynlee curled up and crying.

The two clusters that I don't recognize are similar; three photos, one of the girl crying, and two of her at school. It's inhumane, what I'm seeing. The way they're hung so methodically, so precisely, it's absolutely sickening. There's nothing that doesn't match, nothing out of place.

Well, there is one thing.

In every photo of the girls crying, one thing in particular bothers me. Every girl's shorts look bigger than what would normally fit her petite body, each girl wearing a different pair.

Cade nudged my shoulder, jarring my attention from the first horror to a new terrifying sight. Below the photos sit four petri dishes, three with something in them, and one without. I bent over and examined them, careful not to touch anything.

I've watched enough television to know that you should never touch anything at a crime scene unless you're wearing gloves.

The farthest dish to the right contains a small ring, its ridges lined with particles of brown dirt encrusted along the outer rim. The ring itself appears covered in light pink jewels, Panama City Beach 2016 etched on the inner loop. The dish beside it holds a bracelet, this time gold and bare. It looks unusually tiny, as if it's meant for a child even smaller than any of the girls in the photos. The final dish before the empty one is home to a single earring, one half covered in dried blood, the other only fading in color. The design itself is a unicorn head with a letter on its cheek.

G for Gabriella.

Officer Chesley noticed the petri dishes about the same time Cade did, kneeling beside me to get a closer look. "Something from each of his victims. Makes me sick."

One man ran out of the room and threw up. At what, I don't know for sure, but I can pretty easily guess. Apparently not every cop has as tough of an exterior as we've been led to think. After all, they're just people like the rest of us. And no one, no matter their occupation, should ever have to see evil like this.

No one.

And yet here I am looking evil directly in its cruel eyes. Except this time, I'm not alone. I have a family to get through it with. But those girls on the walls, they have families too, families who may never get to see their beautiful smiles again while on this earth.

Suddenly, Cade spoke, working up the nerve to ask the question we've all been wondering.

"Why is one of the dishes empty?"

Everyone looked around, waiting for someone to answer the question, and finally, someone did.

"That's Brynlee's dish."

"Yeah, but why is there nothing in it?"

"He's not done with her yet."

316

PLEASE
DO NOT
DISTURB

THIS GUEST HAS
ASKED THAT YOU
DO NOT DISTURB
THEM FOR THE
DURATION OF THEIR
STAY.

OLD
GARRETT
INN

Chapter Thirty-Five

September 27, 2023~12:01 AM

"Something doesn't add up. I just can't quite place my finger on it yet."

It's midnight now, and neither Cade nor I have left the Old Garrett Inn since we first arrived. Technically, room three-sixteen isn't a crime scene, since we have no direct proof that any crimes have been committed against those girls unless you include Brynlee and Gabriella, but they still have to process the horrid scene.

Mr. Davidson said that they plan to get a warrant in order to see who rented out the room. They can't legally get that information otherwise. The lady at the front desk, scary as she may be, was actually a bit of help, according to Officer Chesley.

"Clerk described seeing a white male, lean but average height, rent the room from an associate who was on shift last night. He paid cash for the week in full. Oh, and he was bald. That's all I got."

I guess that's better than nothing.

How could someone do something so cruel? Even just seeing the photos makes me sick to the stomach.

"The warrant will take at least another day, especially with no judge in town awake at this hour."

Mr. Davidson says "no judge" as if there are more than a total of two in Stonson, both getting closer to retirement by the hour. I feel as though, considering the circumstances, there has to be some law allowing them to see who paid for the room without a warrant. We just found the jackpot that every detective would kill to find in a case like this, and yet we aren't even able to pursue it for another twenty-four hours. In that time Brynlee could be far away from here, or worse, she could be dead.

"Excuse me! Comin' through guys, just gonna scoot right by you..."

As I turned around, I saw a boy making his way through the crowd of officers and intrigued spectators behind the yellow tape, screaming as he plunders closer. Well, more like shouting into the night, waiting for anyone to acknowledge his cries.

"Kid, you can't come through here." An officer stopped the poor boy just before he crossed the tape, but Mr. Davidson motioned for him to be let in. For a second I wasn't sure why he was being allowed so close to the hotel, but then I realized who the boy was.

Brynlee's ex-boyfriend, TJ.

I guess Mr. Davidson has talked to him about her disappearance prior to tonight, because they already seem quite well-acquainted. TJ can't possibly be more than a hundred and twenty pounds soaking wet, a very scrawny young man. The way he once appeared to me in biology is much different from how he looks now, probably a result of the heartbreaking recent events he's had to endure.

"Sir, I heard that you found her. Is it true? Do you have my Brynlee?"

I stood up from my low seat on the curb and brushed off my legs, heading over to where the two now stand talking. As TJ spoke, his eyes expressed genuine sadness, a clear sign that he's lost a real friend. I guess it's true what they say about relationships; when the other person is gone, you miss the friendship you once shared more than anything else—more than the puppy love, more than the anniversary gifts, more than any of the classic things couples do—you miss the friendship.

Simply the feeling of friendship with his beloved partner, that's what TJ misses the most.

Mr. Davidson sighed and glanced at me, hesitantly turning back to put a comforting hand on TJ's shoulder. "You must've misheard son, she's not here."

TJ sniffled, trying his best to keep from crying. "Well, where is she? I need to see her. I need to make sure she's okay."

"TJ. We haven't found her yet."

In that moment, it seemed as if I was watching his heart break right before my very eyes. I have seen this only once before, on the faces of Brynlee's parents the night of the fire, but this is much more intense than then, because TJ spoke no words as he fell apart inside. Although, in my opinion, his silence is plenty enough for all of us to understand how he feels.

There's that word again, *silence.*

Silence speaks volumes. I know that for certain now.

He walked away with his head drooping, reaching to plug his blue headphones into his small cell phone. Then, he found a comfortable seat on the back of someone's truck bed, although I'm sure this situation is anything but comforting for TJ.

Have you ever simply looked at someone, someone you aren't very close with, and felt the urge to talk to them? In my experience, that's how some of the best friendships and relationships are born. By having real face-to-face conversations rather than discussions through text messages, by being kind and outgoing rather than allowing a peer to sit alone in their own pity during a time when they need people the most.

We all enjoy people in our lives that care, but sometimes we're gratified more by the confirmation of others actually enjoying our presence rather than the feeling of simply having friends.

So I walked over to TJ, his body now slumped down in the truck bed as he bobs his head to a song.

"What's that you're listening to?"

He looked up from his phone for just a second before turning back to it. TJ is clearly just another one of those guys who considers it shameful to cry in front of a girl. I wish he knew how overwhelmingly fine I am with the idea of him crying. Everyone needs to express their emotions somehow. If he needs to cry, it's better to get it out than lock it away inside.

Of all people, I would know.

"It's just a playlist Brynlee made a while back. I don't think she ever meant for me to hear it, but I couldn't help myself."

"I don't think she'll mind."

"Everything she does amazes me. Her creativity and free spirit inspire me more than I tend to admit. I just wanted to see what such a genuine person surrounds herself with, what she listens to in her free time."

"I get that."

"You know, they say the kind of music someone listens to reflects how they feel inside. If that's really true, I'm pretty sure Brynlee had a lot more to say than she was ever given the chance to."

For such a quiet person, TJ sure has a lot to say about Brynlee, even considering she's his ex.

"What's your favorite song she saved? If you don't mind me asking."

He nodded, then took a moment to scroll through the playlist he continues to hold so tight.

"*Something to Someone*, Dermot Kennedy. I can't really explain why I like it so much. I guess it just leaves me with so many questions I wanna ask her, so many things it forces me to think about. That's Bryn for ya, always with a few tricks up her sleeve."

Everything he said made me smile. I can feel myself slowly getting closer to Brynlee just by simply taking part in this heartfelt conversation. I know that TJ made some mistakes while he and Brynlee were dating, but I really think he loves her.

I just hope he gets the chance to tell her that.

"Tatum, right? You know, you aren't as bad as they make you seem."

"What's that supposed to mean?"

He slightly smiled, never answering my question, then continued.

"I don't know why I feel the need to tell you this, but Bryn used to do something else that made me fall in love with her. She keeps a list of principles she tries to live by. Would you by chance wanna see that?"

I laughed as TJ relaxed his shoulders, the same shoulders that have been so tense ever since I walked over.

"Of course I would! I'd love to take a look."

He pulled a small white piece of paper out of his back pocket, uncrumpling it before handing it over. The handwriting on it is faded, a single blue ink stain in the top left corner, but otherwise it's in pretty decent shape.

On the first line, it read "Brynlee Berkley" in an almost cursive font, then began the list directly below it.

- Perception is reality.

- You only realize what you've lost when you try to replace it.

- A woman's heart should be so close to God that a man has to chase Him in order to find her.

- God removes people we love in order to show us what love really means.

• People carry their trauma in different ways...

• Make the effort to love everything that someone hates about themself, it will allow you to see them in a much more forgiving light!

• God gave us two ears and one mouth for a reason. You should listen twice as much as you talk.

• Seeing what someone can be even through their pain isn't a cliche, it's how you stay humane at heart.

• It's only crazy until it happens.

• No man is worth letting go of your faith!

• The right man is someone who you can talk to without hesitation, someone you can have a conversation with and not put in much effort. Effortless, that's what true love is. And it's usually the person who you least expect it to be. Don't try to fight the amazing plan God has for you!

• Trust is something that needs to be earned, except for with God. You can always trust Him.

• God's opinion is the only one that really matters!

• Take things slow, it's usually better that way.

• Evidence is not a substitute for faith.

• Mercy triumphs over judgment

The list was simply that, sixteen of her deepest thoughts and moral pillars. However, one more towards the bottom corner of the page caught my eye, a single asterisk beside it.

Maybe Brynlee is more mature than I've been giving her credit for.

- *The cure to pain isn't something you can buy in a store, it is only found when you close your eyes and fold your hands.

Wow.

"TJ, do you mind if I borrow this for a while? There's something about a bullet she wrote. I want to think it over a little more, if that's okay."

Thankfully, he nodded, and I put the crumpled note inside my weathered pink wallet. I smiled and turned to head back for Cade, looking forward to sharing what I found, but TJ called out just before I got too far.

"Hey, Tatum?"

"Yes?"

He quietly coughed, his sweet southern voice clearing itself as he spoke. "You're a real good person for doin' all this, you know that?"

I smiled, rubbing my finger lightly across the wallet in hand. "Well, I appreciate that." Maybe there is some good left in the world after all, a small sliver of acknowledgement in all of us that recognizes kindness when we see it. The fact that someone I just spoke to for the first time sincerely saw the good in me, means more than TJ will ever know. For once, someone saw something other than a continuous line of red flags.

Thank you, God, for people like TJ. I pray that I can be someone else's TJ one day, but maybe I've already met more than one TJ. I just didn't know it at the time.

A wise friend of mine once told me something that I will never forget. His words were simple, but powerful: "Life can be an amazing adventure if you change your ways and the way that you perceive things. Love over lust, faith over fear, lessons from failures, and stronger from facing adversity."

No one knows exactly how much truth can come from one person's thoughts. The mind is an amazing thing, and the friendships that it brings about should be cherished.

Cherish those memories with Brynlee, TJ, and I promise you will make more someday.

One day.

THE playlist :)

	Song	Time	Artist	Category
	Something to Someone	3:17	Dermot Kennedy	Facts
	Fight the Feeling	3:29	Rod Wave	Cry to
	If I Died Last Night	2:46	Jessie Murph	Scream on the highway
	It Is What It Is	2:08	Jamie Miller	If I could say anything to him

Chapter Thirty-Six

September 27, 2023~8:36 AM

How can they possibly expect me to show up at school the day after something like this happens? Heck, how do they expect anyone to let their child go out at all when there's a rampant killer on the loose?

And yet here I am heading for the building where I more than likely will be committing *social suicide.*

When I got to the school parking lot, it was almost bare, my bike being the only one on our rusted metal rack. I count twenty-two cars, the majority of which are probably teachers.

Looks like people in this town might have some sense after all.

By the time I got to science class, it seemed as if even fewer people were there than I could've imagined, a teacher walking out the front door every ten minutes or so to go home themselves. Only four other kids sit in class with me, one of which is Cade. Beau hasn't shown up, but that isn't a big surprise. Honestly, it's more shocking that Cade came rather than anyone who hasn't, considering the night he just painfully suffered through.

Before we left the inn with Mr. Davidson, a social services worker came and spoke to Cade for over two hours. I wasn't allowed to hear what they discussed for legal reasons, but I know it couldn't have been very good considering Cade came out moping, his eyes puffy beyond recognition. The social worker, Catiey, is someone we've both known for a long time, practically since all this began. She would never have said anything to Cade that was intended to hurt him, but I know she probably had to get into some pretty serious topics during their talk.

She agreed to let Cade stay with Mr. Davidson at his house until they can work out where he should be placed, or in other words, what screwed-up foster home he'll go to until his mom was cleared of any involvement. I'm not sure if Catiey even knows about the situation with Mom and me yet.

Can't wait to see how that discussion goes.

I stayed at Kelly's house for the night, but my excuse for why I need a room won't last much longer.

"My mom went away on a business trip and forgot to leave the key out. Would you mind if I stayed with y'all until she gets back?" Kelly gladly opened up her home to me, Mrs. Gibson overjoyed at the news as well.

"Of course you can! What about your dad? Did he go on the trip too?"

They're still totally oblivious to David and Mom's divorce, so I had to cover that up as well.

"No, he's away visiting some family in Texas. He should be back in a week or so, but my mom will be home before then."

Somehow that load of crap was convincing enough to buy me time underneath the shelter of a safe roof and a warm family, but where I will go permanently is still up in the air. Honestly, both my life and Cade's are goin' up in flames, but neither of us has had a breakdown yet.

Surprising.

"Where is everyone today? I've never had so many kids absent in all my years of teaching. Geez, that made me sound a bit old, no?"

Mr. Daniels has been moving up with us ever since middle school. Every year he swears that he won't be going up a grade, but then right before schedules are released, he proudly announces his new position as a science teacher at our current grade level. Most of us don't mind it, he's a pretty chill guy.

A little odd, but chill.

"Well, there's no point in teaching a lesson with five of you here, so feel free to study whatever you'd like. Or, if you prefer, the other teachers and I are signing a card for the Berkley family. We would love it if some of you students could add your names as well."

What a great idea, although I doubt a card will help much, considering the situation Brynlee is in right now. I can almost guarantee they don't sell cards for this at the general store.

But I signed the card anyhow, and Cade did too, passing it along to a total of three other kids who sit behind us. At least now there's documented proof that we existed during such a time as this, you know, in case all of this blows up in our faces and a news crew catches wind of it. I can see it now: SMALL TOWN HOLDS BIG SECRETS: A KILLER REMAINS UNTAMED AMONGST ITS QUAINT COMMUNITY.

When the clock hit 3:10 and that stupid bell rang through our empty halls, I ran out the front door as fast as my little legs could go. To be honest, I don't even know if I remembered all my stuff.

"Tatum, slow down. You're leavin' me in the dust here."

Oh crap, Cade. I forgot about him.

"I've got to get to the station. They're gonna have that warrant soon."

Cade dropped all his stuff by the curb and aggressively put his hands on his hips, as if he's my father and I his lowly child. "Tatum, you have to let it go. You can't fix every problem that's thrown at you. You can't try to dodge every wave that knocks you over. You, being in the midst of the case, aren't going to do anything other than put both of us in more danger than we're already in. At some point you have to let the professionals handle it. Trust."

That seems like his new favorite thing to say, "trust". What he fails to realize is exactly how hard it is for me to trust anyone after what happened to my dad. But nonetheless, the nerve he has to say such a *demeaning* thing to me, after everything we've gone through to get to this point. We're so close to finding out the truth, to getting every question answered we've spent countless nights pondering over.

And he wants me to just "let it go"?

I'll let it go when I know that Brynlee is alright and that no one is ever going to take away a precious child from her family again, not as long as I can help it.

"So you want me to let the professionals handle it now? Cade, no officer in Stonson, is exactly what I would consider a professional, you know that. If we want anything real to happen, we're gonna have to do it ourselves. And that's what I plan to do, with or without you."

Cade closed his eyes and leaned back his head with a low moan, reluctantly picking up his bags once again.

"I didn't mean it like that. I just want you to know that you don't have to do everything on your own. God gives you friends for a reason. *Embrace* them."

He may piss me off sometimes—actually, he pisses me off a lot—but I know he's usually right. I know I don't have to figure everything out on my own, but it would sure be nice to figure out at least one thing by myself.

"C'mon, you can ride with me. We'll get your bike later."

Cade thinks it's just hilarious that I still ride that old clunker around, but it's my only choice. I don't exactly have the luxury of parents who care enough to buy me a nice car.

Then again, at least mine aren't felons.

We got to his car and headed straight to the station, something we've found ourselves doing much too often recently.

"You know what bothers me?"

Cade always seems to feel more comfortable talking about his thoughts when we're in the car. I think it might be the fact that I can't get up and walk away if I don't like what he's saying.

"What's that?" I can tell he's puzzled by whatever he's about to say, but honestly, what doesn't confuse him at this point?

"The body in the warehouse that we thought was Bryn. How does that fit in? It just doesn't make any sense, Tatum, too much doesn't add up."

He's right, there are way too many moving parts in all this. Someone doesn't just wake up one day and decide they're going to become a murderer. Or are the remaining girls even dead? We don't know, and I don't like that at all.

I don't like not having answers. I've dealt with that feeling for far too long.

Maybe Gabriella's death was a mistake, something our kidnapper didn't account for. The murderer didn't plan for Cade and I to find Gabriella before they could come back and get her. We weren't a part of their itinerary.

So assume the other three girls are still alive, say they're still tucked away from society somewhere. Mr. Davidson said the killer reached out to Mr. Hampton with the proposal to take Gabriella, saying he was impressed with his handiwork on my dad. He wanted help with a project he was planning, but Mr. Hampton only did the one job. As a kind gesture, the two have kept in touch through anonymous emails and burner phone calls. Last week sometime Mr. Hampton received a phone call from his conspicuous friend saying he would soon be in town for a visit. He wanted his help on another "job", but Mr. Hampton was brought in before he could give the killer a final answer.

Something about that story doesn't add up either, it's just too fake. It sounds more like the plot of a horror movie rather than real life. But at this point that's how everything seems, too unreal to actually be true.

And how did Gabriella's killer know Mr. Hampton killed my dad?

"I know. There are a lot of things that've been bugging me too. But for me it isn't Gabriella, it's Brynlee."

Cade squinted, his forehead wrinkling up with small rolls. "What do you mean?"

"The cardigan. If it's true that your dad had nothing to do with Brynlee's disappearance, why was it in your backyard?"

He slowed the car a bit before stopping at the four-way. Deep in thought, he answered, "I've been waiting for one of us to bring that up, but I don't know. It's killing me, Tatum, I can't stand this. Not knowing how long he's lied to me, or if he's lying at all, I don't like it."

"I know, but maybe it's better if he is lying."

"Why do you say that?"

"Because if he is telling the truth, there's still someone out there hurting Brynlee, and we have no idea who it is."

The station was crowded with cars of all colors and models, mild-tempered men smoking cigarettes by the hoods as their concerned wives sit in the passenger seats. It seems as if everyone who wasn't at the high school migrated here.

When we walked inside, a line of angry people by the front desk shoved into us over and over, all waiting for their turn to discuss the town's safety with a willing officer. One woman yelled, "I'd like to file a complaint!" After a moment we heard another agree, someone else quickly shouting, "Our children aren't safe here!"

I can confidently say that an angry mob has officially formed, and it's not a pretty sight. I managed to catch the eye of Bryce behind the front desk, quickly motioning towards Mr. Davidson's office. She gave the thumbs up and buzzed us in, freeing our throbbing ears of the echoing complaints in the lobby.

When we got to his office, Mr. Davidson was on the phone, an intense conversation being held. He waved us in as we took a seat next to an officer whom I do not recognize. Her uniform tag is labeled KAUR, a last name that I recall from one of the files Cade and I reviewed. He kindly placed the caller on hold and introduced us to the woman, who now seems eager to make our acquaintance.

"Cade, Tatum, this is Officer Ziva Kaur, otherwise known as Brynlee's aunt. She has been ever so kind as to personally get us in touch with a judge in Raleigh who can validate our warrant much faster than one here. I'm on the phone with their offices now."

He picked the phone back up and held it out so that we could all hear. The woman on the other line has a strong Jersey accent, very thick and prominent.

"Sir? Are you still there?"

"Yes, I'm here." The line crackled for a second before resuming, a result of Stonson's poor service.

"Good! I have just received approval for your request, warrant 164809, North Carolina, has been signed off on. You can officially access the records needed for your case."

Mr. Davidson's face lit up, but if I was him I wouldn't get too excited just yet. The chances of whoever rented that inn room being someone in town are slim, even less now that so many hours have passed since last night.

"Great! Any chance you can access those records for us, just to save some time? If not, no worries."

The phone line was quiet for a moment, then the woman nervously continued. "I'm not sure if I can do that legally, but I've been reading about what you're dealing with down there. Those poor girls, I can't even begin to imagine what they must be going through. I'll do anything I can to help. Let me just look in the file... I see. It says here that the personnel who signed for room three-sixteen at the

Old Garrett Inn the night in question was one Harrison Lee Daniels. I really hope you catch him. Best of luck."

As the woman hung up, the room quickly grew quiet, Cade and I in shock and the others still comprehending.

And so Cade began the conversation that would soon start connecting all the dots, everything finally beginning to come together.

"Harrison Daniels? As in our teacher, Harrison Daniels?"

"Of course, it all makes sense now. The school photos, the petri dishes. He's been right underneath our noses this whole time."

This is no longer just a story that might end with a big fat question mark. It is now something much more. This is reality, and Brynlee now confronts a much more dire reality than before because, whether we want to admit it or not, someone has been manipulating us this entire time. And not just us, but the entire station and the whole town alike. Mr. Daniels has been a part of this community for over half my life, and the whole time he was a monster hiding behind a basic upper-class citizen's profile. The day we discovered Gabriella, when we thought he was going home to grade that day's pop quiz, he was actually heading out to seek his prey like the predator he really is.

The worst part, unfortunately, is that the man who has been snatching our peers and taunting them is anything but a stranger. In fact, he's considered a friend by more than one of us.

I guess not every relationship is founded on trust, some are founded on lies.

How can someone lie without flinching? How can he possibly lead an entire life, making him appear as if he's nothing more than an innocent victim? He probably gets a kick out of playing us all, and we've been giving him exactly the satisfaction he fiends for.

I won't tell you the words Mr. Davidson used as he ran out in the hallway to get the force ready, but let's just say he must've recently expanded his vocabulary.

Here we go again, on a wild goose chase for someone that, at one point, we all thought we sincerely knew. Except this time it feels different. This is it. No more surprises. Either we find Brynlee or we don't, but no matter what, this is the end of the mystery that has ruled our lives for almost two weeks.

I took a deep breath and grabbed Cade by the hand, his breathing quickening at my touch.

"Here we go."

"She so desperately wanted to share how she loves him.
But rather than telling him how she truly feels,
she closed her lips and sat in silence
as he continued on with his untampered lifestyle.
You think you know someone, she thought,
and yet she could not have been more wrong about
the kind of man she believed him to be.
Otherwise, she would never have fallen in love with him.
Although, to fall in love, it is said that there must be
two people involved.
However, this couple was the exception,
for she so deeply loved him, while he remained
oblivious to her existence.
Or so she thought, for in reality he was just as madly in love
with her as she with him.
That, my friend, is proof that you will
never be able to truly know someone,
no matter how close or far apart you may be.
But you can love them despite the odds—you can

love them with all your heart,
and never once have known their name."
-Unknown

Chapter Thirty-Seven

September 27, 2023~7:27 PM

189 Park Place, Stonson NC. This is where it all started—all the pain and suffering, all the resentment towards each other, all the nights spent in confusion—at the home of Harrison Daniels.

The beautiful ranch sits on over twenty acres of luscious pasture, not a spot without pure green grass, and is occupied by the entire Daniels family. One wife, one child, and a nine-hundred square foot white stable full of beautiful horses that surrounds a luxurious mansion.

And a sick sociopath owns it all.

Such a gorgeous piece of property. Who could've guessed the secrets that lie within its *misleading* beauty?

When we got to the property, the sky was dark, only a single porch light on. The entrance gate can't be less than fifteen yards wide, an electronic code required for entry on our left. The light-colored bronze reflection of the bars stunned my eyes, clearly too expensive for me to even be glancing at. Once you pass through the gate, two marvelous sights surround each side of the car; on the left sits the large stables slightly on a hill leading towards the trees, on the right rows of hay bales and a giant rock lay smack dab in the middle of a field. At first glance, it looks to be an above average estate. A small pink bicycle leans up against the mailbox, but in reality it's more of a dungeon than it is a home.

Mr. Davidson parked his car on the right side of the house, lights still on, but sirens dead. I got out once the officers were standing outside the wraparound driveway and large garage door—actually three large garage doors—and ran discreetly up to a row of bushes lining the back fence. I felt my phone fall out somewhere along the way, but that's the least of my worries right now.

Cade and I sat behind the bushes as we watched the scene unfold, anxious to see Daniels step out and admit to his crimes. Mr. Davidson led the long line of officers as they headed for the front steps, making note of two cars in the driveway. Bang bang bang!

"Harrison Daniels! This is Chief Davidson. Open the door or we'll come in on our own."

A few seconds went by before the door opened, but the person standing before its frame was not who I expected.

"Oh John, hello! Why do you need to speak with my husband at this hour?"

Mr. Davidson clearly hadn't fully prepared himself for an encounter with anyone other than Mr. Daniels himself. He froze at the simple question. Before he could think of an answer, a small figure appeared next to Mrs. Daniels; a young girl in her pajamas.

I forgot about their daughter, a very scrawny but beautiful girl. She reminds me all too much of Cade on that night so many years ago, both just innocent victims about to have their entire lives uprooted, and all because of the sins of their parents. I know that everyone makes mistakes, myself included, but this poor girl has no idea the heartache that's about to hit her.

"Ma'am, as hard as this is for me to inform you, we believe your husband may be involved in the kidnapping of Brynlee Berkley and the murder of Gabriella Hernandez, along with other serious charges. Is he by chance home?"

Mrs. Daniels grabbed her heart, and although I'm too far to see her face, I can tell the news struck her like a knife.

"He isn't here right now, but he just came home and dropped off his stuff from work about an hour ago." She hesitated, somewhat humming, before answering, "He said he was going to get dinner. Listen, I don't know what led you to think he might be involved in this, but I can assure you that my husband had nothing to do with any of those accusations."

Mr. Davidson slowly stepped back, asking permission to search inside the home. She nodded and opened the door a bit further, but made sure to tell him a few things before he entered.

"Please, John, my daughter. She doesn't need to think Harrison is a criminal, especially if he isn't. Be considerate."

He understandingly nodded and squatted down to meet the young girl's eyes.

"Well hey there, what's your name?"

The girl grabbed her mother's arm tightly, only answering after she received the okay to do so. "Madeline. What's yours?"

Her voice was *kind, pure, innocent.* A precious child with a precious name. Her hair is long and thick, blonde all the way from her roots to her tips.

"My name is John. I'm a friend of your Dad. I'm just gonna look around to see if he accidentally took something of mine home with him. Don't worry, I won't keep you from bedtime long."

Madeline nodded, flashing a soft smile that could be seen from even this distance. She's one of those children that is never gonna need braces, no gap apparent in her tiny teeth whatsoever. Mr. Davidson gave one last heartfelt look towards Madeline's mother, then proceeded into the house, three officers following behind while the others remained outside.

Reagan Daniels held her daughter's hand as they searched inside, momentarily shedding a tear that I know she's trying so hard to hide.

I'm sure she doesn't believe the accusations are true, but if there's one thing every mother knows, it's that nothing is certain.

It couldn't have been more than ten minutes before they came back out, Mr. Davidson holding one extra item than he went in with; a leather briefcase, no larger than a decorative pillow, and black. He thanked Mrs. Daniels for her time and motioned that it was okay for her to carry on with putting Madeline to bed. She knows that officers will still be outside when she's done, but family always comes first.

Cade and I finally left our spot behind the brush and joined Mr. Davidson to take a look at what he found. "I don't think y'all can see this. It would be a breach in the chain of evidence."

Of course he has to say that, but after all we've been through together, there's no way he'd take us out of the loop now.

He curled up his lip at our begging faces as a sign of disapproval, but opened the briefcase anyway. Inside lay but one thing: the front page of a newspaper from our local station, the *Carolina Classic*. Its corners appear pinched by small silver clips that attach it to the inner lid, black fuzz matted on in some areas. Except this is not a regular newspaper article. In fact, it isn't a real article at all. The story that fully covers the front page hasn't even happened yet.

Carolina Classic

BREAKING NEWS

STONSON'S KILLER CAUGHT!

Last Monday night, Chief Officer John Davidson finally intersected a break in the case that has haunted his provincial town for almost a month. It all began the night of Stonson's local high school dance when a young girl was abruptly taken from the premises without a trace. Originally, they connected her disappearance to a cold case from over four years ago, where a man named Michael Cassidy fell victim to a brutal murder on Hirsten Court. Fortunately, those responsible for Mr. Cassidy's death have been caught and charged appropriately, but officers still failed to connect the two cases. A true blessing in disguise, the man charged with that murder was able to provide insight into the kidnapping. This not only led to solving the overlooked murder of Gabriella Hernandez, age thirteen, but also to the arrest of a local high school teacher by the name of Harrison Lee Daniels at his residence in Park Place. More details to be released as charges are made.

DEALING WITH SELF-DOUBT IN TODAYS WORLD

Page 42, the story of young girl who struggles with severe anxiety and ADHD. She shares her experiences and how to cope with this diagnosis in such a cruel and modern world.

RENAISSANCE FAIR NOVEMBER 11, 4-11 PM

ON THE BACK OF THE page was a note, written in red marker.

Finally! Welcome each and every one of you, to the game of a lifetime. Congratulations on catching me, for I have no problem being caught, but why not make this fun, no need for second thoughts! She loved me and I loved you, written below is your very first clue:

If you find this paper to soon be true, follow the car whose color is blue.

An officer in the back shouted, "Does he think this is a game?", his peers clearly agreeing. "I refuse to go on a childish scavenger hunt to get this guy."

Mr. Davidson did not take any note of their opinions. He's determined to catch Mr. Daniels, whether it's under child-like circumstances or not.

A perfectly average guy with a beautiful family, revealing his sick mind through an inhumane joke. We should've guessed.

The part that bothers me most about his note is something Mr. Davidson hasn't seemed to acknowledge yet. "Congratulations on catching me, for I have no problem being caught." Daniels has already accepted his fate, that's very clear now, but the reason for the newspaper gimmick is much more confusing to me. It doesn't fit with the rest of the letter, it's out of place.

Daniels has decided that if he has to go out, it must be with a bang. Instead of trying to run, he's making an attempt to grow his status, get more attention turned on himself. The more game-like he makes this feel, the more police will view it as a joke. But the simple fact is that this is no joke, it's just him trying to draw more attention to the work he's still so very proud of. The only way to beat him would be to ignore this stupid charade. But then we risk losing Brynlee.

That is, if we still *have* her.

"We're doing it, no questions asked."

Mr. Davidson seems set on pursuing this lead, but only before he realizes that he has no idea what the clue means. It's pretty easy to follow, find a blue car. But the only blue car in sight is Cade's, and it isn't exactly blue, it's navy. Surely it can't be Cade's car that Daniels referred to, but I have to acknowledge the thought.

I leaned over to Cade and whispered in his ear, just so that no one would think of it before we did.

"Cade, your car is the only one here that's..."

"I know, and that's what scares me."

He walked over to Mr. Davidson to share our discovery, and although it seemed unlikely, they decided to check Cade's car, anyway. He led both Cade and I over to the car, seven or eight officers behind us, some with guns holstered and some still holdin' strong. We stood back while they searched the car, throwing his clothes and belongings out onto the damp grass without a care in the world. Cade cringed as they tossed his things around, but he knows that it's necessary.

Three officers came out saying it seemed to be clear, four more confirming that the outside was safe as well. Then there was of course that one outsider, the one who just had to double-check.

I complain, but without the outsiders of this world, some of us wouldn't be alive.

"Sir, I found something!" The female officer came around from the passenger side of the car, a letter in her hand and a concerned expression on her face. Mr. Davidson took the letter from her, his look now similar to hers. He knows that this may not end well, but he's also aware that he has no choice but to try. For the town, for the Berkley family, and for himself.

He already let a killer slip once. He isn't about to let it happen all over again.

"What's this one gonna say, follow the pot of gold?" The surrounding officers laughed hesitantly, trying not to piss off the chief, but also hiding the fact that they're just as scared as us.

Mr. Davidson's sarcasm is just a mechanism to hide his fear, something I learned about in psychology class. The mind is an interesting thing, every channel set on a "different wavelength". Each part has a unique purpose. It keeps us functioning the way we're supposed to. It really makes you think, what would life be like if everything always functions the way it's supposed to? I know that technically it does, because everything that happens is a part of God's plan, and for that we should all be forever grateful.

But what would it be like if the world was still perfect?

Every situation with only positive outcomes, every boy you like feeling the same way, and every day a good one. No more war, no more anger, no more petty arguments that hurt far past the short time during which the fight was held. Even the little things would be great; the way we make others feel, the almost disguised smile we send in a friend's direction just to cheer them up. If we all threw out one compliment a day to someone we don't know, would our self-esteem sky-rocket?

Maybe then there would be a little extra kindness to go around and a lot fewer tears shed underneath the deafening silence we hear when in private.

Do you ever sit down and look at someone, wondering what could be going on inside their head? Not in a creepy way, but you just can't quite figure them out. Everyone else says they're weird, maybe even antisocial, depending on who you talk to. But you don't think that, because you see that they're just misunderstood. They're smarter than half the population, and they recognize the need for people who simply sit back and observe. Waiting for the perfect time to act, waiting for the right time to talk to the right person.

But how do you know who the right person is?

That's the thing; you don't.

Everyone says when you meet "the one" it will be so obvious that it'll practically do all but smack you across the face, but I'm not sure I completely agree with that. Especially in today's world, it's becoming harder and harder to meet someone who is transparent and genuine. Someone who isn't caught up in social media traps, who isn't flirtatious with every woman they see, someone who is simply themself. You see, opposites attract, but only to a certain extent. You still have to share the same pillars, the same beliefs, and the same values in order to be compatible.

God makes exceptions to this rule, of course, but that's because He knows that they can make it work.

So back to my point, how do you know when you find the one? I think that if I meet that special someone, the person I pray God blesses me with one day, that they will fall for me just as I fell for them. I pray that they will be the easiest person to talk to, someone I can call for hours and hours and never run out of things to talk about. Someone that I so much as see and those unique parts of my brain light up like fireworks, joy pulsing throughout my body. And lastly, I pray that they share those same beliefs with me about my faith and family, and love God. This person wouldn't be afraid to love me just because we don't have the same friends. They wouldn't be scared of judgment from their peers. They would simply enjoy me, love talking to me, and cherish hearing my thoughts.

Now, let's swap around the perspective. Say that you are someone's person, you sweep them off their feet and you care for them deeply. You love them no matter their friend group; you care for them no matter what they think about themselves or about politics. You share the same beliefs, but are also willing to work on the topics you find yourselves in disagreement about. You see them and your day is automatically made better. You don't have to work too hard to smoothly carry on a conversation with them. You don't stand in the hallway waiting to see if they will approach you. You can just run over and start to rant about your day knowing they will know exactly what to say. They don't care when you get a little hyper and act immature, in fact, they match your energy, and you do the same.

That's the kind of person that God wants you to be for your special someone. A compassionate, caring, and observant companion they can always lean on.

Yet here I am, standing next to my special someone, allowing his own mind to get the best of him while I hesitate to step in.

What am I to Cade if not first his friend?

I want to be his person just as he is mine because I know that God is leading us to each other, but how can I be his person if I can't even comfort him when he needs it the most? I can't tell what he's thinking, much less see how he really feels. I used to be able to look into Cade's eyes and read him like a book. His eyes are the only thing he leaves unlocked. He can't hide them. Their blue haze is essentially a window into his mind. They're the most honest part of him. He pushes people out when he needs them the most. He shuts down the minute anything gets hard, but you would never know unless you're close enough to him to understand how his mind works. He appears more distant than most men his age, even when he isn't trying to be.

That's what hurts me the most to see, the fact that no one else notices his pain.

All they see is a goofy, yet extremely tough guy who feels the need to overcompensate in order to keep his image as it is.

But what I see is so much different.

I see a young boy too scared to screw up any more than he already has. He feels responsible for the troubles in his life, and he wants to cling dearly to anyone that's willing to give him a second look, but he doesn't. I don't mean friends; believe it or not, he's actually very picky about his friends. I'm talking about the ones he truly cares about; his family. He wants to do everything perfect, aiming to never let them down. Then, he gets hurt if it doesn't work out. Instead of facing the fact that God didn't want them in his life anymore, he blames the world for his problems.

So when he finally finds someone that is willing to work with him and try her best to bring him closer to God, he freaks out and runs away. "It'll never work. She's just like the rest. This is all a game to her, back out now." That's what he tells himself every time he sees her, every time he sees me. What he doesn't know is just how much my heart hurts when he ignores me, how disappointing it is to see his actions do us both harm. And yet I have no desire to force him to love me as I love him. That's not how my feelings work. I just miss the bond that we shared as children. I miss our friendship more than the thought of a potential relationship.

Everyone tells me to let him go, and essentially I have. But when I see Cade in pain, putting on a fake act in front of his friends just to cover up the guilt he feels inside, it does nothing more than break my heart.

Not because I love him romantically, although I do, but because I love the person he truly is.

I would be happy if he found a girl who loves him too, but she'll never know him like I do. She would never know the stories she missed when we were younger, never know about the Friday night games when he cried alone in the locker room after a loss. She won't know his favorite Bible verse, she won't know the things he fears telling her about. He doesn't want to lose her, so why scare her off by sharing the real guy he hides so deep inside?

She might love the guy he appears to be, but she will never love him like I do.

I love Cade like a sister, but also like a wife. I know that seems dramatic, but I don't mean it to be weird. Allow me to explain; a sister is concerned when she sees her brother cry. She can tell when something is on his mind, but a wife learns his routine, she notices the little things that no one else can. Apart, they create an image of a great man that is recognizably strong. But together, the two know the best and worst of a man they both love.

Different perspectives, but the same deep love for a sheltered soul they see is hurting.

Cade is my sheltered soul, he's the one that I pray I have the rest of my life to fully figure out. Other girls might see him as antisocial or clingy if he grows to care for them. They might see him as a tough guy who focuses on just two things—sports and the gym. But I see him sing with his hands raised in praise every Sunday at church. I see his face when he knows he's in the wrong. I see the joy he feels when laughter fills the room.

If Cade ever didn't love me, I would accept it and move on, but that doesn't mean I wouldn't continue to love him. I would still stop and pray over him if I saw that he was in pain.

And that's the difference between the rest of the world and those who truly love him. We notice his pain, even when he tries so hard to hide it. But no matter the number he can bench in the gym, no matter how fast he can run, that strength doesn't transfer into his emotions, and he knows it. He's aware that his greatest weakness is his emotions. That's why people pray for him, because they see it too.

Sometimes you just need a *friend* rather than a *girlfriend*, someone in sweatpants who cares about you rather than someone in a tight dress and loads of makeup.

That's the difference between true love and plain attraction.

Attraction is a love of the eyes, but true love cannot be weakened by even the worst days. In fact, it's on those days that the bond grows stronger than ever. If there ever comes a day when Cade no longer cares for me, I wouldn't think of him as a boyfriend, but I would still love him.

And that's what I need to be for him right now; a friend rather than a girlfriend, someone who can be his shoulder to cry on when he needs it the most. He may not have been that person for me when I needed it four years ago, but forgiveness isn't always a two-way street.

Cade didn't move as Mr. Davidson read the letter. He only stood and stared at the faded paper and envelope as if it was a newborn child crying for its mother. I leaned over and laid on his shoulder as he remained still, swapping out my lover hat for my friendship one.

"He was in my car, Tatum, he could've done anything. You were in that car, and if anything ever happened to you..."

My turn to step in. "But he didn't, right? Nothing happened."

"But it could have. You don't understand."

"Cade, I'm okay. If he wanted to hurt me, he would've already done it by now."

Silence. He kept those beautiful lips of his tightly shut while I continued to stare at his motionless face as his eyes remained locked on the letter. I smiled, realizing exactly what I need to say to get that angered expression off his face.

"Cade, have I ever lied to you?"

Finally, he smiled, letting out the first laugh I've heard since we arrived at Park Place. Guess he knows now that I really haven't ever lied to him, at least not officially.

"You guys ready?"

I turned away from Cade, sadly breaking my stare with those deep blue eyes.

I love those *deep blue* eyes.

Mr. Davidson patiently waited for the two of us to watch before opening the letter, taking his time to slip on a pair of white crime scene gloves. I nodded, wrapping my hand tighter around Cade's arms, now covered in chills. He opened the letter, glancing over it before proceeding. One eyebrow raised, he concerningly reached out the letter towards Cade.

"Uh, kids, I think this is for you two."

It always makes me smile when he calls us "kids". It's like he still thinks of us as those twelve years old sitting in his lobby eating Fritos. He handed the letter to Cade, a pair of gloves coming before the exchange. Cade slipped them on and moved the letter into both our eyelines, taking a deep breath before reading it aloud.

How proud I am of the new couple finally realizing their true potential!

Who knew that opposites really can attract?

But you aren't exactly opposites, are you?

No, the two of you are essentially the same person who has dealt with the same tragedy.

Which corner you see it from, however, determines how you have chosen to let it affect you.

One of you spent your childhood weighed down by the guilt of not knowing what could have been.

The other, spent everyday learning more about how this tragic world works, and tried your best to make sense of why it all happened.

So, how are you going to let this affect you?

Think about that.

You may not be children anymore, that I am aware of, but you still have those memories.

Use them.

Remember, I'm waiting for you, no tricks.

Good luck, *don't choke.*

"NOW WHAT KIND OF CLUE IS THAT?" Cade is clearly not amused by Mr. Daniels' effort to get inside our heads. In fact, he raised his raspy voice to a level much louder than needed. But maybe he's right to do so, because Mr.Daniels is now getting in his head specifically.

This is no longer just a way for him to prolong capture. It is now a chance for him to play with his two final victims, or targets, if you will. And right about now I can feel that cold bullseye being pinned right across my chest, Cade's too.

Except this clue isn't just directed towards us, but it is also much harder than the last one. All it talks about is our past, particularly. It indirectly hints at my dad's murder, but we already solved that case.

There is one thing that bothers me though. Well, there are a lot of things about this that bother me, but just one leaves my intestines churning, the inside of my gut itching for an answer. Daniels knows way too much about my childhood, about Cade's childhood, about what we went through. It's almost as if he has an odd obsession with what happened to my dad, like he feels that he relates to Cade and I somehow.

Is it even possible to feel an emotional attachment to two people you barely know?

Maybe something happened in his life to make him this way. Maybe he lost h is father too. That must be it, or something close, because he sure seems set on targeting that weakness in Cade and I. But what else is there to notice about my dad's case? All we can assume is that he had knowledge of my dad's murder. Maybe it even sparked his interest in killing.

But oddly enough, I have a feeling that his first kill was much before my dad's death, whether we will ever be able to prove that or not.

"Do you have any idea what it means?" Mr. Davidson leaned over Cade's shoulder and read the letter once more, analyzing it for anything he might've missed the first time.

"No, there ain't even a clue in this one. At least with the first one, we knew what part to figure out."

This may not be a game in real life, but that's how we need to view it. This whole time I've been noticing the importance of perspective, yet I am failing to see the need for it right now.

Perspective, that's it.

"We need to look at it from a different perspective."

Cade tilted his head in confusion—something he's been doing a lot lately. "Like how? Turn it upside down?"

I know that he's being sarcastic, but at this point, even that idea might be worth a shot.

"No, I mean read it as if we're a different person. Well, in this case, as if we're the same person, just in a different time."

"You lost me."

"Look, the whole letter talks about when we were kids; the tragedy we experienced, the memories we shared. It's clearly about our childhood, so we need to look at it as if we're readin' it back then."

I know it doesn't really make sense, but for once I just need Cade to trust me. Not as a sister, and not as a wife, but as a friend.

So we carefully sat the letter down on the grass, reading it from our new point of view. But still nothing stood out, that is, until Cade made a dumb observation. That's usually his specialty.

"The only thing that's out of place is when he tells us not to choke, it's italicized. That's gotta mean somethin', right?"

That's when it hit me, a childish answer for a childish riddle.

"Cade, do you remember summer after fifth grade? When your dad had to call 911?" It's a bit of a stretch, but it's all I've got.

"Yeah, because I choked on a piece of pizza. What a day." He laughed, chuckling at the fondness of when his dad wasn't a convicted killer. That's when it hit him, too. We both had the same thought, but we also both know there's a good chance it means nothing.

"The Italian place!"

Mr. Davidson and the other cops both stand puzzled, but Cade and I must look overjoyed. "Sir, that's where I choked as a kid, a memory both Tatum and I share. That's what Daniels must be talkin' about."

He furrowed his brow once more, simultaneously lost and unsure of what we've discovered.

Sighing, Cade elaborated, "It also happens to be the place where my parents were the night Brynlee disappeared. It can't be a coincidence."

Mr. Davidson scratched his head, moving the emerging gray hairs swiftly to the left with his calloused hands, an obvious sign that he lacks faith in our discovery. But fortunately for us, I can tell in his eyes that he's desperate for anything, drained from the tragic search that has taken up most of his nights.

"I guess it's worth a shot. After all, rule number eleven says there ain't no such thing as a coincidence."

I haven't heard Mr. Davidson reference his infamous set of rules in years. He teaches them to every recruit at his station, even mentioned some to me a few times back when I was younger. He claims that they keep him in line, says God left room for us to interpret our own observations and learn from them. He's right, and I know that, but he's never been more right than he is with that eleventh rule.

I don't believe in coincidences either.

He grabbed the letter from Cade, tucking it into his coat pocket as he walked over to the car. "Everyone head over to Anthony's place."

We have one more chance, our third clue, on the hunt of a lifetime. This is no movie scene, no page out of a bestselling book, and certainly no joke. This is reality, and reality has never felt more deafening than it does right now. Sitting at a desk every day in school, that isn't reality. That's the life we've all been bred to be okay with living, the one where going out of our comfort zone is blatantly frowned upon. But going out of that zone is how we grow, and when we grow, we learn.

Let's just say that both Cade and I are learning a lot tonight; a lot about ourselves, a lot about each other, and a lot about this town. Some of what we learn we may share down the road, some we will never speak of again. And that's how life goes; a mixture of stories and secrets. Some you tell, some you keep. But it is also so much more than just those things. It is a time during which we get the privilege to share the gospel of God with others.

So that's what I'll do. If this has taught me anything, it's the importance of faith. Right now, faith is all that either of us has, and it's that all we need. Well, that and the prayer a certain Italian restaurant is open this late.

"For everything there is a season,
and a time for every matter under Heaven:

a time to be born, and a time to die;
a time to plant, and a time to pluck up what is planted;
a time to kill, and a time to heal;
a time to break down, and a time to build up;
a time to weep, and a time to laugh;
a time to mourn, and a time to dance;
a time to cast away stones, and a time to gather stones together;
a time to embrace, and a time to refrain from embracing;
a time to seek, and a time to lose;
a time to keep, and a time to cast away;
a time to tear, and a time to sew;
a time to keep silence, and a time to speak;
a time to love, and a time to hate;
a time for war, and a time for peace."
Ecclesiastes 3:1-8

JOHN DAVIDSON
THE RULES

1. PRAY
2. OPEN YOUR EARS
3. TALK ONLY WHEN NEEDED
4. BE GRATEFUL
5. ACCEPT THAT YOU DON'T KNOW
6. SOME PEOPLE ARE DECEITFUL, BUT DECEIT IS A TWO-WAY STREET
7. EVERYONE GETS A SECOND CHANCE
8. RESPECT IS EARNED
9. DON'T TRUST YOUR GUT, TRUST GOD
10. NEVER GO TO BED ANGRY
11. THERE ARE NO SUCH THINGS AS COINCIDENCES
12. NEVER GIVE UP
13. ALWAYS PERCEIVE.
14. KEEP AN OPEN MIND
15. KIDS ARE NOT AS STUPID AS THEY SEEM, THEY USUALLY SEE MORE THAN WE EVER WILL
16. IF YOU WANT THE TRUTH ABOUT SOMETHING, NEVER ASK A FEMALE
17. CHOOSE YOUR WORDS CAREFULLY, AND MAKE THEM FEW
18. DON'T ARGUE WITH THE WIFE
19. SOMETIMES, A SMILE IS THE LOUDEST FORM OF ENCOURAGEMENT
20. READ YOUR BIBLE
21. BE PRODUCTIVE
22. IT'S OKAY TO STRUGGLE, BUT DON'T STAY IN THAT WAVE OF HARDSHIP, GET BACK UP
23. GIVE THANKS TO GOD ALWAYS
24. BE PROFESSIONAL
25. SHOW OTHERS THAT YOU REALLY CARE FOR THEM
26. BEING ABLE TO IMAGINE YOURSELF IN SOMEONE ELSE'S SHOES IS ONE OF THE GREATEST BLESSINGS THAT GOD CAN GIVE YOU
27. YOU CAN BE WRONG
28. LEARN
29. GROW
30. SURVIVE THE DAY WITH PRAYER
31. TIME GOES BY FAST, SO MAKE THE BEST OF IT
32. GO FOR IT

Chapter Thirty-Eight

September 27, 2023~9:03 PM

As Rabindranath Tagore once said, "You can't cross the sea merely by standing and staring at the water". I think he's right, in most situations. Nothing in life will ever get better if you just sit and wait, unless, of course, you pray while you wait. However, you could be a world renowned poet or an award-winning actor, you could be a homeless drug addict for all I care, but no matter who you are, I seriously doubt you've said a quote that applies to this situation.

No one has.

When we got to the restaurant it was closed, as it usually is every night in a town this small and redneck. But instead of giving up hope, I watched as Cade got out of the police car and approached the building, fidgeting with all ten of his tan fingers. The single front door was locked, all windows surrounding it covered with flimsy white blinds. Below is something written in chalk, partially washed away from the rising morning dew.

"Cade, what is that?"

I got out of the car and joined him as he stood beside the welcome mat near his feet. He looked at the ground, following my gaze, and noticed the same drawing. An arrow, written in light pink chalk and coated over until it was a thick and bold line, lies perfectly outlined inches from the door's base. The arrow pointed back towards us, but this time, we thankfully aren't the target. It appears intended in the direction of a small key hidden from our original eyeline. Behind a vase to the right of Cade is not only the key, but a small lockbox as well. Pure silver, the lockbox clearly isn't for the restaurant, it has no label or street address.

Mr. Davidson joined us, snatching the lockbox from Cade's ungloved hands and flashing him a look of disapproval. He intently examined the box, along with the key. It's not a regular gold or silver color like your average home key, it appears decorated much like a flower. Blue, red, yellow, and white floral design echo from the center of it all the way out to the tip. Mr. Davidson waved over an officer for two evidence bags, but only after inserting the key into the bottom of the lockbox to see if it fit.

"Let's just hope third time's the charm."

When he unlocked the box, it quickly shot open from the right side, revealing a single slip of paper no bigger than a bottlecap. He squinted to see what it said, but his efforts were pointless. There's nothing to be read. Even far away, I can see what it is, and I immediately pulled out Cade's phone from his back pocket.

"What are you doing?"

He grabbed my hand as I reached for the phone, not aware of what's printed on the slip.

"Look. It's a QR code, you dummy. Now give me the phone."

I'm pretty sure that made Cade feel a little uncomfortable, being yelled at by a girl in front of everyone, but he handed over the phone anyhow, probably because he seems just as impressed with my boldness as he is embarrassed by it.

Mr. Davidson flipped the paper over four times before he confirmed what I observed. It is in fact a QR code, printed only large enough to be detected by a camera. He held out the square as I scanned it, grabbing another officer's flashlight in order to have enough light. The camera slowly brought up a yellow link for me to click on, taking just a second to load before showing us the next clue.

Well, if you'd call it a clue.

"OUR HOMECOMING POSTER?"

The retro themed homecoming poster was a single file not connected to the school's website. Just the file, a singular document that may determine whether or not we move on in this game that Daniels calls a journey.

"Wait, look at the address. That's not the address for the school, it's not even the right street."

Mr. Davidson peered over to the phone, squinting once again to see my discovery.

"Hey kid, you might actually be onto somethin'. Cade, put that address into the shop's navigation."

I stared at the poster a little longer while Mr. Davidson threw Cade the keys to his car. He started it up and plugged the address into the navigation system. 1783 Derek Drive. It sounds familiar, but I'm not sure where I know it from.

"Is everything else right?"

I double checked the poster, confirming that the address is the only thing out of place.

Mr. Davidson eagerly asked, "Have any luck yet?"

Cade sits in the driver's seat of the car, his eyes still set on the bright screen.

"Son, I asked you a question."

He turned to look at us, smiling ecstatically. "For once, we just might. Might have good luck, I mean. You'll never guess where that is."

I waited for him to tell us where we're likely headed next, his grin saying everything except the actual address.

"Trinity Faith Church."

That's where I recognize it from. I should have known. If Daniels is at the church, that means we have a home-court advantage. That place is home to half this town. No one would dare make a joke out of it without putting up a fight.

And that's a fight we're willing to wager.

"Will anyone be there this late?"

I've never gone other than Sunday mornings and the occasional Wednesday nights, and even then it was hard to listen to the sermon or pay attention to my peers knowing that Mom didn't know I was there. I may not have helicopter parents, but I sure have a paranoid one.

Mr. Davidson crumbled up the slip of paper and threw it on the ground, stomping to the car as he did so.

"If Pastor Mike isn't, I know someone who will be."

"Seek out the moments when you felt your heart move.
When something changed forever, even if that moment seems
minuscule compared to the rest of the story.
That will be your five-second moment.
Until you have it, you don't have a story.
When you find it, you're ready to begin crafting your story."
-Matthew Dicks

Chapter Thirty-Nine

September 27, 2023~10:13 PM

White. Such a *pure* color, free of shame and blemish. Full of possibilities, cleanliness, and empathy. Ever wonder why most churches are painted white? It's because the color white makes the building perceivable as holy, therefore, what goes on inside is the same. I understand that theory, but no paint color can change the glorious image of God.

I know now that it is possible for a building of such honor to be made into hunting grounds for evil. Shameful, it's such a shameful thing.

We arrived at the church at 10:13 PM, the moon still hiding patiently behind miles of trees, birds furrowing away within shadows of our southern night sky. The bushes lining the front steps have been freshly trimmed, shavings still lie beneath where they sit. The sign out front displays "IS PRAYER YOUR STEERING WHEEL OR YOUR SPARE TIRE?"

Every week it reads something different, usually a Bible verse or sliver of advice. But instead of the writing being highlighted by a bright white spotlight, it sits beneath the shadows of the haunting moon.

The classic white front door to the church stands wide open, a sign that we are not the only ones here.

We exited Mr. Davidson's vehicle, and both put on jackets from the backseat. Despite the usual summer heat, it grows extremely cold when the sun no longer shines above.

"You both stay here, and I mean it this time. I don't want to see either of you anywhere near that church."

The officers seem very serious this time around, but they should know we're much too invested to stand down now. Mr. Davidson killed the sirens and lights, motioning for his force to do the same.

"No sense in scarin' him off now, although I have a feeling it's gonna take a lot more than a few lights to do much of any scarin.'"

There are more than just twelve officers now. I'd estimate twenty or so just including the ones who drove themselves. They popped their trunks and loaded their weapons, quickly putting on vests and every kind of protection they could find. I guess they've been saving this stuff for a long time, for the perfect moment. This isn't what I would call a perfect moment, per se, but it's definitely a trademark one.

For some of us more than others.

They gathered on the pavement leading towards the front steps of the church, Mr. Davidson in front and three large men in the rear. Without saying a word, he motioned them ahead, and suddenly the sound of boots stomping collectively echoed throughout the wooded land. The minute the last man entered the church, Cade and I ran around to a window on the side of the building.

I used to peek through this window as a kid, just trying to sneak a look at the adult service. I hated the nature walks we'd take in Sunday school. The boys would always try to chase me around with a stick or play with my hair. I wanted to sit next to Daddy in adult service, an experience I only got to do a few times.

We could see Mr. Davidson waving his gun around as he circled the wooden pews that line the entrance. The force followed, making sure there's no sign of our lovely friend Mr. Daniels. After holding up his hand to show the all clear, Mr. Davidson waved for an officer to bring in Cade and I.

"Run over there, quick!"

We sprinted back to the car and sat where we were supposed to be, Officer Chesley coming over to bring us inside.

"It's clear. You guys can follow me."

Cade looked at me, a subtle smile on his face. I miss the days when we played jokes like this on our parents, giggling until we burst out in laughter. But I must admit, the tension in the church makes it a bit harder to laugh than it used to be.

"There's nothing here. Maybe we missed something." Mr. Davidson stood, scratching his head as he looked around the pews once again. One officer pulled out a camera to take photos of the church, another a clipboard to begin the report. Except there ain't nothin' to report yet. There hasn't been since we got here. I would say this was all a hoax, a way to lead us away from the real trail, but I know better than that. Daniels is much too egotistical to send us on a pointless chase. He truly believes that he's too smart to be caught unintentionally. He yearns for attention from others, for someone to acknowledge his deceitful actions. It's why he feels as if he relates to Cade and I.

When he wants us to find him, we will, whether it's on our own terms or not.

"Chesley, canvas the baptism pool. There shouldn't be enough room for anyone to hide there, but check anyhow. I'm not putting anything past this guy. Bring Harley with you to document."

Officer Chesley nodded and headed to the left corner of the stage up front, Officer Harley following close behind. The set of stairs leading into the wall is only a flight or two, ending at a small bath of lukewarm water used for baptism. Mr. Davidson let out a long sigh, then headed in our direction, his face drooping as if he's lost all hope.

"Alright kids, you've gotten us this far. What do we do now?"

I looked at Cade, exchanging the same glance we shared back at the barn only a few days ago; a look of distress, desperation, and curiosity. There has to be a reason why Daniels sent us here. Everything he's done so far has had a rhyme and reason to it.

"I mean no disrespect, but I don't think your team looked hard enough. Daniels is methodical, self-centered, he thinks very highly of himself. Reasoning, that's his motive. Everything he's done up until this point was for a very specific reason. He wouldn't just change his plans for the fun of it."

Just as I finished my rant, Officer Chesley waved from inside the baptism pool meters above us. "Sir! I've got something! I think."

We all hustled towards the bottom of the stairs, both Chesley and Harley beating us there. I did my best to look through the cluster of blue uniforms in front of me, trying to lay eyes on whatever Chesley found.

In his hand sits a small boat made of stationery paper, covered in grease stains. Officer Harley snapped a photo of it, pulling a pair of gloves out of his back pocket. He handed the gloves over to Mr. Davidson, who, without hesitation, handed them to me.

"Are you sure?"

"You were right, only fair you're the first to check it out."

No one has ever thought of me first to do anything, so I gladly put on the latex gloves and examined the boat. Cade peered over my shoulder as I held the fragile object. It felt as if a single gust of wind could tear it apart. The boat itself resembles origami of some sort, tight creases and precise corners wherever it bends. Several angles have small black lines across them, words I can't yet decipher.

"Can I unfold it, or do you need it to stay the way he found it?"

Mr. Davidson looked at Harley and nodded, a sign that they're in agreement. "Do whatever you need. We've already got photos."

I'm not sure how in line with crime scene procedures this is, but I guess they've been given a bit more leeway when it comes to such a serious matter. Cade looked at me, his hand now on my shoulder.

"You got it, babe."

He gave me a thumbs up, looking at the boat as his expression quickly turned from a look of confidence to a declaration of fear.

This reminds me of when Cade first talked to me again, the start of resuming what was once such a great friendship. I guess it's true what they say about things changing with age. It applies to people too. Connections and relationships morph into better or worse versions of themselves as time goes on. In this case, I'm pretty sure it's better rather than worse.

Thank the Lord.

I began to unfold the white paper, its thickness making it harder than I originally thought it would be. Once I got it undone and straightened out most of the creases, I held it up for Harley to take a photo. A list of names ran clearly across the weathered piece of paper, *Honor Roll 2019*, written at the top.

"Can I see that?"

Mr. Davidson took the uncrumpled paper from my hands, no gloves on of any sort. But before he got the chance to look closer at the paper, a voice rang through the now partially empty room.

"So you found it. I am truly proud."

I turned to look at the door, attempting to match the voice to a face, Cade grabbing me by the waist as I did so. He pulled me closer to his chest, tightening his grip as we stepped back.

The man at the door wore a green army-like jacket and black pants, taking a firm stance as we all laid eyes on him. His glasses are gripped tightly in his left hand, a handkerchief along with them.

Harrison Daniels in the flesh.

"I was wondering how long I would have to wait for you to finally give the juniors a chance. You know, they could've figured it out all on their own if necessary. I designed it that way."

Are Cade and I the "juniors" he's referring to?

"Lucky for you, I also designed it in case they needed help. Clearly you thought they did."

His voice is *smooth, calm,* no longer with the accent he used all those years at school. At school he was southern, real country, he fit in. Now he sounds distinguished, intelligent, almost British. It's obvious that he is not shaken, nor unnerved, by his place now at the center of guns drawn. He took a step further into the church, one officer yelling "Stop!" as he put one foot in front of the other. He placed both feet on the ground, directly in line with the third row of brown wooden pews.

"No need to worry. I'm not here to cause any trouble. I just want to talk." He smiled a smug grin as he looked directly at the concerned officers around him.

Mr. Davidson took a step closer, blocking Cade and I with his arm. One hand held a gun, the other occupied the paper that he still squeezes so tightly. I grabbed the paper from his hand, something he didn't seem to mind. Cade pulled me back a step further, putting himself in front as if he's trying to protect me. But for some reason, I know Mr. Daniels does not intend to hurt me, he only does that with his victims. I don't think he sees me as a victim anymore. I'm now someone he relates himself to. It was my dad's death that inspired his methods. I'm the one who he's been watching ever since then. This entire ruse was planned for me. Everyone else involved is merely collateral damage.

"Hands up, back away from the door."

The smile stayed on Daniels' freckled-covered face as the command reached his ears, his feet staying in position.

"Unfortunately, I cannot do that. You see, what you ask of me is not in my best interest. However, Ms. Cassidy can change that. Isn't that right, Tatum?" He tilted his head to catch a peek at me from behind the broad barrier of Cade's body. Cade inched closer to me, his posture straightening a little at the threat.

"She doesn't want anything to do with you."

He may be right to speak for me in any other situation, but this time, he couldn't be more wrong.

Rule thirty-two says to go for it. So here we go.

"Actually, I can change that." I carefully stepped out from behind Cade, his eyes practically bulging as he saw me move. I continued, "But you must do something for me in return."

Daniels took a step closer, lowering his hands behind his back as if in the presence of royalty. He's intrigued by my cooperation, I can tell.

"Anything for you, my dear."

He has taken a liking to me for some reason, and not a perverted one that has to do with my gender or waist size. There are plenty of girls involved in this that he could've chosen to "design for", and yet he picked me. I do not look anything like the girls in his photos, but at the same time, I'm very similar to them; we're all lost, all hurting, and all just trying to make sense of a tragic event. It has nothing to do with our race, our hair color, our social status or political standing.

We're all just hurting souls praying for help.

"No, there will be no discussing anything with her. This is not a negotiation, Harrison." Mr. Davidson aimed his gun a little straighter, taking a step towards the third pew, still twenty or so feet from where Daniels stands.

He subtly flared his nostrils. "I'm talking to Tatum, not you."

While I let them continue on for a moment bickering, I analyzed this whole situation. As you look around, the church officers tremble as they hold their guns. No one is standing even remotely close to

Daniels. Most of these men and women have been in Stonson their whole lives. They've never encountered any real danger like they are right now. If something happens, there's a good chance that none of them will do anything to help.

But one officer in particular stands out more than the rest, a taller man with very large calf muscles. He is farthest from Daniels, but closest to the door, as if he's about to run scared out of his mind. Even on the other end of the church, I can see his torso practically shaking, a literal sound being made from his teeth chattering together. The poor guy looks terrified. I know him from somewhere, it's right on the tip of my tongue. Maybe Cade knows him too.

Before I could inch back to ask him, my brain autopilot jumped back to reality. Thank God. I don't have time to be diagnosing anxiety some officer in the back is dealing with. Right now, I need to be focusing on trying to figure out why Daniels only wants to talk to me.

If you look at all of his victims that we know so far, there's four: Brynlee, Gabriella, and the two other girls from the Old Garrett photos. Compared to them, I'm obviously the oldest, the blondest too. I am past the point in my life where others label me as a little girl. I now have a mind of my own. In hindsight, I've had a mind of my own since I was twelve, but at least now others are finally beginning to recognize that. And yet I don't think that's why Daniels took an interest in me. He relates to me because we are both outcasts in this modern world. Both he and I have the potential to be classified as normal, as average, and yet we choose to see everything through a different lens. There's nothing wrong with that. In fact, I recommend seeing people from a new point of view every once in a while.

The only difference between us is that one was made a victim, and the other is the reason victims exist.

It's time to stop the arguing and get back to my turn with Daniels.

"Answer just one question for me, if you can." I took a step forward, showing myself from behind the wall that is Cade Hampton.

He whispered, "What are you thinking?"

I rubbed his arm to calm him. "Trust me, I know what I'm doing."

A look of desperation on his face, he sighed, "Here, at least take this." Cade reached into the small of his back and pulled something out and into view; a small gun.

"Cade, where did you get this?" I've never touched a firearm before. Nothing good could come from me doing so. My dad was always against guns, used to say they do more harm than good.

"Don't worry about it, just take it."

I reluctantly took the gun from his hand, holding it like I observed Mr. Davidson doing. It may be good for show, but if it comes down to it, I won't know the first step to firing this thing.

I'm surprised Mr. Davidson didn't stop me, or at least take away the gun. He stood there, almost intrigued, as if he wants to see how this plays out.

"Darling, no need for such hostility. Ask me anything you desire." Daniels speaks as if this is a seventies Italian mob film, but quite frankly, it fits the tension in the church.

"Why? That's my question. Why? A simple question, for a complex man."

He took a few steps closer; me doing the same, and no officer saying so much as a word.

"Why what? Why does the sky darken, why does the world revolve? Why do we grow up, why do we say things that we know we will later regret? You must be more clear with your questions. I'm getting duller with age." He seemed delighted by my mistake, but he knows what I meant.

"Why did you do all this? Everything; Brynlee, Gabriella, the other girls. And what about the body in the warehouse? Did you do that too?"

He clicked his tongue, moving his filthy hands back towards his sternum. Wagging his finger back and forth, he approached me. Shaking, I raised the gun up to my eyeline. I can't let him see my fear, because fear, although a coping mechanism, is exactly what men like Daniels prey on.

"A magician never reveals his secrets."

Why did he answer so indirectly? I mean, of course I didn't foresee him confessing to every little thing, but you would think that he'd at least want to acknowledge his kills. If there is anything I've learned from crime shows, it's that killers love to showcase their trophies when given the chance. And this man isn't just a killer, he's an egotistical sociopath. He's clearly very proud that I've figured him out, because he knows that no one else can.

"So if you won't answer my question, do I get to ask a new one?"

"Shoot."

That's ironic for him to say, considering the gun that I hold ever so tightly is still aimed at his sinister expression.

"The last clue, if you will. What is it?"

The fourth clue, the honor roll list that Harley just found. There's nothing else to it other than the fact that a name, or verb, or place is written beside each letter of the alphabet. P is Park Place, T is Tres, C is Carla, H is Hampton, R is Riley, et cetera. The one thing that I did notice, however, was the letter Z. Beside the letter read the word "Zealous", except it's in a much bolder font than A through Y.

Zealous, "showing great energy or enthusiasm in pursuit of a cause or objective". In pursuit of a cause, what a great way to describe Mr. Daniels.

But what exactly is his cause, per se? What's his *endgame*?

Just as I was going to ask him, he answered my question. But not with a sentence, with a song.

"ABCDEFG, what is it that you don't see? HIJKLMNOP, this is how it's got to be. QRSTUVWXY, then there were three."

Everyone around looked at Daniels as if he was crazy, each line coming with its own unique voice crack.

"There were three what?"

All he did was look not at me, but at my hand. And not the hand holding a weapon like you might think, but instead, at the hand beside my stomach.

The hand that holds the list.

I'm too close to Daniels to risk putting down Cade's gun even for a second. And yet, I know what he's hinting for me to do. I know why Z was left out, and I know the reason for the Honor Roll List.

Apples.

I turned to the back corner of the church so that I would be facing an officer towards the back pew. I moved my gun as I moved my eyeline, its line of fire no longer put on Daniels.

"Tatum, what are you doing?"

Officer Chesley came up behind me, something that you should never do to a girl with a gun. He questioned my aim, and yet trusted me enough to follow in my footsteps. Before long, all the unsteady and confused officers had moved their weapons so that they pointed where mine was, directly at Officer Tanner.

Tanner stopped shaking, the noise from his teeth finally coming to an abrupt halt. His eyes remain bulged, still terrified, but now for a different reason.

Turning to face Mr. Davidson across the room, he whimpered, "Sir, I mean no disrespect, but why are you following this kid's lead? She has no idea what she's doing!"

I continue to point my gun at Tanner, leaving Daniels in my peripheral vision as I walk towards him. Mr. Davidson finally saw that it's time to step in, probably realizing the lack of reason for what I'm doing. He'll realize it soon enough. Everyone will.

"Hey Cassidy, whatcha thinkin' here?"

I can hear the confusion in his voice, but he still managed to chuckle as he spoke.

"Tres, it's what the letter T stands for on the list. You all thought it meant three, right?" I waited for everyone to nod in agreement, then continued. "Wrong, it's the name of a stuffed animal I like to have by my side every once in a while. Would y'all like to know when I got that stuffed animal?" Again, I waited for them to nod. It's kind of fun. "The night my dad never came home, actually, it was in the police station, to be more specific."

During my explanation, I'm pretty sure I did nothing more than confuse the police force more than they already were, but Cade still tried to bear with me.

"I remember that night, the basketball bear!"

"Exactly. Officer Tanner, allow me to tell you about a woman I met that night. She sat, waiting for her grandson to finish his shift at the station. Do you remember the woman's name?"

Officer Tanner looked to Mr. Davidson, who now stands behind me, his face beckoning for some backup, or even just an explanation. Realizing that his chief was just as confused as he was, he answered my question. "What are you talking about? What kind of story is this?"

"Carla. The woman's name was Carla. And her grandson's name was David, David Tanner. Although I knew him better as New Cop."

His eyes turned an entirely different color, a different shade of green that I noticed even from five or six feet away, then doubled in size. The man standing before me is none other than New Cop himself, just an aged version. He may not remember the fragile little girl who sat and spoke with him on that tragic night, but now that I understand, I sure remember him.

I reached my left hand backwards towards Cade, no longer worrying about Daniels beside me. He's content with being caught. He won't try to run, and he won't try to hurt me. But at the same time, Daniels wants us to know the full story, the whole truth. If he's going down for this, he's gonna make sure that everyone who helped him goes down too.

I already know what happened. It just took a lot of comprehension to put the jagged pieces together, and now everyone else is about to know the same.

I handed the little slip of paper to Cade; him taking it without hesitation.

"Cade, can you read something for me?"

"Sure."

I closed my eyes to remember which letters said what. My partially photographic memory drained from this chase. "Letters C, D, and T please."

He unfolded the paper, scanning it until he found the first letter I requested. "C is Carla."

Still confused but slowly catching on, a few officers looked at each other in astonishment that the woman from the station was listed on the "honor roll".

Cade announced, "D is David."

Thank God Mr. Davidson realized where I'm going with this. I thought he never would.

"T is Tres."

A few officers gasped, finally catching on. Others stood still as they tried to comprehend, wavering their guns back and forth between Tanner and Daniels. Out of the corner of my eye I can see Mr. Daniels drop his head and smile, proud that I've figured it out. Oddly enough, I found myself relating to him just as he related himself to me. Not in the chaotic way that he displayed earlier, but in the sense that both of us are just trying to deal with the trauma in our past.

I'm just glad I handled mine in a very different way than he handled his.

"Sir, I have no idea what she's talking about. I don't know why my name is on that list, I swear, but I know that I didn't have nothin' to do with any of it, if that's what Hothead here is implying."

Officer Tanner grew very defensive of what I've discovered, which, in case you haven't noticed, is his involvement.

"Mr. Daniels, those three names are on the list for a reason. Are they not?" I turned to him in anticipation of a response, his head slowly lifting itself back to eyeline position.

"Well aren't you just a little fireball? John, I think you should listen to this one more often."

Mr. Davidson is clearly not amused by Daniels' efforts to engage in conversation. In fact, he moved his gun back towards him as he spoke.

"No more games Harrison, explain."

Daniels turned his entire body so that it's now facing Tanner. "I think I'll leave that to my friend David here." He thinks this is all just one big game. That's becoming more clear by the second, but if it gets someone to explain Tanner's involvement, I'm willing to play along.

David Tanner stood beside the back pew for a moment longer, sweat practically dripping off of him. And then there he went, dropping everything and running towards the open door. He didn't get far before his fellow officers took him to the ground. As they tackled and held him down, he yelled, "You try living on a cop's salary with four kids and a wife, then you can shame me for doing what I had to!"

What an awful way to go out, caught in your own pride. We all find ourselves in shameful points at times, but I'm not sure how many would result in involving themselves in what Tanner did.

Daniels stood, smiling, recognizing our need for a further explanation. "Did you really think I could do all this on my own? John, I appreciate the confidence, really, but no one is that good."

He held out his hands, ready for handcuffs, explaining more as Officer Chesley slapped them on. He told of how he reached out to Tanner a few months back, as he did with Cade's dad, eager to enlist his help with a new "project". He would need help from someone on the inside if he wanted to pull off his stunt, taking a girl of such status from Stonson. Brynlee is a pretty girl, sure, but Daniels only took her to show what he was capable of. His plan went far beyond just the one kidnapping, but he still needed a man to fall back on, and unfortunately, Officer Tanner fit that profile. A cop who needed a raise and was willing to do what he had to if it meant putting food on the table for his growing family.

Officer Chesley walked over to Cade and me, his face frozen with a confused expression. "I'm still lost on what just happened."

"Honestly, so am I. We'll figure it out at the station. But hey, guess what?"

Still in shock, Mr. Davidson smiled, "Maybe this is all finally over, and I can sleep for more than an hour at night." He chuckled at his own statement, swearing he'll retire once they wrap this up. He grabbed Mr. Daniels by the arm and headed to his shop, the other officers following behind with Cade and I. I'm glad we've found Daniels, I'm glad the hunt is over. But still, there are a few things that just don't add up.

For starters, the clues. This isn't a crime reality show or children's scavenger hunt. Real life crimes don't happen like this, not with perfectly staged clues and humorous riddles. Looking back, they almost seem like a cruel joke, beyond childish things being used for such evil reasons.

Secondly, Daniels himself. I knew he was the kind of criminal who's willing to give himself up once he's completed his "tasks", as he referred to them, but leading us right to him, and right to Officer Tanner? Something just doesn't make sense. It was too easy. Well, let me reword that. None of this was easy, but considering the steepness of prior events, this part seemed like a cakewalk.

Daniels stopped with Mr. Davidson a few feet away from the car, the two having a short conversation. As I got closer, I could see Mr. Davidson's face in dismay, Daniels turning to look directly at me.

"So Ms. Cassidy, aren't you going to ask me about my photography skills?"

Yep, that's the third thing. The photos; the pictures in Daniels' hotel room of the young girls. When it comes to the first two things, all I know is that they bother me, but I can't figure out why. But as for the photos, I know exactly why they bother me. We all assumed those girls were long gone, innocent children made into his poor victims. But if we know he isn't done with Brynlee, how are we to surely say that he is, in fact, done with the remaining two? Gabriella may be gone, but there's still hope for the others.

Well, maybe.

"Fools, you forget how to properly play a game. In order to win, you must play by the rules. Well, my rules state that I still have something you don't."

"And what might that be?"

"The girl."

Brynlee Berkley, and she isn't a chess piece in some game, like he's making her sound. She's just a girl trying to survive like the rest of us. Except instead of trying to survive the tedious hallways of high school, she's fighting for her life somewhere else all alone.

It's as if everyone got so caught up in the thrill of finding Mr. Daniels, on top of Officer Tanner, we let the biggest concern slip our minds.

Where is Brynlee?

"My friends, no need to fret. I gave you three clues. This is no longer a test. You followed them all, found me and now two, but if you look even closer, I'm sure you'll realize what is true."

And then came the floodgates. Another prolonged session of foul language displayed by none other than Mr. Davidson himself. He continued to yell and scream, inching closer to Daniels with every sentence. But Daniels didn't flinch, not even once. He just kept looking at me as if he's waiting for something to be said from my frozen lips. What is he trying to tell me?

I turned around to Cade and whispered, "Can you pull out the last clue one more time?"

Of course he didn't mind, quickly unfolding the paper and passing it over. I held up the paper to show Mr. Daniels, him nodding his head as I did so. Confused, Mr. Davidson finally paused his frivolous rant, intrigued by what I'm doing.

I scanned the list one more time, nothing obvious sticking out. But of course it won't be obvious. Daniels knew he was essentially already caught when he left us this clue, but he clearly finds more satisfaction in us solving his puzzles rather than staying on the run.

Are there any states? Any restaurants or businesses? Maybe the name of a street? There's none of that on the Honor Roll. In fact, there's only one location on the entire list; Park Place. The fake newspaper article did say the "killer" was caught at his home.

Surely Daniels isn't dumb enough to keep Brynlee at his own home. And even if he was, there are officers searching the house. There's no way they'd miss her. But, keeping that in mind, I also know how Daniels' brain works.

Without a star, there is no movie, and without an antagonist, there is no star.

So, now all I have left to decide is this: Does Daniels see himself as the star, or as the antagonist?

I ran over to Mr. Davidson and showed him with my finger the letter P on our list. He grabbed the sheet and held it up to Daniels, only inches away from his freckled face.

"Congratulations, you finally let the girl do something! Now, see how far you can get when you take my advice?"

He took the back of his hand and hit Mr. Daniels across the face, smiling as he handed him over to another officer. Daniels willingly went to another car, waving to me the best he could through tinted windows. I heard my name being called by a female officer waiting to take Cade and I back to the station while the others head to the Daniels estate in Park Place.

Here we go, the last stretch. I'm finally ready, and so is everyone else. We all want a safe return for Brynlee, but now it is something much more than just that. We want to put the lurking evil to rest once and for all, to stop feeling the need to look over our shoulders every few steps. This is our last chance, and I have a feeling that Stonson isn't the town to throw away a perfectly good fight.

"I will not allow my life's light to be determined
by the darkness around me."
-Sojourner Truth

Honor Roll 2019

- A-Aidan
- B-Brynlee
- C-Carla
- D-David
- E-Emily
- F-Franklin
- G-Gabriella
- H-Hampton
- I-Isabella
- J-Jessica
- K-Kin
- L-Lanie
- M-Mourning
- N-Next
- O-Overview
- P- Park Place
- Q- Quadrupal
- R-Riley
- S-Shelly
- T-Tres
- U-Ultraviolet
- V-Vikings
- W-Worthy
- X-Marks the spot
- Y-Young
- **Z-Zealous**

Details are everything.

Chapter Forty

September 28, 2023~1:14 AM

1:14 AM, officers arrive on scene at the Daniels residence in Park Place. Cade and I were not allowed to go back to the house. Mr. Davidson said the time of day combined with the fact that we're minors would cause problems when Daniels is eventually tried in court. I've never listened to his advice before, but I don't mind just this once.

So we sit back in that small audio room eating bags of chips and downing soda while we wait for the call. He made sure his body camera was turned on and working properly, promising to contact us when he could share the live feed. This way we can watch whatever happens at Park Place without taking the risk of contaminating any evidence they might find.

Suddenly, a light lit up on the computer screen in front of Cade. No call from Mr. Davidson, no knock on the door from another officer, just a single blue light. I clicked on the file beside the light, and sure enough there sat the live feed from Officer John Davidson's body camera.

The feed started with Mr. Davidson approaching a shed towards the back of the Daniels' property. Black paint coats its wooden frame, a faded yellow double door on the front. Stopping only a few feet from the dirt pile that lines the entrance, he motioned for his fellow officers to surround the building from the back so that all points of entry are covered. Then, gun in hand and badge on hip, he kicked in the once locked door with a great deal of force.

The audio suddenly became static, the obnoxious sound of muffled boots against concrete flooring quickly overcoming the station's pristine sound system.

Once Mr. Davidson entered the shed, he turned full three-sixty to "clear the perimeter", as he called it. His accompanying officers confidently nodded their heads in agreement that the coast was clear.

There was nothing in the shed except a few metal shelves and some orange construction buckets. Well, that was until a young officer called Mr. Davidson over to share what she found. Or better yet, what she didn't; a small cutout in the flooring, originally hard to notice, but once you find it, you can't help but recognize that something is clearly awry. A rusted metal handle sticks up from the concrete hatch, black paint splatter apparent on the outer rings, once covered by a dirty car maintenance towel.

When the young officer opened the hatch, Mr. Davidson's camera caught nothing more than a small tunnel leading underneath the shed. We heard him laugh at the thought of crawling down himself, so instead, he motioned for the other officer to go down; her slicked brunette bun popping underneath the floor's surface. He then switched our feed to her body camera rather than his.

Once the second blue light turned on and we double-tapped the new file, we saw not only the shed but also the tunnel. The officer, whose tag read THURMOND, is merely a young girl whose hands prominently shake as she enters the tunnel. She can't be more than twenty-five, only about five foot four. I've seen her once before, at the very first place they looked for Brynlee; the school.

She's very beautiful, brown, thick hair and hazel eyes frame her defined face muscles. A little edge in her ear sticks out from a cartilage piercing, lacking an earring to fill it. She seems pretty observant, considering her discovery of the hatch in the floorboard.

She reminds me of myself in many ways, although I've never officially met her. Someone determined to reach her goals no matter what stereotypes or barriers get in her way.

God led her to become a cop, so she became a cop. If God leads me to become a cop, I'll become a cop. Doing whatever we know is right with God, no matter the opinion it may create in the minds of others.

Once she made her way a few feet into the tunnel, all that could be seen through her camera was a stretch of carved out hollow space appearing to lead nowhere. Dark, brown walls line the straight-away ahead, small particles falling from the ceiling. But Officer Thurmond continued to push forward, all the way until a small glimpse of light flooded through a hole in the muddied earth she crawls on. She punched the hole with her fist, at first nothing moving other than a few specks of dirt above her head. Then, with the thrust of a second punch, the hole easily broke through, revealing what can only be described as a miracle.

Well, a miracle disguised as a *massacre*.

Past the hole in the dirt sits a small room, no bigger than your average bathroom. Inside lay four young women, two not moving, and two curled up beside each other.

"Tatum, look..."

Cade pointed to the computer screen, his face expressing both relief and shock. I'm not even sure what to call that emotion, but it sure exists. That I know. His finger aims at one of the girls curled up in the corner, her dark hair and skin recognizable by just about anyone in Stonson.

Brynlee, alive and the closest to well she's been in weeks.

She looked up from her friend and saw Officer Thurmond, the face of whom I'm sure was astonished. Even though I am not in the room with her, I can tell just by watching that a weight was lifted off of everyone's shoulder as Thurmond climbed in to get each girl one by one. Brynlee broke down into tears, her already bruised and beaten face hitting the ground as she praised God for saving her.

The girl beside her also became emotional, but her tears were not as plentiful. This girl looks even smaller than Brynlee, both of their figures already beyond petite. She had no energy, no will to celebrate being saved. She tried, but it just wasn't in her.

I recognize both that girl and another on the ground from Daniels' hotel room, Panama City Beach ring and gold bracelet, if I recall correctly. All three girls got up from the floor, failing to dust themselves off before running towards Officer Thurmond's compassionate arms. She crawled back up to the top of the tunnel with each girl, Mr. Davidson coming into the camera's view with every handoff. When Thurmond handed Brynlee over to him, I saw even through the blurry camera's image that he shed a few tears himself.

I guess even the toughest of men really do need to cry sometimes. How can we expect someone not to share their feelings with the world, when the world has no problem sharing how it feels about them?

Officer Thurmond got the third girl to the top, surfacing for just a moment before returning to the triggering barricade to retrieve the final girl. The sad reality we face is that this hole in the ground has been those girls' home for God knows how long, even the mere sight makes me feel claustrophobic. I can't imagine how they must've felt.

Just one more girl lays in the small room, but neither Cade nor I recognize her. She doesn't match any of the girls from the photos, all of which have been accounted for. She has auburn hair and fair, long legs. Her eyes remain closed, and yet her mouth is wide open, revealing beautifully straightened teeth.

Officer Thurmond's voice came over the camera's audio. "Sweetie? My name is Officer Kelsi Thurmond. Can you hear me?"

No answer.

"I'm going to come over to you now, okay?"

No response.

In fact, there was no noise at all after that, other than the practically inaudible sound of Officer Thurmond crawling to the young girl's side. She approached on her left, both us and the camera discovering a large cut on her torso. The bleeding has stopped, but her entire bra and shirt are still soaked in blood. Her right eye looks deeply bruised, and her fingers burnt and left blackened. She by far looks the worst out of all four girls. It's obvious she has called this hole home for the longest.

Officer Thurmond's hand came into the frame as she touched the girl's neck, what looks as if she's checking for a pulse. After feeling for a minute or so, she put her ear to the girl's lips, listening for breath, but there was nothing. No sign of life and no apparent warmth in her fingertips or cheeks. She reached for her radio and called into who I assume was Mr. Davidson up above.

"I'm gonna need some help down here. I've got another girl." There was a brief pause, then a short response from the other end of the frequency.

"Thurmond, just bring her up. I don't need to know all the details yet."

Officer Thurmond looked up at the ceiling, almost as if to look at God in desperation. She may be more like me than I thought, trusting God with all she does. I try my best, but she's definitely trying harder.

"No disrespect, but you're not understanding. I can't bring her up just yet. She isn't responding."

"What do you mean, she isn't responding?"

You could hear the fear in Mr. Davidson's voice even through the static line, his mind going to the same dark place as Officer Thurmond's.

"Sir, she's dead."

There was a long stretch of silence after that, everyone too afraid to speak, as if the sound of a singular word would collapse the entire shed on top of them. Even through the camera footage, I felt the vibrant joy of finding the other three girls slowly dwindling away, as the realization that they weren't able to help this girl hit the officers like a freight train.

Then, finally breaking the silence, Mr. Davidson displayed his elite skills for everyone to hear, throwing out foul words left and right. After sharing his talent with quite a few of the officers above, we heard him come to assist Officer Thurmond with the young girl's body.

No one recognizes her, and we all know just about everyone who lives in Stonson.

They brought the girl back up, her frail body light as a feather, a result of lying dormant for some time. She was taken towards the front of the house, where a medical examiner took it from there. And then they cut the camera, no more inside view of the crime scene.

I must admit, I don't like being blind. Especially not in a case like this, when what I am being refused the chance to see is also the only thing I genuinely care to look at.

I don't enjoy the gory that comes with the price of helping, or the trauma that I know will likely follow, but the look of relief on those girls' faces make every tear worth crying. Every time I questioned my competency, every stare in the hallway I was forced to pretend I didn't see. It was all worth it.

Anything and everything Cade and I went through over the past few weeks became overwhelmingly worth it as I saw Brynlee's loving eyes fill up with tears as they met those of her parents in the hospital room. She was rushed to the same hospital that Gabriella had been, the only hospital in Stonson, so Cade and I joined to watch the reunions of the three girls and their families unfold. I have never seen such an embrace as that of which was given to Brynlee when she once again felt her mother and father's love wash over her worn and tired body.

Later on, we were told that the girl in the shed, the one who didn't make it, was Kendel McCoy. She lived in Florida, a long way from our small-town recluse. Apparently, those luscious auburn locks of hair were inherited from the girl's mother, the older sister of Mrs. Daniels herself. Now, of course Mrs. Daniels claimed to have no knowledge that her niece had been kept in her backyard ever since she went missing three years ago. That's only a year or so after my dad died, a coincidence that I don't believe to be true.

In fact, after learning of Mr. Daniels actions, she even filed for a divorce with the state, swearing she wanted nothing to do with her "sorry excuse for a husband". But Daniels simply laughed at that news, as if he's actually going to rat her out whether she was involved or not.

For some reason, all I can think about is their poor daughter, Madeline. Not only about how messed up her life will be but also about something a little more on the sinister side. She looks nothing like the rest of Daniel's victims, who all had darker hair and thinner builds, excluding Kendel. It's interesting to me how he only chose girls that couldn't look less like his own daughter. Not exactly what I would call great news, considering in the end a heartbroken mother in Florida will still receive the call that her little girl has been found, just not in the way she hoped for all those years. But nonetheless, three other families get the good news that their angel is safe and sound, no matter the battle scars they'll carry for the rest of their lives. Brynlee will eventually get to come back to school and bless the lives of so many more people as she has mine once she's been released from the hospital, of course.

We often fail to realize just how big of an impact someone has on us until it's too late to thank them for it. Just as Brynlee once wrote on her list of things to live by, "God removes people we love in order to show us what love really means". I never knew just how right she was until now, standing outside her hospital room, taking in the miracle God has given before me.

Cade leaned closer to me, carefully reaching to hold my hand. He lightly squeezed it, a sign of affection that he tends to offer rather than comforting words. We all express love in different ways, but his is my favorite. It still amazes me every day how genuine he is, how confident he continues to be in himself. But not in a cocky way, in the most honest way possible. He's different from most guys, and I like different.

Different, no matter how frowned upon it may be, is what keeps this world together. God, of course, is the true glue that holds us up, but He made us all a little different for a reason. And I've learned that if God gives you a reason to do something, you do it, no matter how different it may be.

Cade and I started dating a few days after everything ended, if you would consider it an ending at all. I guess even the happiest of endings have their flaws. This one just happens to have quite a few.

Three girls saved, two lost.

I'd say that's better than what we all feared would happen, although nothing will ever bring those two back. They'll never get to celebrate another birthday, never get married, never buy their first house. But you know what they are getting to do? They're getting to see the wonders of Jesus Christ himself in Heaven up above. And that, no matter how hard it may be, is what we must hold on to as we cope with losing loved ones.

The bench just outside the high school entrance feels warm as we sit on it in bittersweet enjoyment, slowly sipping two cherry Cokes Cade bought from the vending machine by the auditorium.

"Okay, peak and valley of your day. Go."

We do this every day, it's our little way of showing appreciation for even the best and worst moments.

I started, "My valley was definitely the psychology test in fourth."

He laughed, agreeing that it was his as well.

"I'd have to say my peak was breakfast this morning. I'm not used to eating like that!" Mr. Davidson got up early to make us pancakes and bacon, a much needed upgrade from my usual fasting or occasional granola bar.

Ever since the Davidson family volunteered to let Cade and I temporarily stay with them after all the devastating family affairs, life has been great. We both finally have people cheering us on during Friday night football games, someone to yell at us for messy rooms when we get home from school, even telling us to do our homework. It's like we're a family for once, although I'm pretty sure Jenny thinks of Cade as much more than a family-friend.

"I agree, but I have another peak that I think might just beat that."

"And what's that?"

Cade smiled, putting his hand on my leg as he shared the highlight of his day. "Right now. Just getting to sit with you. God gave us to each other for a reason, you know."

Cade has always been able to find ways to make me smile, even on the toughest of days. With all that we've been through, this is the first chance we've gotten to just sit down and breathe. We're finally at peace, God by our side.

I looked up to the sky and smiled, closing my eyes as I reached to hold Cade's warming hand. The breeze feels refreshing against my skin, the ends of my hair blowing against the back of the bench.

Silence; it's painfully bliss. A moment of silence speaks louder than the harshest of words, just like wind always goes further than waves.

I felt Cade squeeze my hand as I opened my eyes to meet his. He smiled, leaning against the bookbag that sits between us. "Tatum, can I ask you something?"

I knew that was coming sooner or later. I can tell when Cade has something on his mind, and the sudden declaration of gratitude towards me explains it. He can ask me anything, he knows that.

"Of course, hit me with your worst."

He tilted his head down, laughing, reminding me of how thankful he was for my useless sarcasm. "It's about Brynlee; about her cardigan. What was it doing in my backyard? We never figured that out."

He's right. In all the chaos of finding Brynlee and validating everything Daniels had said, we forgot about the white cardigan that once laid in the forest behind Cade's house. It makes no sense for it to have been there, especially since Daniels admitted to everything involving Brynlee. He never mentioned Carl Hampton in his confession unless it came to Gabriella and the old barn.

So here we are, back at a crossroads. Two paths to choose; one that will let us forget about every minor discrepancy and little question, and another that could very likely throw us both back into a world full of unanswered questions and riddles. The secrets we hide, how they grow and put us to shame.

Knowing myself, there is no way I can live without knowing the whole story. The full story, not just the tip of it. After everything, I refuse to give up on the truth.

So back into a whirlwind we go, a spiraling cluster of relationships each filled to the brink with misplaced trust and fake smiles.

Just another day in the life of a typical high schooler.

I took a deep breath and picked up my bags, headed to Cade's navy Jeep Cherokee parked along the back row of the lot. I can hear his massive feet following close behind, clearly excited to see where my head full of curiosity will lead him now. Another hunt, another list of questions that I refuse to leave unanswered.

Apples.

Acknowledgements

WRITING A BOOK HAS turned out to be harder than ever I thought it would be, yet simultaneously more rewarding than I could've imagined. Special thanks to everyone who inspired the stories, the nicknames, and the many heartfelt concepts found in this book. Without them there would be much less laughter, much less love, and fewer hard truths put in front of me in my daily life. Thank you for standing by me through the entire process of writing *Every Hidden Secret,* and for never once doubting its potential.

My deepest appreciation to the following:

Addie Harper, who encouraged me to lead beyond my comfort zone.

Erin Spinks, for growing my faith in God.

Earl Parker, taken home too soon.

Amy McCoy, a beautiful woman with an even prettier soul. Thank you for staying calm even when I throw tantrums with Carlee at all hours of the night. I really appreciate you encouraging me to finish this, despite living a state away from home. You will forever mean more to me than just my best friend's mother; to me, you are truly a blessing. I am so thankful that God put you and your family in my life, and I pray we get to make hundreds more memories to add to our collection. Remember, when in doubt, put it in "mountain mode".

Gigi, my *forever* role model. I could never have gotten as far as I have without your help. All the late night projects, thrown-together costumes, and breakfast trips have made me more thankful for you than you could possibly imagine. Thank you for encouraging me while I wrote this story!

Ashley Wegmann and Holly Schultz, two teachers each with a heart of nothing but gold. Thank you for helping me through the editing and publishing process, and for offering kind words of advice when I didn't know what steps to take next.

My parents for all the support they have blessed me with. Whether it's on the field or at home, they always know exactly what I need to hear in order to succeed.

Carlee, for everything she's done in contribution to the completion of this book. From every late night phone call, to the encouraging texts, and even to our weekly rant sessions, she's been there for me. She is one of the reasons that I somewhat understand my own complicated life, why I get so excited at the sight of a hedgehog, and why I now live with an irrational fear of rabbits. "Razzle dazzle"...

Lilly, for staying in touch.

Mitchell, always in our hearts and forever in Heaven.

A close friend of mine, because without his help I would have never even began writing this book. His wise words encouraged me when I lost all inspiration, and his genuine conversations are the reason I think so deeply about my actions. He may not know it, but I truly appreciate his friendship and transparency. He isn't like anyone else I've ever had the pleasure of meeting, and I respect his will to stand out. So thank you, for all of the effort you've put into bettering me, and for putting yourself second.

BCR for showing me that others' priorities are not always as we hope for them to me.

Every artist whose music was mentioned in this book; Conway Twitty for "That's My Job", Alabama for "Angels", Bananarama for "Cruel Summer", Dermot Kennedy for "Something to Someone", Jamie Miller for "It Is What It Is", Rod Wave for "Fight the Feeling", Natalie Jane for "Seeing You With Other Girls", and Jessie Murph for "If I Died Last Night". Also, a shout-out to anyone whose work was not specifically mentioned; Tom Hanks, Mark Harmon, Bailey Zimmerman, Kenny Chesney, Billy Ray, Olivia Rodrigo, Taylor Swift, and Kim Novak.

To all personnel whose quotes are mentioned in this novel—dead or alive, your legacies still remain strong; Kristin Armstrong, Victor Borge, David Gemmell, Vivian Greene, Julianne MacLean, Joel Leon, Paula Coehlo, S.C Lourie, George Washington Carver, Thomas Day, Doe Zantamata, Mother Teresa, L.A Meyer, David Leviathan, Edmondo de Amicis, Martin Luther King Jr., Og Mandino, Robyn Schneider, Mitch Albom, Elizabeth Kubler Ross, Matthew Dicks, Albert Einstein, Rabindranath Tagore, Sojourner Truth, Ellen Burstyn Jr., Ranata Suzuki, Bob Dylan, and Erin Hansen for his poem "If I Showed You My Teardrops".

LaReece Stewart for giving me permission to include her Latin class life lessons in this book.

My final thanks to all my friends who helped me finish this and who supported me through the process. You will forever have a special place in my heart.

In Loving Memory Of

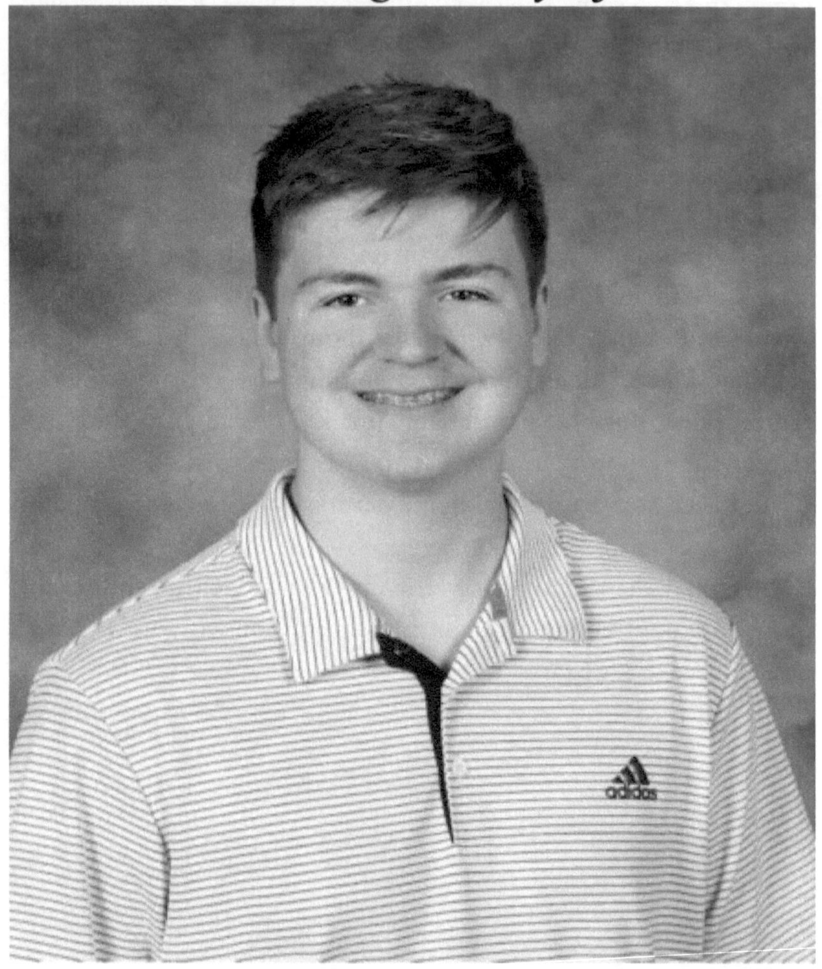

Nolan Thompson

"When God entered my life, my whole life changed. God saved me and set me free. He allows me to live a love filled life. He allowed me to be cleansed of my sins. God means everything to me. He is the word and the light. God should be in everyone's life, and he should mean a lot to you like he does to me."
"Aidan Courier" 2006-2023

Did you love *Every Hidden Secret*? Then you should read *Platonic* by Reese McPherson!

After losing her best friend and platonic soulmate, Eli, seventeen year-old Rowan Walker escapes her grief by spending winter break in Charlotte with her Dad and his newest girlfriend, Tessa. Helping at Tessa's flower shop far from the pain of South Alabama, she doesn't expect the chaotic rhythm of the Bloom Room---or the Braswell brothers next door---to begin softening the edges of her sorrow.

Nineteen year-old Callum Braswell is steady, unreadable, and far too intriguing. Their paths cross in unexpected ways, stirring questions Rowan isn't ready to face as she fights to find pieces of Eli in Callum that simply aren't there. They're nothing alike---one a misunderstood philosopher and the other a blue-collar man of ruggedness. But Cal has his own ghosts, and grief doesn't make room for easy answers.

As the weeks unfold through wilted petals, broken record players, and long walks home, Rowan must decide to either accept that healing has bloomed where she least expected it, or turn away her epiphany that the end of one love may not be the end of all.

Also by Reese McPherson

Every Hidden Secret

About the Author

Reese McPherson was born in Scottsdale, Arizona in July 2007. Growing up as a traveler, she saw many states and countries, along with beautiful scenery, inspiring her love to write stories with unique settings. She celebrates her seventeenth birthday this year, loving friends and family by her side. She is currently a runner at her local high school in Georgia, as well as a cheerleader and member of various clubs. "Every Hidden Secret" is her first novel, an intriguing story of two lovers clinging to their past, struggling with their present, and dreaming of their future.